Lords of the Underworld

In a remote fortress in Budapest, six immortal warriors – each more dangerously seductive than the last – are bound by an ancient curse none has been able to break. When a powerful enemy returns, they will travel the world in search of a sacred relic of the gods – one that threatens to destroy them all.

Gena Showalter's
new paranormal series

LORDS OF THE UNDERWORLD

continues with

DARK BEGINNINGS
containing three stories
and a bonus guide to the Underworld!

Also available in this series

THE DARKEST NIGHT
THE DARKEST KISS
THE DARKEST WHISPER
THE DARKEST PLEASURE

And don't miss the next Lords of the Underworld book

THE DARKEST PASSION

Coming next month from MIRA®

New York Times and *USA Today* bestselling author **Gena Showalter** has been praised for her "sizzling page turners" and "utterly spellbinding stories". She is the author of more than seventeen novels and anthologies, including breathtaking paranormal and contemporary romances, cutting-edge young adult novels, and stunning urban fantasy. Readers can't get enough of her trademark wit and singular imagination.

To learn more about Gena and her books, please visit www.genashowalter.com and www.genashowalter blogspot.com.

Gena Showalter

DARK BEGINNINGS

DID YOU PURCHASE THIS BOOK WITHOUT A COVER?
If you did, you should be aware it is stolen property as it was reported *unsold and destroyed* by a retailer. Neither the author nor the publisher has received any payment for this book.

All the characters in this book have no existence outside the imagination of the author, and have no relation whatsoever to anyone bearing the same name or names. They are not even distantly inspired by any individual known or unknown to the author, and all the incidents are pure invention.

All Rights Reserved including the right of reproduction in whole or in part in any form. This edition is published by arrangement with Harlequin Enterprises II B.V./S.à.r.l. The text of this publication or any part thereof may not be reproduced or transmitted in any form or by any means, electronic or mechanical, including photocopying, recording, storage in an information retrieval system, or otherwise, without the written permission of the publisher.

This book is sold subject to the condition that it shall not, by way of trade or otherwise, be lent, resold, hired out or otherwise circulated without the prior consent of the publisher in any form of binding or cover other than that in which it is published and without a similar condition including this condition being imposed on the subsequent purchaser.

MIRA is a registered trademark of Harlequin Enterprises Limited, used under licence.

Published in Great Britain 2010.
MIRA Books, Eton House, 18-24 Paradise Road,
Richmond, Surrey, TW9 1SR

DARK BEGINNINGS © Harlequin Books SA 2010

The Darkest Fire © Gena Showalter 2008
The Darkest Prison © Gena Showalter 2009
The Darkest Angel © Gena Showalter 2010

ISBN 978 0 7783 0371 8

54-0510

MIRA's policy is to use papers that are natural, renewable and recyclable products and made from wood grown in sustainable forests. The logging and manufacturing processes conform to the legal environmental regulations of the country of origin.

Printed and bound in Spain
by Litografia Rosés S.A., Barcelona

CONTENTS

THE DARKEST FIRE

CHAPTER ONE

EVERY DAY FOR HUNDREDS of years the goddess had visited Hell and every day Geryon had watched her from his station, desire heating his blood more than the flames of damnation beyond his post ever had. He should not have studied her that first time and should have kept his gaze downcast all the times since. He was a slave to the prince of darkness, spawned by evil; she was a goddess, created in light.

He could not have her, he thought, hands fisting. No matter how much he might wish otherwise. She would not want him anyway. This…obsession was pointless and brought him nothing but despair. He did not need more despair.

And yet, still he watched her this day as she floated through the barren cavern, coral-tipped fingers tracing the jagged stones that separated underground from underworld. Golden ringlets flowed down her elegant back and framed a face so perfect, so lovely, Aphrodite herself could not compare. Eyes of starlight narrowed, a rosy color blooming in those cheeks of smooth alabaster.

"The wall is cracked," she said, her voice like a song amid the hiss of nearby flames—and the unnatural screams that always accompanied them.

He shook his head, positive he had merely imagined the words. In all their centuries together, they had never spoken, never deviated from their routine. As the Guardian of Hell, he ensured the gate remained closed until a spirit needed to be cast inside. That way, no one and nothing escaped—and if they tried, he rendered punishment. As the goddess of Oppression, she fortified the physical barrier with only a touch. Silence was never breeched.

Uncertainty darkened her features. "Have you nothing to say?"

She stood in front of him a moment later, though he never saw her move. The scent of honeysuckle suddenly overshadowed the stink of sulfur and melting flesh, and he inhaled deeply, closing his eyes in ecstasy. Oh, that she would remain just as she was....

"Guardian," she prompted.

"Goddess." He forced his lids to open gradually, slowly revealing the glow of her beauty. Up close, she was not as perfect as he had thought. She was better. A smattering of freckles dotted her sweetly sloped nose, and dimples appeared with the curve of her half-smile. Exquisite.

What did she think of *him?* he wondered.

She probably thought him a monster, hideous and misshapen. Which he was. But if she thought so, she did not show it. Only curiosity rested in those starlight eyes. For the wall, he suspected, not for him. Even when he'd been human, women had wanted nothing to do with him. They'd run from him the moment he'd turned his attention to them. He'd been too tall, too brawny, too bumbling. And that was *before* he'd resembled an ogre.

Sometimes he wondered if he'd been tainted at birth.

"Those cracks were not there yesterday," she said. "What has caused such damage? And so swiftly?"

"A horde of Demon Lords rise from the pit daily and fight to break out. They have grown tired of their confinement here and seek living humans to torment."

She accepted the news without reaction. "Have you their names?"

He nodded. He did not need to see beyond the gate to know who visited on the other side; he sensed it. Always. "Violence, Death, Lies, Doubt, Misery. Shall I go on?"

"No," she said softly. "I understand. The worst of the worst."

"Yes. They bang and they claw from the other side, desperate to reach the mortal realm."

"Well, stop them." A command, laced with husky entreaty.

If only. He would have given up the last vestiges of his humanity to do as she wished. Anything to repay the daily gift of her presence. Anything to keep her just where she was, prolonging the sweetness of her scent. "I am forbidden to leave my post, just as I am forbidden to open the gates for any reason but allowing one of the damned inside. I'm afraid I cannot grant your request."

Besides, the only way to stop a determined demon was to kill it, and killing a High Lord was another forbidden act.

A sigh slipped from her. "Do you always do as you're told?"

"Always." Once he had fought the invisible ties that bound him. Once, but no longer. To fight was to invite pain and suffering—not for him, but for others. Innocent humans who resembled his mother, his father and his brothers—because his true mother, father and brothers had already been slain—were brought here and tortured in front of him. The screams…oh, the screams. Far worse than the ones that seeped from Hell. And the sights… He shuddered.

Had the pain and suffering been heaped upon *him,* he would not have cared. Would have laughed and fought all the harder. What was a little more pain? But Lucifer, brother to Hades and prince of the demons, needed him healthy, whole, so had found other ways to gain his cooperation.

The memories would forever haunt him, but might have faded during the night, if he'd required sleep. He remained awake, however, every hour of every day, never able to forget.

"Obedience. I expected differently from you," she said. "You are a warrior, so strong and assured."

Yes, he was a warrior. But he was also a slave. One did not cancel out the other. "I am sorry, goddess. My strength and assurance change nothing."

"I will pay you to help me," she insisted. "Name your price. Whatever you desire shall be yours."

If only, Geryon thought again. He would ask for a single taste of her lips.

Why limit himself, though? he wondered next. *Whatever he desired.* He could ask for a night in her arms. Naked. Touching. Tasting. Yes. *Yes.* Every muscle in his body clenched. In arousal. In desperation.

In despair.

No. He could not risk the suffering of the innocent—*why do you bother with them?*—simply to sate his craving for the lovely goddess. So have a kiss? A night with her? No again.

Finally I know true torture. He ground his teeth. Why did he bother? Because without good, there would be only evil. And he had seen too much evil over the centuries. He would not be responsible for more.

"Guardian?" the goddess prompted. *"Anything."*

CHAPTER TWO

DO NOT SPEAK. DO NOT DO THIS. Geryon gulped. "I am sorry, goddess." *No. Say no more. Ask for that kiss, at the very least.* "As I told you, I cannot help you." *No, no, no.*

How he hated himself just then.

Her delicate shoulders sagged in disappointment, and his self-hatred grew. "But…why? You want to keep the demons in Hell just as much as I do. Right?"

"Right." Geryon didn't want to tell her his reasons for refusing her, was still ashamed after all this time. Tell her, however, he would. Perhaps then she would return to the old ways and pretend he did not exist. As it was, his craving for her was deepening, intensifying, his body hardening. Readying.

She's not for you.

How many times would he need the reminder before this conversation ended?

"I sold my soul," he admitted. He had been one of the first humans to walk the earth. Despite his massive build and bumbling ways, he'd been content with his lot and enraptured by his mate, even though she'd been chosen by his family and, like all the other females of his acquaintance, had not desired him in return.

A year into their marriage, she had grown sick, and he had despaired. Though she had found no joy with him, she had belonged to him, and ensuring her safety and well-being had been his duty. So he had cried out to the gods for assistance.

They had ignored him, and his despair became unbearable.

That was when Lucifer appeared before him. So cunning, that one was.

To save his mate—and perhaps finally win her heart—Geryon had willingly given himself to the dark prince. And found himself transformed from man to beast. Horns had sprouted atop his head, and his hands had become clubs, his nails claws. Dark, carmine fur had covered the skin on his legs, while hooves replaced his feet.

In seconds, he'd been more animal than human.

His wife had healed, as his contract with Lucifer stated, but she had not softened toward Geryon. No, his selfless act had meant nothing to her and she had left him for another man. A man she had apparently been seeing all along.

What a fool he'd been. A cuckold. *All for nothing.*

"What thoughts fill your head, Guardian? Never have you appeared so…broken."

The goddess. His hands fisted, claws digging deep into his palms, as he refocused on her. There had been compassion in her tone. Compassion he must ignore. Unemotional, that's how he had to be. Always. Otherwise, he would not survive his time here.

"My actions are no longer mine to command. No matter how I wish otherwise, I cannot help you. Now please. Don't you have duties to attend to?"

"I am doing my duty now. Are you?"

He flushed.

She sighed. "Forgive my waspishness. I am frazzled." The goddess studied him, her head tilting to the side. He shifted uncomfortably, such scrutiny unnerving given his sickening appearance. To his surprise, revulsion did not darken her lovely gaze as she said, "Your soul belongs to the dark prince?"

"Yes."

"And if your soul was returned to you, you would aid me?"

"Yes," he repeated, the word a croak. Would she still offer him a boon for that aid?

"Very well. I will see what I can do."

His eyes widened in horror. Approach Lucifer? "No, you must—"

She disappeared before he could stop her.

Inner Corridors of Hell

"LUCIFER, HEAR ME WELL. I demand to speak with you. You *will* appear before me. This day, in this room. Alone. I will remain exactly as I am." Kadence, goddess of Oppression, knew to state her wants precisely or the demon prince would "interpret" them however he wished. "And you will be clothed."

Were she simply to demand an audience, he might whisk her to his bed, her arms and legs tied, her clothing gone, a legion of fiends surrounding her.

Several minutes ticked by and there was no response to her summons. But then, she'd known there wouldn't be. He enjoyed making her wait. Made him feel powerful. *Keep busy. Act as if you do not care.*

Kadence eyed her surroundings, as if studying them was exactly what she'd come to do. Rather than stone and mortar, the walls of Lucifer's palace were comprised of flames. Crackling, orange-gold. Deadly.

His throne was comprised of bone, ash and more of those flames. Off to the side was a bloodstained altar. A lifeless body still lay across it—minus a head. The head would reattach all too soon, however, so that the torturing could begin anew. That was the way of it here.

No soul would escape. Even in death.

She hated everything about this place. Plumes of black smoke wafted from the blazes, curling around her like fingers of the damned. So badly she wanted to wave her hand in front of her nose, but she did not. She wouldn't show weakness—even with so small an action.

Did she dare, she knew she would find herself *drowning* in the noxious fumes. Lucifer loved nothing more than exploiting vulnerabilities.

Kadence had learned that lesson well. The first time she had visited, she'd come to inform both Hades and Lucifer that she had been appointed their warden. As one who embodied the essence of subjugation and conquest, there was no one better to ensure that demons and dead alike remained here.

Or so the gods had thought, which was why they'd chosen her for this task.

She had not agreed, but refusing them would have invited punishment. Many times since accepting, however, she'd thought perhaps punishment would have been better. Having stones thrown at her, bloody carcasses left on her doorstep in warning…they hardly compared to spending her days sleeping in a nearby cave—not a true sleep but a watchful one, her mind's eye drifting over the different demon camps. Could hardly compare to spending her nights surveying a wall of rock.

As the Guardian watched.

That, however, was not such a hardship.

For many years, his attention had unnerved her, for he was unlike anyone she had ever met: half man, half beast, all…edge. But then she'd come to find comfort in his detached gaze. He protected her from demons and souls who slipped through the gate, attacking everyone in their path. No matter the harm to himself.

She could do no less for him.

I sold my soul, he'd said. For what? she wondered. What had he received in return? Did he consider the trade a good one? She'd wanted to ask him, but had recalled how uncomfortable he had been with her questions about the wall. He would not have welcomed a discussion about something so personal.

And that was probably for the best. Only her job mattered right now. How could she not have known demon High Lords were determined to escape *forever?*

Had Lucifer somehow blocked her visions of this realm? He was the only one strong enough to do so. If so, what did he hope to gain? Were she to ask, he would merely lie, that much she knew.

She'd never felt more helpless.

No, that wasn't true. During her first visit, Lucifer had sensed her trepidation—and he'd since used every opportunity to nurture it. A fire-coated touch here, a wicked taunt there. Every time she had come here to report an infraction, she had wilted under his attentions.

That had disappointed the gods. They would have called her home, she was sure, had they not already bound her to the wall, an act that had been meant to help with her duties, not hinder them. But not even the gods had known just how deeply the bond would go. Rather than simply sensing when the wall needed fortification, she'd realized it was her reason for living.

Her blood now sang with its essence.

The first time one of the demons had scratched it, she'd felt the sting and had gasped, shocked. Now, it no longer shocked her, though she still felt every contact. When a soul brushed it, her skin felt tickled. When the inferno licked at it, she felt burned. So why had she not sensed these latest ministrations?

Oh, she'd felt her body draining of strength, little by little, pains shooting through her seemingly for no reason, but her visions had been calm. Well, as calm as such visions could be, considering what she was forced to witness on a daily basis.

Now, at least, she knew why she'd hurt. Bound as she was to this dark underworld, that crack in the outer wall was literally killing her.

You are losing focus. Concentrate! Distraction could cost her. Dearly. And the outcome of this meeting was more important than any that had come before it.

From outside the palace she could hear the crazed laughter of the demons, the moans of the tortured and the sizzle of flesh pouring from bone. And the smell…it was a hell all its own.

It was difficult, remaining stoic amidst such vileness. Especially now. The High Lords must have been working on the wall for weeks. Because if her side was cracked, she shuddered to think of the damage on Hell's side. At the very least, she should have seen the demons approach. But again, her visions had remained calm.

Enough of this. Clearly, she could not concentrate.

"Lucifer," she called again. "You heard my demands. Now heed them. Or I will leave and you will miss this opportunity to bargain."

The pound of footsteps suddenly echoed and the flames several feet in front of her parted. Finally. In strolled Lucifer, as carefree as a summer day.

"Yes, I did hear them," he said in the silkiest of voices. He even grinned, the expression pure wickedness. "You mentioned a bargain? What can I do for you, my darling?"

CHAPTER THREE

KADENCE DIDN'T ALLOW herself to shudder.

Lucifer was tall, muscled like a warrior and sensually handsome despite the dark inferno raging in his eyes. But he did not compare to the beast who guarded his domain. The beast whose face was too rough to be considered anything other than savage. The beast whose massive body should have frightened her but only made her feel safe. The beast whose monstrous appearance should have disgusted her but didn't. Instead, his brown eyes—eyes she'd once considered impassive, but after today, now saw as haunted—captivated her. And, of course, his protective nature intrigued her.

She might never have become interested in the Guardian, might have continued to assume he was like every other hated creature here, but then he'd saved her life that first time. Sadly, even immortal goddesses could be slain—a prospect that had never been clearer as the outer gates had parted to welcome a spirit and a minion slipped free, racing toward her, hungry for living flesh.

She'd frozen, knowing her death was imminent.

The Guardian—what was his name?—had intervened, destroying the fiend with one swipe of his poisoned claw before it had made contact with her. He hadn't spoken to her afterward, and she hadn't spoken to him, her belief that he was like all the other creatures in this underworld shaken but not yet completely broken.

She'd begun to study him, though. Over time, she'd become fascinated by his complexities.

He was a destroyer, yet he'd saved her. He had nothing, yet he hadn't asked for anything in exchange. How rare that was. How strange. How…welcome. She now *wanted* to do something for him. Anything, as she'd told him. And for one stolen moment, she'd thought he meant to request a kiss. His gaze had fallen to her lips, and lingered. Utter longing had radiated from him.

Please, she had almost begged. Her heart rate had sped up, her mouth had watered. What would he taste like? But then his expression had cleared, he had looked away and shaken his head. *No.*

Her disappointment had nearly felled her. Push him, however, she would not do. He'd already done so much for her. Still, she couldn't help but wonder, hope…did he favor her in return? For that stolen moment, she would have sworn she saw white-hot flames in his eyes, flames that had nothing to do with the damned.

"Am I so boring you cannot grant me your attention after you summoned me? Twice."

The question returned her to the present, and she could have slapped herself. *Do you* want *to lose this match of wits with the prince of darkness?* "Boring?" She shrugged. To say yes would be asking him to liven things up. To say no would be telling him she enjoyed him. In his mind, at least. Neither would end well for her.

Lucifer regarded her silently as he settled atop his throne. Instantly, swirling, ghostly souls began writhing between the bones and ash. A bejeweled goblet materialized, already clutched in his hand, and he sipped from it. A drop of crimson slid down the corner of his mouth and trickled onto his stark white shirt. Blood.

Revulsion besieged her, but she kept her expression neutral.

"You are disgusted by me but do not show it," he said with another of those wicked smiles. "Where is the mouse who usually visits? The one who trembles and stumbles over her words? I like her better."

Kadence raised her chin. He could call her all the names he wished, but she wouldn't comment. "Your walls have been compromised, and a horde of demons fights to escape."

The prince quickly lost his smile. "You lie. They would not dare."

His agitation was understandable. Without his legions, he would have no one to rule. "You're right. Your band of thieves, rapists and murderers would not dare disobey their sovereign."

His eyes narrowed in a show of anger. One he quickly masked by shrugging casually. "So the walls are compromised. What do you expect me to do about it?"

She should not have been surprised. Always he made things difficult. "The Guardian. He can help me stop the ones responsible. But as you own his soul, he must first gain your permission."

Lucifer snorted. "No. I will not grant it. Not for any reason. I like him where he is."

Yes. Difficult. "Why?"

"I need a reason? Well, then. Let's see. Let's see." He tapped his chin with a fingertip. "What about, my last guard fell victim to a demon's lies and almost allowed a legion to escape."

A lie of his own? The Guardian she knew had been here far longer than she, so she did not know if anyone else had ever stood in his place. "This one could just as easily fall." Now *that* was a lie. No one was more determined. There would be no falling. Not for him.

"No." Lucifer shook his head. "Geryon is impervious to their wiles."

Geryon. Finally. A name. Greek in origin, meaning monster. She didn't like it.

He was more than his appearance. Far more.

"Nothing else to say?" Lucifer asked. "Shall we part, then?"

She barely stopped herself from running her tongue over her teeth. Was this a game he played? He needed the wall repaired as much as she did. Well, not as *much* as she did, she mused. Unlike her, he would not die if the wall crumbled. Still. His resistance grated.

With that thought, she answered her own question. Yes, this was a game. One she would not tolerate. "I am your sovereign," she said. "You will—"

"You are not my sovereign," he growled in another display of anger. Another display he quickly hid. A single breath in and out, and he visibly calmed. "You are my…observer. You watch, you advise and you protect, but you do not command."

Because you are too weak, he did not say. But then, he didn't have to. They both knew it was true.

She wanted to be different. Strong. She truly did. And she should have been. Once, she had been. Her very nature was one of subjugation, after all. For others, though, and not herself. Or that's the way it had been. *Why* was she like this now?

You know the answer, and you would do well to forget it.

She squared her shoulders, realizing she would have to play Lucifer's game, after all. There was no other way. *You can do this. For Geryon.* "I believe I offered to bargain with you, and you were amenable. Shall we begin?" she asked silkily.

He nodded, as if he'd merely been waiting for the question all along. "We shall."

Gates of Hell

"I DO NOT UNDERSTAND," Geryon said, refusing to leave his post. He even crossed his arms over his chest, an action that reminded him of his human days, when he'd been more than guard, more than monster. "Lucifer would never have agreed to release me from his…care."

"I promise you, he agreed. You are free." The goddess cast her gaze to her sandaled feet, saying no more on the subject. "Finally."

Did she hide something? Plan to trick him, for whatever reason? It had been so long since he'd dealt with a female, he wasn't sure how to judge her actions. Her, though, he wanted to believe. Anything and everything she said. And that was what scared him most.

She could destroy him and his poor heart. Or rather, what remained of it. If anything did.

She was paler than usual, he noted, the rosy glow in her cheeks gone, her freckles stark. Her golden ringlets tumbled down her shoulders and arms, and he could see soot woven throughout the fine strands. His hands ached to reach out, to sift those tresses through his fingers.

Would she run screaming if he did so? Probably.

Today she wore a violet robe and matching necklace—a necklace that boasted a teardrop amethyst as large as his fist and as bright as the glistening ice of his homeland. Ice he had not seen in hundreds of years. She had never worn such a thing before; usually she draped herself in white, an angel among evil, with no adornment.

"How?" he persisted. "Why?" *And why do you look so sad?*

"Does it matter?" Her gaze lifted, boring into him with the precision of a spear and cutting just as deep.

There was fury blended with her sadness. He did not like either. This female should only ever be happy. "To me, yes." But only because it was necessary to his survival. Anything else, and he might have caved then and there. Given her whatever she desired. Even follow her into the fires behind him, as she'd first requested.

She gave a little stomp of her foot. "To save the wall, I need your help. Let that be enough of an answer for now. You know Lucifer would not want it to fall." Her fingers beckoned him.

"Come. See the damage that has been done on this side. See why I must cross over."

The goddess did not await his reply. She turned away from him and walked to the far corner of the wall. No, not walked. She glided, a dream of falling stars amid shimmering twilight.

Why do you want to survive? What good does living do you? Geryon hesitated only a moment before following her, breathing deeply of her honeysuckle scent along the way.

To his surprise, no one jumped from the shadows as he walked; no one waited to punish him for daring to leave his post. Was he truly free? Dare he hope?

The goddess didn't face him when he reached her, but traced a fingertip along a thin, jagged groove in the middle stone. A groove that branched into smaller striations, like tiny rivers flowing from a churning ocean.

"It's small, I know, but already it has grown from what I saw yesterday. If the demons continue their abuse, it will continue to grow until the rock splits completely in two, allowing legions to enter the human realm."

"Were a single demon released upon the unsuspecting world," he muttered, "death and destruction would reign." Whether or not a punishment would be delivered to him, he would help her, Geryon decided. He could not allow such a thing to happen. Innocence should never be taken from the undeserving. It was too precious.

"If I do this… If I help you…"

Still she didn't face him. "Yes?" A breathy sigh.

"I will earn that boon? Whatever I desire?" How selfish he was to ask, he thought, but he did not take the words back.

"Yes." No hesitation. Still breathy.

What did she think he would ask for? "Then so be it. I accept. I will lead you into Hell, goddess."

CHAPTER FOUR

THE GODDESS GAVE A STARTLED gasp and flicked him the briefest of glances. "You'll help me? Even knowing you are no longer bound to the prince? That you could leave?"

His chest constricted at that glimpse of starlight eyes and lush red lips. "Yes. Even knowing." If she spoke true and he *was* free, he had no place to go. Too many centuries had passed, and his home was now gone. His family, dead. Without a doubt, he would cause riots with his appearance. Besides, he might crave the very freedom the goddess promised but he still feared trusting her. She might not intend malice, but Lucifer certainly would.

With the prince, there was always a catch. Free today did not necessarily mean free tomorrow. And since his soul had not been returned to him…

No, he dare not hope.

"Thank you. I didn't expect—I— Why did you sell your soul?" she asked softly, tracing the crack again.

A change of subject. One he was not prepared for.

"What would you have me do?" he asked rather than answer. He did not wish to admit the reason for his folly and the subsequent humiliation.

Her arm dropped to her side, and she faced him fully. As his gaze drank her in, her expression softened. "I am Kadence," she said, as though he had asked for her name rather than instruction.

Kadence. How he loved the way the syllables rolled through his mind, smooth as velvet—gods, how long since he'd touched a material so fine?—and sweet as wine. How long since he'd tasted such a drink?

"I am Geryon." Once, he'd had a different name. Upon arriving here, however, Lucifer had given him his current moniker. *Monster* was the literal translation, but in truth it meant Guardian of the Damned, which was what he was and all he would ever be. Soul or not.

Some legends, a demon had once jeered at him, proclaimed him to be a three-headed centaur. Some, a vicious dog. Some, the leavings of a warrior named Hercules. Anything was better than the truth, however, so he did not mind the stories.

"I am yours to command," he said, adding, "Kadence." Tasted even better on his tongue.

Breath caught in her throat; he heard the hitch of it. "You say my name like a prayer." There was no astonishment in her tone. Only…uncertainty?

Had he done so? "I am sorry."

"Don't be." Her cheeks flushed prettily. Then she clapped her hands and brought the conversation back to what should have been their primary concern. "Our first order of business is to patch those cracks."

He nodded but said, "I fear the wall is already compromised." Outer damage was fixable. But not inner. In walls or in immortals, he thought, thinking of the inner scars he must bare. "Patching will merely strengthen it for a time." But might not prevent an eventual fall, he did not add.

What they would do then, he did not know. Chaos would reign. Souls and demons would be able to leave at will.

Something more would have to be done. But again, he did not know what.

"Yes. Knowing demons as I have come to, they will return and inflict more damage." Once more she lifted her gaze to him, kernels of fear swirling where there should only be satisfaction. A crime. "Geryon," she began, only to press her lush lips together.

What was left of his heart skidded to an abrupt stop. She was just so lovely, her gentleness and goodness setting her apart from everything he represented. He wanted to duck his head, hide his ugliness from her. "Yes?"

"I— I—"

Why so uncomfortable? "You may speak freely with me, goddess." Whatever she needed, he would provide.

"Kadence. Please."

"Kadence," he said again, and savored. *So good...*

"I— What boon would you ask of me?"

That was not what she'd meant to ask, he knew it, and could only gape at her, trying not to panic. He had hoped to discuss this *after.* "A...a kiss." He waited for her screech of horror. Her denial.

Instead, she merely opened her mouth in a wide O.

"You may close your eyes and imagine you are with someone else," he rushed out. "Or refuse me. I would understand." *Stop talking. You're only making things worse.*

"I would not refuse," she said softly, huskily.

"I—I—" Now he was the one to stutter. She would not refuse?

She licked her lips. "Shall I give you a kiss now?"

Now? Suddenly he had trouble breathing. Standing. His knees were shaking, his limbs as heavy as boulders. Dark spots winked over his vision. *Now?* he wondered again, wildly this time.

He was not ready. He would make a fool of himself, and she would leave him. No longer want his help. Or worse, she would cast him pitying, disgusted glances the entire time they worked.

"After," he managed to croak.

Was that...disappointment clouding her expression? Surely not.

"Very well," she said. No emotion. "After. But Geryon, I must warn you. There is a chance we will not survive."

"What do you mean?"

"After we have repaired the wall, we must hunt and kill the demons who would destroy it. Are you *sure* you wish to wait?"

Hunt and destroy the demons. Of course. The answer was so clear, he was embarrassed that he had not thought of it. By killing the High Lords, they would be committing a crime, and they would be punished. Perhaps be put to death.

"So…your kiss?" she prompted softly.

Had he not known better, he would almost think her…eager.

But he *did* know better. Agreeing to Lucifer's bargain had been difficult. Or so he'd thought at the time. This was a thousand times more so. "After," he repeated. He would earn that kiss, and hopefully, she would not ever think back on it and consider him unworthy.

She nodded, and once again looked away from him. "Then let us begin our work."

CHAPTER FIVE

FOR HOURS GERYON WORKED at repairing the outer wall, pleading with Kadence all the while to remain behind. Demons were dangerous, he said. Demons liked their prey alive and fresh, he said. What he did not say was that she was fragile, breakable. No, he did not need to say it; she read the thoughts in the ever-growing concern in his eyes.

Through it all, she refused to allow him to be alone. She had not bartered something that would surely earn her the wrath of the gods, only to send him on a mission he could not hope to win without her.

While the demons were not hers to command, she *could* force them to bow to her. She hoped. Besides, she might appear fragile and breakable, but she possessed a core of iron.

Something she'd *finally* proven to Lucifer earlier. As well as herself.

As a child, she had been an indomitable force. A whirlwind that trampled anything and everything in her path. It had not been intentional. She'd simply followed the quiet urgings inside her head. *Dominate. Master.*

Do you really wish to think of this now?

No better time, she supposed. Only other thing to think about was why Geryon had not wanted to kiss her when she'd offered. Why he'd actually looked alarmed. A few ideas came to mind: he did not really want to kiss her—but why then would he have requested one? Or he resented her for asking for his aid—this was the most likely—and last, he was simply desperate for a woman, she was the only one available, yet he had to force his body to react first.

Embarrassing!

Not helping.

She could have helped him rather than simply pondering, but he had shooed her away every time she tried. When she joined him anyway, he'd threatened to leave her if she did not stop. So here she was, doing nothing. Useless.

I am not weak, damn it. Even though, for the most part, I have acted like it.

When, as a child, she'd realized she had chipped away at her own mother's strength of mind, turning the once vibrant goddess into a lifeless shell, she had retreated inside herself, afraid of who and what she was. Afraid of what she could do, unintentional though it was.

Sadly, with those fears came others, as if she'd opened a doorway in her mind and placed a welcome mat out front. Fear of people, places, emotions. For centuries she had acted like the mouse Lucifer had called her.

Underneath the fears, however, she was still the goddess she'd been born to be: Oppression. She conquered. She did not cower. *Please, do not let me cower.* Not any longer.

"I have done all I can for the outer wall," Geryon suddenly said.

Kadence had been perched on a nearby rock, and now stood. Her robe fell to her ankles, swaying.

"Once I pry the gate's boulders apart—" boulders that blocked the cavern from a yawning pit "—we must hurry. We will only have a small slit to pass through, but we cannot let that slow us."

Or someone—or thing—could escape. "I understand," she said, closing the distance between them.

"There will be no ledge for us to stand upon. We must hold on to the boulder and work our way down the pit."

Only after she nodded did he shove and push, creating the aforementioned slit.

Instantly flames and scaled arms reached out. Screams permeated the air. Geryon entered first, commanding all to recede. To her surprise, the demons darted away, the flames died, and the screams quieted as she came through, her body swinging from the natural world into the spiritual one. Part of her wanted to believe they had done so because they'd been afraid of *her.* The other part of her knew they'd feared Geryon's wrath.

She held onto the boulder with every bit of her strength as Geryon closed the slit. To let go was to freefall into Hell, a fiery pit just waiting to gobble them up.

Palms…sweating…

"Ready, goddess?" He inched his way toward her. He had swung to the left of the gate, and she the right. "Ready?" he insisted, reaching for her. To protect her? Aid her?

"Yes." *Finally, I will know his touch. Surely it will not be as divine as my body expects. Nothing could be.* But just before contact, he moved behind her, then away from her, all without touching her. She sighed in disappointment and tightened her grip on the wall, balancing her feet on a rocky protrusion as best she could.

"This way." He motioned toward this side's crack with a tilt of his chin.

"All right. And Geryon? Thank you. For everything." Usually she whisked herself to Lucifer's palace without ever opening the gate, too afraid of *this.* Not today. She couldn't. For she could not whisk Geryon. Or anyone else, for that matter. The ability extended only to herself.

"You are welcome."

As she passed, she waved one hand over the now-closed slit.

Because there was no longer a guardian stationed out front, the extra fortification would be needed—despite the fact that providing it weakened her, forcing her to leave a piece of herself behind.

As fragments of her power adhered to the stones, she was careful to maintain distance from them. Supposedly Geryon was the only one who could touch the handles of the gate without consequence. Well, besides Hades and Lucifer. Anyone else, the stones heaped untold pain and horror upon.

She had never dared test the supposition.

A thought occurred to her, and she tilted her head, studying her companion. Without Geryon at the gate, who would open the stones to allow damned souls inside?

Perhaps Lucifer had already appointed another Guardian. Perhaps? She chuckled without humor. He had. He couldn't leave the gates unguarded, even if he had known Kadence would refortify it.

The knowledge that Geryon would not be the man she saw every day…saddened her. For when the wall was safe—she would not allow herself to believe she would fail in this mission—Geryon could leave, but she would be stuck here.

Do not think about that now. She would cry. If she cried, her vision would blur and if her vision blurred, she would have trouble knowing where to place her hands. Her *still* sweating hands.

She glanced around. The air was smokier here, she noticed, hotter. So hot, in fact, that the sheen of sweat spread up her arms, her neck, even her face. Beads formed, and those beads began trickling down her temples, *blurring her vision.*

"Geryon," she said, nearing a panic.

"I am here, Kadence." In the next instant, he was climbing over her and positioning himself behind again. The scent of decadent, powerful male enveloped her, chasing away the pungent odor of decay. "Are you all right?"

"Yes," she whispered, but gods, what had she gotten herself into?

CHAPTER SIX

"MOVE WITH ME," Geryon told Kadence. "Can you do that?"

"Yes. Of course." Could she? Maintaining a firm grip, she used the jagged stones to edge along, ever conscious of the seemingly endless void awaiting her should she lose her balance—but far more aware of the male still behind her, caging her in, keeping her steady. "Perhaps the wall is not as damaged as I feared. A goddess can hope, at least."

"Yes, a goddess can hope."

How she yearned to rub against him, to drink in his strength, belong to him if only for a moment, but she did not, too afraid of distracting him. Or startling him. Or giving him too much of her weight and causing him to fall.

A rock tumbled from the small ledge on which she had just placed her foot, and she yelped.

"Do not show your fear in any way," he said. "The demons and the flames feed on it, will try to increase it."

"They are alive? The flames, I mean."

"Some of them, yes."

Dear gods. How had she not known? "I did not imagine the climb would be difficult. I wish I could flash us."

"Flash?"

"The ability to move from one location to another with only a thought."

"You have this ability?"

"Yes."

"And you can go anywhere?"

"Anywhere I have already been. To flash somewhere I have not is…dangerous."

He thought for a moment. "Have you been to the bottom of this cavern?"

"No." He had to wonder why she, one of the keepers of Hell, had not physically visited every inch. She had thought herself so clever, merely sending her mind through to watch. But she realized her mistake now.

"Then I ask that you do not try to flash. You might misjudge the distance and end up in a spot without a ledge."

Or underground, but she did not tell him that.

"That is a handy power to possess. I envy you."

Poor man. He'd been stuck at the gates of Hell for countless lifetimes. "If you could flash to anywhere in the world, where would you go?" Once they'd destroyed the demons trying to escape, perhaps she would take him there. She would not be able to remain with him, of course, but seeing his happiness could fuel her fantasies for years to come.

He grunted. "I do not wish to lie to you, goddess, therefore I will not answer your question."

Oh. "I appreciate your honesty." *Why won't he talk to me?*

Curiosity bombarded her. Did his answer embarrass him, perhaps? If so, why? She desperately wanted to know, but let the matter drop. For now.

"We are almost there," he said. Almost at the crack.

"Good." He was still close to her, still behind her, but he made sure not to touch her. Yet he couldn't stop his heat from enveloping her. It was not a heat she minded, even amidst the smoldering furnace that was Hell. His was…heady.

He stopped, forcing her to do the same. "I'm sorry to say it's worse than I thought it would be." His breath trekked over the back of her neck.

"Wh—what?" she asked, horrified. Being near her was worse than he'd thought?

"The wall. What else?"

Thank the gods, she thought, expelling a breath. *Foolish woman.* Her life depended on this wall. She should not care whether a man found her attractive. Or not.

She forced her gaze straight ahead, her mind to center on her job, not the intriguing man behind her. Thick claw marks abounded. And what had appeared to be thin grooves on the other side were massive craters here.

Hope abandoned her.

Irreparable. In every way.

"They are more determined than I realized," was all she said, voice trembling slightly. No reason to speak her fears aloud. Geryon might think she was complaining about his work or doubting his abilities.

He adjusted his grip, his arm just over her shoulder. A tremor raked her. If she stood on her tiptoes, she would feel his skin through her chimation. Though it had been hundreds of years since she'd had a man, she remembered the comfort such simple contact could offer.

"Do not worry, Kadence. I will not allow them to hurt you."

He was using her name more freely now, and that gladdened her. "Just so you know, I will not allow them to hurt you, either." It was a vow.

There was a pause. Then, "Thank you." He sounded unsure.

"You are welcome."

She thought she heard him swallow. "Shall I try and patch this side?"

"No." Too much effort for too little reward. She realized that now. "We should make our way to the bottom. Destroying the High Lords is the only way to prevent *more* damage."

Evil laughter erupted behind them, and they both stiffened. *Demons.*

"Leave us," Geryon snapped.

The laughter increased in volume. Drew closer.

He sighed. "I cannot battle them like this, and they know it," he muttered, latching onto her waist.

She gasped. Finally. He was touching her. It was amazing and wonderful, wild and intense. But there was no comfort in it, as she'd expected. No, instead she experienced white-hot, searing arousal. And a burning desire for more.

"What should we do?"

"Time to fall, Kadence," he said, and then he released the rocks, taking her over the edge with him.

CHAPTER SEVEN

THEY SEEMED TO FALL FOREVER. Geryon retained an iron-edged grip on the trembling Kadence, her hair whipping around them like angry silk ribbons. She didn't scream, something he'd expected, but she did turn and wind her legs around him, something he had not.

It was his first taste of heaven. In this life, and his other.

"I've got you," he said. Her body fit perfectly against his, soft where he was hard, smooth where he was callused.

"When does it end?" she whispered, but still he caught the undercurrents of panic in her voice.

They were not twirling, were merely dropping, but he knew the sensation could be harrowing. Especially, he reflected, for one used to flashing from one place to another.

"Soon." He'd fallen like this only once before, when Lucifer summoned him to the palace to explain his new duties. But he had never forgotten the experience.

Like before, flames kindled all around them, pinpricks of gold in the shuddering darkness. Except before, those flames had flicked like snake tongues, licking at him. That they didn't now…did they fear him? Or the goddess?

She was more *everything* than Geryon had realized. More courageous. More determined. Every minute he spent with her, his desire for her intensified. She was the break of dawn in the bleakness that was his life. She was refreshing ice in smoldering heat.

She is not for you.

Ugly as he was, she would run fast and far if she knew the many fantasies his mind had begun to weave of them. Him, laying her on the ground, stripping her, dancing his tongue over every delicious inch of her. Her, moaning in pleasure as he tasted her core. Crying out in abandon as he filled her with his shaft. Far more than the kiss she would have allowed him.

A kiss born of…pity? Or gratitude?

He found he desired neither. He wanted her to *want* his kiss.

And damn himself to everlasting eternity, why had he not taken her lips when she'd offered them? In pity, gratitude or not. What a fool he was! What a coward.

Did the opportunity arise again, he would pounce.

"What's wrong?" she asked, her still-rising panic evident.

"Nothing's wrong," he lied. "Some have called this the never ending pit, but I assure you, there is an end. Just a little farther and we'll hit. Landing will jar you, but I'll absorb most of the impact." He moved one of his hands up and onto the base of her neck. Offering comfort, he told himself. He'd tried not to touch her, had fought it, but there'd been no other way to protect her inside the pit.

Besides, what was the harm in adjusting a single hand?

"But you stiffened."

I must stop craving her. Her skin was soft, so soft, and he felt little bumps rise under his palm as he gently massaged. To his delight, her muscles relaxed under his ministrations.

Apparently, there was a lot of harm. His shaft hardened unexpectedly, and his cheeks heated. Could she feel the evidence of his arousal? It was buried beneath his only piece of armor, so perhaps she would think the metal responsible.

And you are a fool.

"Tell me what's wrong," she said. "You're hiding something, I can tell. I know this pit is made for souls, not breathing, flesh-and-blood bodies. Are we going to—"

"No. I swear it. We will live." The conversation seemed to calm her, so he said, "Tell me about you. About your childhood."

"I—all right. But there's not much to tell. I was not allowed out of my home as a child. For the greater good," she added, as though the line had been fed to her many times before.

He did not mean to, would have stopped himself if he'd realized, but he found himself hugging her tight, understanding. Because of her nature, she'd been as much an outcast as he was. "Kadence, I—" The air was thickening around them, the flames spraying what looked to be molten teardrops. He recognized the signs; the end was near. "Drop your legs from me, but do not let them touch the ground."

"All righ—"

"Now!"

Too late.

Boom. They smacked into the ground and Geryon planted his feet as the impact vibrated through him. He tried to remain upright to keep the goddess from having to touch the bones littering the area, but his knees soon gave out and he collapsed backward.

Kadence remained in his arms, unwinding her legs as he'd asked, so his back took the brunt of the fall, breath knocking from his lungs.

He lay there for a moment, panting. They were well and truly inside Hell.

There was no going back now.

CHAPTER EIGHT

"GERYON? ARE YOU ALL RIGHT?"

The muted darkness of the pit had given way to bright light, fire illuminating every direction. Kadence hovered over him, like the sun he sometimes glimpsed in his daydreams, bright and glorious. "I am…fine."

"No, you're not. You're wheezing. What can I do to help?"

He was surprised to note she did not scramble off him, now that they were safe. Well, as safe as a person could be inside Hell. "Tell me more about yourself. While I catch my breath."

"Yes, yes, of course." As she spoke, her delicate hands wisped over his brow, his jaw, his shoulders. Searching for injuries? Offering comfort? "What should I tell you?"

"Anything." He was growing stronger by the second, but he did not admit it. Rather, he luxuriated in the sensation of her touch. "Everything. I want to know all about you." Truth.

"All right. I…goodness, this is hard. I guess I'll start at the beginning. My mother is the goddess of Happiness. Odd, I know, that such a woman could give birth to one such as me."

"Why odd?" When looking at Kadence, hearing her voice, breathing in her scent, gave him more joy than he'd ever known?

"Because of what I am," she said, clearly ashamed. "Because of the damage I can cause."

"I have known nothing but—" *pleasure, hunger, desperation* "—kindness at your hands."

Her ministrations ceased, and he could feel her gaze boring into him. "Truly?"

"Yes, truly." *Do not stop touching me.* Centuries had passed since he'd last enjoyed even the slightest hint of contact. This was nirvana, paradise and a dream all wrapped into one delightful package. "My head," he found himself saying on a moan.

"Poor baby," she cooed, massaging his temples.

He nearly smiled. Now was not the time for this. They were inside Hell, out in the open, possible targets. The demons at the gate could have followed them. But he could not help himself, was too desperate, greedy. *Just a little longer.* "Your story," he prompted.

"Where was I? Oh, yes." Her honeysuckle scent enveloped him, chasing away the odor of rot. "I was a mean little girl. I didn't share my toys, and I frequently made the other children cry, unintentionally compelling them to bend to my will. All right, perhaps a few of those times it was not so unintentional. I think that's one of the reasons I was sent to Hell as warden, though it was never said aloud. The gods wanted to be rid of me, once and for all."

How forlorn she sounded. "Every living creature has made a mistake at one point or another. Besides, you were a child. Not yet sensitized to the feelings of others. Do not blame yourself. They should not have. They knew better."

"What of you?" she asked, and this time she sounded more buoyant.

I did that. I encouraged her.

"What would you like to know?" he wondered.

Slowly she grinned. "Anything. Everything."

That grin…one of the gods' finest creations, surely. His gut clenched. His shaft hardened again.

"I need a moment to think." He'd relegated his human memories to a far corner in his mind, never to be considered again. Before, thinking of those days had stung, for he'd known they were forever lost—but he reminded himself that with his wife's desertion, that was a good thing. Today, however, with the essence of Kadence all around him, he experienced only a thrum of sadness for what might have been.

"I was a wild child, untamable, a roamer," he said. "My mother despaired, thinking I would worry her and every member of our family to death." He laughed, her sweetly aged face flashing in his mind. "Then they introduced me to Evangeline. She calmed me, because I wanted to be worthy of her. We married, as both our families desired."

Kadence stiffened. Even paled. The hand she'd been dancing at his temple stilled. "You are…wed?"

"No. She left me."

"I am sorry," she said, but there was relief in her tone.

Relief? Why? "Don't be." Had he not given his soul for Evangeline, she would have died. And had she not left Geryon, he might have fought Lucifer when the time came to become Guardian. And had he fought, he might not have met Kadence.

In that moment, he had never been so glad of something.

Suddenly a frenzied snarl echoed through the distance, trailed by more demon laughter. They had indeed been followed.

Giving up all pretense of being winded, Geryon popped to a stand, lifting the goddess with him and searching the distance.

The horde was several yards away. But as he watched, a fiend separated from the pack and raced straight for them.

CHAPTER NINE

GERYON SHOVED KADENCE behind him. Another touch—*warmth, satin skin, perfection*—and he yearned to revel in it. He didn't, couldn't. He'd agreed to come with her to save the human realm, yes, but also to keep her safe. Not because she was a goddess and not because she was the most beautiful thing he'd ever beheld, but because, in this single day, she had made him feel like a man. Not a beast.

"Remember that I swore to let no harm befall you," he told her. A minute, perhaps two, and the creature would reach them. Fast as it was, there was still a great distance to cover, the streets of Hell stretching endlessly. "I will keep my word."

"Geryon. Perhaps I can—"

"No." He didn't want her involved in this fight. Already she was trembling in fear. She was so scared, in fact, she had yet to realize her hands were resting on his back, twin conductors of inexorable pleasure. Had she known, surely she would have jerked away. "I will fight it." Should she try to do so, it would feed off her fear, becoming more crazed.

As did most minions, the creature coming at them possessed a skeletal face and a muscled body covered in green scales, its forked tongue flicking out as if blood already coated the air. Glowing red eyes glared at them, a thousand sins resting where pupils should have.

Warrior instincts demanded Geryon stride forward and

meet the bastard in the middle. Fight there, like true soldiers. Yet his every *male* instinct demanded he stay where he was. To put any distance between himself and Kadence was to place her in further danger. Another demon could be hiding nearby, waiting for the chance to pounce on her. Another of the horde could separate, circle around and try to take her from behind.

"This is my fault," she said. "No matter that I had begun to relax, my fear of this place is bone-deep. And that fear is like a beacon to them, isn't it?"

He chose not to answer that, too afraid of scaring her further by acknowledging the truth of her words. "When it reaches us, I want you to run backward. Press against the wall and scream for me if you see any hint of another demon."

"No, I want to help you. I—"

"Will do as I said. Otherwise, I will defeat it and leave this place." His tone was uncompromising. Already he regretted bringing her here, whether the wall needed defending or not. Whether innocents needed saving or not.

She was more important, he realized.

She stiffened against him, but didn't offer another protest.

A cry of "Mine, mine, mine" rent the air.

The creature closed in, faster…almost…there. Claws raked at Geryon as he grabbed his opponent by the neck. Multiple stings erupted on his face, followed by the trickle of warm blood. Flailing arms, kicking legs.

Only when the temptation of Kadence's hands fell away did Geryon truly begin to battle. He tossed the creature to the ground and leapt upon it, knees pinning its shoulders. One punch, two, three.

It bucked, wild and feral. Saliva gleamed on its fangs as curses sprang from its bony mouth. Another punch. Still another. But the pounding failed to subdue it in any way.

"Where is Violence? Death? Doubt?" he gritted out. They were why he was here, after all.

The struggling continued, intensified, terror leaping to life in those red eyes. Not fear for what Geryon would do, he knew, but terror for what its brothers-in-evil would do if they learned of any betrayal.

Though Geryon hated for Kadence to see him kill brutally, savagely—again—it could not be helped. He raised his hand, spread his elongating, dripping nails and struck. The poison that coated his nails was a "gift" from Lucifer to aid in his duties and acted swiftly, without mercy, spreading through the creature's body and rotting it from the inside out.

It screamed and screeched in agony, its struggles becoming writhing spasms. Then the scales began to burn away, smoking, sizzling, leaving only more of that ugly bone. But the bones, too, disintegrated and black ash soon coated the air, blowing in every direction.

Geryon stood to shaky legs. "You are next," he shouted to the others.

They quickly scampered away.

How long would they *stay* gone, though?

He should move on. Instead, he kept his back to Kadence for several minutes, waiting, hoping—dreading—that she would say something. What did she think of him now? Would there be any more of her tending? Would she rescind her offer of a kiss?

Finally curiosity got the better of him and he pivoted on his heels.

She stood exactly as he'd commanded, her back pressed against the rocky wall. Those glorious ringlets cascaded around her. Her eyes were wide and filled with…admiration? Surely not.

"Kadence."

"No. Do not speak. Come to me," she said, and crooked her finger.

CHAPTER TEN

KADENCE HAD BEEN UNABLE to hold back her entreaty. Geryon stood several feet away, panting shallowly, his cheeks cut and bleeding, his hands dripping with his opponent's lifeblood.

His dark eyes were more haunted than she'd ever seen them.

"Come to me," she said again. And again, she motioned him over with a wave of her fingers.

The first time, he'd given no reaction. As though he hadn't believed he'd heard her correctly. This time, he blinked. Shook his head. "You wish to…punish me for my actions?"

Silly man. Punish him? When he'd saved her? Yes, part of her was angry that he'd kept her from the fight, that he'd threatened—vowed—to leave without doing what they'd come here to do. Yet again. But part of her was relieved. As the demon had struck at him, she had felt power bloom inside her. Such magnificent, beautiful power. Born of fury, perhaps, but born nonetheless.

I am not a coward. Not anymore. Next time, I will act. No matter his wishes, no matter mine. He deserves that. Deserves to have someone look out for him.

"Kadence," Geryon said, and she realized she had been staring at him, silent.

"I would never punish you for aiding me. No matter your actions. If you learn nothing else about me, learn that."

Again he blinked. "But…I killed. I hurt another creature."

"And you were injured in the process. Come, let me attend to your wounds."

Still he resisted. "But you would have to put your hands on me."

He said it as though the thought should be loathsome to her. "Yes, I know. Does the thought bother you?" *Please don't let it bother you.* "I mean, I have done so already and you did not seem… I mean…"

"Bother *me?*" One hesitant step, two. At that pace, he would never reach her.

Sighing, she closed the rest of the distance herself, twined their fingers—experienced an electric jolt, gasped—and led him to the rocks. "Sit. Please."

As he obeyed, he tugged his hand from her and rubbed where they'd been connected. Had the same jolt pierced him? She hoped it had, for she did not want to be alone in this…attraction. Yes, attraction, she realized. Physical, erotic. The kind that prompted a woman to leave her inhibitions and invite a man into her bed.

Whether that invitation was accepted or not was a different story.

Reluctant as Geryon was, she was positive he would turn her down. As he had done for the kiss. And perhaps that was for the best, she decided now. Her lovemaking tended to scare men away. Because when the pleasure hit her, she could not control her nature. The chains she'd erected broke, unleashing her will with a vengeance.

Physically, her lovers became her slaves. Mentally, they cursed her, knowing she had stolen their freedom of choice, unwitting though it had been.

She had never bedded the same man twice, and, after three tries, had stopped altogether. One she had considered bad luck. Two, a coincidence. Three, undeniably her fault.

How would Geryon respond, though? Would he hate her as

the others had? Probably. Already he knew the horrors of being bound to someone else's will. She would not doubt if freedom was the most precious commodity in his life.

And that was as it should be. Natural. Normal. Both of which he probably craved as well.

She would be more trouble than she was worth.

Sighing, she tore several strips of cloth from the bottom of her robe and knelt in front of him, between his legs. His shaft was hidden by a short skirt of leather and metal filigree. A warrior's cloth. Perhaps it was wanton of her, but she wanted to see him *there.* Despite everything. She licked her lips, thinking maybe, perhaps, what if she did peek? That would not destroy his life and…

As if he could read her mind, he sucked in a breath. "Don't," he said.

"I'm sorry. I—"

"No. Don't stop."

CHAPTER ELEVEN

DON'T STOP. DID HE MEAN for her to move his armor out of the way? Or simply to clean him as she'd promised? Already he was nervous, on edge, and had resisted even the slightest of handling. Afraid to risk a mistake, she leaned in, reached up and mopped the blood from his face with one of the strips of cloth. *Acting the coward again, are we?*

His delectable scent filled her nose, a midnight breeze that inexplicably reminded her of home. A sprawling, opulent home she had not been able to visit since reluctantly agreeing to oversee the fortification of Hell. How she missed it.

"In all the years I have known you," she said, carefully avoiding the deepest gash, "you have never left your post at the gate. Do you eat?" At first contact, he had jumped. But she maintained a steady, casual rhythm and he gradually relaxed.

Perhaps one day he would allow her to do more. Would she enslave him, though, as she had the others? Still the question plagued her. If there was a chance that she wouldn't… *What are you doing?* She'd already told herself she could not risk it, but hope was a silly thing and refused to leave her.

"No," he said. "There's no need for me to eat."

"Really?" Even she, a goddess, needed food. She could survive without it, yes, but she *would* waste away, becoming a mere shell of herself. That was why baskets of fruits and breads were brought to her once a week—along with lectures about her many failures. "How, then, do you survive?"

"I'm not sure. I know only that I stopped needing food the day I was brought here. Perhaps the fire and smoke sustain me."

"So you don't miss it? The tastes and textures, I mean?"

"It's been so long since I've seen even a crumb that I rarely think of food anymore."

She wanted to feed him, she thought. Wanted to sweep him out of this nightmare and into a banquet hall with tables piled high, food of every kind gracing their surfaces. She wanted to watch his face light in ecstasy as he sampled one of everything. No one should be forced to go without such nourishment.

When his face was clean, she switched her attentions to his right arm. Angry claw marks glared at her, and she knew they had to be hurting him. Not by word or deed did he betray it, though. No, he actually seemed…blissful.

"I'm sorry I do not have the proper medicines to ease your pain."

"You have no reason to be sorry. I'm grateful for what you're doing and hope to repay you in kind someday. Not that I desire you to be injured," he added quickly. "I do not." Horror blanched his features. "I would hate such a thing. Truly. I only want to see you healthy and whole."

Her lips curled into a slow smile. "I understood your meaning." Finished with her ministrations, she settled her hands in her lap. She didn't move from her position between his legs, because an idea had taken root in her mind. Perhaps he wasn't ready for her to remove his armor, but that did not mean he would refuse her…other things. And he'd seemed to enjoy having her hands on him.

Careful. "May I ask you a question, Geryon?"

He nodded hesitantly. "You may do anything you like to me."

Had he meant the words to emerge so sensually? So husky

and rich? Butterflies took flight in her belly. "Are you…do you like me?"

He looked away from her and gave another nod. "More than I should," he muttered.

Those butterflies morphed into ravens, flapping their dark wings wildly. "Then I would like very much if you would kiss me at last."

CHAPTER TWELVE

KISS HER? "I SHOULDN'T. I can't." *What are you doing? You just told yourself you would not pass up an opportunity like this again.* Geryon's gaze strayed to her lips. They were lush and red. Glistening. His mouth watered for a taste of them. His horns, sensitive to his emotions as they were, throbbed.

Those pretty lips dipped into a frown. "Why not? You just said you liked me. Did you lie to spare my feelings?"

If only it were that easy. "I would never lie to you. And I do like you. You are beautiful and strong, the finest thing I have ever known."

"You think me beautiful? Strong?" Pleasure lit her expression. "Then why won't you kiss me?"

Yes, you fool. What reasons do you have now? "I will hurt you." Oh. Why hadn't he thought of that before? It was irrefutable. And the only guarantee he would keep his lips to himself.

Her face scrunched adorably in her confusion. "I don't understand. You've never hurt me before."

"My teeth…they are too sharp." He didn't add that his hands were too toxic, his strength too mighty. Were he to lose control of himself and squeeze her, which was a possibility considering how much he desired her, she *would* be hurt. Scared, too. Perhaps even irreparably damaged.

"I'm willing to risk it," she said, placing her palms on his thighs and burning him soul-deep.

He both hated and loved his half-armor at that moment. Hated because it kept him from skin-to-fur contact. Loved because it blocked her gaze from parts of his monstrous form.

"Why?" What reason could she possibly have for wanting to place her luscious lips on something so disgusting? Mere curiosity would not drive a female to such an act. Evangeline had vomited the moment she'd first spied his changed appearance. "I could tolerate what you were, but I cannot tolerate…*this,*" she'd thrown at him.

"Because." Twin pink circles painted Kadence's cheeks, but she didn't turn her gaze.

"Why?" he insisted. He placed his hands atop hers. Gulped at the headiness, the silkiness.

"You saved me."

So she was grateful. Exactly as he had suspected—and had not wanted. His shoulders sagged in disappointment. *Did you truly expect her to desire you?* No, he hadn't expected it—but he had hoped. "It would be dishonorable to kiss you for such a reason."

"But I owe you."

"No. I release you from that vow." *Foolish again!*

"Fine." Though she remained on her knees, she rose until they were merely a whisper apart. "Do it because I'm desperate, needy. Do it because I've suddenly realized how quickly something can be taken from me, and I wish to know some part of you before I'm—"

"Before you're…" he managed to choke out. She was desperate? Needy? For him?

"Do it," she pleaded.

Yes. *Yes.* Geryon could no longer resist, dishonorable or not. Risk or not. He would be careful, he vowed. So careful. He could not resist her. Would not resist her.

He bent the rest of the way, softly pressing his mouth against hers. Exquisite. She didn't pull away. She gasped, lips parting, and he swept his tongue inside. Her taste…so sweet, like a snowstorm after a millennium of fire. *Beyond* exquisite.

"More," she said. "Deeper. Harder."

"Sure?" Please, please, please.

"More than I've ever been."

Thank the gods. Centuries had passed since he'd kissed a woman and never while in this form, but he began thrusting his tongue against hers, rolling them together, retreating, then going back for more. When he felt his teeth scrape hers, he stiffened. And when she moaned, he tried to pull away. But her arms slid up his chest, one anchoring around his neck, the other caressing a horn. He had to grip his thighs, nails sinking deep, to keep his claws off her.

"Like?" she asked.

"Yes," he managed to grit out.

"Good. Me, too." Her lush breasts pressed into his chest, her nipples hard and searching.

She truly enjoyed his kiss? Tremors rocked him, their tongues beginning another dance, his muscles tightening against the strain of remaining exactly as he was. With every moment that passed, every breathy sound that emerged from her, his control snapped a little more. He yearned to toss her down, climb atop her and pound, pound so hard he would brand himself on every inch of her. Inside every cell.

More, more, more. He had to have more. Had to have *all.*

Had already *given* all.

The realization rocked him. "Stop," he finally said. "We must stop." He jerked to his feet, away from her, already mourning the loss of her taste. Shaking. He kept his back to her, panting, his heart racing.

"Did I do something wrong?" she asked softly, and there was a catch in her voice.

Oh, yes. You stole a heart I could not afford to give. He'd promised never to lie to her, however, so he merely said, "Come. We have waited long enough. We have demons to hunt."

CHAPTER THIRTEEN

THEY STOPPED AT THE FIRST building they came to: a tavern. An actual, honest-to-gods tavern, where blood was served rather than alcohol and body parts were the snacks. Kadence had known such things existed down here, but it still struck her as odd. Demons, acting as humans. In their eerie way.

She and Geryon had had a two-mile trek from the pit's entrance to here. A two-mile trek she had spent remembering his earth-shattering kiss, cursing him for stopping it and fretting about his reasons for doing so.

Throughout her endless life, she had welcomed only those three lovers into her bed, and all three had been gods. If gods had not been able to handle her, there was no way Geryon could. But she had hoped. For once, during that too-short span, she'd had no thoughts of controlling her nature, only enjoying. Oh, had she enjoyed. His taste was divine, his tongue hot and wet, his body a work of art and muscle. So badly she had wanted him to touch her. To strip her and penetrate her. To *claim* her.

Yet Geryon had walked away from her, just as the others had.

Am I so terrible? So horrible a person?

More than the others, she had wanted Geryon to find pleasure with her because he *meant* more. She liked who she was with him. Liked how she felt when he was near. Worthy. Precious. Instead, she had…disgusted him? Repelled him? Failed to arouse him in even the slightest way?

"Stay by my side," he said as he shoved open the tavern's swinging double doors. They were the first words he had uttered since reminding her of their quest. "And keep your hood over your head. Just in case. Actually, are you versed in glamour?"

His voice was deep and rough and caressed every one of her weeping senses. Surely she did not disgust him. Surely she did not repel him. He had held himself back during their kiss, had stopped it, but when he looked at her, he made her feel as if she were the only woman in the world. The most beautiful, the most desired.

He paused before entering. "Kadence?" Cleared his throat. "Goddess?"

"I will glamour myself and stay by your side," she told him, though inside she beseeched, *Tell me why you continually push me away.* She only wanted to draw closer.

He didn't, of course. He nodded and stepped forward. She stayed close, as promised, mentally projecting the image of bones and scales. Anyone who glanced in her direction would think they saw one of their own. She could only hope her fear was masked as well. They would not hesitate to devour one of their own.

Taunting laughter and pain-filled cries immediately assaulted her ears. Gulping, she sent her gaze around the room. So many demons…they came in every shape and size. Some were like the image she projected, bones and scales. Some were half man, half bull. Some were winged like dragons with snouts to match. Yet all of them crowded a stone slab. A moving slab?

No, not moving, she realized, horror claiming her in a bruising grip and nearly crushing her lungs. Human spirits were atop the slab. The demons were ripping them apart, eating their insides. Dear gods.

Unfortunately, there was no peace for the damned. Only endless torture.

"Disgusting," she couldn't help but breathe. "How can we defeat a horde of these?"

"All we can do is try."

Yes. Sadly, they had no guarantee of success. *But I told Geryon I would protect him, and I will.*

"Over here." He edged them to the side and out of the way, and she knew it was so that they could observe the happenings without drawing notice. "The creatures you see here are minions, soldiers and servants. They are not what we will be fighting."

That's right, she thought, stomach sinking. Violence, Death and the like were Demon Lords. While minions enjoyed their prey's agony, their main focus was the fulfillment of a single, basic need: hunger.

The Lords cared only for the agony. Prolonging it, increasing it to the depths of insanity. And the more agony they inflicted, the more screams they elicited, the stronger they became.

Oh, yes. They were far worse than anything here.

She would never be able to keep Geryon safe.

CHAPTER FOURTEEN

"SSSMELL GOOD, LIKE FEAR," something suddenly growled beside Kadence. "Mmm, hungry."

Startled, she gasped. *I've already given myself away?* She'd just decided to do something, anything to force Geryon to return to the gate. Now this. Hell. No, she thought.

Geryon tried to pull her behind him, but she resisted. This time, she wouldn't sink into the background, forcing him to do all the work, take all the risks. This time, she fought.

"Move away or die," she told the demon.

It frowned at her. "Look like me ssso why you sssmell so good?" It licked its lips, saliva dripping from the corners of its paper-thin mouth. It was covered in yellow scales and only reached her navel. And while it appeared lean, she suspected unyielding strength rested underneath those scales.

A tremor moved through her. *Remember who you are. Remember what you can do.*

It stepped closer. "Tassste."

"You were warned," she said, bracing herself.

"Wait outside, Kadence. Please." Geryon tried to move in front of her. "I will handle this."

She blocked him, not facing him. "No. You will not fight them alone."

As they spoke, the demon continued to inch toward them, its claws lengthening.

"Please, Kadence." Geryon tugged at her. "I need to know you're safe. Otherwise, I'll be distracted, and a distracted warrior is a defeated warrior."

Defeat would not be theirs. "I cannot act the coward. Not anymore. Besides, if this works, you will not have to fight him at all." She was Hell's warden; it was past time she acted like it. Past time she ruled rather than merely observed.

"*If* isn't good enough. Not when it comes to your safety."

She did not have time to bask in his beautiful concern. Any moment the creature would cease its stalking and spring. She knew it, felt it. Kadence reached inside herself as she angled her chin to stare deep into its eyes, surprised to find her power easily accessible. She shouldn't have been surprised, though. She might *try* to suppress it, but it was always there, never silent, a churning sea inside her.

Hadn't Geryon's earlier fight proven that?

"Stay," she said, and the creature locked in place, its mind still active but every part of its physical form hers to command.

For a long while, she simply drank in her handiwork, amazed. *I did it.* Not once did the fiend try and approach her again—even though murder gleamed in those beady eyes.

"Something's happened," Geryon said, sounding confused.

"*I* happened," she said, proud of herself. "Watch." To the demon she said, "Raise your arms over your head."

Instantly, it obeyed, shooting both arms into the air without a word of complaint. But then, she had possession of its mouth, as well.

Joy burst through her. For once, she had used her ability for good: to save someone she greatly lo—admired. Dear gods. Love? Did she love Geryon? She loved being with him, loved the way he made her feel, but did that mean she had given him her heart? Surely not. Surely she was not that foolish.

Soon they would part.

"Look, Kadence." Geryon pointed to the slab. "Look what's happened."

She followed the direction of his finger and gasped. *Every* demon had frozen in place, their hands in the air. Even the spirits had stopped writhing. There was no laughter, no cries. Only the sound of her own breathing could be heard.

"You did this?" Geryon asked.

"I—yes."

"I am amazed. Awed."

Her joy intensified. He admired her. Was perhaps even proud of her. "Thank you."

"Can they hear me?" When she nodded, he slowly grinned and shouted to the creatures, "Hear me well. Go forth and tell every Demon Lord the Guardian is here and that I plan to destroy them." To Kadence he added, "You may release them now."

"Are you sure? I could command their bodies to wither and die." And those bodies would obey. Power…so sweet…

"I am sure. They are here to punish, so they do serve a purpose. More than that, they will now bring the Lords to us."

Though she wanted to protest, Kadence did as he'd asked. In less than a blink, the creatures were racing from the building as fast as possible, leaving her and Geryon alone. "We must prepare," Geryon said gravely.

"For?"

"War."

There would be no taking him back, she realized. Unless she ordered him to return. Which she could do, and he would now be forced to obey. *Power…* But he would return, she was sure. Too much determination rested in his smoldering eyes.

You can protect him now, she thought next, and grinned.

"War," she said with a nod. "That sounds fun."

CHAPTER FIFTEEN

GERYON FORTIFIED the building against attack as best as he was able, given the lack of supplies and tools. Kadence remained at his side, lending a spiritual touch whenever needed, forcing the planks and stones to bow to her will. He noticed she grew paler with every minute that passed. A paleness all the more stark when compared to the authority she'd wielded over those demons.

Why was she weakening?

Did he have the right to ask? She was a goddess, after all. But that growing paleness did not speak of typical fatigue; it spoke of something more. Something deeper.

"What's our battle plan?" she asked when they finished, settling against the far wall. The only place without blood or…other things on it.

Keeping you alive, by whatever means necessary. He joined her, careful not to touch her. One touch, and he would pull her back into his arms. He needed to be alert, on guard. "The moment they enter, you'll lock them in place and I'll slay them with my poison."

"Quick and easy," she said with a ring of satisfaction in her tone.

He was surprised she was not more fearful, despite her show of power. Maybe because he wanted her fearful. Just a bit, just enough. That was the only way to keep her out of the action. Safe. "But we must wait until they all arrive, otherwise they will hear of the devastation we have caused and run. And if they run, we might never be able to find them."

She absorbed his words. "How long do you think we have before they begin arriving?"

"A few hours. It will take a while for news of my arrival and intentions to spread. Longer still for the Lords to gather their forces and plan an attack." Geryon raked a claw across the floorboard to mar the curse etched there, shards flying into the air. "I have a question for you."

"Ask."

Did he dare?

Yes, he thought, glancing at her beauty. He dared. "I understand why Lucifer wishes you to destroy the demons trying to leave Hell and thereby prevent all other demons from following them, but why does it matter so much to you? You were born in the heavens. You could be frolicking there, in the clouds and amid the ambrosia."

"Many times I have wished to return. But I willingly agreed to do this job, and do it, I shall. Besides, when I agreed to enter this realm, I became…connected to it."

"Connected? What do you mean?"

"If the wall crumbles, I…die."

She would *die?* "Why did you not tell me before now?" he growled. "And why would you connect to such a thing? Why would you come here willingly?"

She twisted the fabric of her gown. "Had I remained in the heavens, I would have been punished every minute of every day. No one is crueler in that respect than the gods. They wanted me here, so here I came. But I had no idea how permanent the bonding would be. How powerful. As to why I didn't tell you before…" She shrugged. "You had permission to finally leave your post yet you chose to help me. I didn't want to burden you further. Now you've saved me, again, and I don't wish to lie to you. Even by omission."

"Kadence," he said, then shook his head. He could not

believe this was happening. That he could lose her—and be able to do nothing about it. "I should have remained at the inside of the gate, without you, and slayed the Lords as they approached. Now the wall is without protection, and you are in more danger than ever."

"No. They would have seen you and stayed away, for there is no place to hide above the pit."

"And that would have been fine with me. That would have kept you safe."

"Yet that is no kind of life for you, simply lying in wait."

"It is the life I am used to." Truth. But knowing what he did was for her…there was no greater purpose.

"But you deserve more!" Looking away from him, she traced a fingertip over the area he had clawed. "We had to do this. Or rather, I did. But I want you to know that if I fall, the wall will remain as it is, for *it* isn't bound to *me.* I know because I have been hurt many times over the years, yet it did not show signs of damage."

"I don't care about the damn wall!" Again, truth.

Her eyes widened. Then she gulped and continued as if he hadn't spoken. Or yelled. "Without me, there will be no one who senses when something is wrong. The gods will have to find someone new. I know you are now free, but would you remain there, vigilant, until that person is found? Even if Lucifer has already appointed a new guardian?"

"You are not going to die, damn it. Now tell me why Lucifer allowed you inside? Clearly, he needs you *outside.*"

Color fused her cheeks. Embarrassment? Guilt? "He also needs his wall protected at any cost."

Guilt, most definitely. It was there in her voice, echoing off the walls. "He could have destroyed or imprisoned the Demon Lords."

"If he could catch them."

Geryon didn't want to, but he nodded. "I'll give you that." He tapped two fingers against his chin, pondering the situation. "Lucifer allows nothing, even those things he needs, without demanding some form of payment." Which meant Kadence had had to pay. "What did he demand of you? And why did he allow you my services? Why release my soul? And where is my soul now, if Lucifer no longer has it?" Even as he asked the questions, a few of the answers shaped in his mind. He snarled low in his throat. "You *bought* me from him."

That color in her cheeks deepened. "Geryon, I—"

"Didn't you?"

"Yes," she whispered. Her eyelashes fluttered shut, the length of them casting spiky shadows over her cheeks. One of her hands rubbed at the amethyst dangling between her breasts. "I'm not sorry, either."

Was his soul inside that stone? "Did you buy me with… yourself?" If so, he would slay the prince before allowing one evil finger to touch this woman's precious body.

A pause, her eyes slowly opening. Then, "No. I do not wish to discuss this, though."

"I don't care. Tell me." Anger was building inside of him. Anger with her, with Lucifer, with himself that this could have happened. What had this prized woman given up? *Why* had she given it up? He placed his hand over hers, not to hold her in place—powerful as he now knew she was, he doubted he could have done so—but to offer reassurance. He was here, he wasn't leaving. Nothing she said would send him running. "Please."

Her chin trembled. "I—I gave him a year on earth, unimpeded, to do as he wished."

"Oh, Kadence," Geryon said, knowing the other gods would have to honor her bargain—and would make her suffer for it. Everything inside him rebelled at the thought. If they hurt her…*you can do nothing.* Powerless fool. "Why would you do such a thing?" A savage whisper. Run, no. He still would not.

Tears beaded in her eyes. "To save you. To save me. To save the world beyond our reach. I could think of no other way. A single year to wreak his havoc seemed a small thing to trade in comparison to an eternity of demons roaming free." Her mouth opened, but rather than words she gave a pained cry.

Quick as a snap, her skin leached of color and she doubled over.

Concern instantly rocked him. "What's wrong, sweet? Tell me."

"The demons…I think…I think they're at the wall. I think they're killing me."

CHAPTER SIXTEEN

HAD LUCIFER TOLD THE DEMONS of her bond to the wall? Kadence wondered, pain slicing through her. Rather than come here to fight, they had gone there. Why would they do such a thing unless they knew she would weaken, die?

Or perhaps they had hoped to draw Geryon to them, leaving her here, alone and seemingly vulnerable to ambush. Or did they want *her* to come to them? So many alternatives. All of them grim.

The prince probably found the entire situation vastly amusing. He probably—a sudden thought nearly paralyzed her. If she were killed, he could have more than the agreed upon year on the earth, bartering for souls, causing untold havoc. He could have forever, if he so desired, and he could bring his demons with him, ruling his minions *and* humans.

He was a god, a brother to the sovereign. Because of that, there was no guarantee he would be captured and sent back.

Of course. The perfect plan. He'd wanted her to come here. He'd wanted her to bring Geryon. He'd wanted them both—his only hindrances—to die.

Oh, gods. She was sickened, for she had unwittingly helped him every step of the way. *What kind of fool am I?* More than sickened, she was so ashamed.

So easy. She'd made it so easy for him.

"Kadence, speak to me. Tell me what's wrong," Geryon

insisted. He popped to his knees and swung around, kneeling between her legs. One of his claws gently, tenderly brushed away the damp hair clinging to her brow.

Her gaze lifted to his. Seeing him with so much concern in his beautiful brown eyes, the sickness and the shame left her—the pain, though, remained. She suddenly could not regret the choices she'd made. No matter what happened, he would be free. This proud, strong man would finally be free. As he'd always deserved.

"I…am…fine," she managed to gasp out. Gods, she felt shredded inside, as though her organs were being ripped to ribbons.

"No, you're not. But you will be." He scooped her into his arms and carried her to the back. To a room the owner must have used. He laid her on a thin pallet of fur. "May I?" he asked, lifting the amethyst that housed his soul.

"Yes." She had planned to present it to him once their mission was completed, a gift for his aid, but she nodded. Right now, there was a good chance she would not complete anything.

"Is my soul inside?"

"Yes. All you must do is hold the stone over your heart."

"That easily?"

"Yes," she repeated. She wasn't capable of more.

Slowly, carefully, he worked the stone from around her neck and placed it over his heart as she'd instructed. His eyes closed. He was probably unsure what would happen. And at first, nothing did. Then, in gradual degrees, the jewel began to glow.

A frown pulled at Geryon's lips, and he grunted. "Burns."

"I'll hold it for y—"

The glow exploded into a thousand pinpricks of light, and he roared, loud and long.

After the last echo sounded, everything quieted. The lights faded. Only the chain that had held the jewel remained in his hand.

His frown was lifting into a smile as his eyes opened. But when he studied his arms and then his body, the frown returned, deeper, more intense. “I should have…I did not…I had hoped to return to my former visage.”

“Why?” She loved him, just as he was. Horns, fangs, claws and all. Loved. Unquestionably. She had considered it before, but had discarded the idea. Now, there could be no discarding. The emotion was there, undeniable as Death stared her in the face.

No man had ever been more perfectly suited for her. He was not disgusted by her nature, he reveled in it. He did not fear what she could do, but found pride in it. He delighted her, amused her, tempted her.

“It is my hope that…that…” He gulped. “If you bond with something else, something besides the wall, perhaps your ties to it will lessen and your strength will return. Perhaps the pain will ease.”

Something else? “You?” she asked, suddenly breathless for reasons that had nothing to do with pain.

“Yes. Me. I would understand if you choose not to do such a thing. I wanted only to offer the possibility so that—”

“Geryon?”

“Yes?”

“Shut up and kiss me.”

CHAPTER SEVENTEEN

GERYON REMAINED IN PLACE, looking away from her. "First, hear me out. I know I'm ugly. I know the thought of being with me in such a manner is abhorrent, but I—"

"You aren't ugly," Kadence interjected, "and I do not like that you think you are. I do not like when you demean yourself like that."

His attention whipped back to her and he blinked at her, astonishment shining in his expression.

She continued, "The thought of being with you is welcome. I promise you. *Now* can we kiss?"

Now his mouth opened and closed. "Welcome?"

She supposed not. "Yes. But I don't want you to bond with me simply to save me." She had once been too afraid to admit she craved his body, had pretended merely to be grateful to get a kiss. There would be no more pretending. "I want you to want to do this. Because I…I want you inside of me, becoming part of me, more than I want another tomorrow. I want to be your woman, now and always."

Before he could respond, another pain slicked through her, raining like poisoned hail and curling her into a ball. Another crack had just slithered through the wall; she saw it in her mind.

"Geryon?" she panted. "You must decide."

His gaze bore into her. "I once swore that were I ever lucky enough to regain my soul, I would never, for any reason, trade it again. I have just realized that I would willingly trade it for you, Kadence. So yes, I want to do this. *Now* we can kiss."

AS THEIR MOUTHS WORKED hungrily, Geryon slowly divested Kadence of her robe, careful not to hurt her with his razor-sharp nails. She was already in pain and he doubted she could bear much more. *Beautiful, precious woman.* She deserved only pleasure.

For whatever reason, she desired him. Desired forever. Together. She had given him the thing he'd thought he valued most—his soul—but he had not known until he'd watched her curl into a ball that he valued *her* more. Far more. He'd longed to take her pain into himself. For her, anything. She cared not that he was a beast. She saw to the heart of him, and liked it.

Amazing.

When she was naked, he pulled back and drank her in. Alabaster skin dusted with the sweetest hint of rose. Lush breasts, a curved waist, a navel his mouth watered to sample. Legs that stretched for miles. He bent and licked one of her nipples, laving his tongue around the delectable tip, his hands traveling all over her body.

The closer his fingers came to her core, the more she purred a deep sigh of satisfaction, her pain seeming to melt away. "The pleasure, it's replacing the pain," she said, confirming his thoughts.

Thank the gods. He moved his attention to her other nipple, sucking, allowing the tip of a fang to graze it ever so gently. She moaned.

"Still helping?" All the while his fingers teased just above her clitoris, not touching, only teasing. Was he doing this right? Please, gods, let him be doing this right.

"Still helping. But I want to see *you,*" she said, giving his armor a pointed stare.

He lifted his head and peered into her eyes. "Are you sure? I could take you without removing a single piece of armor."

"I want all of you, Geryon." Her features were luminescent. "All."

Beautiful, precious woman, he thought again. "Whatever you desire, you shall have." He only hoped she did not change her mind when she saw him.

"Do not fear my reaction. You are beautiful to me."

Such sweet words. But…he'd lived with his insecurities so long, they were a part of him. "How can I be? Look at me. I am a beast. A monster. Something to be feared and reviled."

"I *am* looking at you and you are something to be praised. You may not bear the appearance of other men, but you have strength and courage. Besides," she added, licking her lips, "animal magnetism is a very good thing. Now, show your future bride what she wants to see."

CHAPTER EIGHTEEN

GERYON REMOVED HIS BREAST cloth and tossed it aside, his too-corded chest with its scars, fur and over-large bones revealed. His hands shook as he then unwound the leather wrapped around his waist, as well as the rounded piece of armor, slowly revealing his hardened shaft, his scarred and fur-lined thighs.

He tensed, waiting for the inevitable gasp of horror, even though Kadence had assured him of his "animal magnetism."

"Beautiful," she said reverently. "A true warrior. My warrior." She reached up and ran her fingertips through that fur. "Soft. I like. No. I love."

Breath seeped from his parted lips, breath he had not realized he'd been holding until just then. "Kadence. Sweet Kadence," he rasped. She was…she was…everything. What had he ever done to deserve her? If he hadn't fallen in love with her already, he would have fallen then.

"Want to taste you."

"Please."

As the hottest thrum of desire he'd ever experienced pounded through him, he kissed his way down her stomach, stopping only to dip his tongue inside her navel. She trembled. When he reached the apex of her thighs, he worshipped her, sipping, licking, nibbling, *loving,* and the trembling became writhing.

"Amazing," she gasped, fisting his hair. "Don't stop. Please don't stop."

He could feel the power of her, wrapping around him, trying to drive his actions. He wasn't sure if he could have disobeyed and he didn't care. He wanted to devour her, possess her, and he did.

Only when she came apart, screaming her pleasure, did he rise above her. He was proud and honored to have given her such ecstasy. But he was trembling now himself, his body on fire. Desperate. Aching. For her, only her.

"Pain?"

"Gone."

The fact that this bonding could save her might be the reason he'd dared broach the subject, but he had never been happier. She would be his. She would live.

Her legs wound around him, and she cupped his cheeks, staring deep into his eyes. "Please don't change your mind. I need more of you."

He had stilled, he realized, poised at her entrance. "Never change my mind. *Must* have you. Ready?"

"Always."

He entered her an inch, one blessed inch. Stopped, gave her time to adjust. He'd go slowly if it killed him. And it might. Torture. The sweetest kind of torture. But he would make this good for her, the best.

"Why do I not feel the need to master you?" she purred into his ear. She bit the lobe.

Sweet fire. "That's how it was, before?" Sweat beaded all over him and dripped onto her.

She nodded, arching her hips to take more of him. Another inch.

He had to cut off a groan. "Perhaps because my heart is so completely yours, there's nothing left to master."

"Oh, Geryon. *Please.*" She stroked his horns, circling a fingertip over the hard points. "Take me all the way. Give me everything."

He could deny her nothing.

Releasing his fierce grip on control, he pounded forward and she cried out. Not in pain, but in joy, he realized. Their souls—he had a soul, he truly had a soul—were dancing together, intertwining…joining. Yes. Yes. Over and over he filled her, giving her all of him. Their wills intermingled so completely, it was impossible to tell who wanted what. Pleasure was the only goal.

His nails raked the floor beside her head, his teeth even nipped her, but she loved it all, urging him on, still begging for more. And when he spilled his seed inside her, her inner walls clutching him in her own surge of satisfaction, he shouted the words that had been building inside of him since the moment he'd met her. "I love you!"

To his surprise, she gave a shout of her own. "Oh, Geryon. I love you, too."

They were mated.

They were bound.

THEY QUICKLY DRESSED. Kadence was still weak, but at least the pain had stopped.

"Are they still at the gate?" Geryon asked. He was ready to end this. To take her away from this realm and cherish her always.

What if she still could not leave?

The thought drifted through his head but he ignored it. He would finally have a happy ending. Because they were together. Because they loved.

"Oh, yes," she said. "They're working it feverishly."

He kissed her lips, and he reveled in another taste of this woman he loved. "We will hike there. The moment you spy them, lock them in place, and I will do the rest."

"I hope this works," she said, "because I couldn't bear the thought of being parted from you."

Neither could he. "It will. It has to."

CHAPTER NINETEEN

THE HIKE TOOK AN HOUR, a slow torturous hour as well as a too-quick span, and then Geryon found himself standing a few yards from the wall. When he comprehended the carnage around him, he couldn't quite believe his eyes. The demons had worked so fervently, they had bled all over the stones—stones that had been shredded, almost paper thin. A hole was imminent.

Worse, the horde of Demon Lords was still there. They were huge, all of them at least seven foot, their bodies so broad that even Geryon, massive as he was, would not be able to stretch his arms wide enough to measure them. Skeletons were visible underneath the translucent skin. A few had wings, a few scales, and all were grotesque in their evil. Red eyes, horns like Geryon and fingers like knives.

"Kadence," he said.

"I'm trying, Geryon, I swear I am." Each word was softer, weaker. "But…"

One of the…things spotted them. Laughed, a sound that raised every hair on his body.

"Now," he shouted to Kadence. Please.

"Freeze, demons. I demand that you freeze."

They did not.

"Try again."

"Am." She glared over at them—nothing. Pointed her hands

at them—nothing. Groaned with the force of her will—but still nothing happened. The Lords did not freeze in place. "I can't," she gasped out.

"What's wrong?" He glanced at her, even as he moved in front of her, repositioning his arm around her waist. She had paled, as she had while working in the bar, and her trembling had returned. Had his arm not been around her, he knew she would have fallen. Had the bonding not worked, then? "Talk to me, sweetheart."

He watched the demons as they rallied together, watching *him.* Laughing. Imagining how they would kill him?

"I'm bound to you *and* the wall. I can feel your strength, its weakness, and it's tearing me apart," she cried. "I'm sorry. So sorry. All of this was for nothing, Geryon. Nothing! I'm doomed. I was doomed all along."

"Not nothing, never nothing. We have each other." But for how long? "I won't let you die."

"Nothing can be done."

Slowly the demons stalked forward, predators locked on prey. Eerie delight radiated from them. "I'll kill them all. We'll run. We'll—"

"You are the best thing that ever happened to me," she said weakly, leaning her cheek against his back.

"I forbade you to talk like that, Kadence." To say goodbye. For that's what she was doing, he knew it was.

"Kill them and run, just as you planned. Live in peace and freedom, my love. Both are yours. You deserve them."

No. *No!* "You will not die." But even as he said it, the wall, so badly damaged, began to crack, to crumble, the hole appearing. Widening. "Swear to me that you will not die."

Kadence's knees finally gave out, and he turned, roaring, easing her to the ground. Her eyes were closed. "So…sorry. Love."

"No. You will live. Do you hear me? You will live!"

Her head lolled to the side. Then, nothing.

"Kadence." He shook her. "Kadence!"

No response. But there *was* a rising and falling of her chest. She lived still. Thank gods, thank gods, thank gods.

"Tell me how to help you, Kadence. Please."

Again, nothing.

"Please." Tears burned his eyes. He had not cried for the wife that left him, had not cried for the life he'd lost, but he cried for this woman. *I need you.* She wanted him to stop the demons from leaving this realm, and then leave himself, but Geryon couldn't bring himself to move from her side.

Without her, he had no reason to go on.

Something sharp scraped at his neck, and he jerked his head to the side. The Lords flew around them, cackling with glee. "Leave us," he growled. He would spend however long was necessary, holding her until it was safe enough to move her.

"Kill her," one demon beseeched.

"Destroy her."

"Maim her."

"Too late. She's gone."

More laughter.

Bastards! One of them swooped down and raked a claw over her cheek, drawing blood before Geryon realized what was happening. She did not react. But he did. He roared with so much fury, the sound scraped at his ears.

The rest of the demons scented the lifeblood and purred in delight. Then there was a moment of absolute stillness and quiet. The calm before the storm. For, in the next instant, they attacked in a frenzy.

Geryon roared again, throwing himself over Kadence to take the brunt of their assault. Soon his back was in tatters, one of his horns chewed loose, a tendon severed. All the while he swung out his arm, hoping to slay as many as he could with his poison, but only one failed to dodge his blow.

On and on the laughter and abuse continued.

"I love you," Kadence suddenly whispered in his ear. "Your scream…pulled me from…darkness. Had to…tell you."

She had awakened? His muscles spasmed in shock and relief. "I love you. Stay with me. Don't leave me. Please. If you stay awake, just long enough to defend yourself, I can kill them. We can leave."

"I'm…sorry. Can't."

Then he would find a way to save her *and* continue protecting her. He never would have brought her into Hell had he known this would happen. He would have spent his entire existence at the gate, fighting to protect it. Her.

Wait. Fighting to protect. These demons wanted to escape. That's why they were here.

"Go," he screamed to them. "Leave this place. The mortal realm is yours." He didn't care anymore. Only Kadence mattered.

As if the wall had merely been waiting for his permission, it finally toppled completely. Which meant—

"No," he screamed. "I did not mean for you to collapse. I only meant for the demons to fly through." But it was too late, the damage was done.

Gleeful, the Demon Lords abandoned him and flew into the cave, then disappeared from view.

A new stream of tears burned Geryon's eyes as he gathered Kadence in his bleeding arms. "Tell me the wall no longer matters. Tell me I can now carry you to safety. That we can be together."

"Goodbye, my love," she said, and died in his arms.

CHAPTER TWENTY

SHE WAS DEAD. KADENCE was dead. And there was nothing he could do to save her. He knew it as surely as he knew he would take his next breath. An unwanted, hated breath. Those stinging tears slid down his cheeks, mocking reminders that he lived—and she did not.

I failed her. Damn this, I failed her!

She had wanted his help to save the wall, to save her. She had wanted his help to keep the Demon Lords inside Hell, yet he had failed her on all counts. Failed, failed, failed.

"I am so sorry, Geryon."

At this newest sound of her voice, he blinked. What the—as he watched, her spirit began to rise from her motionless body. She was…she was… Hope fluttered inside his chest. Hope and joy and shock.

He had not truly lost her, after all!

Her body was destroyed, but her spirit would live on. Of course. He should have known. Every day he encountered such spirits, though none had been as pure and vibrant as hers. They could still be together.

He pushed to his feet, facing her, heart drumming madly, legs shaking. She smiled sadly at him.

"I'm so sorry," she repeated. "I should not have bound myself to you. Should never have asked for your aid."

"Why?" When he'd never been happier? She was here, with

him. "You have nothing to be sorry for, sweetheart. It is I who failed you."

"Never say such a thing. Had you been stationed at the gate as you had wanted, this would not have happened."

"That isn't so. The demons would have ruined the wall, and thereby ruined you, but I would not have had the opportunity, no, the pleasure, of bonding with you. I cannot regret what happened." Not anymore. Not with her spirit just in front of him.

"Geryon—"

"What of the demons?" he asked, cutting her off. He would not have her lamenting her supposed mistakes. She had made none.

"I suppose the gods will attempt to gather them, bemoaning me as a failure forevermore."

He shook his head. "You are not a failure, love. You did everything within your power to stop them. Most would never even have entered the gates." His head tilted to the side as he studied her more intently. She was as lovely as ever, like a dream of her former self. Glittery, translucent, fragile. Still she possessed those golden curls. Still she looked at him with those bright eyes.

Before her, his life had been a wasteland. A single moment without her would have been…well, hell.

"Thank you, my sweet Geryon. But even if the wall is repaired, even if the demons are somehow captured, I fear the gods will be unable to contain those demons here." She sighed. "They have now tasted freedom. They will always fight to escape."

"The gods will find a way," he assured her. "They always do." He reached out to hug her to him, but his hand misted through her and he frowned, some of his happiness draining. Touching her was a necessity; he would not be able to live without her warmth, her softness.

Better he do without her touch and her warmth, though, than without *her.*

"You understand now," she said in that sad tone. "We can never be together again. Not truly."

"I don't care."

"But I do." Tears filled her eyes. "After everything you have suffered, you deserve more. So much more."

"I only want you."

She continued as if he had not spoken. "I will leave you and wander the earth alone." She gave a firm shake of her head. Those tears splashed onto her cheeks. "I know gods and goddesses are allowed to choose where they wish to reside in the afterlife, but I have no desire to return to heaven or stay in Hell."

As she spoke, an idea sprang into his mind. A wild idea he did not discard, but rather embraced.

Are you really going to do this?

He looked at her again, their gazes colliding and thought, *Yes. I really am going to do this.* "When I bonded to you, Kadence, it was forever and another eternity. I will not give you up now."

"But you will never again be able to touch me. You will never—"

"I will. I promise." And with that, he sank his own poisoned claws into his chest, felt the toxin burn him, blistering, scorching. He screamed at the anguish, black winking over his eyes.

He was…dying…

When the pain eased, the blackness faded. He was nothing. A void.

No, not true. There was a light. A bright light. He ran toward it, huffing and puffing for mile after mile, almost… there…

His eyelids fluttered open and he saw that his body was gone, a pile of ash, his spirit floating beside Kadence. Her eyes were wide, her mouth hanging open.

So many times over the centuries, he'd considered taking just such an action. Anything to end the monotony of his existence. But he had clung to life, for Kadence. To see her, to imagine caressing her and hope for the chance.

Now, that chance was a reality.

"You are…Geryon…you are just the same."

He looked down at himself. There were his claws, his fur, his hooves. "Are you disappointed?"

"No. I am overjoyed! I love you just as you are and do not want you to ever change. But you should not have given up your life for me," she sputtered through tears—and a grin she could not hide.

"I, too, am now free," he said. "Truly free. To be with you. And I would die all over again for just such an outcome." He jerked her into his arms, grinning, too, because he could feel her again. She was not as warm, there was a coldness to them both now, but he was holding her. He could deal. "You are my everything, sweetheart. I am lost without you."

"I love you so much," she said, raining little kisses all over his face. "But whatever will we do now?"

"Live. Finally, we will live."

And they did.

WHEN THE GODS REALIZED that the wall between earth and Hell had been breeched and a horde of Demon Lords let loose upon earth, they sent an immortal army to repair the damage—but no one could catch the fiends. And even if they could, the gods knew that locking them back inside Hell would merely invite another rebellion.

Something had to be done.

Though the stone barrier had fallen, the goddess of Oppression's body was still bound to the wall of Hell. And so the gods rebuilt the wall and then created a box-sized prison from Kadence's bones, confident that the powers she had tapped into hours before her death still resided deep in the marrow.

They were proven right.

Once opened, the box drew the demons from their hiding places, holding them captive as even Hell had been unable to do.

Of course, the gods were pleased with their handiwork and gave the box to Pandora, the strongest female warrior of her time, to guard. But that is a story for another time.

* * * * *

THE DARKEST PRISON

PROLOGUE

REYES, ONCE AN IMMORTAL warrior for the gods, now possessed by the demon of Pain and living in Budapest, entered his bedroom. He was drenched in sweat and panting from the force of his workout. Because he could not experience pleasure without physical suffering, the burn in his muscles had excited him. *Was* exciting him.

As always, his gaze sought out his woman, and he palmed the blade they preferred to use during their loveplay. She was sitting at the edge of their big bed, lovely features drawn tight as she studied the canvas in front of her. A canvas she'd propped on an easel and lowered so that she had a direct view. Blond hair fell to her shoulders in wild disarray, as if she'd tangled her fingers through the thick mass multiple times, and she was chewing on her bottom lip.

Sex could wait, he decided then. She was troubled, and he would be unable to think of anything else until he'd solved this dilemma for her. Whatever it was. He sheathed the blade.

"Something wrong, angel?"

Her eyes lifted and landed on him, worry in their emerald depths. She offered him a small smile. "I'm not sure."

"Well, why don't I help you figure it out?" Anything that bothered her, he would dispatch. No hesitation. For her happiness, he would do anything, kill anyone.

"I would like that, thank you."

"Shall I shower before I join you?"

"No. I like you just how you are."

Darling woman. But he didn't like the thought of dirtying her pretty clothes. He quickly grabbed a towel from the bathroom and rubbed himself dry. Only then did he settle behind his woman, his legs encasing hers, his arms wrapping around her waist. Breathing deeply of her wild storm scent, he rested his chin in the hollow of her neck and followed the direction of her gaze.

What he saw surprised him.

It shouldn't have. Her paintings were always vivid. As the All-Seeing Eye, an oracle of the gods and one of their most cherished aides, she could peer into heaven and Hell. And did, every night, though she had no control over what she witnessed. Past, present, future, it didn't matter. Every morning, she painted what she'd seen.

This one was of a man. A warrior, clearly. With that muscle mass, he had to be. A gold collar circled his neck, cinching tight. He was on his knees, legs spread. His arms rested on his thighs, palms raised. His dark head was thrown back, and he was roaring up at a domed ceiling. In pain, perhaps. Maybe even fury. There was blood smeared all over his chest, seeping from multiple wounds. Wounds that looked as if his skin had been carved away.

"Who is he?" Reyes asked.

"I don't know. I've never seen him before."

Then they would reason this out as best they were able. "Was he from heaven or Hell?"

"Heaven. Definitely. I think he's in Cronus's throne room."

A god, then? A few months ago, Titans had overthrown the Greeks and seized control of the divine throne. So, if this man was in Cronus's throne room, chained up, hurt, and Cronus was leader of the Titans, that must mean the warrior was a Greek. A slave who had been punished, perhaps?

"You saw only this image?" Reyes asked. "Not what got him to this point?"

"Correct," Danika said with a nod. "I heard him scream, though. It was…" She shuddered, and his arms squeezed her in comfort. "I felt so sorry for him. Never have I heard so much rage and helplessness."

"We can summon Cronus." Cronus wasn't too fond of Reyes and his fellow Lords of the Underworld—the very men who had opened Pandora's box, unleashing the evil from inside. The men who had then been cursed to carry that evil inside themselves. But the god king hated their enemy, the Hunters, more, because Danika had seen Galen, the leader of the Hunters, chop off Cronus's head in a vision. Now the god king was determined to kill Galen before Galen could kill him. Even if that meant soliciting the aid of the Lords. "We can ask him if he knows this man."

A moment passed while Danika pondered his suggestion. Finally, she sighed, nodded. "Yes. I'd like that." Then she surprised him by turning to him and offering the sweetest smile he'd ever seen. Well, all of her smiles were that way. "But it's too early in the morning to summon anyone, and besides, I think you had other things on your mind when you entered the room. Why don't you tell me about them?" she suggested huskily.

He was rock hard in seconds—that's what she did to him. "That would be my pleasure, angel."

She pushed him to his back, smile widening. "And mine."

CHAPTER ONE

"BE STILL, NIKE. YOU'RE ONLY making this worse for yourself." Atlas, Titan god of Strength, stared down at the bane of his existence. Nike, *Greek* goddess of Strength. And Victory, he inwardly sneered. She loved to remind him that many called her the goddess of Strength *and* Victory. As if she were better than him. In reality, she was his godly counterpart. His equal. His enemy. And an all-around grade-A bitch.

Two of his best men held her arms and two held her legs. They should have been able to pin her without incident. She was collared, after all, and that collar prevented her from using any of her immortal powers. Even her legendary strength—strength that was *not* on par with his, thank you. But never had a female been more stubborn—or more determined to fell him. She continually struggled against their hold, punching, kicking and biting like a cornered animal.

"I will kill you for this," she growled at him.

"Why? I'm not doing anything to you that you didn't once have done to me." Motions clipped, Atlas tore his shirt over his head and tossed the material aside, revealing his chest, the ropes of his stomach. There, in the center, in big black letters spanning from one tiny brown nipple to the other, was her name, spelled out for all the world to see. N-I-K-E.

She'd branded him, reduced him to her property.

Had he deserved it? Maybe. Once, he'd been a prisoner in

this bleak realm. In Tartarus, a divine dungeon. He'd been a god overthrown and locked away, forgotten, no better than rubbish. He'd wanted out, and he had been willing to do anything to see it done. *Anything.* So he had seduced Nike, one of his guards, using her amorous feelings for him against her.

Though she would deny it now, she truly had fallen a little in love with him. The proof: she'd arranged his escape, a crime punishable by death. Yet she'd been willing to risk it. For him. Only, just before she could remove his collar, allowing him to flash himself away—moving from one place to another with only a thought—she discovered that he had also seduced several *other* female guards.

Why rely on one to get the job done when four could serve him better?

He'd counted on the fact that none of the Greek females would want their affair with an enslaved Titan known. He'd counted on their silence.

What he should have done was count on their jealousy. *Women.*

Nike had realized she'd been used, that his emotions had never really been engaged. Rather than throw him back into his cell and pretend he did not exist, rather than have him beaten, she'd had him held down and marked permanently.

For years he'd dreamed of returning the favor. Sometimes he thought the desire was the only thing that kept him sane as he whiled away century after century in this hellhole. Alone, darkness his only companion.

Imagine his delight when the prison walls began to crack. When the defenses began to crumble. When their collars fell away. It had taken a while, but he and his brethren had finally managed to work their way free. They'd attacked the Greeks, brutally and without mercy.

In a matter of days, they had won.

The Greeks were defeated and now locked exactly where

they'd locked the Titans. Atlas had volunteered to oversee the realm and had thankfully been placed in charge. Finally, his day of vengeance had arrived. Nike would forever bear *his* mark.

"You should be grateful you're alive," he told her.

"Fuck you."

He smiled slowly, evilly. "You've done that, remember?"

Her struggles increased. Increased so viciously she was soon panting and sweating right alongside his men. "You bastard! I will flay you alive. I will torch you to ash. Bastard!"

"Flip her over," he ordered the guards over her curses. No mercy. Atlas didn't have the patience to wait until she tired. "And a warning to you, Nike. You had best be still. I'll just keep tattooing until my name is clear enough to satisfy me."

With a frustrated, infuriated screech, she finally settled down. She knew he spoke true. He always spoke true. Threats were not something he wasted his breath uttering. Only promises.

"Bastard," she rasped again.

He'd been called worse. And by her, no less. "That's a good girl." Atlas strode forward and ripped the cloth from her back. The skin was tanned, smooth. Flawless. Once, he'd caressed this back. Once, he'd kissed and licked it. And yes, being with her had been more satisfying than being with any of the others, because she'd looked at him with such adoration, such hope and awe. He'd felt…humbled. Lucky to be there, touching her. But he would not be ruled by his dick and release her before branding her, all in the hopes that he could get her into bed again.

He *would* do this.

"Ready?" he asked her.

"That's not what I did to you," Nike growled. "I didn't mark your back."

"You would rather I brand your lovely breasts?"

At that, she held her tongue.

Good. He didn't want to mar her chest. Her breasts were a work of art, surely the world's finest creation. "No need to thank me," he muttered. He held out his hand and someone slapped the needed supplies in his palm. "At least you won't have to look at my name every day of your too-long life." As he had to do. "Everyone else will, though. They'll see." *And they'll know who mastered her at last.*

"Every lover I choose, you mean."

He popped his jaw. "Not another word from you. It is time."

"Don't do this," she suddenly cried. "Please. *Don't.*" She turned her head and there were tears in her brown eyes.

She wasn't a beautiful woman. Could barely be called pretty. Her nose was a little too long, and her cheeks a little too sharp. She had ordinary brown hair cut to hit her too-wide shoulders, and no true curves to speak of. Besides her breasts. No, she had the body of a warrior. But there was something about her that had always drawn him.

"Please, Atlas. Please."

He rolled his eyes. "Dry the fake tears, Nike." And he knew they were fake. She wasn't prone to displays of emotion. "They don't affect me and they certainly don't become you."

Instantly her eyelids narrowed, the tears miraculously gone. "Fine. But I *will* make you regret this. I vow it."

"I'm looking forward to your attempts." Truth. Sparring with her had always excited him. She should know that by now.

Without a single beat of hesitation, he pressed the ink gun just below her shoulder blade. His grip was steady as he etched the outline of the first letter. *A.* Not once did she flinch. Not once did she act as if she felt a single ounce of pain. He knew it hurt, though. Oh, did he know. To permanently mark an immortal, ambrosia had to be mixed into the colored liquid and that ambrosia burned like acid.

She remained silent as he finished each of the outlines.

Silent, still, as he filled in the letters. When he finished, he sat back on his haunches and surveyed his work: A-T-L-A-S.

He expected satisfaction to overtake him, so long had he waited for this moment. It didn't. He expected relief to overwhelm him; finally vengeance had been achieved. It didn't. What he didn't expect was a white-hot sweep of possessiveness, but that's exactly what he experienced. *Mine.*

Nike now belonged to him. Forever. And all the world would know it.

CHAPTER TWO

NIKE PACED THE CONFINES of her cell. A cell she shared with several others. Knowing her temper as intimately as they did, they were careful to stay out of her way. Still. Roommates sucked. She could feel their eyes boring into her robe-clad back, as if they could see the name now branded there.

A-T-L-A-S.

If they dared say a single word about it… *I will kill them!*

There hadn't been enough cells to contain all of the Greeks, so they'd been crammed into each chamber in groups. Male, female, it hadn't mattered. Maybe the Titans hadn't cared about the mixing of the sexes, or maybe they'd done it to increase the torment of each prisoner. The latter was probably the case. Husbands had not been paired with wives and friend had not been paired with friend. No, rival had been paired with rival.

For her, that rival was Erebos, the minor god of Darkness. Once, Erebos had treated her like a queen. Once, she'd really liked him. Had even considered marrying him. But then she'd fallen in love with Atlas—that womanizing, lying bastard Atlas—so she'd cut Erebos loose. *Then* she'd discovered that Atlas had never really wanted her, that Atlas had only been using her.

Love had quickly morphed into rage.

The rage, though, had eventually cooled. She'd forgotten him. For the most part. *Liar.* Now, with his name decorating her back, she hated him with every fiber of her being.

Maybe—*maybe*—she'd overreacted when she'd done the same to him. Branded him forever. Impulsiveness had always been her downfall. For years, she'd even regretted her decision. Not that she would ever admit such a thing to him. Regret was not what she felt now, however.

She hadn't lied to him. She *would* kill him for this.

First, she would have to find a way to remove the stupid collar around her neck. As long as she wore it, she was powerless. The thick gold did not remove her god-given abilities, but merely muted them. Substantially. Too substantially. Second, she would have to find a way to escape this realm.

The first, in theory, should have been easy. Yet she'd already tried clawing and beating at it, and had even attempted to melt it from her neck. All she'd done was cut her skin, bruise her tender flesh and singe her hair off. She should have known that's what would happen. How many times had she watched Titan prisoners try the same things? The second, in theory *and* reality, seemed impossible.

Her gaze circled her surroundings. After the Titans had escaped, they'd reinforced everything. How, she didn't know. The prison was supposedly bound to Tartarus, the Greek god of Confinement who'd once kept guard over the Titans, and when he'd begun to weaken for no apparent reason, the realm had weakened, as well. Everything in it became structurally unsound. But now, Tartarus was missing. The Titans didn't have him and no one knew where he was. There was no reason the realm should be as strong as it was in his absence.

The walls and floor were comprised of godly stone, something only special godly tools—tools she didn't have—could break through. And yet, even without Tartarus's presence, there was not a crack in sight.

The thick silver bars that allowed a glimpse of the guard's station below had been constructed by Hephaistos, and only

Hephaistos could melt such a metal. Unfortunately, he resided somewhere else. As with Tartarus, no one knew where. Still, without Tartarus, she should have been able to bend that metal. She couldn't; she'd already tried.

"Could you settle the hell down?" Erebos grumbled from one of the cots.

Nike flicked him a glance. From his dark hair to his dark skin, from his handsome features to his strong body, he was the picture of unhappy male, and all of that unhappiness was directed at her.

"No," she replied. "I can't."

"We're trying to plan an escape here."

They were always planning an escape.

"Besides," he continued, "your ugly face is giving me a headache."

"Go suck yourself," she replied. Though she'd been the one to hurt him all those centuries ago—*unintentionally*—he'd repaid her a thousand times over. Purposely. Not emotionally, but physically. He liked nothing better than to "accidentally" trip her, bump into her and send her flying, as well as to eat what little portion of food was meant for her before she could fight her way to the front of the line, starving her.

If she hadn't been wearing the collar, he never would have been able to do those things. She would have been too strong. And he would have been too scared. Another reason to despise her captivity.

"Sucking myself would probably elicit better results than when you did it," he retorted.

The handful of gods and goddesses around him snickered.

"Whatever," she said, as if the taunt didn't bother her. Except, her cheeks did flush. She was the epitome of Strength—or she was supposed to be—and she'd always been more mannish than feminine. That was why Atlas's attentions had so surprised and delighted her. That gorgeous man could have won anyone, yet he'd chosen her. Or so she'd thought. And she'd fallen for his act because he'd somehow made her feel like a delicate, beautiful woman.

Stupid. I was so stupid.

From the corner of her eye, she saw a black-clad male stride into the guard's station. She didn't have to see him to know who it was. Atlas. She *felt* him. Always she felt his heat.

When her gaze found him, she discovered that he had his arm wrapped around a leggy blonde. A blonde who cuddled herself into his side as if she belonged there—and had rested there many times before.

The thought angered Nike. It shouldn't have; she despised Atlas with all of her being and didn't care who he slept with. Didn't care who he pleasured. And yes, he would have pleasured the blonde with those talented hands and seeking lips. He was an amazing lover whose touch still haunted Nike's dreams. But there it was. Anger.

She didn't mean to, but found herself striding to the bars and gripping them for a better, closer look at him. Three other guards stood around him, all talking and laughing. While prisoners wore white, guards wore black, and he wore that darkness well. It was the perfect complement to his dark, chopped hair and sea-colored eyes.

His face had been chiseled by a master artist, everything about him perfectly proportioned. His eyes were the perfect distance apart, his nose the perfect length, his cheeks the perfect sharpness, his lips the perfect shape and color and his chin a perfect, stubborn square.

He was perfect while she was nothing but flaws.

She should have known he was playing her the moment he'd turned those dangerous eyes on her and they lit with "interest." Men just didn't look at her like that. Not even Erebos had, and he had loved her.

"Bastard," she muttered, the curse for both the men in her past.

As if he heard her, Atlas lifted his gaze. The moment their eyes met, she wanted to release the bars. She wanted to step away, out of sight. But she didn't allow herself that luxury. That would have been cowardly, and this man had seen her weak one too many times.

Just to taunt him, and hopefully make him feel as out of control as he always made her feel, she allowed her attention to fall to his chest, exactly where her name rested. She smiled smugly before raising her gaze and arching a brow.

Score. A muscle ticked in his jaw.

What does your lover think of your mark? she wanted to shout. *What does the blonde think of my name on your body?*

He jerked the stupid blonde deeper into his side and, without breaking eye contact with Nike, planted a lush, wet kiss on her mouth. Of course, the bitch reacted as any other woman would have. She wrapped her arms around him and held on for dear life. As Nike well knew, that man could make a woman come with the expertise of his kiss.

Nike's anger intensified. Had she been able, she would have stomped down there and ripped them apart. Then she would have killed them both. Not because she wanted Atlas for herself—she didn't—but because he was clearly using yet another woman. Passion did not glow from his expression. Only determination did.

Nike would be doing the female population a favor by snuffing him out.

"Erebos," she called. "Come here. I want to kiss you."

"What?" he gasped out, his shock clear.

"Do you want a kiss or not? Get over here. Quickly."

There was a rustling of clothing behind her and then her former lover was beside her. He was a prisoner, and sex was a rarity. He would take what he could get, even from someone he loathed. That much she knew.

Nike turned to him; he was already leaning down. Like the blonde, she wrapped her arms around her companion's neck and held on tight. Only, she didn't enjoy the kiss, familiar as it was. Erebos's taste was too…what? Different from Atlas's, she realized, and that ratcheted her anger another notch. No man should have that much power over her.

Still. She let Erebos continue. Atlas needed to realize that she no longer desired him. He needed to realize that he would never, *never* play her emotions again. She was not an idealistic little girl anymore.

He'd made sure of that.

CHAPTER THREE

RAGE. ABSOLUTE RAGE FILLED Atlas. He released his companion—he couldn't recall her name—and she gasped in protest at the abruptness of his actions. He didn't bother explaining what he was about as he stomped away from her. The rage continued to spread as he climbed the stairs that led to the prisoners' cages and to the cell holding Nike.

His name was on her back. How dare she allow another man to put his lips on her?

When he reached his destination, he raised his arm, and the sensor he'd had embedded in his wrist caused the bars to slide open. Several prisoners were seated against the far wall. Rapturous longing colored their faces as they watched the minor god of Darkness and the goddess of Strength clean each other's tonsils. So absorbed were they, in fact, that they didn't rush Atlas and try to escape. Or maybe that had something to do with the pain they would feel if they did so. He had only to press a button, and their collars would ravage their brains.

Nike moaned, as if she really liked what was being done to her. Red flickered through Atlas's vision. How. Dare. She. Teeth grinding, he grabbed Nike by the collar of her robe and jerked her into the hard line of his body, away from Erebos.

A gasp escaped her. Unlike when the blonde had gasped, he did not remain unaffected. He wanted to swallow the sound—and do something, anything, to cause Nike to make it again.

What's wrong with me?

"Hey," Erebos snapped, foolishly reaching for her to finish what had been started. "We were busy."

Scowling, Atlas kicked him in the chest. The smaller man flew backward, slamming into his fellow prisoners. The minor god jumped to his feet to attack, saw who had rendered the blow and stilled, nostrils flaring, hands fisting.

"Touch her again," Atlas said calmly, though he was gritting the words out as if they were being pushed through a meat grinder, "and I'll remove your collar. Right along with your head."

The god paled, perhaps even whimpered. "I won't go near her. She wasn't worth it, anyway."

Atlas might kill him for such an insult, as well. Her kisses were heaven, damn it.

"What the hell do you think you're doing?" Nike demanded, suddenly coming to life and drawing his attention. She whirled on him, glaring up at him. "I can sleep with whoever I want. And hey, guess what? I might even pick one of your friends. What do you think of that?"

Despite her heated claims, she wasn't breathless as she would have been if Atlas had been the one kissing her, and her cheeks weren't flushed. Her nipples weren't even hard.

Finally, something cooled the hottest flames of his rage.

"Just zip your mouth." He latched on to Nike's upper arm and dragged her out of the cell with him. Automatically, the bars closed behind him.

"What the hell do you think you're doing?" she said again, tugging against his hold. She'd never been one to obey him.

"What the hell did you think *you* were doing?" he countered. When he reached the bottom of the steps, he stopped. The blonde, who just happened to be the goddess of Memory—damn it, what was her name? Kneemah? No, but close. Nee Nee? Closer. Mnemosyne. Yes, that was it—Mnemosyne, as well as the three other warriors chosen to guard Tartarus today, were gaping at him.

"What?" he snapped. At least Nike stopped resisting him. She stilled at his side, attention darting from him to the others, the others to him.

"You can't just remove a prisoner," Hyperion, god of Light, said. He was a handsome man, though as pale as his title suggested, and Nike had better not be eyeing him as a possible bedmate.

"I'm not removing her," Atlas replied stiffly. "I'm relocating her." To a cell of her own, where no one could put their dirty, disgusting lips on her. Where no one could put their roving hands on her body. There was nothing…possessive about this decision, either. He simply didn't want her experiencing any type of pleasure. She didn't deserve it.

"Why?" Mnemosyne regarded him curiously, not a single thread of upset or jealousy in her expression.

Why? he wondered himself. Mnemosyne been eager to date him for months, summoning him constantly. Last night, she'd even shown up at his home naked. She was beautiful, yes, and he'd almost given in and slept with her. His body had been worked into a frenzy after what had transpired with Nike, after all, and he'd been desperate for release. But before he sealed the deal, he'd sent the determined goddess away. He'd felt too guilty to continue. As if he were cheating on Nike. Which was ridiculous. The only relationship he had with Nike was one of hate.

Besides, who wanted to spend time with a female who would never forget your mistakes? A female who would remember your every transgression? A female who could spin new, false memories into your mind, making you believe whatever she wished. Not him. Yet he'd flashed to Mnemosyne's home this morning and asked her to spend the day with him, just so he could bring her to the prison this morning. He'd been strangely jubilant at the thought of parading her in front of Nike.

So again, he wondered why Mnemosyne did not feel as if Nike were a threat. Most females didn't, he knew. He'd heard them talk. Nike was too tall, too muscled, they said. She was too hard, and too coarse. But those were the things that had first sparked his interest in her. She could handle his strength. She gave as good as she got. She would never wither under his glare. She would never run from his anger. She would always face him head-on. And he liked that. A lot. No other female he'd ever encountered had that kind of courage.

And she *was* pretty, he thought. Yes, only yesterday he'd thought her barely so, but, just now, that seemed wrong on every level. Only a short while ago, when he'd first walked into the prison, he'd felt her gaze on him and had looked up. For a second, only a second, her defenses had been lowered. She hadn't known he'd been watching her, so she hadn't guarded her expression. An expression that had been soft, wistful, her eyes luminous.

The sight of her had heated his blood as if he'd been caught on fire.

That still didn't mean he desired her, his enemy. The fact that his name was spelled across her back was simply playing havoc with his mind, he was sure.

"Well," Mnemosyne prompted.

"Yeah," Nike said. "We're waiting for an answer."

"Shut up, prisoner," Mnemosyne snapped. She was sister to Rhea, the god queen, and an elitist. Always had been. She loved power and strength above all else, and viewed most people as beneath her.

He wanted to scold her for using that tone with Nike, but didn't. They were waiting for an answer to what? he wondered, thinking back over the conversation. Oh, yeah. Why was he moving Nike? He raised his chin, refusing to look down at her. Not that he would have had to look far. At six feet, she was nearly as tall as he was. "I don't need a reason. I'm responsible for this prison and everyone in it. Therefore, if I want to move you, I can."

The last was meant for the Titans. They would do well not to question him.

Without another word, he dragged Nike away.

"But Atlas," Mnemosyne called.

He ignored her. Where should he take Nike? There were not many private places in this doomed structure. All of the cells were filled to capacity. That left—his office, he decided.

"You're lucky I don't have that bastard slain," he said when they snaked a corner and he was sure the others couldn't hear him.

Nike didn't have to ask who "that bastard" was. "What for? He did nothing wrong."

Nothing wrong? *He touched what's mine.* "He didn't have permission to consort with you." There. An answer to pacify. Truthful, yet misleading. Atlas snaked another corner, and there at the end of the hallway was his door.

"Consort with me?" She laughed without humor. "Oh, wait. I get it. You can screw anyone you want, but I can't."

Good. They were on the same page. "That's right." He pushed his way inside, kicked the door shut and finally released her. His hands itched to return to her, but he kept them at his sides. Rather than settle behind his desk, he faced her, placing them nose to nose. "You are to suffer in solitude." Gods, she smelled good. Like passion. Pure, white-hot passion.

"As if. I have more fun with myself, anyway."

The image those words evoked nearly sent him to his knees. He should back away from her. Before he did something foolish.

Her eyes narrowed. "You haven't changed, you know. You're as much of an ass now as you were years ago."

"However," he continued, as if she hadn't just insulted him. Foolishness be damned. She was here, and they were alone. "If you need to be kissed, I'll take care of it."

And, godsdamn it, that was the absolute truth.

CHAPTER FOUR

THERE WAS NO TIME to protest. In less time than it took to blink, Nike found herself smashed into the wall, Atlas pressing against her, solid chest to soft breasts, his hands pinning her temples, his mouth slamming into hers. His tongue thrust deep, without warning, forcing its way past her teeth.

She could have bitten him. Wanted to bite him, actually, and not in affection. She wanted to draw blood, pain. Instead, her body instantly became his slave, as if centuries of hatred hadn't passed, and she welcomed him inside. She wound her arms around him and arched into his erection. Erection? Oh, yes. He was hard. Hard and long and thick. Just as she remembered.

His taste was decadent, wild and burning, like dark spices. His muscles were tensed under her palms. Up she moved them, until her fingers were tangled in his hair. The short spikes abraded deliciously, causing her to shiver.

Touch me, she wanted to shout. It had been so long, so damned long, since she'd experienced this. Oh, she'd been with other men since giving herself so foolishly to Atlas, because she'd been searching for something as intense as what they had shared. Something to soothe her, heal her even. But each experience had left her hollow and unsatisfied. She'd actually felt worse. And then she had been captured—by Atlas himself—and unceremoniously stuffed into this prison.

With the lack of privacy, there'd been no opportunities to find companionship. Not that she would have wanted to or had even tried. No one drew her anymore. No one but Atlas, damn him.

Yes, damn him. *Him.* The man who had held her down only yesterday and etched his name into her flesh. What was she doing, allowing this? He would think she still cared for him. He would think she still pined for him, dreamed of him…craved him. That might be true, curse it, but she would never allow him to know it.

Panting, she tore her mouth away. *How dare you stop,* her body cried. "I don't want you," she lied. "Let me go. Now." *Hold me forever.*

A low growl erupted from his throat. "I don't want you, either." Once, twice, he rubbed his shaft against her. "But I'm not letting you go."

Thank you.

Stupid body.

Tremors slid the length of her spine. Sweet heaven. He'd hit her sweet spot, and sensation rocketed through her. Then one of his hands lowered and cupped her breast, and her knees almost buckled.

"Why?" The word was a mere whimper. And why was she allowing him the choice? Why wasn't she ripping away from him? *You are Strength. Act like it.*

"Why won't I let you go?" He rolled her hardened nipple between his fingers.

That was why she remained as she was, she thought, dazed. The pleasure was building, flowing through her veins, burning her up, recreating her into a new being. Someone who lived for satisfaction alone. Someone who didn't care that the one responsible for her desire was an enemy.

"Yes."

"I just…I…" Those fingers tightened, stinging her a little. "Just shut up and kiss me again."

"Yes," she replied before she could stop herself.

Their mouths met again, and this time she rose on her tiptoes to meet him. As their tongues clashed and warred, he cupped her ass and lifted her feet off the floor. So strong he was. Forcing him to hold her weight would have been fun, but not nearly as pleasurable as winding her legs around his waist and pressing her needy core against his shaft.

Clever girl.

With her braced against the wall, he was able to tunnel both of his hands under her robe. Their bodies were too close together for him to reach her slick center, where she wanted him most, but having his hands on her cheeks, wanting skin against fiery skin, was almost as welcome. He was hotter than she remembered.

His lips left hers, but before she could moan her disappointment, he was kissing and licking his way down her neck.

"Yes," she gasped. "Yes. Like that."

"More?" His nose nuzzled the golden slave collar as if it were a trinket rather than a device that could kill her. For once, *she* even liked the collar.

"Yes." More. At the moment, that was the only word she was capable of. Unless...did he think to make her beg?

Fury suddenly blended with desire. Well, she would show him. She would beg for nothing. Not even this. Especially this. Not for him.

"Then more you shall have," he said, shocking her. She had not begged, yet he was giving her what she wanted. He tugged the fabric of her robe down, revealing her breasts. Air hissed through his teeth. "So lovely. So perfect." His tongue flicked out and circled the nipple he'd pinched just a short while ago. "So mine."

Her head fell back, and her nails scratched at his back. So *good.* The heat...the wetness...the—"Yes!" The suction. He was sucking at her so forcefully, her stomach muscles were quivering. No one else had been physically powerful enough to suit her. Their caresses had felt like whispers, barely there, utterly unsatisfying. "Atlas," she groaned. "Don't stop." A command, not a plea.

"I won't. I can't." He straightened, his narrowed gaze suddenly pinning her in place far more effectively than his body. "I want you. All of you."

She struggled to regain her breath. Her senses. "You mean sex?" *Yes, yes, yes.* Here, now.

A clipped nod was the only answer she received. She opened her mouth to reply, but somehow found the strength to stop herself. She drank in the sight of him—a sight that delighted her almost as much as it angered her. Angered? Why? Her delight should be all-consuming. His nostrils were flared, his lips pulled tight. He looked as if he barely had himself under control. Nothing like he'd looked with Mnemosyne.

He truly wants me.

But…why? she wondered. Or was he merely that good an actor?

Yes, she mused darkly. He was that good an actor. And that was where the anger sprang from. He'd looked at her like that once before, the last time they'd had sex. That look had been the catalyst to her decision to free him, despite the consequences to herself. Consequences that could have resulted in a death sentence. *But,* she'd thought, *he truly loves me with the same intensity that I love him.* She'd thought *anything* worth the risk of freeing him. Of possibly being with him for eternity.

How they would have managed that, she hadn't known. But she'd wanted to try. He had not.

Thank the gods she'd encountered one of the members of his skank parade mere minutes after escorting him from the building and into the clouds outside, where he would have been able to flash away. He'd still had his collar on—she hadn't wanted to remove it until they'd bypassed every single guard. That way, everyone who saw them walking together would have assumed she was simply moving a prisoner.

But outside, they'd been seen. No one could flash out of or into the prison itself, so everyone had to walk through the front door. Aergia, the goddess of Laziness, of all things, had decided to come to work early, surprise, surprise—just to be with Atlas again. She'd stopped Nike to question where he was being taken.

I'm taunting him with what he can never have again, Nike had claimed.

The goddess had frowned. *Well, take him to my office when you're done.*

Why?

The frown became a slow, sensual smile. *So I can dish my brand of...punishment to him.*

Dread had sparked inside her. *And how do you punish him?*

How do you think? But don't worry. I'll leave him begging for more. I always do.

Atlas had tried to run then, mowing right over them both, but with his collar still in place, he hadn't gotten far. Nike had locked him back up and, suspicious, questioned all the female guards. Nearly every single one of them had had a go at him. And he'd told them all the same thing: *You are beautiful. I want to spend my life with you. All I need is my freedom, and I will be your slave for eternity.*

So, have sex with him again? "Hell, no."

"You want me," he snapped. His grip tightened on her, his fingers digging deep, bruising. "I know you do."

Just like that, she knew what this little make-out session was about. He planned to sleep with her, make her fall in love with him all over again, and then dump her. He'd grind up her pride, spit it out and stomp all over it. Again. All to punish her, she was sure, for daring to tattoo him as she had. Marking her with his name clearly wasn't enough.

"Wanting you dead and wanting your body aren't the same things." With a sugar-sweet grin, she patted his cheek. "And I can promise you that while I do want the first, I was only teasing you about the second." Now who was playing who? "So…if we're done here…? I believe there is a minor god awaiting my return."

Atlas ran his tongue over his teeth. His arms fell away from her, and he stepped back. She nearly collapsed, but managed to shift her legs and absorb her own weight. Unaffected. That's how she had to appear.

"We're done," he said, his tone clipped. "We are definitely done."

Good, she thought. So why did she suddenly want to cry for real?

CHAPTER FIVE

ATLAS HAD TO EMPTY A CELL of its seven occupants and place those gods and goddesses within other, already cramped cells to make a place for Nike. The time and effort was worth it, though. He couldn't tolerate the thought of her with that bastard Erebos, doing the same things to him that she'd once done to Atlas.

Not. Going. To. Happen.

Ever.

And maybe, perhaps, there was a slight chance it had nothing to do with punishing her and everything to do with the pleasure he'd earlier denied. In her arms, he'd come alive. That had happened last time, too, but he'd written it off as prisoner insanity. Now, he couldn't write it off. He wasn't a prisoner; he was a warden. He'd come alive, and he needed more. Of her, only her. Yet she claimed she'd merely been playing him.

Fucking *playing* him. He wanted that to be a lie more than he wanted to take his next breath. Which he really wanted to take. He didn't understand this. She was doomed to spend eternity hidden away, which meant they could not have any kind of life together. Not even if he freed her. *He* would then be locked away or put to death. Unlike her, that was not something he was willing to risk.

But that she had been, all those centuries ago…it was *humbling*. He still could not get over the emotion.

Surely she still wanted him.

For a week, Atlas lamented his plight and pondered what to do. All the while, he stayed away from Nike's new cell. That didn't stop him from thinking about her, however. What was she doing? Did *she* think of *him?* Did she dream of him and that shattering kiss?

He did. Every time he closed his eyes, he saw the passion glowing from her face. A face that was exquisite. From barely passable, to pretty, to exquisite, all in a week's time. He shook his head in wonder. But she deserved the praise. Her lashes were long and as rich as black velvet. Velvet that framed sensual chocolate eyes. Her cheeks were smooth, perfect for caressing, and her lush, red lips were sweeter than ambrosia. And all that strength…his shaft filled and lengthened just remembering it. She'd gripped and scratched him with savage abandon. He still bore the marks.

Fine. He had lied to her. They definitely weren't done. Not even close. He had to experience that again.

Finally, he could stand the separation no longer. Thankfully, his shift was over. A shift that had consisted of walking the prison halls, watching the prisoners inside their cells and ensuring everyone remained calm.

That should have bored him. After all, he was a warrior. But bore him it didn't. And *that* should have irritated him. After all, he'd spent countless centuries in this place and had sworn never to return once he'd escaped. But again, irritation was not what he felt. He'd wanted this job to be close to Nike. To have his vengeance, he'd once told himself. Now, he wasn't so sure. Today, and all week really, he'd walked the halls invigorated, knowing all he had to do to catch sight of her was turn a corner.

He hadn't allowed himself to do so. Until now. Finally, he would see her.

The moment she came into view, his blood heated, blistering. His breath followed suit, flaming his lungs to ash. She sat atop her cot, arms gripping the rail, knees drawn up while she leaned slightly forward. Her hair was finger-combed to perfection, and her eyes were narrowed, shielding her irises and the emotion banked there, but at least he could see the shadows her lashes cast over her cheeks. Shadows he might trace with a fingertip. Or his tongue.

Oh, yes. She was exquisite.

"Where's your girlfriend?" Her voice was smooth as silk. Just beneath that silk, however, he thought he caught a tendril of fury.

Was she mad that he'd come? Or mad that he'd stayed away so long?

"I don't have a girlfriend." Though Mnemosyne was still trying to change that.

Even though he pushed her away every damn time.

Nike shrugged. "Too bad for you that whores never commit."

He knew he was the whore that she spoke of, and popped his jaw. But he deserved that, he supposed. "I did what I had to do to escape, Nike. That doesn't mean I didn't feel—" No. Oh, no. He would not go down that road. He hadn't wanted to feel anything for her, but he had. That hadn't stopped him from using her, so she'd never like what he had to say about the matter. "I'm sure you'd do anything to escape, as well."

Her expression darkened, but she did not refute his words. "So, did you come to free me?"

"Hardly."

"Then why are you here? We have nothing more to say to each other."

Because you're all I think about anymore. He never should have marked her. This might have been avoided. Or not. He might have slept with others all those years ago because he'd been desperate to flee this place, but it had been her face he'd imagined when he'd done so.

Without looking away from her, he leaned back against the bar behind him and crossed his arms over his chest. "There's plenty to say. About the kiss."

She yawned, patting her beautiful mouth. A mouth he wanted all over his body. "I'd rather sleep."

So. She still wanted him to think she had been unaffected. Part of him believed it. An insecure part of him that had never really known how to deal with her, his equal in every way. Yes, even strength, though he often liked to deny it. The other part of him, the masculine part, knew she had liked everything he'd done. She'd shouted his name, for gods' sake, and he hadn't even made her climax.

"You're saying you don't want me?" he asked as silkily as she had.

"Not even a little."

"Really?" He rested his fingers at the waist of his pants, twisting the button, and her eyes followed the movement. His cock was already hard, already straining, rising over the top. Moisture glistened there. "Not even a tiny, tiny bit?"

She gulped. "N-no." The word was croaked. "But you are. Tiny, that is."

Liar. She did. She wanted him. And he was huge, thank you very much. He stretched her. The sense of possessiveness returned, all the more intense because it was joined by satisfaction.

"I'll have you yet, Nike. That I promise you."

"Just…go away," she said, suddenly sounding almost… dejected. She eased to her side, then rolled to her back, facing away from him. "We're done with each other. Remember?"

Wrong move. Seeing her back, even covered by that baggy robe, reminded him of what he'd done and that set fire to his blood anew. Whatever he had to do, he *was* going to have this woman.

"I guess we'll find out," he told her before walking away.

To think. To plan.

CHAPTER SIX

ATLAS PUSHED PAST the double doors that led into Cronus's throne room. Armed guards, immortal warriors Cronus himself had created, were stationed along the edges of the walls. Each held a spear, and swords swung from the sheaths at their waists. They stood at attention, waiting for an order or a threat. They would spring into action for both.

Of course, there were also warriors lining both sides of the purple lamb's fleece carpet that led to the bejeweled dais, crowding Atlas as he made his way forward. His weapons had already been removed, but they were taking no chances, eyeing his every movement with distrust.

He wondered if, when she had been a free woman, Nike had ever been summoned to this room, albeit to meet with Zeus, *her* king. And if she had, had it been for a reward or a punishment?

Stop thinking about her. Concentrate on Cronus. He's wily, that one. The god king was not the same man he'd been before his incarceration. The thousands of years inside Tartarus had changed him; he was harder, harsher. Utterly unforgiving. Any weakness, he pounced upon.

Nowadays, Cronus refused to stay in the heavens without an army to shield him. But then, a man at war with his own wife couldn't be too careful. Especially when that wife was a queen with powerful abilities and allies of her own. A wife who—

Dizziness spun through Atlas's head, fragmenting his

thoughts, and he frowned. Frowned but didn't stop until he reached the end of the fleece. He kept his attention, foggy as it was, fixed on Cronus. What was wrong with him?

The king was seated atop a throne of solid gold. Dark strands were threaded through his silver hair, and his beard had thinned since the last time Atlas had seen him. Some of the age lines had even disappeared from his weathered features. He wore a long white robe, much like the prisoners of Tartarus. Why? Atlas had often wondered.

Only two explanations made any sense. Cronus had worn the garment for centuries and now felt most comfortable in it. Or he did not want to forget what he'd once been—and could be again if he weren't careful. Atlas had been more than happy to shed his own robe. Would Nike do the same, if ever she gained her freedom? Not that she would.

You're thinking about her again.

A woman stood beside the throne. She possessed one of the plainest faces Atlas had ever seen, and had pale, freckled skin. She was reed thin, with dark, curling hair and delicate shoulders. Power did not hum from her. Rather, she seemed...insubstantial. Ethereal, as he imagined a ghost might look. There, but see-through. There, but wavering. Her eyes were shadowy, vacant, as if no one was home.

When she reached up and brushed a lock of hair from her brow, he could only gape. The elegance of the movement was awe inspiring. More graceful than a dancer, more delicate than a butterfly wing. Someone was indeed home, she just didn't care about what was happening around her.

Atlas pulled his attention from the female and studied the chamber. There were thousands of chandeliers overhead, each dripping with glistening teardrops. Multihued glitter sparkled in the air. Odd, he thought, head tilting to the side for a better view. That air was even sweetly scented with—he inhaled deeply—ambrosia. Ah. Now he understood the dizziness *and* the glitter. Dried ambrosia was being pumped through the room. To keep him docile?

"Atlas, god of Strength," Cronus said with a nod of greeting, drawing him from his musings.

Atlas bowed, as was proper. "My king. It's an honor to have this audience with you."

Cronus leaned forward, silver eyes bright with anxiety. "All is well in Tartarus, yes?"

"Most assuredly."

Relief instantly replaced the anxiety. "Why, then, did you request this meeting?"

There was no one who hated the Greeks more than this man, this Titan sovereign, and with very good reason. They'd stripped him of his power, humiliated him in front of his people. Even Nike had been a participant.

Just tell him. Get this over with. "I want to remove a woman from the prison and set her up—"

"Stop. Stop there." Scowling, Cronus raised a hand. "There will be no removing *anyone* from Tartarus. It is too dangerous."

He'd expected that answer. However, he persevered. "Perhaps the reward is worth the danger. I would keep her locked inside my home, Majesty. I would never remove her collar—" well, except to whisk her to his home, for she couldn't be flashed out of Tartarus with it on, but he would recollar her the moment they reached their destination "—and she would be my personal slave. I would ensure her misery." His first lie of the day, but probably not his last. He only wanted to give Nike pleasure.

Had he forgiven her for what she'd done to him? He wasn't sure. All he knew was that he no longer wanted to kill her when he thought about it. He would tire of her eventually, and he looked forward to the day. Until then, this was his only recourse.

The king ran his tongue over his teeth. "Of which *her* do you speak?"

"Nike. Greek goddess of Strength." He did not allow a single bit of affection to lace his tone.

The king's eyes widened. "The one who…" Now those eyes dropped to Atlas's chest, where his shirt covered his tattoos.

"Yes. The very one." *Hear my anger, only my anger.* Except, what she'd done no longer angered him. The marks were as much a part of him now as his were a part of her.

"Interesting." Cronus leaned back in the throne, the picture of contemplation. "Do you not think she is being made to suffer enough inside Tartarus?"

Time for his second lie. "No. I do not." In truth, as dejected as she'd sounded at their last meeting, the goddess was suffering. And he didn't like it.

"And what will you do to *increase* her suffering?"

"Much as she hates me—" desires me, he added inside his head, so that he wouldn't reveal the depths of irritation thoughts of her possible loathing elicited "—she will take particular displeasure in cleaning my home, preparing my food and warming my bed."

The king smiled up at the ghostly girl. "What you'd like to do to your Paris, eh, my Sienna? Make him your slave."

Her expression never changed. She offered no response, either.

Paris, the demon-possessed immortal who used to haul new prisoners into Tartarus? Atlas wondered, and then shrugged. He didn't care. Nike was his only concern at the moment.

"My king?" Atlas prompted. "I lack only your permission to begin Nike's torment. My determination is unparalleled. You will not be disappointed in the results."

Cronus faced him once again, his smile falling away. A minute passed in silence, then another. Then the king sighed.

"I'm afraid my answer has to be no. While I like the thought of Nike's anguish intensified at your hands, I'm unwilling to risk the removal of her collar, even for the few seconds required to flash her. She is Strength, and were she to somehow escape you and free her brethren, another heavenly war would erupt. I cannot afford to have my attention divided now. Well, not any more than it already is. I find I spend most of my time observing the Lords of the Underworld."

The Lords of the Underworld. So. The girl named Sienna *did* wish to enslave the immortal Paris. Atlas had never dealt with the man or any of his friends, as they'd been his enemy and he'd already been incarcerated before Zeus created them.

But he'd heard stories and knew they were vicious… brutal.

"My king. If you will just—"

"I have declared my answer, Strength. I do not understand why you are still here."

Atlas's own sense of dejection—and fury—bloomed. He wanted to stalk up that dais, grab the king and shake him. How dare his request be denied? How dare his desires be discarded? Instead, he said, "Very well, my king. I thank you for your time," and pivoted on his heel. To do otherwise would have invited punishment.

He strode from the chamber, his determination overshadowing all else. He'd already decided that nothing would keep him from claiming Nike. Now he realized that not even this would do so. The king's will be damned. He would have his woman, just as he wanted.

CHAPTER SEVEN

"COME WITH ME."

Nike's heart raced at the sound of that deep voice. Hesitant, she rolled over on her cot. Sure enough, her skin tingled when her gaze found Atlas. Gorgeous as ever, he stood at the bars—bars that were now open. His hand was extended, and he was waving her over. There was fury in his too-tight expression.

What had she done this time?

She'd tried to ignore him. She'd tried to pretend that she felt nothing for him. Anything to stop the madness. But gods, she couldn't stop thinking about their kiss. She couldn't stop wishing she'd allowed him to take her all the way. That she'd have experienced *everything* before being taken back to nothing.

So what if he would have tired of her afterward? So what if he would have been smug about her capitulation? So what if he found someone else and paraded her before Nike? For a few blessed hours—who was she kidding?—for a few blessed minutes, because it wasn't as if either one of them would last beyond that, she would have known the joy of being with him again. Of simply feeling, giving, taking, sharing…loving.

Have all the rest, common sense piped up, *but deny the love.*

That would be my pleasure. But I have to get him to offer *me the rest first.* She still would not beg. A girl had her pride, after all.

Pride will not make you come.

"Come," he repeated.

What did he have planned? Did it matter? Anything was better than this monotony.

Slowly she sat up. Her hair was in desperate need of a brush, and gods, the rest of her needed a shower. How long since she'd had one? Prisoners were given a bowl of water each day and that was it.

"Why?"

A muscle twitched in his jaw. "Do you want to spend a few hours outside the prison or not?"

Wait. What? *Leave* Tartarus? She was on her feet before her brain could process what she was doing. Her knees almost buckled, she'd spent so much time prone, bored, but she managed to stay upright. She even reached out and twined their fingers together. The heat of his skin should not have shocked her, but it did. The calluses should not have ignited a fire in her blood, but they did.

"You're taking me outside?"

"Yes. But do not say a word when we reach the guard's station. Understand?"

"Yes." This could be a trick. A trick to build up her hopes only to dash them cruelly, but she didn't care. If there was a chance, slight though it was, that he would actually stay true to his word, she would do anything he asked.

Without a word, he led her from the cell and down the hall. Other prisoners spotted her and gasped. Some began to murmur amongst themselves, gossiping as they'd once enjoyed doing in the heavens. Some gripped their bars and simply watched her through wistful eyes.

Erebos even shouted, "Hey, where are you going with her now?"

Atlas ignored him, and Nike followed suit. A sense of

urgency pounded through her. If Atlas did this, took her outside, even for a few hours… Why would he do such a thing?

"Did you get permission for this?" she asked. "And we're not at the guard's station yet, so it's okay that I'm talking."

"No. I didn't get permission." His words were curt, clearly meant to end the conversation.

As if she'd ever done what was expected of her. "Then why are you—"

"Just be quiet."

"Or what?"

"Or I'll shut you up my favorite way."

Her mouth fell open. Did he mean he'd shut her up with a kiss? Or by pushing a button on her collar and shooting painful lances through her brain? It was fifty-fifty, she thought. His proclamation had the desired results, however. She was too busy pondering his meaning to talk.

In the guard's station, two Titans were laughingly making bets about the prisoners. They looked up at Atlas and nodded politely in greeting—only to freeze when they spotted her. As promised, she remained quiet.

"She try to escape?" one demanded, obviously ready to beat her for doing so.

"No. But I'm taking her out for a bit," Atlas replied.

"Why?" the other gasped out. "There's nothing out there."

"Her viper's tongue offends me. Therefore, she deserves a new punishment. To that end, I plan to taunt her with what she cannot have."

The very words she'd once offered Aergia, the goddess of Laziness. He'd remembered.

Still the guard persisted. "Has this been cleared with—"

"*I'm* in charge of this prison and the people inside it. Now shut up and do your job." With that, Atlas ushered her out of the building and into the daylight. No one else tried to stop him.

As the first ray hit her skin, she jerked free of his hold and stopped, simply basking in the moment. Clouds. Sun. She closed her eyes, head thrown back, arms splayed. The warmth, followed by a cooling breeze…the brightness—her skin soaked them up greedily. Oh, how she'd missed them. She would have loved to have seen temples and golden streets and people, as well, but she would take what she could get without complaint.

Strong arms suddenly banded around her. "You're beautiful," Atlas whispered, his nose nuzzling her ear, practically purring. "Do you know that?"

"I know what I look like." Her lashes fluttered open. The clouds enveloped him, creating a dream haze. Her heart was hammering against her ribs, and she couldn't have stopped herself from flattening her hands on his chest to save her life. His own heart was racing, she realized with astonishment. Was he…could he be as affected by her as she was by him? "And beautiful is not a word that describes me."

His head lifted, and he gazed down at her. Tenderness softened his expression, and she thought he'd never been more appealing. "Then you don't see yourself as I do."

How did he see her? As much as he hated her—but did he hate her still? How could he, when he'd just escorted her to paradise?—she would have guessed he pictured her with horns, fangs and a tail.

She cleared her throat, too afraid to ask. "Why did you do this for me?" A much easier question, with an answer that probably wouldn't destroy what little was left of her feminine pride.

"I have my reasons," was all he said. "Now, as much as I'd love to stay in this exact spot with you, we only have a short amount of time. Do you want to spend it here or eating the food I've prepared, as well as bathing? I know those are the two things I missed most during my tenure here."

"Eat…eating. Bathing." Was this really happening? Or was

she merely dreaming about him again? Nothing else explained this change in him, in her situation.

He kissed the tip of her nose. "Then food and a bath you shall have. Come. Since I can't flash you outside of this realm, and there are no homes, inns or shops here, I've set up camp a mile north, out of view of the prison."

Dreaming, surely. Perhaps a trick, as she'd first supposed. But she allowed him to lead her through the clouds without protest.

CHAPTER EIGHT

BY THE TIME THEY REACHED the camp he'd set up, Atlas was hard and aching. Nike had been pressed against his side the entire mile, her female scent in his nose, her heat radiating into his body.

When she spied the tent he'd erected, she gasped. Wide brown eyes flicked up to him with wonder before she raced forward, not slowing as she barreled through the front flap. He heard another gasp.

Grinning, Atlas followed her inside. He liked this softer side of her. She stood in the center, twirling, clearly trying to take everything in at once. He'd spread furs on the floor and had even carted a small round table here and piled it high with her favorite foods. There was a porcelain tub already filled with steaming water, rose petals floating on the surface.

Never let it be said that the Titan god of Strength did not know how to romance a woman.

Nike's hand fluttered over her heart, her gaze glued to the plate of strawberries and feta. "How did you know I liked those?"

Because he'd always been hyperaware of her every action. He'd watched her from his cell while she'd eaten them with her friends and he'd fumed that he was not the one with her, basking in her good humor. That was not something he'd admit to, however.

"Good guess," he finally said.

She peered down at the rug and kicked out her bare, dirty foot. "I don't understand why you're doing this, Atlas."

"That makes two of us," he replied gruffly.

"But—"

"Just enjoy it, Nike. It's all I can give you."

Her lashes fluttered up, and her gaze pinned him. "But why would you want to give me anything?"

"Stop analyzing my reasons. This isn't a ploy or a punishment, I promise you. And the food is not poisoned, if that's what you're thinking." He closed the distance between them, placed his hands on her shoulders and urged her to the table.

There, they ate in silence. The rapture on her face, rapture that increased with every bite, delighted him. The wine she savored sip by sip, moaning with every swallow.

Bringing her here was worth the risk of Cronus's wrath, he thought.

Although, to get technical, Cronus had merely ordered him to keep her in Tartarus. Which he had done. The clouds around the prison were part of the realm. So really, he had not broken any rules. Cronus, though, being Cronus, would not see it that way.

Still, Atlas couldn't regret it. He had never seen this joyful, eager side of the Greek goddess, and he found that he liked it just as much as he liked everything else about her. Which was way more than he should have.

When every crumb had been consumed, she turned her attention to the bath. "That's for me?" Utter longing radiated from her, yet she didn't move toward it.

"Yes. But I can't leave you. You know that, right?"

She chewed on her bottom lip and nodded. "What you're saying is, I can bathe with you watching or not at all."

"Exactly."

He expected her to fight him on that. Hell, she could have

refused outright. What he did not expect was for her to push to her feet and discard her robe without hesitation. At the sight of her nakedness, he hissed in a breath. Already he'd thought her exquisite…but now, now…holy gods. She was the finest creature the gods had ever produced.

Her skin, so golden and smooth, covered lean muscle and succulent breasts. Those breasts were soft, perfect for his hands, and her nipples were as pretty a pink as he remembered. His mouth watered for them.

She walked to the tub and stepped inside. Her ass, her back… his name. He was on his feet before he realized what he'd done. He wanted to kiss those tattoos, something she would probably fight him over. He wouldn't apologize for having given them to her, though. Hell, no. He liked them too much.

Nike pivoted slowly, and her gaze met his as she sank into the water. There was no hiding the desire he felt—it consumed him, ate him up and left him as bare as she was. Her expression, however, was blank.

Slowly, she worked the bar of soap he'd brought her over her entire body. She seemed completely unabashed as the suds danced over her, sliding down those magnificent breasts hiding beneath the rose petals. She washed her hair, too, and soon the locks were dripping down her face and shoulders.

With every move she made, he inched a little closer to her. He just couldn't help himself. Finally she finished and stood. Another feast for his eyes. All the strength he craved more than anything else in the world was now wet, and he wanted to lick away every drop.

"What are you thinking about?" she asked, stepping from the tub. Her voice was as devoid of emotion as her expression. Why?

"I need you," he managed to croak past the lump in his throat.

Finally. A reaction. Relief and desire, such intense desire, claimed her, and she grinned a siren's smile. "Then have me you shall."

They were a mimic of his earlier words, and completely unexpected. Why the change in her? *Doesn't matter.* As he'd told her earlier, there was no good reason to analyze a change of heart. Not in either of them. Not now.

He had the distance between them defeated a split second later. Had his arms wrapped around her, jerking her into him, a second after that. Their lips met in a wild tangle, their tongues seeking, rolling together. On and on the kiss continued, drowning him in all that she was.

He hated to stop, even for a moment, but he had to remove his clothes. If he didn't experience skin-to-skin contact soon, he was going to ignite into flames. Panting, he tore away his shirt, his boots, then his pants.

She moaned. "Atlas."

He pulled her back into his embrace. Finally. Blessedly. Skin to skin. Both of them groaned at the headiness. Her nipples rubbed against his chest, his tattoos, while their lower bodies thrust together. Then she was bending down, tracing those letters with her tongue—and gods, he had never been happier that he had them.

After she'd traced the last one, she kissed her way down his stomach. She dropped to her knees.

Was she going to…please, please, please…but she didn't like him enough to do it. Did she? "What are you—"

She sucked his cock deep into her mouth.

His head fell back, and he roared. All that wet heat was ecstasy, surely the first he'd ever truly known, for nothing had ever felt this damned good. Except her, that first time he claimed her. Up and down she moved, allowing him to hit the back of her throat.

"Gods! Don't make me come."

She laughed, pulled off and licked his sac. "When have I ever listened to you?"

"Vixen."

"Why can't I make you come?"

"Because I want inside you." With a growl, he dropped to his knees, as well. She could taste his seed. Later. He hadn't lied to her. More than anything, even more of that ecstasy, he wanted inside her, and he didn't want to have to wait for it. "Spread your legs for me."

The moment she obeyed, he had two fingers buried deep. More wet heat. And to his delight…"You're ready for me." Never had he been more proud that he'd brought a female to this point. And that he'd done so with kisses, only kisses.…

She trembled, had to grip his shoulders to remain upright. "I'm ready for you every damn time I see you."

And she didn't like it, he could tell from her tone, but he could only bask in the admission. "It's the same for me."

At first, she blinked, as if she couldn't allow herself to believe him. So vulnerable she appeared, so—dare he wish?—hopeful. Then she placed a sweet kiss on his lips and breathed him in. "Don't say things like that," she whispered.

"Why not? I spoke true."

"Because they affect me."

Headier words had never been spoken. "Let's finish this before I combust, sweetheart."

"Please."

He was sweating, panting, as he settled back on his ass, reached out and cupped hers. He jerked her onto his lap, forcing her to wrap her thighs around his waist. As her hands tangled in his hair, he lifted her, placing her eager core at the tip of his erection.

"Ready?" he asked hoarsely. This was it. The moment he felt he'd been waiting forever for.

"Ready."

He thrust up and she pushed down, and then he was all the way in, surrounded by the very thing he had defied his king, his sovereign, to possess. It was better than he remembered, better than he could have imagined. He couldn't pause, couldn't give her time to adjust. Over and over he pushed in, pulled out, too overwhelmed by pleasure to do anything but ride out the storm. Perhaps it was the same for her. Her nails scored his back, and her moans rang in his ears.

Gods, he was close. On fire. Burning. Desperate. He reached between their bodies and pressed his thumb against his new favorite place.

"Atlas," she shouted, her inner walls suddenly milking him.

She was climaxing, lost to all that he was, and the thought drove him over the last bit of the edge, as well. He jetted inside her, lost to all that *she* was, the most intense orgasm of his life claiming him.

An eternity later, his spasms stopped. Together, they fell backward, onto the softness of the fur. He kept his arms around her, unwilling to let her go. Now…always?

Yes, always, he thought, and his eyes widened. He wanted her always. Wanted more of this. *Had* to have more of this. When he'd forgiven her completely, he didn't know. When he'd softened, he didn't know, either. He only knew that she'd become an important part of his life. Perhaps she always had been; he'd just been too foolish to realize it.

What the hell was he going to do?

They could be together each night after his shift, but they'd never have privacy, and her pride would soon chafe at his amorous attentions, all while he refused to set her free. It would have been the same for him when the situation had been reversed. Besides, she was too precious to hurt in that way. But the problem was, he couldn't be without her. He'd proven that already.

Damn, he thought next, suddenly sick to his stomach. Damn!

He'd finally found the one woman for him, but they were doomed.

CHAPTER NINE

SHE LOVED HIM, NIKE THOUGHT. Again. *I'm hopeless.*

He'd just…he'd been so amazing. He'd whisked her away, given her everything she'd craved: food, water and his body. Gods, had he given her that delectable body. She'd savored every moment. Savored his taste, his touch, the feel of him pounding inside her.

Four days had since passed, but she craved more. Always she craved more. She'd spent the time locked inside her cell, pacing, trying to think of ways for them to be together. If he still wanted her, that is. Atlas had come by at least once a day to make sure she was properly fed and that her basin of water was filled, but he'd never said a word to her. Actually, they hadn't spoken since leaving the tent.

At the time, she'd felt too raw, too exposed. She'd feared her feelings for him had been shining in her eyes. He was everything she'd ever wanted in a mate. His strength matched hers. She would never have to worry about hurting him. He was witty and charming. He was a protector, a warrior. He was deliciously vengeful, she knew firsthand.

She smiled, wishing she could reach between her shoulder blades and feel his name. She was certain the letters would be as hot as the man himself. But…

Why hadn't he spoken to her?

Why didn't you speak to him?

Because she hadn't known what to say. Did he still want her? Did he feel anything for her? How would she react if he didn't, which was most likely the case? Part of her wanted to take anything he would give her. The other part of her knew her pride wouldn't allow her to do such a thing. But there at the end, when they'd returned to Tartarus and he'd closed the bars to her cell, she had thought she'd glimpsed regret. Regret that he had to seal her inside. Regret that they couldn't spend more time together—in bed and out.

Nike tugged at her collar and screeched. Damn this. She was the epitome of strength, yet was as helpless as a babe. How could she win a man's heart when she couldn't even win her own freedom?

ATLAS HEARD A SCREECH of frustration and knew immediately who had uttered it. Nike. His Nike. His beautiful Nike. He'd deliberated about what to do, how they could be together, for four days. Well, the time for thinking was over, it seemed. She was close to her breaking point. She'd tasted freedom; being sequestered now had to be a thousand times worse than before.

He hated that she was locked up, and he knew they could never be together while she was. He also knew they could not be together if he released her. She would most likely run, and he would most definitely be punished.

Maybe she loved him, maybe she didn't. Maybe she'd stay with him. Or try to. She liked him and was attracted to him, he would go so far as to say. After everything that had transpired between them, she wouldn't have slept with him otherwise. But love? He wasn't sure.

And it didn't matter, really. *He* loved *her.* Perhaps he always had. He'd never felt so strongly about a woman. He'd never wanted to spend his every waking minute with someone before, had never wanted to cuddle someone into his side for every sleeping minute. He'd never wanted to eat every meal together. To talk and laugh about their days. To spar, verbally and physically. But he did with her.

And since they couldn't be together, no matter what way things panned out, there was only one thing to do.

Dread. That's what he felt as he pounded up the stairs and to her cell. Also…relief. She was banging a fist into the wall, plumes of dust forming around her. The sight of her nearly undid him. He wanted to kiss her, put his fingers all over her, sink inside her. *Harden your heart. Do what is needed.* His hand was shaking as he lifted the sensor.

She heard the slide of the bars and turned. A gasp parted her beautiful lips. Without a word, he held out his palm.

"What—"

"Just take it."

She frowned as she accepted.

Still silent, he pulled her along the same path he had just taken. The same path they'd taken those four days ago. No one tried to stop him this time. In fact, as he passed the guard's station, the two gods on duty rolled their eyes.

Outside, with the clouds all around him, he whirled on Nike. He still wanted to kiss her, but knew that if he did so, he would not be able to let her go. And he had to let her go.

"Atlas," she said with a seductive grin. She tried to wrap her arms around his neck. "Another outing? I'm glad."

He shook his head and placed his fingers on the designated indentations in the collar. Cool metal met his touch. Then he leaned down and fit his lips over the center.

Her grin fell away. A tremor moved through her. "Wh-what are you doing?"

"Be still." He drew in a deep breath, held it…held it…and then slowly released it. As that breath slithered through the inside of the collar, the metal loosened…finally splitting down the center and tumbling to the ground. Such a simple thing, the removal. Touch and breath. Yet only an uncollared god could do so, a fact that had to taunt the incarcerated. Perhaps that's why the bands had been designed as they had.

Eyes wide, she reached up, felt her bare neck. "I don't understand what's happening," she said. They were the same words she'd spoken before. He hadn't had an answer then. He did now. He loved her, but he could never tell her that.

"Go," he said. "Flash somewhere. Maybe earth. And whatever you do, stay hidden. Do you understand me?"

"Atlas…no." She shook her head violently, even fisted his shirt. "No, I can't. When they discover I'm gone for good, and they will, you'll be charged with a crime. You'll be locked away, placed with the Greeks who hate you. Or, if you're lucky, you'll be killed."

She felt, he realized, both amazed and saddened. She cared for him, which meant she would suffer without him. If anything, that only increased his determination to save her. She did not deserve a life behind bars.

He forced his expression to harden. Forced himself to jerk away from her. "I can't stand to look at you anymore. I've had you, and now I'm bored with you."

Her arms dropped to her sides as if weighed down by rocks, but she quickly pulled them around her middle. "Then keep me locked up and stay away from me. You don't want to do this."

Still willing to give up her freedom to be near him? Damn her. He fell a little more in love with her. "Go! Did you not hear me? I can't stand the sight of you anymore. Don't you get it? You make me sick, Nike."

"Shut up." Tears filled her eyes. Real godsdamned tears. "You don't mean that. You *can't* mean that." The last was whispered brokenly.

His heart constricted painfully. *Do it. Finish it.* "I'd rather be killed or locked away than look at you another moment. Because every time I look at you, I'm reminded of what we did and I—I want to vomit. I was using you, wanting to punish you, but I took things too far. Even for me." Hating himself, he turned away from her. "So do us both a favor and go."

For a long while, she didn't speak. He knew she didn't flash away, either, for he heard no rustle of clothing. But then, he *did* hear a whimper. A sob. More of those tears must be falling.

Gods, he couldn't do it. He couldn't send her away like this. He spun, meaning to grab on to her and tell her the truth, to force her to listen. To make her leave another way. But she was gone before their eyes could meet and his hands encountered only air.

"YOU INSOLENT FOOL!"

Atlas peered up at the fuming Cronus. Not like he could do anything else. His wrists were chained to poles, forcing him to remain on his knees. The very collar he'd removed from Nike was now wrapped around his own neck.

He'd known this would happen, but he hadn't cared. He still didn't. Nike was free, and that was all that mattered.

"Have you nothing to say for yourself?"

"No."

"One Greek can raise an army. That army can attack us. Ruin us. I told you that, and still you defied me."

"Nike won't do that," he said confidently. He trusted her to disappear. Even as angry as she had to be with him, she would not endanger herself to save people she had never truly liked.

Cronus slammed his fist against the arm of his throne, ever the petulant child. "You can't know that! You aren't my All-Seeing Eye."

Atlas arched a brow, refusing to be cowed. "Would you risk being imprisoned again to help your fellow Titans? I may not be able to see all the secrets of the heavens and Hell, yet I know you would not. She will not, either."

The king had no response to that, but that didn't stop him from growling. "You disobeyed a direct order, and for that you will be punished."

"I understand." He offered the statement without hesitation. It was the truth. He understood that the god king had to make an example out of him. Otherwise, others would see Cronus as weak. They would disobey him as Atlas had.

"I think you actually do." Some of Cronus's fury abated. "Only this morning I saw a portrait of you. A portrait painted by my Eye. With it, she showed me exactly how to punish you." The king smiled evilly and looked to the ghostlike girl still standing at his side. "You know what to do, sweet Sienna."

Sienna strode forward, a knife appearing in her hand. She stopped in front of Atlas and dropped to her knees, placing them eye to eye. So this was it, he thought. The end. As an immortal, he'd never thought to reach this point. Still. He found he only regretted that he hadn't had more time with Nike, that he hadn't gotten the chance to apologize for his harsh words the last time they were together and that he would never have the chance to confess his love.

With absolutely no emotion on her face, the girl dug the tip of the blade into his wrist and cut out his sensor, rather than chop off his head. That's when he realized Cronus meant to lock him away rather than kill him. Good. More time to think about Nike and what could have been.

But then Sienna moved the blade to his chest and pressed, slicing. It stung, but that was not what made him struggle against her ministrations. No, it was the fact that she began carving away Nike's name. He roared loud and long, fighting for all he was worth. Guards were called over and hard hands settled over him, pressing him down, holding him steady. Still he fought, but in the end, they managed to remove all four letters.

As each person walked away from him, he glanced down at himself through burning, watery eyes. Blood poured down his chest and four open wounds stared up at him, the muscles torn, the skin completely gone. He might have hated that brand at one point in his life, but he'd grown to love it as much as the woman who'd given it to him. More than that, it had been the last remaining evidence of her presence.

His hands fisted, and his back straightened. Blood and sweat mingled, stinging further. Another roar burst from his lips, and he tossed it to the domed ceiling. He didn't stop until his throat was shredded from the strain.

"Are you quite finished?" Cronus asked him.

His gaze fell to the dais, narrowing. "I will destroy you for this," his vowed brokenly. "One day you will die by my hand."

"Not likely. Take him to Tartarus," the king told his guards, unconcerned. "Where he will rot for all eternity."

CHAPTER TEN

IT TOOK HER TWO DAYS, but Nike finally located Atlas's home, a sprawling estate in Olympus. Or Titania, as Cronus had renamed the city. The amount of wealth Atlas had needed to acquire such a place astonished her—and she knew exactly how much he'd paid because *she* had once owned it. But then, she supposed he'd considered every cent worth it. After living in a tiny cell for thousands of years, he'd most likely wanted every bit of space he could get. And every amenity.

There was a swimming pool, more than thirty bedrooms, two winding, marble staircases and four fireplaces, and all the walls were comprised of solid gold. None of that interested her, however. Only his bedroom did.

There, she discovered more about the man who had sent her on her way. A man who would not have risked *this* just to avoid her face, as he'd claimed. A man who would not have risked his life for anything other than love.

Nearly everything was as she'd left it. A huge bed covered with black silk sheets. The walls were painted with murals of the sun and sky, and the furniture smelled of rich mahogany. There were multiple bookcases, each filled with leather-bound books. Her books. Beaded pillows were strategically placed along the floor. Places for him to lounge and read, as she had done.

What held her attention, however, was the only difference. A portrait hung above the hearth. A portrait of *her.*

He must have commissioned it after their time inside that tent, for she was reclined in a porcelain tub, bubbles sliding over her shoulders and chest, her hair soaked. She would have looked as plain and masculine as always, except he'd had the artist add a sensual light to her dark eyes and a come-and-get-me curve to her lips.

Finally she knew how he saw her. As someone beautiful. He'd once told her so, but she'd had trouble believing him. Now…

Only a man in love would do such a thing. Only a man in love would keep such a thing in such a prominent place. Only a man in love would want to see a woman's portrait every night before he fell asleep, then wake up looking at it.

Oh, yes. He loved her. As she loved him.

There, outside of Tartarus, she'd thought, hoped, that he did so, but she had let his words scrape against her already low self-esteem. How could so beautiful and sensual a man want her? she'd wondered. But he did. He loved her. Proof: he'd risked everything for her.

She could do no less for him.

Nike strode through the bedroom, knowing her lover would have a weapons case stashed somewhere—and knowing exactly what to do with it.

ATLAS WAS NOT GIVEN A CELL of his own—not at first. Still bleeding and frantic, fighting, he had been thrust into a cell with Erebos. Of course, that's who had been chosen as his cell mate, he'd thought, rage filling him. A male who had once thought to claim his Nike. A male who had then stolen food from her, pushed her around and called her terrible names.

Atlas had seen it happen on numerous occasions. He hadn't done anything about it then, telling himself she deserved what she got, but he'd wanted to. And there was no better time than now.

Even with his strength corralled by the collar and half his

blood dried to his chest, even with his still-seeping wounds splitting open with every move he made, Atlas managed to defeat Erebos in record time. He punched, he kicked, he did not play fair, kneeing the god in the balls while he was down. In the end, a broken, bloody Erebos lay crying on the dirty floor, right alongside everyone who had tried to save him.

That's when Atlas was moved to the empty cell Nike had occupied. He stretched out on the cot, simply breathing in her lingering essence. His sweet, sweet Nike. He would have to spend eternity without her. Without even her brand. Once again, he roared.

What was she doing now? If she sought solace in the arms of another man, even in the years to come, he would tear this prison apart stone by stone and kill the bastard. *As if. You sent her on her way to do just that. You want her happy.*

"What's all the racket? Seriously."

Gods, he was hearing her voice now. Locked up two days, and he was already headed into insanity.

His bars rattled, slid open. He rolled to his side, determined to send whoever it was away. When he caught sight of his beloved Nike, he blinked. Oh, yes, he was indeed going insane. She stood before him, clad in a black leather bra top and black leather pants. Her hair was slicked back in a smooth ponytail. Blood splattered her cheeks. Never had she looked more beautiful, her strength there for all to see.

She was holding someone's arm. Without their body. For the sensor in the wrist?

His hallucinations were certainly detailed.

"Well?" she said, clearly impatient. She tossed the arm aside. "Aren't you going to say anything?"

Slowly he sat up. He didn't want this moment to end. Didn't want to lose sight of her. "I missed you. So much."

"And I wanted an apology. Stupid me. I much prefer this."

She grinned, practically beaming. "I missed you, too, but we'll have to catch up later." Her gaze fell to his chest, and she gaped in astonishment. Then she growled. "Did the god king cut my name off you?"

"Yes."

She was holding a knife, he saw, and her knuckles bleached of color. "I. Will. Kill. Him."

"Already promised to do so."

"We'll do it together, then. After we get out of here." Her attention flicked behind her, urgent, before returning to him. "Come on. We have to go before someone realizes what I've done."

"Just let me look at you. Just let me enjoy this moment. Let me apologize for what I said to you. You said you wanted an apology, yes? I didn't mean it, not a word I said that last day, but I—"

She closed the distance between them and slapped him. Hard. The blow knocked him back against the cot and caused stars to wink over his vision.

Once more, he blinked at her. "You hit me."

"Yeah, and I'll do it again if you don't get your ass in gear."

"You're real."

"Yes."

"But you're *real.*" He sat up, saying the words but not truly absorbing them. This couldn't be happening.

She dropped to her knees so that they were eye to eye. "Again, yes." Just as he'd once done to her, she placed her fingers over his collar and blew into the center. As the metal softened, he finally understood what his brain had been trying to tell him. Nike was here. She was really here. And she was saving his life.

With a scowl, he jumped to his feet. "I told you to go to earth, damn it."

"Okay, not the reaction I expected." She stood and pressed

a swift kiss to his lips. "Good thing I never listen to you. Now let's go. I've already taken out the guards below. And no, I didn't kill your friends. Just made them wish they were dead." As she spoke, she latched on to his hand and dragged him out of the cell. "Cronus could realize what's going down at any moment and appear, and then we'll both be in trouble. As long as we're here, we're easy pickings."

True. Nike was a fugitive now; he wanted her out of this prison, out of this realm, as soon as possible. "You risked your life to save me, you fool."

"Well, you risked your life to save *me*."

Down the stairs they pounded and, sure enough, all three of the guards were flat on their faces, motionless. One of them was missing an arm—and he knew exactly where to find it. Not that he'd take the time to tell. The arm, lost or not, would grow back. "But you were free. You had what you wanted."

"Not everything," she threw over her shoulder.

Okay, wow. She'd just admitted she wanted him more than freedom. Atlas couldn't help himself. He gave a tug, propelling her backward, into his arms. "I love you," he finally proclaimed, and mashed their lips together. His tongue thrust deep, tasting, demanding. "I mean it. I love you more than anything. Anyone."

She only allowed the kiss for a few seconds, her hands fisting his hair and taking everything he had to give, before she pulled away, panting. "I love you, too. But let's get the hell out of here. I need your pretty head connected to your amazing body."

Once again, they surged forward. Still, he almost couldn't believe this was happening. It was so much like a dream. "I'm going to spend the rest of eternity making up for what I did to you."

"Good. I think I'll like seeing you grovel. But just for the record, I love my tattoo and I know why you said those nasty things. Sure, I would have found a better way to get you to safety, but then, I'm smarter than you are, so really, I can't blame you."

He laughed. Gods, he loved this woman. "Vixen."

"Your vixen."

"Mine. Always. You'll mark me again just as soon as my skin heals."

"Already planned on it."

Good. He wouldn't feel complete until she did. "So where are we going to live?" he asked. "We can't stay in the heavens."

"You ordered me to hide on earth. I thought we could do so—together. Though I hate that you have to give up your amazing house."

"You've been there?" He found he really liked the thought of her there, surrounded by his things, breathing in his essence. "You know where I chose to live?"

"Yes. Why did you? Choose there, I mean."

"To feel closer to you."

"Well, you're about to be a *lot* closer to me."

A laugh boomed from him. There was no woman more perfect for him. "The only thing I'll miss from that house is the portrait of you. But now I have the real thing." He placed a swift kiss on her lips. "Back to our new living arrangements. There are other gods out there, Greeks like you, who are in hiding. Cronus has never been able to find them. That means there are places he can't see."

"Maybe we'll find them and join them. We are Strength, after all. And Victory."

"Yes. Victory."

"We can succeed where he has failed."

"In the meantime, we might even try to find the Lords of the Underworld. Cronus mentioned being distracted by them. If they are his enemies, they might be good friends for us to have."

Her eyes widened. "I know of whom you speak. They were Zeus's immortal warriors long ago, but now they house the demons once locked inside Pandora's box. Cronus will have his hands tied for a long, *long* time with them. They would be *very* good friends to have."

They reached the door and burst outside, all without incident. Clouds instantly enveloped them, the sun shining brightly. Nike whirled and threw herself in his arms, placing nips and kisses all over his face.

"We did it. Now take us somewhere. Anywhere. As long as we can be together."

"I love you," he said again, then did exactly as his woman had ordered.

* * * * *

THE DARKEST ANGEL

CHAPTER ONE

FROM HIGH IN THE HEAVENS, Lysander spotted his prey. *At last. Finally, I will end this.* His jaw clenched and his skin pulled tight. With tension. With relief. Determined, he jumped from the cloud he stood upon, falling quickly…wind whipping through his hair…

When he neared ground, he allowed his wings, long and feathered and golden, to unfold from his back and catch in the current, slowing his progress.

He was a soldier for the One True Deity. One of the Elite Seven, created before time itself. With as many millennia as he'd lived, he'd come to learn that each of the Elite Seven had one temptation. One potential downfall. Like Eve with her apple. When they found this…thing, this abomination, they happily destroyed it before it could destroy them.

Lysander had finally found his.

Bianka Skyhawk.

She was the daughter of a Harpy and a phoenix shape-shifter. She was a thief, a liar and a killer who found joy in the vilest of tasks. Worse, the blood of Lucifer—his greatest enemy and the sire of most demon hordes—flowed through her veins. Which meant *Bianka* was his enemy.

He lived to destroy his enemies.

However, he could only act against them when they broke a heavenly law. For demons, that involved escaping their fiery prison to walk the earth. For Bianka, who had never been condemned to hell, that would have to involve something else. What, he didn't know. All he knew was that he'd never experienced what mortals referred to as "desire."

Until Bianka.

And he didn't like it.

He'd seen her for the first time several weeks ago, long black hair flowing down her back, amber eyes bright and lips bloodred. Watching her, unable to turn away, a single question had drifted through his mind: Was her pearl-like skin as soft as it appeared?

Forget desire. He'd never wondered such a thing about *anyone* before. He'd never cared. But the question was becoming an obsession, discovering the truth a need. And it had to end. Now. This day.

He landed just in front of her, but she couldn't see him. No one could. He existed on another plane, invisible to mortal and immortal alike. He could scream, and she would not hear him. He could walk through her, and she would not feel him. For that matter, she would not smell or sense him in any way.

Until it was too late.

He could have formed a fiery sword from air and cleaved her head from her body, but didn't. As he'd already realized and accepted, he could not kill her. Yet. But he could not allow her to roam unfettered, tempting him, a plague to his good sense, either. Which meant he would have to settle for imprisoning her in his home in the sky.

That didn't have to be a terrible ordeal for him, however. He could use their time together to show her the right way to live. And the right way was, of course, his way. What's more, if she did not conform, if she *did* finally commit that unpardonable sin, he would be there, at last able to rid himself of her influence.

Do it. Take her.

He reached out. But just before he could wrap his arms around her and fly her away, he realized she was no longer alone. He scowled, his arms falling to his sides. He did not want a witness to his deeds.

"Best day ever," Bianka shouted skyward, splaying her arms and twirling. Two champagne bottles were clutched in her hands and those bottles flew from her grip, slamming into the ice-mountains of Alaska surrounding her. She stopped, swayed, laughed. "Oopsie."

His scowl deepened. A perfect opportunity lost, he realized. Clearly, she was intoxicated. She wouldn't have fought him. Would have assumed he was a hallucination or that they were playing a game. Having watched her these past few weeks, he knew how much she liked to play games.

"Waster," her sister, the intruder, grumbled. Though they were twins, Bianka and Kaia looked nothing alike. Kaia had red hair and gray eyes flecked with gold. She was shorter than Bianka, her beauty more delicate. "I had to stalk a collector for days—days!—to steal that. Seriously. You just busted Dom Pérignon White Gold Jeroboam."

"I'll make it up to you." Mist wafted from Bianka's mouth. "They sell Boone's Farm in town."

There was a pause, a sigh. "That's only acceptable if you also steal me some cheese tots. I used to highjack them from Sabin every day, and now that we've left Budapest, I'm in withdrawal."

Lysander tried to pay attention to the conversation, he really did. But being this close to Bianka was, as always, ruining his concentration. Only her skin was similar to her sister's, reflecting all the colors of a newly sprung rainbow. So why didn't he wonder if *Kaia's* skin was as soft as it appeared?

Because she is not your temptation. You know this.

There, atop a peak of Devil's Thumb, he watched as Bianka plopped to her bottom. Frigid mist continued to waft around her, making her look as if she were part of a dream. Or an angel's nightmare.

"But you know," Kaia added, "stealing Boone's Farm in town doesn't help me now. I'm only partially buzzed and was hoping to be totally and completely smashed by the time the sun set."

"You should be thanking me, then. You got smashed last night. And the night before. And the night before that."

Kaia shrugged. "So?"

"So, your life is in a rut. You steal liquor, climb a mountain while drinking and dive off when drunk."

"Well, then yours is in a rut, too, since you've been with me each of those nights." The redhead frowned. "Still. Maybe you're right. Maybe we need a change." She gazed around the majestic summit. "So what new and exciting thing do you want to do now?"

"Complain. Can you believe Gwennie is getting married?" Bianka asked. "And to Sabin, keeper of the demon of Doubt, of all people. Or demons. Whatever."

Gwennie. Gwendolyn. Their youngest sister.

"I know. It's weird." A still-frowning Kaia eased down beside her. "Would you rather be a bridesmaid or be hit by a bus?"

"The bus. No question. That, I'd recover from."

"Agreed."

Bianka did not like weddings? Odd. Most females *craved* them. Still. *No need for the bus,* Lysander wanted to tell her. *You will not be attending your sister's wedding.*

"So which of us will be her maid of honor, do you think?" Kaia asked.

"Not it," Bianka said, just as Kaia opened her mouth to say the same.

"Damn it!"

Bianka laughed with genuine amusement. "Your duties

shouldn't be too bad. Gwennie's the nicest of the Skyhawks, after all."

"Nice when she's not protecting Sabin, that is." Kaia shuddered. "I swear, threaten the man with a little bodily harm, and she's ready to claw your eyes out."

"Think we'll ever fall in love like that?" As curious as Bianka sounded, there was also a hint of sadness in her voice.

Why sadness? Did she want to fall in love? Or was she thinking of a particular man she yearned for? Lysander had not yet seen her interact with a male she desired.

Kaia waved a deceptively delicate hand through the air. "We've been alive for centuries without falling. Clearly, it's just not meant to be. But I, for one, am glad about that. Men become a liability when you try and make them permanent."

"Yeah," was the reply. "But a fun liability."

"True. And I haven't had fun in a long time," Kaia said with a pout.

"Me, either. Except with myself, but I don't suppose that counts."

"It does the way I do it."

They shared another laugh.

Fun. Sex, Lysander realized, now having no trouble keeping up with their conversation. They were discussing sex. Something he'd never tried. Not even with himself. He'd never wanted to try, either. Still didn't. Not even with Bianka and her amazing (soft?) skin.

As long as he'd been alive—a span of time far greater than their few hundred years—he'd seen many humans caught up in the act. It looked…messy. As un-fun as something could be. Yet humans betrayed their friends and family to do it. They even willingly, happily gave up hard-earned money in exchange for it. When not taking part themselves, they became obsessed with it, watching others do it on a television or computer screen.

"We should have nailed one of the Lords when we were in Buda," Kaia said thoughtfully. "Paris is hawt."

She could only be referring to the Lords of the Underworld. Immortal warriors possessed by the demons once locked inside Pandora's box. As Lysander had observed them throughout the centuries, ensuring they obeyed heavenly laws—since their demons had escaped hell before those laws were enacted, no one having thought escape possible, they had not been killed but thrust into that box first, and the Lords second—he knew that Paris was host to Promiscuity, forced to bed a new person every day or weaken and die.

"Paris is hot, yes, but I liked Amun." Bianka stretched to her back, mist again whipping around her. "He doesn't speak, which makes him the perfect man in my opinion."

Amun, the host of the demon of Secrets. So. Bianka liked him, did she? Lysander pictured the warrior. Tall, though Lysander was taller. Muscled, though Lysander was more so. Dark where Lysander was light. He was actually relieved to know the Harpy preferred a different type of male than himself.

That wouldn't change her fate, but it did lessen Lysander's burden. He hadn't been sure what he would have done if she'd *asked* him to touch her. That she wouldn't was most definitely a relief.

"What about Aeron?" Kaia asked. "All those tattoos…" A moan slipped from her as she shivered. "I could trace every single one of them with my tongue."

Aeron, host of Wrath. One of only two Lords with wings, Aeron's were black and gossamer. He had tattoos all over his body, and looked every inch the demon he was. What's more, he had recently broken a spiritual covenant. Therefore, Aeron would be dead before the upcoming nuptials.

Lysander's charge, Olivia, had been ordered to slay the warrior. So far she had resisted the decree. The girl was too soft-hearted for her own good. Eventually, though, she would do her duty. Otherwise, she would be kicked to earth, immortal no longer, and that was not a fate Lysander would allow.

Of all the angels he'd trained, she was by far his favorite. As gentle as she was, a man couldn't help but want to make her happy. She was trustworthy, loyal and all that was pure; she was the type of female who should have tempted him. A female he might have been able to accept in a romantic way. Wild Bianka…no. Never.

"However will I choose between my two favorite Lords, B?" Another sigh returned Lysander's focus to the Harpies.

Bianka rolled her eyes. "Just sample them both. Not like you haven't enjoyed a twofer before."

Kaia laughed, though the amusement didn't quite reach her voice. Like Bianka, there was a twinge of sadness to the sound. "True."

Lysander's mouth curled in mild distaste. Two different partners in one day. Or at the same time. Had Bianka done that, too? Probably.

"What about you?" Kaia asked. "You gonna hook up with Amun at the wedding?"

There was a long, heavy pause. Then Bianka shrugged. "Maybe. Probably."

He should leave and return when she was alone. The more he learned about her, the more he disliked her. Soon he would simply snatch her up, no matter who watched, revealing his presence, his intentions, just to save this world from her dark influence.

He flapped his wings once, twice, lifting into the air.

"You know what I want more than anything else in the world?" she asked, rolling to her side and facing her sister. Facing Lysander directly, as well. Her eyes were wide, amber irises luminous. Beams of sunlight seemed to soak into that glorious skin, and he found himself pausing.

Kaia stretched out beside her. "To co-host *Good Morning America?*"

"Well, yeah, but that's not what I meant."

"Then I'm stumped."

"Well…" Bianka nibbled on her bottom lip. Opened her mouth. Closed her mouth. Scowled. "I'll tell you, but you can't tell anyone."

The redhead pretended to twist a lock over her lips.

"I'm serious, K. Tell anyone, and I'll deny it then hunt you down and chop off your head."

Would she truly? Lysander wondered. Again, probably. He could not imagine hurting his Olivia, whom he loved like a sister. Maybe because she was not one of the Elite Seven, but was a joy-bringer, the weakest of the angels.

There were three angelic factions. The Elite Seven, the warriors and the joy-bringers. Their status was reflected in both their different duties and the color of their wings. Each of the Seven possessed golden wings, like his own. Warriors possessed white wings merely threaded with gold, and the joy-bringers' white wings bore no gold at all.

Olivia had been a joy-bringer all the centuries of her existence. Something she was quite happy with. That was why everyone, including Olivia, had experienced such shock when golden down had begun to grow in her feathers.

Not Lysander, however. He'd petitioned the Angelic Council, and they'd agreed. It had needed to be done. She was too fascinated by the demon-possessed warrior Aeron. Too…infatuated. Ridding her of such an attraction was imperative. As he well knew.

His hand clenched into a fist. He blamed himself for Olivia's circumstances. He had sent her to watch the Lords. To study them. He should have gone himself, but he'd hoped to avoid Bianka.

"Well, don't just lie there. Tell me what you want to do more than anything else in the world," Kaia exclaimed, once again drawing his attention.

Bianka uttered another sigh. "I want to sleep with a man."

Kaia's brow scrunched in confusion. "Uh, hello. Wasn't that what we were just discussing?"

"No, dummy. I mean, I want to sleep. As in, conk out. As in, snore my ass off."

A moment passed in silence as Kaia absorbed the announcement. "What! That's forbidden. Stupid. Dangerous."

Harpies lived by two rules, he knew. They could only eat what they stole or earned, and they could not sleep in the presence of another. The first was because of a curse on all Harpy-kind, and the second because Harpies were suspicious and untrusting by nature.

Lysander's head tilted to the side as he found himself imagining holding Bianka in his arms as she drifted into slumber. That fall of dark curls would tumble over his arm and chest. Her warmth would seep into his body. Her leg would rub over his.

He could never allow it, of course, but that didn't diminish the power of the vision. To hold her, protect her, comfort her would be…nice.

Would her skin be as soft as it appeared?

His teeth ground together. There was that ridiculous question again. *I do not care. It does not matter.*

"Forget I said anything," Bianka grumbled, once more flopping to her back and staring up at the bright sky.

"I can't. Your words are singed into my ears. Do you know what happened to our ancestors when they were stupid enough to fall asl—"

"Yes, okay. Yes." She pushed to her feet. The faux fur coat she wore was bloodred, same as her lips, and a vivid contrast to the white ice around her. Her boots were black and climbed to her knees. She wore skintight pants, also black. She looked wicked and beautiful.

Would her skin be as soft as it appeared?

Before he realized what he was doing, he was standing in front of her, reaching out, fingers tingling. *What are you doing? Stop!* He froze. Backed several steps away.

Sweet heaven. How close he'd come to giving in to the temptation of her.

He could not wait any longer. Could not wait until she was alone. He had to act now. His reaction to her was growing stronger. Any more, and he *would* touch her. And if he liked touching her, he might want to do more. That was how temptation worked. You gave in to one thing, then yearned for another. And another. Soon, you were lost.

"Enough heavy talk. Let's get back to our boring routine and jump," Bianka said, stalking to the edge of the peak. "You know the rules. Girl who breaks the least amount of bones wins. If you die, you lose. For, like, ever." She gazed down.

So did Lysander. There were crests and dips along the way, ice bounders with sharp, deadly ridges and thousands of feet of air. Such a jump would have killed a mortal, no question. The Harpy merely joked about the possibility, as if it were of no consequence. Did she think herself invulnerable?

Kaia lumbered to her feet and swayed from the liquor still pouring through her. "Fine, but don't think this is the last of our conversation about sleeping habits and stupid girls who—"

Bianka dove.

Lysander expected the action, but was still surprised by it. He followed her down. She spread her arms, closed her eyes, grinning foolishly. That grin…affected him. Clearly she reveled in the freedom of soaring. Something he often did, as well. But she would not have the end she desired.

Seconds before she slammed into a boulder, Lysander allowed himself to materialize in her plane. He grabbed her, arms catching under hers, wings unfolding, slowing them. Her legs slapped against him, jarring him, but he didn't release his hold.

A gasp escaped her, and her eyelids popped open. When she spotted him, amber eyes clashing with the dark of his, that gasp became a growl.

Most would have asked who he was or demanded he go away. Not Bianka.

"Big mistake, Stranger Danger," she snapped. "One you'll pay for."

As many battles as he'd fought over the years and as many opponents as he'd slain, he didn't have to see to know she had just unsheathed a blade from a hidden slit in her coat. And he didn't have to be a psychic to know she meant to stab him.

"It is you who made the mistake, Harpy. But do not worry. I have every intention of rectifying that." Before she could ensure that her weapon met its intended target, he whisked her into another plane, into his home—where she would stay. Forever.

CHAPTER TWO

BIANKA SKYHAWK GAPED at her new surroundings. One moment she'd been tumbling toward an icy valley, intent on escaping her sister's line of questioning, as well as winning their break-the-least-amount-of-bones game, and the next she'd been in the arms of a gorgeous blond. Which wasn't necessarily a good thing. She'd tried to stab him, and he'd blocked her. Freaking blocked her. No one should be able to block a Harpy's deathblow.

Now she was standing inside a cloud-slash-palace. A palace that was bigger than any home she'd ever seen. A palace that was warm and sweetly scented, with an almost tangible sense of peace wafting through the air.

The walls were wisps of white and smoke, and as she watched, murals formed, seemingly alive, winged creatures, both angelic and demonic, soaring through a morning sky. They reminded her of Danika's paintings. Danika—the All-Seeing Eye who watched both heaven and hell. The floors, though comprised of that same ethereal substance, allowing a view of the land and people below, were somehow solid.

Angelic. Cloud. Heaven? Dread flooded her as she spun to face the male who had grabbed her. "Angelic" described him perfectly. From the top of his pale head to the strength in that leanly muscled, sun-kissed body, to the golden wings stretching from his back. Even the white robe that fell to his ankles and the sandals wrapped around his feet gave him a saintly aura.

Was he an angel, then? Her heart skipped a beat. He wasn't human, that was for sure. No human male could ever hope to compare to such blinding perfection. But damn, those eyes… they were dark and hard and almost, well, empty.

His eyes don't matter. Angels were demon assassins, and she was as close to a demon as a girl could get. After all, her great-grandfather was Lucifer himself. Lucifer, who had spent a year on earth unfettered, pillaging and raping. Only a few females had conceived, but those that had soon gave birth to the first of the Harpies.

Unsure of what to do, Bianka strode around her blond; he remained in place, even when she was at his back, as if he had nothing to fear from her. Maybe he didn't. Obviously he had powers. One, he'd blocked her—she just couldn't get over that fact—and two, he'd somehow removed her coat and all her weapons without touching her.

"Are you an angel?" she asked when she was once again in front of him.

"Yes." No hesitation. As if his heritage wasn't something to be ashamed of.

Poor guy, she thought with a shudder. Clearly he had no idea the crappy hand he'd been dealt. If she had to choose between being an angel and a dog, she'd choose the dog. They, at least, were respectable.

She'd never been this close to an angel before. Seen one, yes. Or rather, seen what she'd thought was an angel but had later learned was a demon in disguise. Either way, she hadn't liked the guy, her youngest sister's father. He considered himself a god and everyone else beneath him.

"Did you bring me here to kill me?" she asked. Not that he'd have any luck. He would find that she was not an easy target. Many immortals had tried to finish her off over the years, but none had succeeded. Obviously.

He sighed, warm breath trekking over her cheeks. She had accidentally-on-purpose closed some of the distance between them; he smelled of the icecaps she so loved. Fresh and crisp with just a hint of earthy spice.

When he realized that only a whisper separated them, his lips, too full for a man but somehow perfect for him, pressed into a mulish line. Though she didn't see him move, he was suddenly a few more inches away from her. Huh. Interesting. Had he increased the distance on purpose?

Curious, she stepped toward him.

He backed away.

He had. Why? Was he scared of her?

Just to be contrary, as she often was, she stepped toward him again. Again, he stepped away. So. The big, bad angel didn't want to be within striking distance. She almost grinned.

"Well," she prompted. "Did you?"

"No. I did not bring you here to kill you." His voice was rich, sultry, a sin all its own. And yet, there was a layer of absolute truth to it, and she suspected she would have believed anything he said. As if whatever he said was simply fated, meant to be. Unchangeable. "I want you to emulate my life. I want you to learn from me."

"Why?" What would he do if she touched him? The tiny gossamer wings on her own back fluttered at the thought. Her T-shirt was designed especially for her kind, the material loose to keep from pinning those wings as she jolted into superspeed. "Wait. Don't answer. Let's make out first." A lie, but he didn't need to know that.

"Bianka," he said, his patience clearly waning. "This is not a game. Do not make me bind you to my bed."

"Ohh, now that I like. Sounds kinky." She darted around him, running her fingertips over his cheek, his neck. "You're as soft as a baby."

He sucked in a breath, stiffened. "Bianka."

"But better equipped."

"Bianka!"

She patted his butt. "Yes?"

"You will cease that immediately!"

"Make me." She laughed, the amused, carefree sound echoing between them.

Scowling, he reached out and latched on to her upper arm. There wasn't time to evade him; shockingly, he was faster than she was. He jerked her in front of him, and dark, narrowed eyes stared down at her.

"There will be no touching. Do you understand?"

"Do you?" Her gaze flicked to his hand, still clutching her arm. "At the moment, you're the one touching me."

Like hers, his gaze fell to where they were connected. He licked his lips, and his grip tightened just the way she liked. Then he released her as if she were on fire and once again increased the distance between them.

"Do you understand?" His tone was hard and flat.

What was the problem? He should be begging to touch her. She was a desirable Harpy, damn it. Her body was a work of art and her face total perfection. But for his benefit, she said, "Yeah, I understand. That doesn't mean I'll obey." Her skin tingled, craving the return of his. *Bad girl. Bad, bad girl. He's a stupid angel and therefore not an appropriate plaything.*

A moment passed as he absorbed her words. "Are you not frightened of me?" His wings folded into his back, arcing over his shoulders.

"No," she said, raising a brow and doing her best to appear unaffected. "Should I be?"

"Yes."

Well, then, he'd have to somehow grow the fiery claws of her father's people. That was the only thing that scared her.

Having been scratched as a child, having felt the acid-burn of fire spread through her entire body, having spent days writhing in agonizing, seemingly endless pain, she would do anything to avoid such an experience again.

"Well, I'm still not. And now you're starting to bore me." She anchored her hands on her hips, glaring up at him. "I asked you a question but you never answered it. Why do you want me to be like you? So much so, that you brought me into heaven, of all places?"

A muscle ticked below one of his eyes. "Because I am good and you are evil."

Another laugh escaped her. He frowned, and her laughter increased until tears were running from her eyes. When she quieted, she said, "Good job. You staved off the boredom."

His frown deepened. "I was not teasing you. I mean to keep you here forever and train you to be sinless."

"Gods, how—oops, sorry. I mean, golly, how adorable are you? 'I mean to keep you here forever and train you,'" she said in her best impersonation of him. There was no reason to fight about her eventual escape. She'd prove him wrong just as soon as she decided to leave. Right now, she was too intrigued. With her surroundings, she assured herself, and not the angel. Heaven was not a place she'd ever thought to visit.

His chin lifted a notch, but his eyes remained expressionless. "I am serious."

"I'm sure you are. But you'll find that you can't keep me anywhere I don't want to be. And me? Without sin? Funny!"

"We shall see."

His confidence might have unnerved her had she been less confident in her own abilities. As a Harpy, she could lift a semi as if it were no more significant than a pebble, could move faster than the human eye could see and had no problem slaying an unwelcome host.

"Be honest," she said. "You saw me and wanted a piece, right?"

For the briefest of moments, horror blanketed his face. "No," he croaked out, then cleared his throat and said more smoothly, "No."

Insulting bastard. Why such horror at the thought of being with her? *She* was the one who should be horrified. He was clearly a do-gooder, more so than she'd realized. *I am good and you are evil,* he'd said. Ugh.

"So tell me again why you want to change me. Didn't anyone ever tell you that you shouldn't mess with perfection?"

That muscle started ticking below his eye again. "You are a menace."

"Whatever, dude." She liked to steal—so what. She could kill without blinking—again, so what. It wasn't like she worked for the IRS or anything. "Where's my sister, Kaia? She's as much a menace as I am, I'm sure. So why don't you want to change her?"

"She is still in Alaska, wondering if you are buried inside an ice cave. And you are my only project at the moment."

Project? Bastard. But she did like the thought of Kaia searching high and low but finding no sign of her, almost like they were playing a game of Hide and Seek. Bianka would totally, finally win.

"You appear…excited," he said, head tilting to the side. "Why? Does her concern not disturb you?"

Yep. A certified do-gooder. "It's not like I'll be here long." She peeked over his shoulder; more of that wisping white greeted her. "Got anything to drink here?"

"No."

"Eat?"

"No."

"Wear?"

"No."

Slowly the corners of her lips lifted. "I guess that means you like to go naked. Awesome."

His cheeks reddened. "Enough. You are trying to bait me and I do not like it."

"Then you shouldn't have brought me here." Hey, wait a minute. He'd never really told her why he'd chosen her as his *project,* she realized. "Be honest. Do you need my help with something?" After all, she, like many of her fellow Harpies, was a mercenary, paid to find and retrieve. Her motto: if it's unethical and illegal and you've got the cash, I'm your girl! "I mean, I know you didn't just bring me here to save the world from my naughty influence. Otherwise, millions of other people would be here with me."

He crossed his arms over his massive chest.

She sighed. Knowing men as she did, she knew he was done answering that type of question. Oh, well. She could have convinced him otherwise by annoying him until he caved, but she didn't want to put the work in.

"So what do you do for fun around here?" she asked.

"I destroy demons."

Like you, she finished for him. But he'd already said he had no intention of killing her, and she believed him—how could she not? That voice… "So you don't want to hurt me, you don't want to touch me, but you do want me to live here forever."

"Yes."

"I'd be an idiot to refuse such an offer." That she sounded sincere was a miracle. "We'll pretend to be married and spend the nights locked in each other's arms, kissing and touching, our bodies—"

"Stop. Just stop." And, drumroll please, that muscle began ticking under his eye again.

This time, there was no fighting her grin. It spread wide and proud. That tic was a sign of anger, surely. But what would it take to make that anger actually seep into his irises? What would it take to break even a fraction of his iron control?

"Show me around," she said. "If I'm going to live here, I need to know where my walk-in closet is." During the tour, she could accidentally-on-purpose brush against him. Over and over again. "Do we have cable?"

"No. And I cannot give you a tour. I have duties. Important duties."

"Yeah, you do. My pleasure. That should be priority one."

Teeth grinding together, he turned on his heel and strode away. "You will find it difficult to get into trouble here, so I suggest you do not even try." His voice echoed behind him.

Please. She could get into trouble with nothing but a toothpick and a spoon. "If you leave, I'll rearrange everything." Not that there was any furniture to be seen.

Silence.

"I'll get bored and take off."

"Try."

It was a response, at least. "So you're seriously going to leave me? Just like that?" She snapped her fingers.

"Yes." Another response, though he didn't stop walking.

"What about that bed you were going to chain me to? Where is it?"

Uh-oh, back to silence.

"You didn't even tell me your name," she called, irritated despite herself. How could he abandon her like that? He should hunger for more of her. "Well? I deserve to know the name of the man I'll be cursing."

Finally, he stopped. Still, a long while passed in silence and she thought he meant to ignore her. Again. Then he said, "My name is Lysander," and stepped from the cloud, disappearing from view.

CHAPTER THREE

LYSANDER WATCHED AS TWO newly recruited warrior angels—angels under his training and command—finally subdued a demonic minion that had dug its way free from hell. The creature was scaled from head to hoof and little horns protruded from its shoulders and back. Its eyes were bright red, like crystallized blood.

The fight had lasted half an hour, and both angels were now bleeding, panting. Demons were notorious for their biting and scratching.

Lysander should have been able to critique the men and tell them what they had done wrong. That way, they would do a better job next time. But as they'd struggled with the fiend, his mind had drifted to Bianka. What was she doing? Was she resigned to her fate yet? He'd given her several days alone to calm and accept.

"What now?" one of his trainees asked. Beacon was his name.

"You letsss me go, you letsss me go," the demon said pleadingly, its forked tongue giving it a lisp. "I behave. I return. Ssswear."

Lies. As a minion, it was a servant to a demon High Lord—just as there were three factions of angels, there were three factions of demons. High Lords held the most power, followed by Lords, who were followed by the lowest of them all, minions. Despite this one's lack of status, it could cause untold damage among humans. Not only because it was evil, but also because it was a minion of Strife and took its nourishment from the trouble it caused others.

By the time Lysander had sensed its presence on earth, it had already broken up two marriages and convinced one teenager to start smoking and another to kill himself.

"Execute it," Lysander commanded. "It knew the consequences of breaking a heavenly law, yet it chose to escape from hell anyway."

The minion began to struggle again. "You going to lisssten to him when you obviousssly ssstronger and better than him? He make you do all hard work. He do nothing hissself. Lazy, if you asssk me. Kill *him*."

"We do not ask you," Lysander said.

Both angels raised their hands and fiery swords appeared.

"Pleassse," the demon screeched. "No. Don't do thisss."

They didn't hesitate. They struck.

The scaled head rolled, yet the angels did not dematerialize their swords. They kept the tips poised on the motionless body until it caught flame. When nothing but ash remained, they looked to Lysander for instruction.

"Excellent job." He nodded in satisfaction. "You have improved since your last killing, and I am proud of you. But you will train with Raphael until further notice," he said. Raphael was strong, intelligent and one of the best trackers in the heavens.

Raphael would not be distracted by a Harpy he had no hopes of possessing.

Possessing? Lysander's jaw clenched tightly. He was not some vile demon. He possessed nothing. Ever. And when he finished with Bianka, she would be glad of that. There would be no more games, no more racing around him, caressing him and laughing. The clenching in his jaw stopped, but his shoulders sagged. In disappointment? Couldn't be.

Perhaps *he* needed a few days to calm and accept.

HE'D LEFT HER ALONE for a week, the sun rising and setting beyond the clouds. And each day, Bianka grew madder—and madder. And madder. Worse, she grew weaker. Harpies could only eat what they stole (or earned, but there was no way to earn a single morsel here). And no, that wasn't a rule she could overlook. It was a curse. A godly curse her people had endured for centuries. Reviled as Harpies were, the gods had banded together and decreed that no Harpy could enjoy a meal freely given or one they had prepared themselves. If they did, they sickened terribly. The gods' hope? Destruction.

Instead, they'd merely ensured Harpies learned how to steal from birth. To survive, even an angel would sin.

Lysander would learn that firsthand. She would make sure of it. Bastard.

Had he planned this to torture her?

In this palace, Bianka had only to speak of something and it would materialize before her. An apple—bright and red and juicy. Baked turkey—succulent and plump. But she couldn't eat them, and it was killing her. Liter—fucking—ally.

At first, Bianka had tried to escape. Several times. Unlike Lysander the Cruel, she couldn't jump from the clouds. The floor expanded wherever she stepped and remained as hard as marble. All she could do was move from ethereal room to ethereal room, watching the murals play out battle scenes. Once she'd thought she'd even spied Lysander.

Of course, she'd said, "Rock," and a nice-size stone had appeared in her hand. She'd chucked it at him, but the stupid thing had fallen to earth rather than hit him.

Where was he? What was he doing? Did he mean to kill her like this, despite his earlier denial? Slowly and painfully? At least the hunger pains had finally left her. Now she was merely consumed by a sensation of trembling emptiness.

She wanted to stab him the moment she saw him. Then set

him on fire. Then scatter his ashes in a pasture where lots of animals roamed. He deserved to be smothered by several nice steaming piles. Of course, if he waited much longer, *she* would be the one burned and scattered. She couldn't even drink a glass of water.

Besides, fighting him wasn't the way to punish him. That, she'd realized the first day here. He didn't like to be touched. Therefore, touching him was the way to punish him. And touch him she would. Anywhere, everywhere. Until he begged her to stop. No. Until he begged her to continue.

She would make him *like* it, and then take it away.

If she lasted.

Right now, she could barely hold herself up. In fact, why was she even trying?

"Bed," she muttered weakly, and a large four-poster appeared just in front of her. She hadn't slept since she'd gotten here. Usually she crashed in trees, but she wouldn't have had the strength to climb one even if the cloud had been filled with them. She collapsed on the plush mattress, velvet coverlet soft against her skin. Sleep. She'd sleep for a little while.

FINALLY LYSANDER COULD STAND it no more. Nine days. He'd lasted nine days. Nine days of thinking about the female constantly, wondering what she was doing, what she was thinking. If her skin was as soft as it looked.

He could tolerate it no longer. He would check on her, that was all, and see for himself how—and what—she was doing. Then he would leave her again. Until he got himself under control. Until he stopped thinking about her. Stopped wanting to be near her. Her training had to begin sometime.

His wings glided up and down as he soared to his cloud. His heartbeat was a bit…odd. Faster than normal, even bumping against his ribs. Also, his blood was like fire in his veins. He didn't know what was wrong. Angels only sickened when they were infected with demon poison, and as Lysander had not been bitten by a demon—had not even fought one in weeks—he knew that was not the problem.

Blame could probably be laid at Bianka's door, he thought with a scowl.

First thing he noticed upon entering was the food littering the floor. From fruits to meats to bags of chips. All were uneaten, even unopened.

Scowl melting into a frown, he folded his wings into his back and stalked forward. He found Bianka inside one of the rooms, lying atop a bed. She wore the same clothing she'd been clad in when he'd first taken her—red shirt, tights that molded to her perfect curves—but had discarded her boots. Her hair was tangled around her, and her skin worryingly pale. There was no sparkle to it, no pearl-like gleam. Bruises now formed half-moons under her eyes.

Part of him had expected to find her fuming—and out for his head. The other part of him had hoped to find her compliant. Not once had he thought to find her like *this.*

She thrashed, the covers bunched around her. His frown deepened.

"Hamburger," she croaked.

A juicy burger appeared on the floor a few inches from the bed, all the extras—lettuce, tomato slices, pickles and cheese—decorating the edges of the plate. The manifestation didn't surprise him. That was the beauty of these angelic homes. Whatever was desired—within reason, of course—was provided.

All this food, and she hadn't taken a single bite. Why would she request— It wasn't stolen, he realized, and for the first time in his endless existence, he was angry with himself. And scared. For her. He hated the emotion, but there it was. She hadn't eaten in these last nine days because she couldn't. She was truly starving to death.

Though he wanted her out of his head, out of his life, he hadn't wanted her to suffer. Yet suffer she had. Unbearably. Now she was too weak to steal anything. And if he force-fed her, she would vomit, hurting more than she already was. Suddenly he wanted to roar.

"Blade," he said, and within a single blink, a sharp-tipped blade rested in his hand. He stalked to the side of the bed. He was trembling.

"Fries. Chocolate shake." Her voice was soft, barely audible.

Lysander slashed one of his wrists. Blood instantly spilled from the wound, and he stretched out his arm, forcing each drop to fall into her mouth. Blood was not food for Harpies; it was medicine. Therefore her body could accept it. He'd never freely given his blood to another living being and wasn't sure he liked the thought of something of his flowing inside this woman's veins. In fact, the thought actually caused his heart-beat to start slamming against his ribs again. But there was no other way.

At first, she didn't act as if she noticed. Then her tongue emerged, licking at the liquid before it could reach her lips. Then her eyes opened, amber irises bright, and she grabbed on to his arm, jerking it to her mouth. Her sharp teeth sank into his skin as she sucked.

Another odd sensation, he thought. Having a woman drink from him. There was heat and wetness and a sting, yet it was not unpleasant. It actually lanced a pang of…something un-nameable straight to his stomach and between his legs.

"Drink all you need," he told her. His body would not run out. Every drop was replaced the moment it left him.

Her gaze narrowed on him. The more she swallowed, the more fury he saw banked there. Soon her fingers were tightening around his wrist, her nails cutting deep. If she expected some sort of reaction from him, she would not get it. He'd been alive too long and endured far too many injuries to be affected by something so minor. Except for that pang between his legs… *What* was that?

Finally, though, she released him. He wasn't sure if that gladdened him or filled him with disappointment.

Gladdened, of course, he told himself.

A trickle of red flowed from the corner of her mouth, and she licked it away. The sight of that pink tongue caused another lance to shoot through him.

Definitely disap—uh, gladdened.

"You bastard," she growled through her panting. "You sick, torturing bastard."

He moved out of striking distance. Not to protect himself, but to protect her. If she were to attack him, he would have to subdue her. And if he subdued her, he might hurt her. And accidentally brush against her. *Blood…heating…*

"It was never my intent to harm you," he said. And now, even his voice was trembling. Odd.

"And that makes what you did okay?" She jerked to a sitting position, all that dark hair spilling around her shoulders. The pearl-like sheen was slowly returning to her skin. "You left me here, unable to eat. Dying!"

"I know." Was that skin as soft as it looked? He gulped. "And I am sorry." Her anger should have overjoyed him. As he'd hoped, she would no longer laugh up at him, her face lit with the force of her amusement. She would no longer race around him, petting him. Yes, he should have been overjoyed. Instead, the disappointment he'd just denied experiencing raced through him. Disappointment mixed with shame.

She was more a temptation than he had realized.

"You know?" she gasped out. "You know that I can only

consume what I steal or earn and yet you failed to make arrangements for me?"

"Yes," he admitted, hating himself for the first time in his existence.

"What's more, you left me here. With no way home."

His nod was stiff. "I have since made restitution by saving your life. But as I said, I am sorry."

"Oh, well, you're sorry," she said, throwing up her arms. "That makes everything better. That makes almost dying acceptable." She didn't wait for his reply. She kicked her legs over the bed and stood. Her skin was at full glow now. "Now you listen up. First, you're going to find a way to feed me. Then, you're going to tell me how to get off this stupid cloud. Otherwise I will make your life a hell you've never experienced before. Actually, I will anyway. That way, you'll never forget what happens when you mess with a Harpy."

He believed her. Already she affected him more than anyone else ever had. That was hell enough. Proof: his mouth was actually watering to taste her, his hands itching to touch her. Rather than reveal these new developments, however, he said, "You are powerless here. How would you hurt me?"

"Powerless?" She laughed. "I don't think so." One step, two, she approached him.

He held his ground. He would not retreat. Not this time. *Assert your authority.* "You cannot leave unless I allow it. The cloud belongs to me and places my will above yours. Therefore, there is no exit for you. You would be wise to curry my favor."

She sucked in a breath, paused. "So you still mean to keep me here forever? Even though I have a wedding to attend?" She sounded surprised.

"When did I ever give you the impression that I meant otherwise? Besides, I heard you tell your sister you didn't want to go to that wedding."

"No, I said I didn't want to be a bridesmaid. But I love my baby sis, so I'll do it. With a smile." Bianka ran her tongue over her straight, white teeth. "But let's talk about you. You like to eavesdrop, huh? That sounds a little demonic for a goody-goody angel."

Over the years he'd been called far worse than demonic. The goody-goody, though… Was that how she saw him? Rather than as the righteous soldier he was? "In war, I do what I must to win."

"Let me get this straight." Her eyes narrowed as she crossed her arms over her middle. Stubbornness radiated from her. "We were at war before I even met you?"

"Correct." A war he would win. But what would he do if he failed to set her on the right path? He would have to destroy her, of course, but for him to legally be allowed to destroy her, he reminded himself, she would first have to commit an unpardonable sin. Though she'd lived a long time, she had never crossed that line. Which meant she would have to be encouraged to do so. But how? Here, away from civilization—both mortal and immortal—she couldn't free a demon from hell. She couldn't slay an angel. Besides him, but that would never happen. He was stronger than she was.

She could blaspheme, he supposed, but he would never—never!—encourage someone to do that, no matter the reason. Not even to save himself.

The only other possibility was for her to convince an angel to fall. As she was *his* temptation, and as he was the only angel of her acquaintance, he was the only one she could convince. And he wouldn't. Again, not for any reason. He loved his life, his Deity, and was proud of his work and all he had accomplished.

Perhaps he would simply leave Bianka here, alone for the rest of eternity. That way, she could live but would be unable to cause trouble. He would visit her every few weeks—perhaps months—but never remain long enough for her to corrupt him.

A sudden blow to the cheek sent his head whipping to the side. He frowned, straightened and rubbed the now-stinging spot. Bianka was exactly as she'd been before, standing in front of him. Only now she was smiling.

"You hit me," he said, his astonishment clear.

"How sweet of you to notice."

"Why did you do that?" To be honest, he should not have been surprised. Harpies were as violent by nature as their in-human counterparts the demons. Why couldn't she have looked like a demon, though? Why did she have to be so lovely? "I saved you, gave you my blood. I even explained why you could not leave, just as you asked. I did not have to do any of those things."

"Do I really need to repeat your crimes?"

"No." They were not crimes! But perhaps it was best to change the subject. "Allow me to feed you," he said. He walked to the plate holding the hamburger and picked it up. The scent of spiced meat wafted to his nose, and his mouth curled in distaste.

Though he didn't want to, though his stomach rolled, he took a bite. He wanted to gag, but managed to swallow. Normally he only ate fruits, nuts and vegetables. "This," he said with much disgust, "is mine." Careful not to touch her, he placed the food in her hands. "You are not to eat it."

By staking the verbal claim, the meal did indeed become his. He watched understanding light her eyes.

"Oh, cool." She didn't hesitate to rip into the burger, every crumb gone in seconds. Next he sipped the chocolate shake. The sugar was almost obscene in his mouth, and he did gag. "Mine," he repeated faintly, giving it to her, as well. "But next time, please request a healthier meal."

She flipped him off as she gulped back the ice cream. "More."

He bypassed the French fries. No way was he going to defile his body with one of those greasy abominations. He found an apple, a pear, but had to request a stalk of broccoli himself. After claiming them, he took a bite of each and handed them over. Much better.

Bianka devoured them. Well, except for the broccoli. That, she threw at him. "I'm a carnivore, moron."

She hardly had to remind him when the unpleasant taste of the burger lingered on his tongue. Still, he chose to overlook her mockery. "All of the food produced in this home is mine. Mine and mine alone. You are to leave it alone."

"That'd be great if I were actually staying," she muttered while stuffing the fries in her mouth.

He sighed. She would accept her fate soon enough. She would have to.

The more she ate, the more radiant her skin became. Magnificent, he thought, reaching out before he could stop himself.

She grabbed his fingers and twisted just before contact. "Nope. I don't like you, so you don't get to handle the goods."

He experienced a sharp pain, but merely blinked over at her. "My apologies," he said stiffly. Thank the One True Deity she'd stopped him. No telling what he would have done to her had he actually touched her. Behaved like a slobbering human? He shuddered.

She shrugged and released him. "Now for my second order. Let me go home." As she spoke, she assumed a battle stance. Legs braced apart, hands fisted at her sides.

He mirrored her movements, refusing to admit, even to himself, that her bravery heated his traitorous blood another degree. "You cannot hurt me, Harpy. Fighting me would be pointless."

Slowly her lips curled into a devilish grin. "Who said I was going to try and hurt you?"

Before Lysander could blink, she closed the distance between them and pressed against him, arms winding around his neck and tugging his head down. Their lips met and her tongue thrust into his mouth. Automatically, he stiffened. He had seen humans kiss more times than he could count, but he'd never longed to try the act for himself.

Like sex, it seemed messy—in every way imaginable—and unnecessary. But as her tongue rolled against his, as her hands caressed a path down his spine, his body warmed—far more than it had when he'd simply thought of being here with her—and the tingle he'd noticed earlier bloomed once more. Only this time, that tingle grew and spread. Like the shaft between his legs. Rising…thickening…

He'd wanted to taste her and now he was. She was delicious, like the apple she'd just eaten, only sweeter, headier, like his favorite wine. He should make her stop. This was too much. But the wetness of her mouth wasn't messy in the least. It was electrifying.

More, a little voice said in his head.

"Yes," she rasped, as if he'd spoken aloud.

When she rubbed her lower body against his, every sensation intensified. His hands fisted at his sides. He couldn't touch her. Shouldn't touch her. Should stop this as she'd stopped him, as he'd already tried to convince himself.

A moan escaped her. Her fingers tangled in his hair. His scalp, an area he'd never considered sensitive before, ached, soaking up every bit of attention. And when she rubbed against him again, *he* almost moaned.

Her hands fell to his chest and a fingertip brushed one of his nipples. He did moan; he did grab her. His fingers gripped her hips, holding her still even though he wanted to force her to rub against him some more. The lack of motion didn't slow her kiss. She continued to dance their tongues together, leisurely, as if she could drink from him forever. And wanted to.

He should stop this, he told himself yet again.

Yes. Yes, he would. He tried to push her tongue out of his mouth. The pressure created another sensation, this one new and stronger than any other. His entire body felt aflame. He started pushing at her tongue for an entirely different reason, twining them together, tasting her again, licking her, sucking her.

"Mmm, yeah. That's the way," she praised.

Her voice was a drug, luring him in deeper, making him crave more. More, more, more. The temptation was too much, and he had to—

Temptation.

The word echoed through his mind, a sword sharp enough to cut bone. She was a temptation. She was *his* temptation. And he was allowing her to lead him astray.

He wrenched away from her, and his arms fell to his sides, heavy as boulders. He was panting, sweating, things he had not done even in the midst of battle. Angry as he was—at her, at himself—his gaze drank in the sight of her. Her skin was flushed, glowing more than ever. Her lips were red and swollen. And he had caused that reaction. Sparks of pride took him by surprise.

"You should not have done that," he growled.

Slowly she grinned. "Well, you should have stopped me."

"I wanted to stop you."

"But you didn't," she said, that grin growing.

His teeth ground together. "Do not do it again."

One of her brows arched in smug challenge. "Keep me here against my will, and I'll do that and more. Much, much more. In fact..." She ripped her shirt over her head and tossed it aside, revealing breasts covered by pink lace.

Breathing became impossible.

"Want to touch them?" she asked huskily, cupping them with her hands. "I'll let you. I won't even make you beg."

Holy...Lord. They were lovely. Plump and mouth-watering.

Lickable. And if he did lick them, would they taste as her mouth had? Like that heady wine? *Blood...heating...again...*

He didn't care what kind of coward his next action made him. It was either jump from the cloud or replace her hands with his own.

He jumped.

CHAPTER FOUR

LYSANDER LEFT BIANKA alone for another week—bastard!—but she didn't mind. Not this time. She had plenty to keep her occupied. Like her plan to drive him utterly insane with lust. So insane he'd regret bringing her here. Regret keeping her here. Regret even being alive.

That, or fall so in love with her that he yearned to grant her every desire. If that was the case—and it was a total possibility since she was *insanely* hot—she would convince him to take her home, and then she would finally get to stab him in the heart.

Perfect. Easy. With her breasts, it was almost too easy, really.

To set the stage for his downfall, she decorated his home like a bordello. Red velvet lounges now waited next to every door—just in case he was too overcome with desire for her to make it to one of the beds now perched in every corner. Naked portraits—of her—hung on the misty walls. A decorating style she'd picked up from her friend Anya, who just happened to be the goddess of Anarchy.

As Lysander had promised, Bianka had only to speak what she wanted—within reason—to receive it. Apparently furniture and pretty pictures were within reason. She chuckled. She could hardly wait to see him again. To finally begin.

He wouldn't stand a chance. Not just because of her (magnificent) breasts and hotness—hey, no reason to act as if she didn't know—but because he had no experience. She had been his first kiss; she knew it beyond any doubt. He'd been stiff at first, unsure. Hesitant. At no point had he known what to do with his hands.

That hadn't stopped her from enjoying herself, however. His taste…decadent. Sinful. Like crisp, clean skies mixed with turbulent night storms. And his body, oh, his body. Utter perfection with hard muscles she'd wanted to squeeze. And lick. She wasn't picky.

His hair was so silky she could have run her fingers through it forever. His cock had been so long and thick she could have rubbed herself to orgasm. His skin was so warm and smooth she could have pressed against him and slept, just as she'd dreamed about doing before she'd met him. Even though sleeping with a man was a dangerous crime her race never committed.

Stupid girl! The angel wasn't to be trusted, especially since he clearly had nefarious plans for her—though he still refused to tell her exactly what those plans were. Teaching her to act like him had to be a misdirection of the truth. It was just too silly to contemplate. But his plans didn't matter, she supposed, since he would soon be at her mercy. Not that she had any.

Bianka strode to the closet she'd created and flipped through the lingerie hanging there. Blue, red, black. Lace, leather, satin. Several costumes: naughty nurse, corrupt policewoman, devil, angel. Which should she choose today?

He already thought her evil. Perhaps she should wear the see-through white lace. Like a horny virgin bride. Oh, yes. That was the one. She laughed as she dressed.

"Mirror, please," she said, and a full-length mirror appeared in front of her. The gown fell to her ankles, but there was a slit between her legs. A slit that stopped at the apex of her thighs. Too bad she wasn't wearing any panties.

Spaghetti straps held the material in place on her shoulders and dipped into a deep vee between her breasts. Her nipples, pink and hard, played peek-a-boo with the swooping make-me-a-woman pattern.

She left her hair loose, flowing like black velvet down her back. Her gold eyes sparkled, flecks of gray finally evident, like in Kaia's. Her cheeks were flushed like a rose, her skin devoid of the makeup she usually wore to dull its shimmer.

Bianka traced her fingertips along her collarbone and chuckled again. She'd summoned a shower and washed off every trace of that makeup. If Lysander had found himself attracted to her before—and he had, the size of his hard-on was proof of that—he would be unable to resist her now. She was nothing short of radiant.

A Harpy's skin was like a weapon. A sensual weapon. Its jewel-like sheen drew men in, made them slobbering, drooling fools. Touching it became all they could think about, all they lived for.

That got old after a while, though, which was why she'd begun wearing full body makeup. For Lysander, though, she would make an exception. He deserved what he got. After all, he wasn't just making Bianka suffer. He was making her sisters suffer. Maybe.

Was Kaia still looking for her? Still worried or perhaps thinking this was a game as Bianka had first supposed? Had Kaia called their other sisters and were the girls now searching the world over for a sign of her, as they'd done when Gwennie went missing? Probably not, she thought with a sigh. They knew her, knew her strength and her determination. If they suspected she'd been taken, they would have confidence in her ability to free herself. Still.

Lysander was an ass.

And most likely a virgin. Eager, excited, she rubbed her hands together. Most men kissed the women they bedded. And if she had been his first kiss, well, it stood to reason he'd never bedded anyone. Her eagerness faded a bit. But that begged the question, why hadn't he bedded anyone?

Was he a young immortal? Had he not found anyone he desired? Did angels not often experience sexual need? She didn't know much about them. Fine, she didn't know anything about them. Did they consider sex wrong? Maybe. That would explain why he hadn't wanted to touch her, too.

Okay, so it made more sense that he simply hadn't experienced sexual need before.

He'd definitely experienced it during their kiss, though. She went back to rubbing her hands together.

"*What* are you wearing? Or better yet, not wearing?"

Heart skidding to a stop, Bianka whipped around. As if her thoughts had summoned him, Lysander stood in the room's doorway. Mist enveloped him and for a moment she feared he was nothing more than a fantasy.

"Well?" he demanded.

In her fantasies, he would not be angry. He would be overcome with desire. So…he was here, and he was real. And he was peering at her breasts in open-mouthed astonishment.

Astonishment was better than anger. She almost grinned.

"Don't you like it?" she asked, smoothing her palms over her hips. *Let the games begin.*

"I—I—"

Like it, she finished for him. With the amount of truth that always layered his voice, he probably couldn't utter a single lie.

"Your skin…it's different. I mean, I saw the pearlesque tones before, but now…it's…"

"Amazing." She twirled, her gown dancing at her ankles. "I know."

"You know?" His tongue traced his teeth as the anger she'd first suspected glazed his features. "Cover her," he barked.

A moment later, a white robe draped her from shoulders to feet.

She scowled. "Return my teddy." The robe disappeared, leaving her in the white lace. "Try that again," she told him, "and I'll just walk around naked. You know, like I am in the portraits."

"Portraits?" Brow furrowing, he gazed about the room. When he spotted one of the pictures of her, sans clothing, reclining against a giant silver boulder, he hissed in a breath.

Exactly the reaction she'd been hoping for. "I hope you don't mind, but I turned this quaint little cloud into a love nest so I'd feel more at home. And again, if you remove anything, my redesign will be a thousand times worse."

"What are you trying to do to me?" he growled, facing her. His eyes were narrowed, his lips thinned, his teeth bared.

She fluttered her lashes at him, all innocence. "I'm afraid I don't know what you mean."

"Bianka."

It was a warning, she knew, but she didn't heed it. "I think it's my turn to ask the questions. So where do you go when you leave me?"

"That is not your concern."

Was he panting a little? "Let's see if I can make it my concern, shall we?" She sauntered to the bed and eased onto the edge. Naughty, shameless girl that she was, she spread her legs, giving him the peek of a lifetime. "For every question you answer, I'll put something on," she said in a sing-song voice. "Deal?"

He spun, but not before she saw the shock and desire that played over his harshly gorgeous face. "I do my duty. Watch the gates to hell. Hunt and kill demons that have escaped. Deliver punishment to those in need. Guard humans. Now cover yourself."

"I didn't say what item of clothing I'd don, now did I?" She gave herself a once-over. "One shoe, please. White leather, high heel, open toe. Ties up the calf." The shoe materialized on her foot, and she laughed. "Perfect."

"A trickster," Lysander muttered. "I should have known."

"How did I trick you? Did you ask for specifics? No, because you were secretly hoping I wouldn't cover myself at all."

"That is not true," he said, but for once, she did not hear that layer of honesty in his voice. Interesting. When he lied, or perhaps when he was unsure about what he was saying, his tone was as normal as hers.

That meant she would always know when he lied. Did things get any better than that?

This was going to be even easier than she'd anticipated. "Next question. Do you think about me while you're gone?"

Silence. Thick, heavy.

Wait. She could hear him breathing. In, out, harsh, shallow. He *was* panting.

"I'll take that as a yes," she said, grinning. "But since you really didn't answer, I don't have to add the other shoe."

Again, he didn't reply. Thankfully, he didn't leave, either.

"Onward and upward. Are angels allowed to dally?"

"Yes, but they rarely want to," he rasped.

So she'd been right. He didn't have firsthand knowledge of desire. What he was now feeling had to be confusing him, then. Was that why he'd brought her here? Because he'd seen her and wanted her, but hadn't known how to handle what he was feeling? The thought was almost…flattering. In a stalkerish kind of way, of course. That didn't change her plans, however. She would seduce him—and then she would slice his heart in two. A symbolic gesture, really. An inside joke between them. Well, for herself. He might not get it.

Still, she couldn't deny that she liked the idea of being his first. None of the women after her would compare, of course, and that— Hey, wait. Once he tasted the bliss of the flesh, he would want more. Bianka would have escaped him and stabbed him—and he would have recovered because he was an immortal—by then. He could go to any other female he desired.

He would kiss and touch that female.

"I'm waiting," he snapped.

"For?" she snapped back. Her hands were clenched, her nails cutting her palms. He could be with anyone; it wouldn't bother her. They were enemies. Someone else could deal with his Neanderthal tendencies. But gods, she might just kill the next woman who warmed his bed out of spite. Not jealousy.

"I answered one of your questions. You must add a garment to your body. Panties would be nice."

She sighed. "I'd like the other shoe to appear, please." A moment later, her other foot was covered. "Back to business. Did you return so that I'd kiss you again?"

"No!"

"Too bad. I wanted to taste you again. I wanted to touch you again. Maybe let you touch me this time. I've been aching since you left me. Had to bring myself to climax twice just to cool the fever. But don't worry, I imagined it was you. I imagined stripping you, licking you, sucking you into my mouth. Mmm, I'm so—"

"Stop!" he croaked out, spinning to face her. "Stop."

His eyes, which she'd once thought were black and emotionless, were now bright as a morning sky, his pupils blown with the intensity of his desire. But rather than stalk to her, grab her and smash his body into hers, he held out his hand, fingers splayed. A fiery sword formed from the air, yellow-gold flames flickering all around it.

"Stop," he commanded again. "I do not want to hurt you, but I will if you persist with this foolishness."

That layer of truth had returned to his voice.

Far from intimidating her, his forcefulness excited her. *I thought you didn't like his Neanderthal tendencies.*

Oh, shut up.

Bianka leaned back, resting her weight against her elbows. "Does Lysandy like to play rough? Should I be wearing black leather? Or is this a game of bad cop, naughty criminal? Should I strip for my body-cavity search?"

He stalked to the edge of the bed, his thick legs encasing her smaller ones, pressing her knees together. He was hard as a rock, his robe jutting forward. Those golden flames still flickering around the sword both highlighted his face and cast shadows, giving him a menacing aura.

Just then, he was both angel and demon. A mix of good and evil. Savior and executioner.

Her wings fluttered frantically, readying for battle—even as her skin tingled for pleasure. She could be across the room before he moved even a fraction of an inch. Still. She had trouble catching her breath; it was like ice in her lungs. And yet her blood was hot as his sword. This mix of emotions was odd.

"You are worse than I anticipated," he snarled.

If this progressed the way she hoped, he would be very happy about that one day. But she said, "Then let me go. You'll never have to see me again."

"And that will purge you from my mind? That will stop the wondering and the craving? No, it will only make them worse. You will give yourself to others, kiss them the way you kissed me, rub against them the way you rubbed against me, and I will want to kill them when they will have done nothing wrong."

What a confession! And she'd thought her blood hot before… "Then take me," she suggested huskily. She traced her tongue over her lips, slow and measured. His gaze followed. "It'll feel sooo good, I promise."

"And discover if you are as soft and wet as you appear? Spend the rest of eternity in bed with you, a slave to my body? No, that, too, will only make my cravings worse."

Oh, angel. You shouldn't have admitted that. A slave to his body? If that was his fear, he more than craved her. He was falling. Hard. And now that she knew how much he wanted her…he was as good as hers. "If you're going to kill me," she said, swirling a fingertip around her navel, "kill me with pleasure."

He stopped breathing.

She sat up, closing the rest of the distance between them. Still he didn't strike. She flattened her palms on his chest. His nipples were as beaded as hers. He closed his eyes, as if the sight of her, looking up at him through the thick shield of her lashes, was too much to bear.

"I'll let you in on a little secret," she whispered. "I'm softer and wetter than I appear."

Was that a moan?

And if so, had it come from him? Or her? Touching him like this was affecting her, too. All this strength at her fingertips was heady. Knowing this gorgeous warrior wanted her—her, and no other—was even headier. But knowing she was the very first to tempt him, and so strongly, was the ultimate aphrodisiac.

"Bianka." Oh, yes. A moan.

"But if you'd like, we can just lie next to each other." Said the spider to the fly. "We don't have to touch. We don't have to kiss. We'll lie there and think about all the things we dislike about each other and maybe build up an immunity. Maybe we'll stop *wanting* to touch and to kiss."

Never had she told such a blatant lie, and she'd told some big ones over the centuries. Part of her expected him to call her on it. The other part of her expected him to grasp on to the silly suggestion like a lifeline. Use it as an excuse to finally take what he wanted. Because if he did this, simply lay next to her, one temptation would lead to another. He wouldn't be thinking about the things he disliked about her—he would be thinking about the things he could be doing to her body. He would feel her heat, smell her arousal. He'd want—need—more from her. And she'd be right there, ready and willing to give it to him.

She fisted his robe and gently tugged him toward her. "It's worth a try, don't you think? *Anything*'s worth a try to make this madness stop."

When they were nose to nose, his breath trickling over her face, his gaze fastened on her lips, she began to ease backward. He followed, offering no resistance.

"Want to know one of the things I dislike about you?" she asked softly. "You know, to help get us started."

He nodded, as if he were too entranced to speak.

She decided to push a little faster than anticipated. He already seemed ready for more. "That you're not on top of me." Just a little more persuasion, and that would be remedied. Just a little… "How amazing would it feel to be that close?"

"Lysander," an unfamiliar female voice suddenly called. "Are you here?"

Who the hell? Bianka scowled.

Lysander straightened, jerking away from her as if she had just sprouted horns. He stepped back, disengaging from her completely. But he was trembling, and not from anger.

"Ignore her," she said. "We have important business to attend to."

"Lysander?" the woman called again.

Damn her, whoever she was!

His expression cleared, melted to steel. "Not another word from you," he barked, backing away. "You tried to lure me into bed with you. I don't think you meant to make me dislike you at all. I think you meant to—" A low snarl erupted from his throat. "You are not to try such a thing with me again. If you do, I will finally cleave your head from your body."

Well, this battle was clearly over. Not one to give up, however, she tried a different strategy. "So you're going to leave again? Coward! Well, go ahead. Leave me helpless and bored. But you know what? When I'm bored, bad things happen. And next time you come back here, I just might throw myself at you. My hands will be all over you. You won't be able to pry me off!"

"Lysander," the girl called again.

He ground his teeth. "Return to your *cloud,*" he threw over his shoulder. "I will meet you there."

He was going to meet another girl? At her cloud? Alone, private? Oh, hell, no. Bianka hadn't worked him into a frenzy so that someone else could reap the reward.

Before she could inform him of that, however, he said, "Give Bianka whatever she wants." Talking to his own cloud, apparently. "Anything but escape and more of those…outfits." His gaze intensified on her. "That should stave off the boredom. But I only agree to this on the condition that you vow to keep your hands to yourself."

Anything she wanted? She didn't allow herself to grin, the girl forgotten in the face of this victory. "Done."

"And so it is," he said, then spun and stalked from the room. His wings expanded in a rush, and he disappeared before she could follow. But then, there was no need to follow him. Not now.

He had no idea that he'd just ensured his own downfall. *Whatever she wants,* he'd said. She laughed. She didn't need to touch him or wear lingerie to win their next battle. She just needed his return.

Because then, *he* would become *her* prisoner.

CHAPTER FIVE

HE'D ALMOST GIVEN IN.

Lysander could not believe how quickly he'd almost given in to Bianka. One sultry glance from her, one invitation, and he'd forgotten his purpose. It was shameful. And yet, it was not shame that he felt. It was more of that strange disappointment—disappointment that he'd been interrupted!

Standing before Bianka, breathing in her wicked scent, feeling the heat of her body, all he'd been able to recall was the decadent taste of her. He'd wanted more. Wanted to finally touch her skin. Skin that had glowed with health, reflecting all those rainbow shards. She'd wanted that, too, he was sure of it. The more aroused she'd become, the brighter those colors had glowed.

Unless that was a trick? What did he truly know of women and desire?

She was worse than a demon, he thought. She'd known exactly how to entrance him. Those naked photos had nearly dropped him to his knees. Never had he seen anything so lovely. Her breasts, high and plump. Her stomach, flat. Her navel, perfectly dipped. Her thighs, firm and smooth. Then, being asked to lie beside her and think of what he disliked about her...both had been temptations, and both had been irresistible.

He'd known his resolve was crumbling and had wanted to rebuild it. And how better to rebuild than to ponder all the things he disliked about the woman? But if he had lain next to her, he would not have thought of what he disliked—things he couldn't seem to recall then or now. He might have even thought about what he *liked* about her.

She was brilliant. She'd had him.

He'd never desired a demon. Had never secretly liked bad behavior. Yet Bianka excited him in a way he could not have predicted. So, what did he like most about her at the moment? That she was willing to do anything, say anything, to tempt him. He liked that she had no inhibitions. He liked that she gazed up at him with longing in those beautiful eyes.

How would she look at him if he actually kissed her again? Kissed more than her mouth? How would she look at him if he actually touched her? Caressed that skin? He suddenly found himself wanting to watch mortals and immortals alike more intently, gauging their reactions to each other. Man and woman, desire to desire.

Just the thought of doing so caused his body to react the way it had done with Bianka. Hardening, tightening. Burning, craving. His eyes widened. That, too, had never happened before. He was letting her win, he realized, even though there was distance between them. He was letting his one temptation destroy him, bit by bit.

Something had to be done about Bianka, since his current plan was clearly failing.

"Lysander?"

His charge's voice drew him from his dark musings. "Yes, sweet?"

Olivia's head tilted to the side, her burnished curls bouncing. They stood inside her cloud, flowers of every kind scattered across the floor, on the walls, even dripping from the ceiling.

Her eyes, as blue as the sky, regarded him intently. "You haven't been listening to me, have you?"

"No," he admitted. Truth had always been his most cherished companion. That would not change now. "My apologies."

"You are forgiven," she said with a grin as sweet as her flowers.

With her, it was that easy. Always. No matter how big or small the crime, Olivia couldn't hold a grudge. Perhaps that was why she was so treasured among their people. Everyone loved her.

What would other angels think of Bianka?

No doubt they would be horrified by her. *He* was horrified.

I thought you were not going to lie? Even to yourself. He scowled. Unlike the forgiving Olivia, he suspected Bianka would hold a grudge for a lifetime—and somehow take that grudge beyond the grave.

For some reason, his scowl faded and his lips twitched at the thought. *Why* would that amuse him? Grudges were born of anger, and anger was an ugly thing. Except, perhaps, on Bianka. Would she erupt with the same amount of unrelenting passion she brought to the bedroom? Probably. Would she want to be kissed from her anger, as well?

The thought of kissing her until she was happy again did *not* delight him.

Usually he dealt with other people's anger the way he dealt with everything else. With total unconcern. It was not his job to make people feel a certain way. They were responsible for their own emotions, just as he was responsible for his. Not that he experienced many. Over the years, he'd simply seen too much to be bothered. Until Bianka.

"Lysander?"

Olivia's voice once more jerked him from his mind. His hands fisted. He'd locked Bianka away, yet she was still managing to change him. Oh, yes. His current plan was failing.

Why couldn't he have desired someone like sweet Olivia? It would have made his endless life much easier. As he'd told

Bianka, desire wasn't forbidden, but not many of their kind ever experienced it. Those that did only wanted other angels and often wed their chosen partner. Except in storybooks, he had never heard of an angel pairing with a different race—much less a demon.

"—you go again," Olivia said.

He blinked, hands fisting all the tighter. "Again, I apologize. I will be more diligent the rest of our conversation." He would make sure of it.

She offered him another grin, though this one lacked her usual ease. "I only asked what was bothering you." She folded her wings around herself and plucked at the feathers, carefully avoiding the strands of gold. "You're so unlike yourself."

That made two of them. Something was troubling her; sadness had never layered her voice before, yet now it did. Determined to help her, he summoned two chairs, one for him and one for her, and they sat across from each other. Her robe plumed around her as she released her wings and twined her fingers together in her lap. Leaning forward, he rested his weight on his elbows.

"Let us talk about you first. How goes your mission?" he asked. Only that could be the cause. Olivia found joy in all things. That's why she was so good at her job. Or rather, her former job. Because of him, she was now something she didn't want to be. A warrior angel. But it was for the best, and he did not regret the decision to change her station. Like him, she'd become too fascinated with someone she shouldn't.

Better to end that now, before the fascination ruined her.

She licked her lips and looked away from him. "That's actually what I wanted to speak with you about." A tremor shook her. "I don't think I can do it, Lysander." The words emerged as a tortured whisper. "I don't think I can kill Aeron."

"Why?" he asked, though he knew what she would say. But

unlike Bianka, Aeron had broken a heavenly law, so there could be no locking him away and leading him to a righteous path.

If Olivia failed to destroy the demon-possessed male, another angel would be tasked with doing so—and Olivia would be punished for her refusal. She would be cast out of the heavens, her immortality stripped, her wings ripped from her back.

"He hasn't hurt anyone since his blood-curse was removed," she said, and he heard the underlying beseeching.

"He helped one of Lucifer's minions escape hell."

"Her name is Legion. And yes, Aeron did that. But he ensures the little demon stays away from most humans. Those she does interact with, she treats with kindness. Well, her version of kindness."

"That doesn't change the fact that Aeron helped the creature escape."

Olivia's shoulders sagged, though she in no way appeared defeated. Determination gleamed in her eyes. "I know. But he's so…nice."

Lysander barked out a laugh. He just couldn't help himself. "We are speaking of a Lord of the Underworld, yes? The one whose entire body is tattooed with violent, bloody images no less? That is the male you call *nice?*"

"Not all of the etchings are violent," she mumbled, offended for some reason. "Two are butterflies."

For her to have found the butterflies amid the skeletal faces decorating the man's body meant she'd studied him intently. Lysander sighed. "Have you…felt anything for him?" Physically?

"What do you mean?" she asked, but rosy color bloomed on her cheeks.

She had, then. "Never mind." He scrubbed a hand down his suddenly tired face. "Do you like your home, Olivia?"

She blanched at that, as if she knew the direction he was headed. "Of course."

"Do you like your wings? Do you like your lack of pain, no matter the injury sustained? Do you like the robe you wear? A robe that cleans itself and you?"

"Yes," she replied softly. She gazed down at her hands. "You know I do."

"And you know that you will lose all of that and more if you fail to do your duty." The words were harsh, meant for himself as much as for her.

Tears sprang into her eyes. "I just hoped you could convince the council to rescind their order to execute him."

"I will not even try." Honest, he reminded himself. He had to be honest. Which he preferred. Or had. "Rules are put into place for a reason, whether we agree with those reasons or not. I have been around a long time, have seen the world—ours, theirs—plunged into darkness and chaos. And do you know what? That darkness and chaos always sprang from one broken rule. Just one. Because when one is broken, another soon follows. Then another. It becomes a vicious cycle."

A moment passed as she absorbed his words. Then she sighed, nodded. "Very well." Words of acceptance uttered in a tone that was anything but.

"You will do your duty?" What he was really asking: Will you slay Aeron, keeper of Wrath, whether you want to or not? Lysander wasn't asking more of her than he had done himself. He wasn't asking what he *wouldn't* do himself.

Another nod. One of those tears slid down her cheek.

He reached out and captured the glistening drop with the tip of his finger. "Your compassion is admirable, but it will destroy you if you allow it so much power over you."

She waved the prediction away. Perhaps because she did not believe it, or perhaps because she believed it but had no plans to change and therefore didn't want to discuss it anymore. "So who was the woman in your home? The one in the portraits?"

He…blushed? Yes, that was the heat spreading over his cheeks. "My…" How should he explain Bianka? How could he, without lying?

"Lover?" she finished for him.

His cheeks flushed with more of that heat. "No." Maybe. No! "She is my captive." There. Truthful without giving away any details. "And now," he said, standing. If she could end a subject, so could he. "I must return to her before she causes any more trouble." He must deal with her. Once and for all.

OLIVIA REMAINED IN PLACE long after Lysander left. Had that blushing, uncertain, distracted man truly been her mentor? She'd known him for centuries, and he'd always been unflappable. Even in the heat of battle.

The woman was responsible, she was sure. Lysander had never kept one in his cloud before. Did he feel for her what Olivia felt for Aeron?

Aeron.

Just thinking his name sent a shiver down her spine, filling her with a need to see him. And just like that, she was on her feet, her wings outstretched.

"I wish to leave," she said, and the floor softened, turning to mist. Down she fell, wings flapping gracefully. She was careful to avoid eye contact with the other angels flying through the sky as she headed into Budapest. They knew her destination; they even knew what she did there.

Some watched her with pity, some with concern—as Lysander had. Some watched her with antipathy. By avoiding their gazes, she ensured no one would stop her and try and talk sense into her. She ensured she wouldn't have to lie. Something she hated to do. Lies tasted disgustingly bitter.

Long ago, during her training, Lysander had commanded her to tell a lie. She would never forget the vile flood of acid in her mouth the moment she'd obeyed. Never again did she wish to experience such a thing. But to be with Aeron…maybe.

His dark, menacing fortress was perched high on a mountain and finally came into view. Her heart rate increased exponentially. Because she existed on another plane, she was able to drift through the stone walls as if they were not even there. Soon she was standing inside Aeron's bedroom.

He was polishing a gun. His little demon friend, Legion, the one he'd helped escape from hell, was darting and writhing around him, a pink boa twirling with her.

"Dance with me," the creature beseeched.

That was dancing? That kind of heaving was what humans did as they were dying.

"I can't. I've got to patrol the town tonight, searching for Hunters."

Hunters, sworn enemy of the Lords. They hoped to find Pandora's box and draw the demons out of the immortal warriors, killing each man. The Lords, in turn, hoped to find Pandora's box and destroy it—the same way they hoped to destroy the Hunters.

"Me hate Huntersss," Legion said, "but we needsss practice for Doubtie'sss wedding."

"I won't be dancing at Sabin's wedding, therefore practice isn't necessary."

Legion stilled, frowned. "But we dance at the wedding. Like a couple." Her thin lips curved downward. Was she…pouting? "Pleassse. We ssstill got time to practice. Dark not come for hoursss."

"As soon as I finish cleaning my weapons, I have to run an errand for Paris." Paris, Olivia knew, was keeper of Promiscuity and had to bed a new woman every day or he would weaken and die. But Paris was depressed and not taking proper care of himself, so Aeron, who felt responsible for the warrior, procured females for him. "We'll dance another time, I promise." Aeron didn't glance up from his task. "But we'll do it here, in the privacy of my room."

I want to dance with him, too, Olivia thought. What was it like, pressing your body against someone else's? Someone strong and hot and sinfully beautiful?

"But, Aeron…"

"I'm sorry, sweetheart. I do these things because they're necessary to keep you safe."

Olivia tucked her wings into her back. Aeron needed to take time for himself. He was always on the go, fighting Hunters, traveling the world in search of Pandora's box and aiding his friends. As much as she watched him, she knew he rarely rested and never did anything simply for the joy of it.

She reached out, meaning to ghost a hand through Aeron's hair. But suddenly the scaled, fanged creature screeched, "No, no, no," clearly sensing Olivia's presence. In a blink, Legion was gone.

Stiffening, Aeron growled low in his throat. "I told you not to return."

Though he couldn't see Olivia, he, too, always seemed to know when she arrived. And he hated her for scaring his friend away. But she couldn't help it. Angels were demon assassins and the minion must sense the menace in her.

"Leave," he commanded.

"No," she replied, but he couldn't hear her.

He returned the clip to his weapon and set it beside his bed. Scowling, he stood. His violet eyes narrowed as he searched the bedroom for any hint of her. Sadly, it was a hint he would never find.

Olivia studied him. His hair was cropped to his scalp, dark little spikes barely visible. He was so tall he dwarfed her, his shoulders so wide they could have enveloped her. With the tattoos decorating his skin, he was the fiercest creature she'd ever beheld. Maybe that was why he drew her so intensely. He was passion and danger, willing to do anything to save the ones he loved.

Most immortals put their own needs above everyone else's. Aeron put everyone else's above his own. That he did so never failed to shock her. And she was supposed to destroy him? She was supposed to end his life?

"I'm told you're an angel," he said.

How had he known what—the demon, she realized. Legion might not be able to see her, either, but as she'd already realized, the little demon knew danger when she encountered it. Plus, whenever Legion left him, she returned to hell. Fiery walls that could no longer confine her but could welcome her any time she wished. Olivia's lack of success had to be a great source of amusement to that region's inhabitants.

"If you are an angel, you should know that won't stop me from cutting you down if you dare try and harm Legion."

Once again, he was thinking of another's welfare rather than his own. He didn't know that Olivia didn't need to bother with Legion. That once Aeron was dead, Legion's bond to him would wither and she would again be chained to hell.

Olivia closed the distance between them, her steps tentative. She stopped only when she was a whisper away. His nostrils flared as if he knew what she'd done, but he didn't move. Wishful thinking on her part, she knew. Unless she fell, he would never see her, never smell her, never hear her.

She reached up and cupped his jaw with her hands. How she wished she could feel him. Unlike Lysander, who was of the Elite, she could not materialize into this plane. Only her weapon would. A weapon she would forge from air, its heavenly flames far hotter than those in hell. A weapon that would remove Aeron's head from his body in a mere blink of time.

"I'm told you're female," he added, his tone hard, harsh. As always. "But that won't stop me from cutting you down, either. Because, and here's something you need to know, when I want something, I don't let anything stand in the way of my getting it."

Olivia shivered, but not for the reasons Aeron probably hoped. Such determination…

I should leave before I aggravate him even more. With a sigh, she spread her wings and leapt, out of the fortress and into the sky.

CHAPTER SIX

"YOU, CLOUD, BELONG TO ME," Bianka said. That was not an attempt to escape, nor another sexy outfit, therefore it was acceptable. "Lysander gave you to me, so as long as I don't touch him, I get what I want. And I want you. I want you to obey me, not him. Therefore, you have to heed my commands rather than his. If I tell you to do something and he tells you not to, you still have to do it. *That's* what I want."

And oh, baby, this was going to be fun.

The more she thought about it, the happier she was that she couldn't touch Lysander again. Really. Seducing—or rather, trying to seduce—him had been a mistake. She'd basically ended up seducing herself. His heat…his scent…his strength… *Give. Me. More.*

Now, all she could think about was getting his weight back on top of her. About how she wanted to teach him where she liked to be touched. Once he'd gotten the hang of kissing, he'd teased and tantalized her mouth with the skill of a master. It would be the same with lovemaking.

She would lick each and every one of his muscles. She would hear him moan over and over again as *he* licked *her.*

How could she want those things from her enemy? How could she forget, even for a moment, how he'd locked her away? Maybe because he was a challenge. A sexy, tempting, frustrating challenge.

Didn't matter, though. She was done playing the role of sweet, horny prisoner. She still couldn't kill him; she'd be stuck here for eternity. Which meant she'd have to make him want to get rid of her. And now, as master of this cloud, she would have no problem doing so.

She could hardly wait to begin. If he stuck to past behavior, he'd be gone for a week. He'd return to "check on" her. Operation Cry Like A Baby could begin. Tomorrow she'd plan the specifics and set the stage. A few ideas were already percolating. Like tying him to a chair in front of a stripper pole. Like enforcing Naked Tuesdays.

Chuckling, she propped herself against the bed's headboard, yawned and closed her eyes.

"I'd like to hold a bowl of Lysander's grapes," she said, and felt a cool porcelain bowl instantly press atop her stomach. Without opening her eyes, she popped one of the fruits into her mouth, chewed. Gods, she was tired. She hadn't rested properly since she'd gotten here—or even before.

She couldn't. There were no trees to climb, no leaves to hide in. And even if she summoned one, Lysander could easily find her if he returned early—

Wait. No. No, he wouldn't. Not if she summoned hundreds of them. And if he dismissed all the trees, she would fall, which would awaken her. He would not be able to take her unaware.

Chuckling again, Bianka pried her eyelids apart. She polished off the grapes, scooted from the bed and stood. "Replace the furniture with trees. Hundreds of big, thick, green trees."

In the snap of her fingers, the cloud resembled a forest. Ivy twined around stumps and dew dripped from leaves. Flowers of every color bloomed, petals floating from them and dancing to the ground. She gaped at the beauty. Nothing on earth compared.

If only her sisters could see this.

Her sisters. Winning a game or not, she missed them more with every second that passed. Lysander would pay for that, too.

She yawned again. When she attempted to climb the nearest oak, her lingerie snagged on the bark. She straightened, scowled—reminded once again of the way her dark angel had stalked to her, leaned into her, hot breath trekking over her skin.

"I want to wear a camo tank and army fatigues." The moment she was dressed, she scaled to the highest bough, fluttering wings giving her speed and agility, and reclined on a fat branch, peering up into a lovely star-sprinkled sky. "I'd like a bottle of Lysander's wine, please."

Her fingers were clutching a flagon of dry red a second later. She would have preferred a cheap white, but whatever. Hard times called for sacrifices, and she drained the bottle in record time.

Just as she summoned a second, she heard Lysander shout, "Bianka!"

She blinked in confusion. Either she'd been up here longer than she'd thought or she was hallucinating.

Why couldn't she have imagined a Lord of the Underworld? she wondered disgustedly. Oh, oh. How cool would it be if Lysander oil-wrestled a Lord? They'd be wearing loincloths, of course, and smiles. But nothing else.

And she could totally have that! This was her cloud, after all. She and Lysander were now playing by her rules. And, because she was in charge, he couldn't rescind his command that she be obeyed without her permission.

At least, she prayed that was the way this would work.

"Remove the trees," she heard him snap.

She waited, unable to breathe, but the trees remained. He couldn't! Grinning, she jolted upright and clapped. She'd been right, then. This cloud belonged to her.

"Remove. The. Trees."

Again, they remained.

"Bianka!" he snarled. "Show yourself."

Anticipation flooded her as she jumped down. A quick scan of her surroundings revealed that he wasn't nearby. "Take me to him."

She blinked and found herself standing in front of him. He'd been shoving his way through the foliage and when he spotted her, he stopped. He clutched that sword of fire.

She backed away, remaining out of reach. No touching. She wouldn't forget. "That for me?" she asked, motioning to the weapon with a tilt of her chin. She'd never been so excited in her life and even the sight of that weapon didn't dampen the emotion.

A vein bulged in his temples.

She'd take that for a yes. "Naughty boy." He'd come to kill her, she thought, swaying a little. That was something else to punish him for. "You're back early."

His gaze raked her newest outfit, his pupils dilated and his nostrils flared. His mouth, however, curled in distaste. "And you are drunk."

"How dare you accuse me of such a thing!" She tried for a harsh expression, but ruined it when she laughed. "I'm just tipsy."

"What did you do to my cloud?" He crossed his arms over his chest, the picture of stubborn male. "Why won't the trees disappear?"

"First, you're wrong. This is no longer your cloud. Second, the trees will only leave if I tell them to leave. Which I am. Leave, pretty trees, leave." Another laugh. "Oh my gods. I said leave to a tree. I'm a poet and I didn't know it." Instantly, there was nothing surrounding her and Lysander but glorious white mist. "Third, you're not going anywhere without my permission. Did you hear that, cloud? He stays. Fourth, you're wearing too many clothes. I want you in a loincloth, minus the weapon."

His sword was suddenly gone. His eyes widened as his robe disappeared and a flesh-colored loincloth appeared. Bianka tried not to gape. And she'd thought the forest gorgeous. Wow. Just…wow. His body was a work of art. He possessed more muscles than she'd realized. His biceps were perfectly proportioned. Rope after rope lined his stomach. And his thighs were ridged, his skin sun-kissed.

"This cloud is mine, and I demand the return of my robe." His voice was so low, so harsh, it scraped against her eardrums.

The sweet sound of victory, she thought. He remained exactly as she'd requested. Laughing, she twirled, arms splayed wide. "Isn't this fabulous?"

He stalked toward her, menace in every step.

"No, no, no." She danced out of reach. "We can't have that. I want you in a large tub of oil."

And just like that, he was trapped inside a tub. Clear oil rose to his calves, and he stared down in horror.

"How do you like having your will overlooked?" she taunted.

His gaze lifted, met hers, narrowed. "I will not fight you in this."

"Silly man. Of course you won't. You'll fight…" She tapped her chin with a fingernail. "Let's see, let's see. Amun? No. He won't speak and I'd like to hear some cursing. Strider? As keeper of Defeat, he'd ensure you lost to prevent himself from feeling pain, but that would be an intense battle and I'm just wanting something to amuse me. You know, something light and sexy. I mean, since I can't touch you, I want a Lord to do it for me."

Lysander popped his jaw. "Do not do this, Bianka. You will not like the consequences."

"Now that's just sad," she said. "I've been here two weeks,

but you don't know me at all. Of course I'll like the consequences." Torin, keeper of Disease? Watching him fight Torin would be fun, 'cause then he'd catch that black plague. Or would he? Could angels get sick? She sighed. "Paris will have to do, I guess. He's handsy, so that works in my favor."

"Don't you dare—"

"Cloud, place Paris, keeper of Promiscuity, into the tub with Lysander."

When Paris appeared a moment later, she clapped. Paris was tall and just as muscled as Lysander. Only he had black hair streaked with brown and gold, his eyes were electric blue and his face perfect enough to make her weep from its beauty. Too bad he didn't stir her body the way Lysander did. Making out with him in front of the angel would have been fun.

"Bianka?" Paris looked from her to the angel, the angel to her. "Where am I? Is this some ambrosia-induced hallucination? What the hell is going on?"

"For one thing, you're overdressed. You should only be wearing a loincloth like Lysander."

His T-shirt and jeans were instantly replaced with said loincloth.

Best. Day. Ever. "Paris, I'd like you to meet Lysander, the angel who abducted me and has been holding me prisoner up here in heaven."

Instantly Paris morphed from confusion to fury. "Return my weapons and I'll kill him for you."

"You are such a sweetie," she said, flattening a hand over her heart. "Why is it we haven't slept together yet?"

Lysander snarled low in his throat.

"What?" she asked him, all innocence. "He wants to save me. You want to subjugate me for the rest of my long life. But anyway, let me finish the introductions. Lysander, I'd like you to meet—"

"I know who he is. Promiscuity." Disgust layered Lysander's voice. "He must bed a new woman every day or he weakens."

Another grin lifted the corners of her lips, this one smug. "Actually, he can bed men, too. His demon's not picky. I do hope you'll keep that in mind while you guys are rubbing up against each other."

Lysander took a menacing step toward her.

"What's going on?" Paris demanded again, glowering now. Bianka knew he was picky even if his demon wasn't.

"Oh, didn't I tell you? Lysander gave me control of his home, so now I get whatever I want and I want you guys to wrestle. And when you're done, you'll find Kaia and tell her what's happened, that I'm trapped with a stubborn angel and can't leave. Well, I can't leave until he gets so sick of me he allows the cloud to release me."

"Or until I kill you," he snapped.

She laughed. "Or until Paris kills *you.* But I hope you guys will play nice for a little while, at least. Do you have any idea how sexy you both are right now? And if you want to kiss or something while rolling around, don't let me stop you."

"Uh, Bianka," Paris began, beginning to look uncomfortable. "Kaia's in Budapest. She's helping Gwen with the wedding, and thinks you're hiding to get out of your maid of honor duties."

"I am not maid of honor, damn it!" But at least Kaia wasn't worried. *The bitch,* she thought with affection.

"That's not what she says. Anyway, I don't mind fighting another dude to amuse you, but seriously, he's an angel. I need to return to—"

"No need to thank me." She held out her hands. "A bowl of Lysander's popcorn, please." The bowl appeared, the scent of butter wafting to her nose. "Now then. Let's get this party started. Ding, ding," she said, and settled down to watch the battle.

CHAPTER SEVEN

LYSANDER COULD NOT BELIEVE what he was being forced to do. He was angry, horrified and, yes, contrite. Hadn't he done something similar to Bianka? Granted, he hadn't stripped her down. Hadn't pitted her against another female.

There was the tightening in his groin again.

What was wrong with him?

"I will set you free," he told Bianka. And sweet Holy Deity, she looked beautiful. More tempting than when she'd worn that little bit of nothing. Now she wore a green and black tank that bared her golden arms. Were those arms as soft as they appeared? *Don't think like that.* Her shirt stopped just above her navel, making his mouth water, his tongue yearn to dip inside. *What did I just say? Don't think like that.* Her pants were the same dark shades and hung low on her hips.

He'd come here to fight her, to finally force her hand, and judging by that outfit, she'd been ready for combat. That…excited him. Not because their bodies would have been in close proximity—really—and not because he could have finally gotten his hands on her—again, really—but because, if she injured him, he would have the right to end her life. Finally.

But he'd come here and she'd taught him a quick yet unforgettable lesson instead. He'd been wrong to whisk her to his home and hold her captive. Temptation or not. She might be his enemy in ways she didn't understand, but he never should have put his will above hers. He should have allowed her to live her life as she saw fit.

That's why he existed in the first place. To protect free will.

When this wrestling match ended, he would free her as he'd promised. He would watch her, though. Closely. And when she made a mistake, he would strike her down. And she would. Make a mistake, that is. As a Harpy, she wouldn't be able to help herself. He wished it hadn't come to that. He wished she could have been happy here with him, learning his ways.

The thought of losing her did not sadden him. He would not miss her. She'd placed him in a vat of oil to wrestle with another man, for Lord's sake.

There was suddenly a bitter taste in his mouth.

"Bianka," he prompted. "Have you no response?"

"Yes, you will set me free," she finally said with a radiant grin. She twirled a strand of that dark-as-night hair around her finger. "After. Now, I do believe I rang the starting bell."

Her words were slightly slurred from the wine she'd consumed. A drunken menace, that's what she was. And he would not miss her, he told himself again.

The bitterness intensified.

A hard weight slammed into him and sent him propelling to his back. His wings caught on the sides of the pool as oil washed over him from head to toe, weighing him down. He grunted, and some of the stuff—cherry-flavored—seeped into his mouth.

"Don't forget to use tongue if you kiss," Bianka called helpfully.

"You don't lock women away," Paris growled down at him, a flash of scales suddenly visible under his skin. Eyes red and bright. Demon eyes. "No matter how irritating they are."

"Your friends did something similar to their women, did they not? Besides, the girl isn't your concern." Lysander shoved, sending the warrior hurtling to *his* back. He attempted to use his wings to lift himself, but their movements were slow and sluggish so all he could do was stand.

Oil dripped down his face, momentarily shielding his vision. Paris shot to his feet, as well, hands fisted, body glistening.

"So. Much. Fun," Bianka sang happily.

"Enough," Lysander told her. "This is unnecessary. You have made your point. I'm willing to set you free."

"You're right," she said. "It's unnecessary to fight without music!" Once again she tapped her chin with a nail, expression thoughtful. "I know! We need some Lady Gaga in this crib."

A song Lysander had never heard before was playing through the cloud a second later. Like a siren rising from the sea, Bianka began swaying her hips seductively.

Lysander's jaw clenched so painfully the bones would probably snap out of place at any moment. Clearly there would be no reasoning with Bianka. That meant he had to reason with Paris. But who would ever have thought he'd have to bargain with a demon?

"Paris," he began—just as a fist connected with his face.

His head whipped back. His feet slipped on the slick floor and he tumbled to his side. More of the cherry flavor filled his mouth.

Paris straddled his shoulders, punched him again. Lysander's lip split. Before a single drop of blood could form, however, the wound healed.

He frowned. He now had the right to slay the man, but he couldn't bring himself to do it. He did not blame Paris for this battle; he blamed Bianka. She had forced them into this situation.

Another punch. "Are you the one who's been watching Aeron?" Paris demanded.

"Hey, now," Bianka called. No longer did she sound so carefree. "Paris, you are not to use your fists. That's boxing, not wrestling."

Lysander remained silent, not understanding the difference. A fight was a fight.

Another punch. "Are you?" Paris growled.

"Paris! Did you hear me?" Now she sounded angry. "Use your fists like that again and I'll cut off your head."

She'd do it, too, Lysander thought, and wondered why she was so upset. Could she, perhaps, care for his health? His eyes widened. Was *that* why she preferred the less intensive wrestling to the more violent boxing? Would she want to do the same to him if he were to punch the Lord? And what would it mean if she did?

How would he feel about that?

"Are you?" Paris repeated.

"No," he finally said. "I'm not." He worked his legs up, planted his feet on Paris's chest and pressed. But rather than send the warrior flying, his foot slipped and connected with Paris's jaw, then ear, knocking the man's head back.

"Use your hands, angel," Bianka suggested. "Choke him! He deserves it for breaking my rules."

"Bianka," Paris snapped. He lost his footing and tumbled to his butt. "I thought you wanted me to destroy him, not the other way around."

She blinked over at them, brow furrowed. "I do. I just don't want you to hurt him. That's my job."

Paris tangled a hand through his soaked hair. "Sorry, darling, but if this continues, I'm going to unleash a world of hurt on your frienemy. Nothing you say will be able to stop me. Clearly, he doesn't have your best interests at heart."

Darling? Had the demon-possessed immortal just called Bianka *darling?* Something dark and dangerous flooded Lysander—*mine* echoed through his head—and before he realized what he was doing, he was on top of the warrior, a sword of fire in his hand, raised, descending…about to meet flesh.

A firm hand around his wrist stopped him. Warm, smooth skin. His wild gaze whipped to the side. There was Bianka, inside the tub, oil glistening off her. How fast she'd moved.

"You can't kill him," she said determinedly.

"Because you want him, too," he snarled. A statement, not a question. Rage, so much rage. He didn't know where it was coming from or how to stop the flow.

She blinked again, as if the thought had never entered her mind, and that, miraculously, cooled his temper. "No. Because then you would be like me and therefore perfect," she said. "That wouldn't be fair to the world."

"Stop talking and fight, damn you," Paris commanded. A fist connected with Lysander's jaw, tossing him to the side and out of Bianka's reach. He maintained his grip on the sword and even when it dipped into the oil, it didn't lose a single flame. In fact, the oil heated.

Great. Now he was hot-tubbing, as the humans would say.

"What'd you do that for, you big dummy?" Bianka didn't wait for Paris's reply but launched herself at him. Rather than scratch him or pull his hair, she punched him. Over and over again. "He wasn't going to hurt you."

Paris took the beating without retaliating.

That saved his life.

Lysander grabbed the Harpy around the waist and hefted her into the hard line of his body. Soaked as they both were, he had a difficult time maintaining his grip. She was panting, arms flailing for the demon-possessed warrior, but she didn't try to pull away.

"I'll teach you to defy me, you rotten piece of shit," she growled.

Paris rolled his eyes.

"Send him away," Lysander commanded.

"Not until after I—"

He splayed his fingers, spanning much of her waist. He both rejoiced and cursed that he couldn't feel the texture of Bianka's skin through the oil. "I want to be alone with you."

"You—what?"

"Alone. With you."

With no hesitation, she said, "Go home, Paris. Your work here is done. Thanks for trying to rescue me. That's the only reason you're still alive. Oh, and don't forget to tell my sisters I'm fine."

The sputtering Lord disappeared.

Lysander released her, and she spun around to face him. She was now grinning.

"So you want to be alone with me, do you?"

He ran his tongue over his teeth. "Was that fun for you?"

"Yes."

And she wasn't ashamed to admit it, he realized. Captivating baggage. "Return the cloud to me and I will take you home."

"Wait. What?" Her grin slowly faded. "I thought you wanted to be alone with me."

"I do. So that we can conclude our business."

Disappointment, regret, anger and relief played over her features. One step, two, she closed the distance between them. "Well, I'm not giving you the cloud. That would be stupid."

"You have my word that once you return it to me, I will take you home. I know you hear the truth in my claim."

"Oh." Her shoulders sagged a little. "So we really would be rid of each other. That's great, then."

Did she still not believe him? Or… No, surely not. "Do you want to stay here?"

"Of course not!" She sucked her bottom lip into her mouth, and her eyes closed for a moment, an expression of pleasure consuming her features. "Mmm, cherries."

Blood…heating…

Her lashes lifted and her gaze locked on him. Determination replaced all the other emotions, yet her voice dipped sexily. "But I know something that tastes even better."

So did he. Her. A tremor slid the length of his spine. "Do not do this, Bianka. You will fail." He hoped.

"One kiss," she beseeched, "and the cloud is yours."

His eyes narrowed. Hot, so hot. "You cannot be trusted to keep your word."

"That's true. But I want out of this hellhole, so I'll keep it this time. Promise."

Hold your ground. But that was hard to do while his heart was pounding like a hammer against a nail. "If you wanted out, you would not insist on being kissed."

Her gaze narrowed, as well. "It's not like I'm asking for something you haven't already given me."

"Why do you want it?" He regretted the question immediately. He was prolonging the conversation rather than putting an end to it.

Her chin lifted. "It's a goodbye kiss, moron, but never mind. The cloud is yours. I'll go home and kiss Paris hello. That'll be more fun, anyway."

There would be no kissing Paris! Lysander had his tongue sliding into her mouth before he could convince himself otherwise. His arms even wound around her waist, pulling her closer to him—so close their chests rubbed each time they breathed. Her nipples were hard, deliciously abrading.

"Out of the oil," she murmured. "Clean."

He was still in the loincloth, but his skin was suddenly free of the oil, his feet on soft yet firm mist. The cloud might belong to him once more, but she could still make reasonable demands.

Bianka tilted her head and took his possession deeper. Their tongues dueled and rolled and their teeth scraped. Her hands were all over him, no part of him forbidden to her.

Goodbye, she had said.

This was it, then. His last chance to touch her skin. To finally know. Yes, he planned to see her again, to watch her from afar, to wait for his chance to rid himself of her permanently, but never again would he allow himself to get this close to her. And he had to know.

So he did it.

He glided his hands forward, tracing from her lower back to her stomach. There, he flattened his palms, and her muscles quivered. Dear Deity of Light and Love. She was softer than he'd realized. Softer than anything else he'd ever touched.

He moaned. *Have to touch more.* Up he lifted, remaining under her shirt. Warm, smooth, as he'd already known. Still soft, so sweetly soft. Her breasts overflowed, and his mouth watered for a taste of them. Soon, he told himself. Then shook his head. This was it; the last time they would be together. Goodbye, pretty breasts. He kneaded them.

More soft perfection.

Trembling now, he reached her collarbone. Her shoulders. She shivered. Still so wonderfully soft. More, more, more, he had to have more. Had to touch all of her.

"Lysander," she gasped out. She dropped to her knees, working at the loincloth before he realized what she was doing.

His shaft sprang free, and his hands settled atop her shoulders to push her away. But once he touched that soft skin, he was once again lost to the sensation. Perfection, this was perfection.

"Going to kiss you now. A different kind of kiss." Warm, wet heat settled over the hard length of him. Another moan escaped him. Up, down that wicked mouth rode him. The pleasure…it was too much, not enough, everything and nothing. In that moment, it was necessary to his survival. His every breath hinged on what she would do next. There would be no pushing her away.

She twirled her tongue over the plump head; her fingers

played with his testicles. Soon he was arching his hips, thrusting deep into her mouth. He couldn't stop moaning, groaning, the gasping breaths leaving him in a constant stream.

"Bianka," he growled. "Bianka."

"That's the way, baby. Give Bianka everything."

"Yes, yes." Everything. He would give her everything.

The sensation was building, his skin tightening, his muscles locking down on his bones. And then something exploded inside him. Something hot and wanton. His entire body jerked. Seed jetted from him, and she swallowed every drop.

Finally she pulled away from him, but his body wouldn't stop shaking. His knees were weak, his limbs nearly uncontrollable. That was pleasure, he realized, dazed. That was passion. That was what human men were willing to die to possess. That was what turned normally sane men into slaves. *Like I am now.* He was Bianka's slave.

Fool! *You knew this would happen.* Fight. It was only as she stood and smiled at him tenderly—and he wanted to tug her into his arms and hold on forever—that a measure of sanity stole back into his mind. Yes. Fight. How could he have allowed her to do that?

How could he still want her?

How could he want to do that to her in return?

How could he ever let her go?

"Bianka," he said. He needed a moment to catch his breath. No. He needed to think about what had happened and how they should proceed. No. He tangled a hand in his hair. What should he do?

"Don't say anything." Her smile disappeared as if it had never been. "The cloud is yours." Her voice trembled with… fear? Couldn't be. She hadn't showed a moment of fear since he'd first abducted her. But she even backed away from him. "Now take me home. Please."

He opened his mouth to reply. What he would say, he didn't know. He only knew he did not like seeing her like that.

"Take me home," she croaked.

He'd never gone back on his word, and he wouldn't start now. He nodded stiffly, grabbed her hand, and flew her back to the ice mountain in Alaska, exactly as he'd found her. Red coat, tall boots. Sensual in a way he hadn't understood then.

He maintained his grip on her until the last possible second—until she slipped away from him, taking her warmth and the sweet softness of her skin with her.

"I don't want to see you again." Mist wafted around her as she turned her back on him. "Okay?"

She…what? After what had happened between them, *she* was dismissing *him?* No, a voice roared inside his head. "Behave, and you will not," he gritted out. A lie? The bitter taste in his mouth had returned.

"Good." Without meeting his gaze, she twisted and blew him a kiss as if she hadn't a care in the world. "I'd say you were an excellent host, but then, you don't want me to lie, do you?" With that, she strolled away from him, dark hair blowing in the wind.

CHAPTER EIGHT

FIRST THING BIANKA DID after bathing, dressing, eating a bag of stolen chips she had hidden in her kitchen, painting her nails, listening to her iPod for half an hour and taking a nap in her secret basement was call Kaia. Not that she had dreaded the call and wanted to put it off or anything. All of those other activities had been necessary. Really.

Plus, it wasn't like her sister was worried about her anymore. Paris would already have told her what was going on. But Bianka didn't want to discuss Lysander. Didn't even want to think about him and the havoc he was causing her emotions—and her body and her thoughts and her common sense.

After making out with him a little, she'd wanted to freaking stay with him, curl up in his arms, make love and sleep. And that was unacceptable.

The moment her sister answered, she said, "No need to throw me a Welcome Home party. I'm not sticking around for long." *Do not ask me about the angel. Do not ask me about the angel.*

"Bianka?" her twin asked groggily.

"You were expecting someone else to call in the middle of the night?" It was 6:00 a.m. here in Alaska. Having traveled between the two places multiple times since Gwen had gotten involved with Sabin, she knew that meant it was 3:00 a.m. there in Budapest.

"Yeah," Kaia said. "I was."

Seriously? "Who?"

"Lots of people. Gwennie, who has become the ultimate bridezilla. Sabin, who is doing his best to soothe the beast but whines to me like I care." She rambled on as if Bianka had never been abducted and she'd never been worried. Sure, she'd thought Bianka was merely shirking her duties, but was a little worry too much to ask for? "Anya, who has decided she deserves a wedding, too. Only bigger and better than Gwen's. William, who wants to sleep with me and doesn't know how to take no for an answer. He's not possessed by a demon so he's not my type. Shall I go on?"

"Yes."

"Shut up."

She imagined Kaia high in a treetop, clutching her cell to her ear, grinning and trying not to fall. "So really, you were *sleeping?* While I was missing, my life in terrible danger? Some loving sister you are."

"Please. You were on vacay, and we both know it. So don't give me a hard time. I had an…exciting day."

"Doing who?" she asked dryly. Only two weeks had passed since she'd last seen Kaia, but suddenly a wave of homesickness—or rather, sistersickness—flooded her. She loved this woman more than she loved herself. And that was a lot!

Kaia chuckled. "I wish it was because of a *who.* I'm waiting for two of the Lords to fight over me. Then I'll comfort them both. So far, no luck."

"Idiots."

"I know! But I mentioned Gwen has become the bride from hell, right? They're afraid I'll act just like her, so no one's willing to take a real chance on me."

"Bride from hell, how?"

"Her dress didn't fit right. Her napkins weren't the right color. No one has the flowers she wants. Whaa, whaa, whaa."

That didn't sound like the usually calm Gwen. "Distract her. Tell her the Hunters captured me and performed a hand-botomy on me like they did on Gideon." Gideon, keeper of Lies. A sexy warrior who dyed his hair as blue as his eyes and had a wicked sense of humor.

The thought of seducing him didn't delight her as it once might have. Stupid angel. *Do not think about him.*

"She wouldn't care if you were chopped up into little pieces. You're too much like me and apparently we take nothing seriously so we deserve what we get," Kaia said. "She's driving me freaking insane! And to top off my mountain-o-crap, I was totally losing our game of Hide and Seek. So anyway, why'd you decide to rescue yourself? I'm telling you, you have a better chance of survival in the clouds than here with Gwen."

"Survival schmival. It wasn't fun anymore." A lie. Things had just started to heat up the way she'd wanted. But how could she have known that would scare her so badly?

"Good going, by the way. Allowing yourself to be taken into the clouds where I couldn't get to you. Brilliant."

"I know, *right?*"

"So was it terrible? Being spirited away by a sexy angel?"

She twirled a strand of hair around her finger and pictured Lysander's glorious face. The desire he'd leveled at her while she'd sucked him dry had been miraculous. *You don't want to talk about him, remember?* "Yes. It was terrible." Terribly wonderful.

"You bringing him to Buda for the wedding?"

The words were sneered, clearly a joke, but Bianka found herself shouting, "No!" before she could stop herself. A Harpy dating an angel? Unacceptable!

And anyway, allowing the demon-possessed Lords of the Underworld to surround a warrior straight from heaven would be stupid. Not that she feared for Lysander. Guy could handle himself, no problem. The way he formed a sword of fire from nothing but air was proof of that. But if something were to happen to Gwennie's precious Sabin, like, oh, decapitation, the festivities would be somewhat dimmed.

"I'll be there, though," she added in a calmer tone. "I kinda have to, you know. Since I'm the maid of honor and all."

"Oh, hell, no. I am, remember?"

She grinned slowly. "You told me you'd rather be hit by a bus than be a bridesmaid."

"Yeah, but I want to have a bigger part than you, so…here I am, in Budapest, helping little Gwennie plan the ceremony. Not that she's taking my suggestions. Would it kill her to at least *consider* making everyone come naked?"

They shared a laugh.

"Well, you and I can attend naked," Bianka said. "It'll certainly liven things up."

"Done!"

There was a pause.

Kaia pushed out a breath. "So you're fine?" she asked, a twinge of concern finally appearing in her voice.

"Yeah." And she was. Or would be. Soon, she hoped. All she had to do was figure out what to do about Lysander. Not that he'd tried to stick around, the jerk. He hadn't been able to get away from her fast enough. Sure, she'd pushed him away. But dude could have fought for her attention after what she'd done for him.

"You're gonna make the angel pay for taking you without permission, right? Who am I kidding? Of course you are. If you wait till after the wedding, I can help. Please, please let me help. I have a few ideas and I think you'll like them. Picture this. It's midnight, your angel is strapped to your bed, and we each rip off one of his wings."

Nice. But because she didn't know whether Lysander was watching and listening or not—was he? It was possible, and just the thought had her skin heating—she said, "Don't worry about it. I'm done with him."

"Wait, what?" Kaia gasped out. "You can't be done with him. He abducted you. Held you prisoner. Yeah, he oil-wrestled Paris and I'm pissed I didn't get to see, but that doesn't excuse his behavior. If you let him off without punishment, he'll think it's okay. He'll think you're weak. He'll come after you again."

Yes. Yes, he would, she thought, suddenly trying not to grin. "No, he won't," she lied. *Are you listening, Lysander, baby?*

"Bianka, tell me you don't like him. Tell me you aren't lusting for an angel."

Abruptly her smile faded. This was exactly the line of questioning she'd hoped to avoid. "I'm not lusting for an angel." Another lie.

Another pause. "I don't believe you."

"Too bad."

"Mom thought Gwen's dad was an angel and she regretted sleeping with him all these years. They're too good. Too…different from us. Angels and Harpies are not meant to mix. Tell me you know that."

"Of course I know it. Now, I've gotta go. Tell the bridezilla to go easy on you. Love you and see you soon," she replied and hung up before Kaia could say anything else.

Despite her fear of what Lysander made her feel, Bianka wasn't done with him. Not even close. But she'd been on his turf before and therefore at a disadvantage. If he wasn't here, she needed to get him here. Willingly.

She'd told him to leave her alone, she thought, and that could be a problem. Except…

With a whoop, she jumped up and spun around. That wouldn't be a problem at all. That was actually a blessing and she was smarter than she'd realized. By telling him to stay away from her, she'd surely become the forbidden fruit. Of course he was here, watching her.

Men never could do what they were told. Not even angels.

So. Easy.

Even better, she'd given him a little taste of what it was like to be with her. He would crave more. But also, she hadn't allowed him to pleasure her. His pride would not allow her to remain in this unsatisfied state for long, while he had enjoyed such sweet completion.

And if that wasn't the case, he wasn't the virile warrior she thought he was and he therefore wouldn't deserve her.

How long till he made an actual appearance? They'd only been apart half a day, but she already missed him.

Missed him. Ugh. She'd never missed a man before. Especially one who wanted to change her. One who despised what she was. One who could only be labeled *enemy.*

You have to avoid him. You want to sleep in his arms. You were protective of him while he fought Paris. He angered you but you didn't kill him. And now you're missing him? You know what this means, don't you?

Her eyes widened, and her excitement drained. Oh, gods. She should have realized…should at least have suspected. Especially when she'd protected him, defended him.

Lysander, a goody-goody angel, was her consort.

Her knees gave out and she flopped onto the floor. As long as she'd been alive, she'd never thought to find one. Because, well, a consort was a meant-to-be husband. Some nights she'd dreamed of finding hers, yes, but she hadn't thought it would actually happen.

Her consort. Wow.

Her family was going to flip. Not because Lysander had abducted her—they'd come to respect that—but because of what he was. More than that, she didn't trust Lysander, would never trust him, and so could never do any actual sleeping with him.

Sex, though, she could allow. Often. Yes, yes, she could make this work, she thought, brightening. She could lure him to the dark side without letting her family know she was spending time with him. Humiliation averted!

Decided, she nodded. Lysander would be hers. In secret. And there was no better time to begin. If he was watching as she suspected, there was only one way to get him to reveal himself.

She dressed in a lacy red halter and her favorite skinny jeans and drove into town. Only reason she owned a car was because it made her appear more human. Flying kind of gave her away. Though her arms and navel were exposed, the frigid wind didn't bother her. Chilled her, yes, but that she could deal with. She wanted Lysander to see as much of her as possible.

She parked in front of The Moose Lodge, a local diner, and strode to the front door. Because it was so early and so cold, no one was nearby. A few streetlamps illuminated her, but she wasn't worried. She unlocked the door—she'd stolen the key from the owner months ago—and disabled the alarm.

Inside, she claimed a pecan pie from the glassed refrigerator, grabbed a fork and dug in while walking to her favorite booth. She'd done this a thousand times before.

Come out, come out, wherever you are. He wouldn't have just left her to her evil ways without thinking to protect the world from her. Right? She wished she could feel him, at least sense him in some way. His scent perhaps, that wild, night sky scent. But as she breathed deeply, she smelled only pecans and sugar. Still. She hadn't sensed him when he'd snatched her from mid-free fall, so it stood to reason she wouldn't sense him now.

Once the pie was polished off, the pan discarded and her fork licked clean, she filled a cup with Dr. Pepper. She placed a few quarters in the old jukebox and soon an erratic beat was echoing from the walls. Bianka danced around one of the tables, thrusting her hips forward and back, arching, sliding around, hands roving over her entire body.

For a moment, only a brief, sultry moment, she thought she felt hot hands replace her own, exploring her breasts, her stomach. Thought she felt soft feathered wings envelop her, closing her in. She stilled, heart drumming in her chest. So badly she wanted to say his name, but she didn't want to scare him away. So…what should she do? How should she—

The feeling of being surrounded evaporated completely.

Damn him!

Teeth grinding, not knowing what else to do, she exited the diner the same way she'd entered. Through the front door, as if she hadn't a care. That door slammed behind her, the force of it nearly shaking the walls.

"You should lock up after yourself."

He was here; he'd been watching. She'd known it! Trying not to grin, she spun around to face Lysander. The sight of him stole her breath. He was as beautiful as she remembered. His pale hair whipped in the wind, little snow crystals flying around him. His golden wings were extended and glowing. But his dark eyes were not blank, as when she'd first met him. They were as turbulent as an ocean—just as they'd been when she'd left him.

"I thought I told you to stay away from me," she said, doing her best to sound angry rather than aroused.

He frowned. "And I told you to behave. Yet here you are, full of stolen pie."

"What do you want me to do? Return it?"

"Don't be crass. I want you to pay for it."

"Moment I do, I'll start to vomit." She crossed her arms over her middle. *Close the distance. Kiss me.* "That would ruin my lipstick, so I have to decline."

He, too, crossed his arms over his middle. "You can also earn your food."

"Yeah, but where's the fun in that?"

A moment passed in silence. Then, "Do you have no morals?" he gritted out.

"No." *No sexual boundaries, either. So freaking kiss me already!* "I don't."

He popped his jaw in frustration and disappeared.

Bianka's arms dropped to her sides and she gazed around in astonishment. He'd left? Left? Without touching her? Without kissing her? Bastard! She stomped to her car.

LYSANDER WATCHED AS Bianka drove away. He was hard as a rock, had been that way since she'd paraded around her cabin naked, had lingered in a bubble bath and then changed into that wicked shirt. His shaft was desperate for her.

Why couldn't she be an angel? Why couldn't she abhor sin? Why did she have to embrace it?

And why was the fact that she did these things—steal, curse, lie—still exciting him?

Because that was the way of things, he supposed, and had been since the beginning of time. Temptation seeped past your defenses, changed you, made you long for things you shouldn't.

There had to be a way to end this madness. He couldn't destroy her, he'd already proven that. But what if he could change *her?* He hadn't truly tried before, so it *could* work. And if she embraced his way of life, they could be together. He could have her. Have more of her kisses, touch more of her body.

Yes, he thought. Yes. He would help her become a woman he could be proud to walk beside. A woman he could happily claim as his own. A woman who would not be his downfall.

CHAPTER NINE

AS LYSANDER HAD NEVER had a...girlfriend, as the humans would say, he had no idea how to train one. He knew only how to train his soldiers. Without emotion, maintaining distance and taking nothing personally. His soldiers, however, *wanted* to learn. They were eager, his every word welcomed. Bianka would resist him at every turn. That much he knew.

So. The first day, he followed her, simply observing. Planning.

She, of course, stole every meal, even snacks, drank too much at a bar, danced too closely with a man she obviously did not know, then broke that man's nose when he cupped her bottom. Lysander wanted to do damage of his own, but restrained himself. Barely. At bedtime, Bianka merely paced the confines of her cabin, cursing his name. Not for a minute did she rest.

How lovely she was, dark hair streaming down her back. Red lips pursed. Skin glowing like a rainbow in the moonlight. So badly he wanted to touch her, to surround her with his wings, making them the only two people alive, and simply enjoy her.

Soon, he promised himself.

She'd given him release, yet he had not done the same for her. The more he thought about that—and think about it he did, all the time—the more that did not sit well with him. The more he thought about it, in fact, the more embarrassed he was.

He didn't know how to touch her to bring her release, but he was willing to try, to learn. First, though, he had to train her as planned. How, though? he wondered again. She seemed to respond well to his kisses—his chest puffed up with pride at that. He'd never rewarded his soldiers for a job well done, but perhaps he could do so for Bianka. Reward her with a kiss every time she pleased him.

A failproof plan. He hoped.

The second day, he was practically humming with anticipation. When she entered a clothing store and stuffed a beaded scarf into her purse, he materialized in front of her, ready to begin.

She stilled, gaze lifting and meeting his. Rather than bow her head in contrition, she grinned. "Fancy meeting you here."

"Put that back," he told her. "You do not need to steal clothing to survive."

She crossed her arms over her middle, a stubborn stance he knew well. "Yeah, but it's fun."

A human woman who stood off to the side eyed Bianka strangely. "Uh, can I help you?"

Bianka never looked away from him. "Nope. I'm fine."

"She cannot see me," Lysander told her. "Only you can."

"So I look insane for talking with you?"

He nodded.

She laughed, surprising him. And even though her amusement was misplaced, he loved the sound of her laughter. It was magical, like the strum of a harp. He loved the way her mirth softened her expression and lit her magnificent skin.

Have to touch her, he thought, suddenly dazed. He took a step closer, intending to do just that. *Have to experience that softness again.* And in doing so, she could begin to know the delights of his rewards.

She gulped. "Wh-what are you—"

"Are you sure I can't help you?" the woman asked, cutting her off.

Bianka remained in place, trembling, but tossed her a glare. "I'm sure. Now shut it before I sew your lips together."

The woman backed away, spun and raced to help someone else.

Lysander froze.

"You may continue," Bianka said to him.

How could he reward her for such rudeness? That would defeat the purpose of her training. "Do you not care what people think of you?" he asked, head tilting to the side.

Her eyes narrowed, and she stopped trembling. "No. Why should I? In a few years, these people will be dead but I'll still be alive and kicking." As she spoke, she stuffed another scarf in her purse.

Now she was simply taunting him. "Put it back, and I'll give you a kiss," he gritted out.

"Wh-what?"

Stuttering again. He was affecting her. "You heard me." He would not repeat the words. Having said them, all he wanted to do was mesh their lips together, thrust his tongue into her mouth and taste her. Hear her moan. Feel her clutch at him.

"You would willingly kiss me?" she rasped.

Willingly. Desperately. He nodded.

She licked her lips, leaving a sheen of moisture behind. The sight of that pink tongue sent blood rushing into his shaft. His hands clenched at his sides. Anything to keep from grabbing her and jerking her against him.

"I—I—" She shook her head, as if clearing her thoughts. Her eyes narrowed again, those long, dark lashes fusing together. "Why would you do that? You, who have tried to resist me at every turn?"

"Because."

"Why?"

"Just put the scarves back." *So the kissing can begin.*

She arched a brow. "Are you trying to bribe me? Because you should know, that won't work with me."

Rather than answer—and lie—he remained silent, chin jutting in the air. Blood…heating.

Still watching him, she reached out, palmed a belt and stuffed it in her purse, as well. "So what do you plan to do to me if I keep stealing? Give me a severe tongue-lashing? Too bad. I *don't* accept."

Fire slid the length of his spine even as his anger spiked. He closed the distance until the warmth of her breath was fanning over his neck and chest. "You could not get enough of me in the heavens, yet now that you are here, you want nothing to do with me. Tell me. Was your every word and action up there a lie?"

"Of course my every word and action was a lie. That's what I do. I thought you knew that."

So…did she desire him or not? Two days ago she'd told her sister, Kaia, that she wanted nothing to do with him. At the time, he'd thought she was merely saying that for Kaia's benefit. Now, he wasn't so sure.

"You could be lying now," he said. At least, that's what he hoped. And who would have thought he'd ever wish for a lie?

Excitement sparked in her eyes and spread to the rest of her features. She patted his cheek, then flattened her palm on his chest. "You're learning, angel."

He sucked in a breath. So hot. So soft.

"Here's a proposition for you. Steal something from this store and *I'll* kiss *you.*"

Wait. Her words from a moment ago drifted through his head. *You're learning, angel. He* was learning? "No," he croaked out. He would not do such a thing. Not even for her. "These people need the money their goods provide. Do you care nothing for their welfare?"

A flash of guilt joined the excitement. "No," she said.

Another lie? Probably. That guilt…it gave him hope. "Why do you need to steal like this, anyway?"

"Foreplay," she said with a shrug.

Blood…heating…again.

"Ma'am, I need you to come with me."

At the unexpected intrusion, they both stiffened. Bianka's gaze pulled from his; together they eyed the policeman now standing beside her.

She frowned. "Can't you see that I'm in the middle of a conversation?"

"Doesn't matter if you're talking to God Himself." The grim-faced officer latched on to her wrist. "I need you to come with me."

"I don't think so. Lysander," she said, clearly expecting him to do something.

Instinct demanded he save her. He wanted her safe and happy, but this would be good for her. "I told you to put the items back."

Her jaw dropped as the officer led her away. And, if Lysander wasn't mistaken, there was pride in her gaze.

ARRESTED FOR SHOPLIFTING, Bianka thought with disgust. Again. Her third time that year. Lysander had watched the policeman usher her in back, empty her purse and cuff her. All without a word. His disapproval had said plenty, though.

She hadn't let it upset her. He'd stood his ground, and she admired that. Was turned on by it. This wouldn't be an easy victory, as she'd assumed. Besides, for the first time in their relationship, he'd offered to kiss her. *Willingly* kiss her.

But only if she replaced her stolen goods, she reminded herself darkly. Didn't take a genius to figure out that he wanted to change her. To condition her to his way of life.

It was exactly what she wanted to do to him. Which meant he wanted her as desperately as she wanted him.

It also meant it was time to take this game to the next level. She, however, would not be the one to cave. The six hours she'd spent behind bars had given her time to think. To form a strategy.

She was whistling as she meandered down the station steps. Lysander had finally posted her bail, but he hadn't hung around to speak with her. Well, he hadn't needed to. She knew he was following her.

At home, she showered, lingering under the hot spray, soaping herself more slowly than necessary and caressing her breasts and playing between her legs. Unfortunately, he never appeared. But no matter.

Just in case her shower hadn't gotten him in the mood, she read a few passages from her favorite romance novel. And just in case *that* hadn't gotten him in the mood, she decorated her navel with her favorite dangling diamond, dressed in a skintight tank and skirt and knee-high boots, and drove to the closest strip club.

"I only have a few days left. Then I'm traveling to Budapest for Gwen's wedding and you are not invited. Do you hear me? Try and come and I'll make your life hell. So, if you want a go at me, now's the time," she said as she got out of the car.

Again, he didn't appear.

She almost screeched in frustration. So far, her strategy sucked. What was he doing?

The night was cold yet the inside of the club was hot and stuffy, the seats packed with men. Onstage, a redhead—clearly not a natural redhead—swung around a pole. The lights were dimmed, and smoke clung to the air.

"You gonna dance, darling?" someone asked Bianka.

"Nope. Got better things to do." She did, however, steal the stranger's wallet, sneak a beer from the bar and settle into a table in the back corner. Alone. "Enjoy," she whispered to Lysander, toasting him with the bottle.

"Have you no shame?" he suddenly growled from behind her.

Finally! Every muscle in her body relaxed, even as her blood heated with awareness. But she didn't turn to face him. He would have seen the triumph in her eyes. "You have enough shame for both of us."

He snorted. "That does not seem to be the case."

"Really? Well, then, let's loosen you up. Do you want a lap dance?" She held up the cash she'd taken. "I'm sure the redhead onstage would love to rub against you."

His big hands settled on her shoulders, squeezing.

"Or maybe you'd like a beer?"

"I would indeed," the stranger she'd stolen from said, now in front of her table. He reached into his back pocket. Frowned. "Hey, my wallet's gone." His gaze settled on the small brown leather case resting on her tabletop. His frown deepened. "That looks like mine."

"How odd," she said innocently. "So do you want me to buy you a beer or not?"

Lysander's grip tightened. "Give him back his wallet and I'll kiss you."

Her breath caught in her throat. Gods, she wanted his kiss. More than she'd ever wanted anything. His lips were soft, his taste decadent. And if she allowed him to kiss her, well, she knew she could convince him to do other things.

But she said, "Steal his watch and I'll kiss you."

"What are you talking about?" the guy asked, brow furrowed. "Steal whose watch?"

She rolled her eyes, wishing she could shoo him away.

Lysander leaned down and cupped her breasts. A tremor moved through her, her nipples beading, reaching for him. Sweet heaven. Her stomach quivered, jealous of her breasts, wanting the touch lower.

"Give him back the wallet."

Suddenly she wanted to do just that. Anything for more of Lysander and this sultry side of him. She didn't need the money, anyway. Wait. *What are you doing? Caving?* She straightened her spine. "No, I—"

"I'll kiss you all over your body," Lysander added.

Oh… Hell. He'd decided to take their game to the next level, as well.

Damn, damn, damn. She couldn't lose. If she did, he would control her with sex. He would expect her to be good like him. All the damn time. There would be no more stealing, no more cursing, no more *fun.* Well, except when they were in bed—but would he expect her to be good there, too?

Life would become boring and sinless, everything a Harpy was taught to fight against.

She stood to shaky legs and turned, finally facing him. His hands fell away from her. She tried not to moan in disappointment. His expression was blank.

She blanked hers, as well, reached out and cupped *him.* Though he showed no emotion, he couldn't hide his hardness. "Steal something, anything at all, and I'll kiss *you* all over." Her voice dipped huskily. "Remember last time? You came in my mouth, and I loved every moment of it."

His nostrils flared.

"Yes!" the guy behind her exclaimed. "Give me five minutes and I'll have stolen something."

"You aren't trainable, are you?" Lysander asked stiffly.

"No," she said, but suddenly she didn't feel like smiling. There'd been resignation in his tone. Had she pushed him too far again? Was he going to leave her? Never return? "That doesn't mean you should stop trying, though."

"Wait. Trying what?" the stranger asked, confused.

Gods, when would he leave?

"Lysander," she prompted.

"That's not my name."

"Get lost," she growled.

Lysander's gaze lifted, narrowed on the human. Then Bianka heard footsteps. Her angel hadn't said anything, hadn't revealed himself, but had somehow managed to make the human leave. He had powers she hadn't known about, then. Why was that even more exciting?

"If you won't give the wallet back and I won't steal anything, where does that leave us?" he asked.

"At war. I don't know about you, but I do my best fighting in bed," she said, and then threw her arms around his neck.

CHAPTER TEN

WIND WHIPPED THROUGH Bianka's hair, and she knew that Lysander was flying her somewhere with those majestic wings. She had her eyes closed, too busy enjoying him—finally!—to care where he took her. His tongue made love to hers. His hands clutched her hips, fingers digging sharply. Then she was tipping over, a cool, soft mattress pressing into her back. His weight pinned her deliciously.

And it shouldn't have been delicious. This was not a position she allowed. Ever. It caged her wings, and her wings were the source of her strength. Without them, she was almost as weak as a human. But this was Lysander, honest to a fault, and she'd wanted him forever, it seemed. And as wary as he'd been about this sort of thing, she was afraid any type of rebuke would send him flying away.

Besides, he could do anything he wanted to her like this…

"No one is to enter," he said roughly.

Moaning, she wound her legs around his waist, tilted her head to receive his newest kiss and enjoyed a deeper thrust of his tongue. White lightning, the man was a fast learner. Very fast. He was now an expert at kissing. The best she'd ever had. By the time she finished with him, he'd be an expert at *everything* carnal.

His cock, hard and long and thick, rode the apex of her thighs. She could feel every inch of him through the softness of his robe. His arms enveloped her, and when she opened her eyes—they were inside his cloud, she realized—she saw his golden wings were spread, forming a blanket over them.

She tangled her hands in his hair and pulled from the kiss. "Are you going to get into trouble for this?" she asked, panting. Wait. What? Where had that thought come from?

His eyes narrowed. "Do you care?"

"No," she lied, forcing a grin. No, no, no. That wasn't a lie. "But that adds a little extra danger, don't you think?" There. Better. That was more like her normal self. She didn't like his goodness, didn't want to preserve it and keep him safe.

Did she?

"Well, I will not get into trouble." He flattened his palms at her temples, boxing her in and taking the bulk of his own weight. "If that is the only reason you are here, you can leave."

How fierce he appeared. "So sensitive, angel." She hooked her fingers at the neck of his robe and tugged. The material ripped easily. But as she held it, it began to weave itself back together. Frowning, she ripped again, harder this time, until there was a big enough gap to shove the clothing from his shoulders and off his arms. "I was only teasing."

His chest was magnificent. A work of art. Muscled and sun-kissed and devoid of any hair. She lifted her head and licked the pulse at the base of his neck, then traced his collarbone, then circled one of his nipples. "Do you like?"

"Hot. Wet," he rasped, lids squeezed tight.

"Yeah, but do you like?"

"Yes."

She sucked a peak until he gasped, then kissed away the sting. A tremor of pleasure rocked him, which caused a lance of pride to work through her. "Why do you desire me, angel? Why do you care if I'm good or not?"

A pause. A tortured, "Your skin…"

Every muscle in her body stiffened, and she glared up at him. "So any Harpy will do?" She tried to hide her insult, but didn't quite manage it. The thought of another Harpy—hell, any other woman, immortal or not—enjoying him roused her most vicious instincts. Her nails lengthened, and her teeth sharpened. A red haze dotted her line of vision. *Mine,* she thought. She would kill anyone who touched him. "We all have this skin, you know?" The words were guttural, scraping her throat.

His lashes separated as his eyes opened. His pupils were dilated, his expression tightening with…an emotion she didn't recognize. "Yes, but only yours tempts me. Why is that?"

"Oh," was all she could first think to say, her anger draining completely. But she needed to respond, had to think of something light, easy. "To answer your question, you want me because I'm made of awesome. And guess what? I will make you so happy you said that, warrior."

Warrior, rather than angel. She'd never called him that before. Why? And why now?

"No. I will make *you* happy." He ripped her shirt just as she had done his robe. She wasn't wearing a bra, and her breasts sprang free. Another tremor moved through him as he lowered his head.

He licked and sucked one nipple, as she had done to him, then the other, feasting. Savoring. Soon she was arching and writhing against him, craving his mouth elsewhere. Her skin was sensitized, her body desperate for release. Yet she didn't want to rush him. She was still afraid of scaring him away. But damn him, if he didn't hurry, didn't touch her between her legs, she was going to die.

"Lysander," she said on a trembling breath.

His wings brushed both her arms, up and down, tickling, caressing, raising goosebumps on her flesh. Holy hell, that was good. So damn good.

He lifted from her completely.

"Wh-what are you doing? I wasn't going to tell you to leave," she screeched, bracing her weight on her elbows.

"I do not want anything between us." He shoved the robe down his legs until he was gloriously naked. Moisture gleamed at the head of his cock, and her mouth watered. Reaching out, he gripped her boots and tore them off. Her jeans quickly followed. She, of course, was not wearing any panties.

His gaze drank her in, and she knew what he saw. Her flushed, glowing skin. The aching juncture between her legs. Her rose-tinted nipples.

"I want to touch and taste every inch," he said and just kind of fell on her, as if his will to resist had abandoned him completely.

"Touch and taste every inch next time." Please let there be a next time. She tried to hook her legs around his waist again. "I need release *now*."

He grabbed her by the knees and spread her. Her head fell back, her hair tangling around her, and he kissed a path to her breasts, then to her stomach. He lingered at her navel until she was moaning.

"Lysander," she said again. Fine. She'd jump on this grenade if she had to; if he wanted to taste, he could taste. "More. I need more."

Rather than give it to her, he stilled. "I…took care of myself before following you this day," he admitted, cheeks pinkening. "I thought that would give me resistance against you."

Her eyes widened, shock pouring through her. "You pleasured yourself?"

A stiff nod.

"Did you think of me?"

Another nod.

"Oh, baby. That's good. I can picture it, and I love what I see." His hand on his cock, stroking up and down, eyes closed, features tight with arousal, body straining toward release. Wings spread as he fell to his knees, the pleasure too much. Her, naked in his mind. "What did you think about doing?"

Another pause. A hesitant response. "Licking. Between your legs. Tasting you, as I said."

She arched her back, hands skimming down her middle to her thighs. Although he already held her open, she pushed her legs farther apart. "Then do it. Lick me. I want it so bad. Want your tongue on me. See how wet I am?"

He hissed in a breath. "Yes. Yes." Leaning down, he started at her ankles and kissed his way up, lingering at the back of her knees, at the crease of her legs.

"Please," she said, so on edge she was ready to scream. "Please. Do it."

"Yes," he whispered again. "Yes." Finally he settled over her, mouth poised, ready. His tongue flicked out. Then, sweet contact.

She expected the touch, but nothing could have prepared her for the perfection of it. She did scream, shivered. Begged for more. "Yes, yes, yes. Please, please, please."

At first, he merely lapped at her, humming his approval at her taste. Thank the gods. Or God. Or whoever was responsible for this man. If he hadn't liked her in that way, she wasn't sure what she would have done. In that moment, she wanted—needed—to be everything *he* wanted—needed. She wanted him to crave every part of her, as she craved every part of him.

Even his goodness?

Yes, she thought, finally admitting it. Yes. Just then, she had no defenses; she'd been stripped to her soul. His goodness somehow balanced her out. She'd fought against it—and still had no plans to change—but they were two extremes and actually complemented each other, each giving the other what he or she lacked. In her case, the knowledge that some things were worth taking seriously. In his, that it wasn't a crime to have fun.

"Bianka," he moaned. "Tell me how…what…"

"More. Don't stop."

Soon his tongue was darting in and out of her, mimicking the act of sex. She grasped at the sheets, fisting them. She writhed, meeting his every thrust. She screamed again, moaned and begged some more.

Finally, she splintered apart. Bit down on her bottom lip until she tasted blood. White lights danced over her eyes—from her skin, she realized. Her skin was so bright it was almost blinding, glowing like a lamp, something that had never happened before.

Then Lysander was looming above her. "You are not fertile," he rasped. Sweat beaded him.

That gave her fuzzy mind pause. "I know." Her words were as labored as his. Harpies were only fertile once a year and this wasn't her time. "But how do you know that?"

"Sense it. Always know that kind of thing. So…are you ready?" he asked, and she could hear the uncertainty in his voice.

He must not know proper etiquette, the darling virgin. He would learn. With her, there was no etiquette. Doing what felt good was the only thing that drove her.

"Not yet." She flattened her hands on his shoulders and pushed him to his back, careful of his wings. He didn't protest or fight her as she straddled his waist and gripped his cock by the base. Her wings fluttered in joy at their freedom. "Better?"

He licked his lips, nodded. *His* wings lifted, enveloped her, caressing her. Her head fell, the long length of her hair tickling his thighs. He trembled.

Would he regret this? she suddenly wondered. She didn't want him to hate her for supposedly ruining him.

"Are *you* ready?" she asked. "There's no taking it back once it's done." If he wasn't ready, well, she would…wait, she realized. Yes, she would wait until he *was* ready. Only he would do. No other. Her body only wanted him.

"Do not stop," he commanded, mimicking her.

A grin bloomed. "I'll be careful with you," she assured him. "I won't hurt you."

His fingers circled her hips and lifted her until she was poised at his tip. "The only thing that could hurt me is if you leave me like this."

"No chance of that," she said, and sank all the way to the hilt.

He arched up to meet her, feeding her his length, his eyes squeezing shut, his teeth nearly chewing their way through his bottom lip. He stretched her perfectly, hit her in just the right spot, and she found herself desperate for release once more. But she paused, his enjoyment more important than her own. For whatever reason.

"Tell me when you're ready for me to—"

"Move!" he shouted, hips thrusting so high he raised her knees from the mattress.

Groaning at the pleasure, she moved, up and down, slipping and sliding over his erection. He was wild beneath her, as if he'd kept his passion bottled up all these years and it had suddenly exploded from him, unstoppable.

Soon, even that wasn't enough for him. He began hammering inside her, and she loved it. Loved his intensity. All she could do was hold on for the ride, slamming down on him, gasping. Her nails dug into his chest, her moans blended with his. And when her second orgasm hit, Lysander was right there with her, roaring, muscles stiffening.

He grabbed her by the neck and jerked her down, meshing their lips together. Their teeth scraped as he primitively, savagely kissed her. It was a kiss that stripped her once more to her soul, left her raw, agonized. Reeling.

He was indeed her consort, she thought, dazed. There was no denying it now. He was it for her. Her one and only. Necessary. Angel or not. She laughed, and was surprised by how carefree it sounded. Tamed by great sex. It figured. After this, no other man would do. Ever. She knew it, sensed it.

She collapsed atop him, panting, sweating. Scared. Suddenly vulnerable. How did he feel about her? He didn't approve of her, yet he had gifted her with his virginity. Surely that meant he liked her, just as she was. Surely that meant he wanted her around.

His heart thundered in his chest, and she grinned. Surely.

"Bianka," he said shakily.

She yawned, more replete than she'd ever been. *My consort.* Her eyelids closed, her lashes suddenly too heavy to hold up. Fatigue washed through her, so intense she couldn't fight it.

"Talk…later," she replied, and drifted into the most peaceful sleep of her life.

CHAPTER ELEVEN

FOR HOURS LYSANDER HELD Bianka in the crook of his arm while she slept, marveling—this was what she'd craved most in the world and *he* had given it to her—and yet, he was also worrying. He knew what that meant, knew how difficult it was for a Harpy to let down her guard and sleep in front of another. It meant she trusted him to protect her, to keep her safe. And he was glad. He *wanted* to protect her. Even from herself.

But could he? He didn't know. They were so different.

Until they got into bed, that is.

He could not believe what had just happened. He had become a creature of sensation, his baser urges all that mattered. The pleasure…unlike anything he'd ever experienced. Her taste was like honey, her skin so soft he wanted it against him for the rest of eternity. Her breathy moans—even her screams—had been a caress inside his ears. He'd loved every moment of it.

Had he been called to battle, he wasn't sure he would have been able to leave her.

Why her, though? Why had *she* been the one to captivate him?

She lied to him at every opportunity. She embodied everything he despised. Yet he did not despise her. For every moment with her, he only wanted more. Everything she did excited him. The pleasure she'd found in his arms…she had been unashamed, uninhibited, demanding everything he had to give.

Would he have been as enthralled by her if she had led a

blameless life? If she had been more demure? He didn't think so. He liked her exactly as she was.

Why? he wondered again.

By the time she stretched lazily, sensually against him, he still did not have the answers. Nor did he know what to do with her. He'd already proven he could not leave her alone. And now that he knew all of her, she would be even more impossible to resist.

"Lysander," she said, voice husky from her rest.

"I am here."

She blinked open her eyes, jolted upright. "I fell asleep."

"I know."

"Yeah, but I feel asleep." She scrubbed a hand down her beautiful face, twisted and peered down at him with vulnerable astonishment. "I should be ashamed of myself, but I'm not. What's wrong with me?"

He reached up and traced a fingertip over her swollen lips. How hard had he kissed her? "I'm…sorry," he said. "I lost control for a moment. I shouldn't have taken you so—"

She nipped at his finger, her self-recrimination seeming to melt away in favor of amusement. "Do you hear me complaining about that?"

He relaxed. No, he did not hear her complaining. In fact, she appeared utterly sated. And he had done that. He had given her pleasure. Pride filled him. Pride—a foolish emotion that often led to a man's downfall. Was that how Bianka would make him fall? For as his temptation, she *would* make him fall.

With a sigh, she flopped back against him. "You turned serious all of the sudden. Want to talk about it?"

"No."

"Do you want to talk about *anything?*"

"No."

"Well, too bad," she grumbled, but he heard a layer of satisfaction in her tone. Did she enjoy making him do things he didn't want to do—or didn't think he wanted to do? "Because you're going to talk. A lot. You can start with why you first abducted me. I know you wanted to change me, but why me? I still don't know."

He shouldn't tell her; she already had enough power over him, and knowing the truth would only increase that power. But he also wanted her to understand how desperate he'd been. Was. "At the heart of my duties, I am a peacekeeper, and as such, I must peek into the lives of the Lords of the Underworld every so often, making sure they are obeying heavenly laws. I…saw you with them. And as I have proven with my actions this day, I realized you are my one temptation. The one thing that can tear me from my righteous path."

She sat up again, faced him again. Her eyes were wide with…pleasure? "Really? I alone can ruin you?"

He frowned. "That does not mean you should try and do so."

Laughing, she leaned down and kissed him. Her breasts pressed against his chest, once again heating his blood in that way only she could do. But he was done fighting it, done resisting it. "That's not what I meant. I just like being important to you, I guess." Her cheeks suddenly bloomed with color. "Wait. That's not what I meant, either. What I'm trying to say is that you're forgiven for whisking me to your palace in the sky. I would have done the same thing to you had the situation been reversed."

He had not expected forgiveness to come so easily. Not from her. Frown intensifying, he cupped her cheeks and forced her to meet his gaze. "Why were *you* with *me?* I know I am not what your kind views as acceptable."

She shrugged, the action a little stiff. "I guess you're my temptation."

Now he understood why she'd grinned over his proclamation. He wanted to whoop with satisfied laughter.

"If we're going to be together—" She stopped, waiting. When he nodded, she relaxed and continued, "Then I guess I could only steal from the wicked."

It was a concession. A concession he'd never thought she would make. She truly must like him. Must want more time with him.

"So listen," she said. "My sister is getting married in a week, as I told you before. Do you want to, like, come with me? As my guest? I know, I know. It's short notice. But I didn't intend to invite you. I mean, you're an angel." There was disgust in her voice. "But you make love like a demon so I guess I should, I don't know, show you off or something."

He opened his mouth to reply. What he would say, he didn't know. They could not tell others of their relationship. Ever. But a voice stopped him.

"Lysander. Are you home?"

Lysander recognized the speaker immediately. Raphael, the warrior angel. Panic nearly choked him. He couldn't let the man see him like this. Couldn't let any of his kind see him with the Harpy.

"We must discuss Olivia," Raphael called. "May I enter your abode? There is some sort of block preventing me from doing so."

"Not yet," he called. Was his panic in his voice? He'd never experienced it before, so didn't know how to combat it. "Wait for me. I will emerge." He sat up and slipped from the bed, from Bianka. He grabbed his robe, or rather, the pieces of it, from the floor and wrapped it around himself. Immediately it wove back together to fit his frame. The material even cleaned him, wiping away Bianka's scent.

The latter, he inwardly cursed. *For the best.*

"Let him in," Bianka said, fitting the sheet around her, oblivious. "I don't mind."

Lysander kept his back to her. "I do not want him to see you."

"Don't worry. I've covered my naughty nakedness."

He gave no reply. Unlike her, he would not lie. And if he did not lie to her, he would hurt her. He did not want to do that either.

"So call him in already," she said with a laugh. "I want to see if all angels look like sin but act like saints."

"No. I don't want him inside right now. I will go out to meet him. You will stay here," he said. Still he couldn't face her.

"Wait. Are you jealous?"

He gave no reply.

"Lysander?"

"Stay silent. Please. Cloud walls are thin."

"Stay…silent?" A moment passed in the very silence he'd requested. Only, he didn't like it. He heard the rustle of fabric, a sharp intake of breath. "You don't want him to know I'm here, do you? You're ashamed of me," she said, clearly shocked. "You don't want your friend to know you've been with me."

"Bianka."

"No. You don't get to speak right now." With every word, her voice rose. "I was willing to take you to my sister's wedding. Even though I knew my family would laugh at me or view me with disgust. I was willing to give you a chance. Give us a chance. But not you. You were going to hide me away. As if *I'm* something shameful."

He whirled on her, fury burning through him. At her, at himself. "You *are* something shameful. I kill beings like you. I do not fall in love with them."

She didn't say anything. Just looked up at him with wide, hurt-filled eyes. So much hurt he actually stumbled back. A sharp pain lanced *his* chest. But as he watched, her hurt mutated into a fury that far surpassed his.

"Kill me, then," she growled.

"You know I will not."

"Why?"

"Because!"

"Let me guess. Because deep down you still think you can change me. You think that I will become the pure, virtuous woman you want me to be. Well, who are you to say what's virtuous and what isn't?"

He merely arched a brow. The answer was obvious and didn't need to be stated.

"I told you that from now on I'd only hurt the wicked, right? Well, surprise! That's what I've done since the beginning. The pie you watched me eat? The owner of that restaurant cheats at cards, takes money that doesn't belong to him. The wallet I stole? I took it from a man cheating on his wife."

He blinked down at her, unsure he'd heard correctly. "Why would you have kept that from me?"

"Why should it change how you feel about me?" She tossed back the cover and stood, glorious in her nakedness. Her skin was still aglow, multihued light reflecting off it—he'd touched that skin. Dark hair cascaded around her—he'd fisted that hair.

"I want to be with you," he said. "I do. But it has to be in secret."

"I thought the same. Until what we just did," she said as she hastily dressed. Her clothes were not like his, did not repair on their own, and so that ripped shirt revealed more than it hid.

He tried again. Tried to make her understand. "You are everything my kind stands against, Bianka. I train warriors to hunt and kill demons. What would it say to them were I to take you as my companion?"

"Here's a better question. What does it say to them that you hide your sin? Because that's how you view me, isn't it? Your sin. You are such a hypocrite." She stormed past him, careful not to touch him. "And I will not be with a hypocrite. That's worse than being an angel."

He thought she meant to race to Raphael and flaunt her presence. Shockingly enough, she didn't. And because he hadn't commanded her to stay, when she said, "I want to leave," the cloud opened up at her feet.

She disappeared, falling through the sky.

"Bianka," he shouted. Lysander spread his wings and jumped after her. He passed Raphael, but at that point, he didn't care. He only wanted Bianka safe—and that hurt and fury wiped away from her expression.

She'd turned facedown to increase her momentum. He had to tuck his wings into his back to increase his own. Finally, he caught her halfway and wrapped his arms around her, her back pressed into his stomach. She didn't flail, didn't order him to release her, which he'd been prepared for.

When they reached her cabin, he straightened them, spread his wings and slowed. Snow still covered the ground and crunched when they landed. She didn't pull away. Didn't run. Something else he'd been prepared for.

Clearly he knew very little about her.

"It's probably best this way, you know," she said flatly, keeping her back to him. The wind slapped her hair against his cheeks. "That was my afterglow talking earlier, anyway. I never should have invited you to the wedding. We're too different to make anything work."

"I was willing to try," he said through gritted teeth. *Don't do this,* he projected. *Don't end us.*

She laughed without humor, and he marveled at the difference between this laugh and the one she'd given inside his cloud. Marveled and mourned. "No, you were willing to hide me away."

"Yes. Therefore I was *trying* to make something work. I want to be with you, Bianka. Otherwise I would not have followed you. I would have left you alone from the first. I would not have tried to show you the light."

"You are such a pompous ass," she spat. "Show me the light? Please! You want me to be perfect. Blameless. But what happens when I fail? And I will, you know? Perfection just isn't in me. One day I will curse. Like now. Fuck you. One day I will take something just because it's pretty and I want it. Would that ruin me in your eyes?"

"It hasn't so far," he spat back.

She laughed again, this one bleaker, grim. "The scarves I took were made by child laborers. So I haven't really done anything too terrible yet. But I will. And you know what? If you were to do something nauseatingly righteous, I wouldn't have cared. I would still have wanted to take you to the wedding. That's the difference between us. Evil or not, good or not, I wanted you."

"I want you, too. But that was not always the case, and you know it. You *would* care." He tightened his grip on her. "Bianka. We can work this out."

"No, we can't." Finally, she twisted to face him. "That would require giving you a second chance, and I don't do second chances."

"I don't need a second chance. I just need you to think about this. To realize our relationship must stay hidden."

"I'm not going to be your secret shame, Lysander."

His eyes narrowed. She was trying to force his hand, and he didn't like it. "You steal in secret. You sleep in secret. Why not this?"

"That you don't know the answer proves you aren't the warrior I thought you were. Have a nice life, Lysander," she said, jerking from his hold and walking away without a backward glance.

CHAPTER TWELVE

LYSANDER SAT IN THE BACK of the Budapest chapel, undetectable, watching Bianka help her sisters and their friends decorate for the wedding. She was currently hanging flowers from the vaulted ceiling. Without a ladder.

He'd been following her for days, unable to stay away. One thing he'd noticed: she talked and laughed as if she was fine, normal, but the sparkle was gone from her eyes, her skin.

And he had done that to her. Worse, not once had she cursed, lied or stolen. Again, his fault. He'd told her she was unworthy of him. He'd been—*was,* right?—too embarrassed of her to tell his people about her.

But he couldn't deny that he missed her. Missed everything about her. That much he knew. She excited him, challenged him, frustrated him, consumed him, drew him, made him *feel.* He did not want to be without her.

Something soft brushed his shoulder. He barely managed to tear his gaze from Bianka to turn and see that Olivia was now sitting beside him.

What was wrong with him? He hadn't heard her arrive. Normally his senses were tuned, alert.

"Why did you summon me here?" she asked. She glanced around nervously. Her dark curls framed her face, rosebuds dripping from a few of the strands.

"To Budapest? Because you are always here anyway."

"As are you these days," she replied dryly.

He shrugged. "Did you just come from Aeron's room?"

She gave a reluctant nod.

"Raphael came to me," he said. The day he'd lost Bianka. The worst day of his existence.

"Those flowers aren't centered, B," the redheaded Kaia called, claiming his attention and stopping the rest of his speech to his charge. "Shift them a little to the left."

Bianka expelled a frustrated sigh. "Like this?"

"No. *My* left, dummy."

Grumbling, Bianka obeyed.

"Perfect." Kaia beamed up at her.

Bianka flipped her off, and Lysander grinned. Thank the One True Deity he had not killed all of her spirit.

"I think they're perfect, too," her youngest sister, Gwendolyn, said.

Bianka released the ceiling panels and dropped to the floor. When she landed, she straightened as if the jolt had not affected her in any way. "Glad the princess is finally happy with something," she muttered. Then, more loudly, "I don't understand why you can't get married in a tree like a civilized Harpy."

Gwen anchored her hands on her fists. "Because my dream has always been to be wed in a chapel like any other normal person. Now, will someone please remove the naked portraits of Sabin from the walls? Please."

"Why would you want to get rid of them when I just spent all that time hanging them?" Anya, goddess of Anarchy and companion to Lucien, keeper of Death, asked, clearly offended. "They add a little something extra to what would otherwise be very boring proceedings. *My* wedding will have strippers. Live ones."

"Boring? Boring!" Fury passed over Gwen's features, black bleeding into her eyes, her teeth sharpening.

Lysander had watched this same change overtake her multiple times already. In the past hour alone.

"It won't be boring," Ashlyn, companion to Maddox, the keeper of Violence, said soothingly. "It'll be beautiful."

The pregnant woman rubbed her rounded belly. That belly was larger than it should have been, given the early state of her pregnancy. No one seemed to realize it, though. They would soon enough, he supposed. He just hoped they were ready for what she carried.

What would a child of Bianka's be like? he suddenly wondered. Harpy, like her? Angel, like him? Or a mix of both?

A pang took root and flourished in his chest.

"Boring?" Gwen snarled again, clearly not ready to let the insult slide.

"Great!" Bianka threw up her arms. "Someone get Sabin before Gwennie kills us all in a rage."

A Harpy in a rage could hurt even other Harpies, Lysander knew. As Gwen's consort, Sabin, keeper of Doubt, was the only one who could calm her.

With that thought, Lysander's head tilted to the side. He had never seen Bianka erupt, he realized. She'd viewed everything as a game. Well, not true. Once, she had gotten mad. The time Paris had punched him. Lysander had been her enemy, but she'd still gotten mad over his mistreatment.

Lysander had calmed her.

The pang grew in intensity, and he rubbed his breastbone. Was he Bianka's consort? Did he want to be?

"No need to search me out. I'm here." Sabin strode through the double doors. "As if I'd be more than a few feet away when she's so sensitiv—uh, just in case she needed my help. Gwen, baby." There at the end, his tone had lowered, gentled. He reached her and pulled her into his arms; she snuggled against him. "The most important thing tomorrow is that we'll be together. Right?"

"Lysander," Olivia said, drawing his attention from the now-cooing couple. "The wait is difficult. Raphael came to you and…what?"

Lysander sighed, forcing himself to concentrate. "Answer a few questions for me first."

"All right," she said after a brief hesitation.

"Why do you like Aeron when he is so different from you?"

She twisted the fabric of her robe. "I think I like him *because* he is so different from me. He has thrived amid darkness, managing to retain a spark of light in his soul. He is not perfect, is not blameless, but he could have given in to his demon long ago and yet still he fights. He protects those he loves. His passion for life is…" She shivered. "Amazing. And really, he only hurts people when his demon overtakes him—and only if they are wicked, at that. Innocents, he leaves alone."

It was the same with Bianka. Yet Lysander had tried to make her ashamed of herself. Ashamed when she should only be proud of what she had accomplished, thriving amid darkness, as Olivia had said. "And you are not embarrassed for our kind to know of your affection for him?"

"Embarrassed of Aeron?" Olivia laughed. "When he is stronger, fiercer, more alive than anyone I know? Of course not. I would be proud to be called his woman. Not that it could ever happen," she added sadly.

Proud. There was that word again. And this time, something clicked in his mind. *I'm not going to be your secret shame, Lysander,* Bianka had said. He'd reminded her that she committed all her other sins in secret. Why not him? She hadn't told him the answer, but it came to him now. Because she'd been proud of him. Because she'd wanted to show him off.

As he should have wanted to show *her* off.

Any other man would have been proud to stand beside her. She was beautiful, intelligent, witty, passionate and lived by her own moral code. Her laughter was more lovely than the song of a harp, her kiss as sweet as a prayer.

He'd considered her the spawn of Lucifer, yet she was a gift from the One True Deity. He was such a fool.

"Have I answered your questions sufficiently?" Olivia asked.

"Yes." He was surprised by the rawness of his voice. Had he ruined things irreparably between them?

"So answer a few now for me."

Unable to find his voice, he nodded. He had to make this right. Had to try, at least.

"Bianka. The Harpy you watch. Do you love her?"

Love. He found her among the crowd and the pang in his chest grew unbearable. She was currently adding a magic marker mustache to one of Sabin's portraits while Kaia added…other things down below. Kaia was giggling; Bianka looked like she was just going through the motions, taking no joy.

He wanted her happy. Wanted her the way she'd been.

"You think you are embarrassed of her," Olivia continued when he gave no response.

"How do you know?" He forced the words to leave him.

"I am—or was—a joy-bringer, Lysander. It was my job to know what people were feeling and then help them see the truth. Because only in truth can one find real joy. You were never embarrassed of her. I know you. You are embarrassed by nothing. You were simply scared. Scared that *you* were not what *she* needs."

His eyes widened. Could that be true? He'd tried to change her. Had tried to make her what he was so that she, in turn, would *like* what he was? Yes. Yes, that made sense, and for the second time in his existence, he hated himself.

He had let Bianka get away from him. When he should have sung her praises to all of the heavens, he had cast her aside. No man was more foolish. Irreparable damage or not, he had to try and win her back.

He jumped to his feet. "I do," he said. "I love her." He wanted to throw his arms around her. Wanted to shout to all the world that she belonged to him. That she had chosen him as her man.

His shoulders slumped. Chosen. Key word. Past tense. She would not choose him again. She did not give second chances, she'd said.

She often lies…

For the first time, the thought that his woman liked to lie caused him to smile. Perhaps she had lied about that. Perhaps she would give him a second chance. A chance to prove his love.

If he had to grovel, he would. She was his temptation, but that did not have to be a bad thing. That could be his salvation. After all, his life would mean nothing without her. Same for her. She had told him that he was her own temptation. He could be *her* salvation.

"Thank you," he told Olivia. "Thank you for showing me the truth."

"Always my pleasure."

How should he approach Bianka? When? Urgency flooded him. He wanted to do so now. As a warrior, though, he knew some battles required planning. And as this was the most important battle of his existence, plan his attack he would.

If she forgave him and decided to be with him, they would still have a tough road ahead. Where would they live? His duties were in the heavens. She thrived on earth, with her family nearby. Plus, Olivia was destined to kill Aeron, who would essentially be Bianka's brother-in-law after tomorrow. And if Olivia decided not to, another angel would be chosen to do the job.

Most likely, that would be Lysander.

One thing his Deity had taught him, however, was that love truly could conquer all. Nothing was stronger. They could make this work.

"I've lost you again," Olivia said with a laugh. "Before you rush off, you must tell me why you summoned me. What Raphael said to you."

Some of his good mood evaporated. While Olivia had just given him hope and helped him find the right path, he was about to dash any hopes of a happily-ever-after for her.

"Raphael came to me," he repeated. *Just do it; just say it.* "He told me of the council's unhappiness with you. He told me they grow weary of your continued defiance."

Her smile fell away. "I know," she whispered. "I just…I haven't been able to bring myself to hurt him. Watching him gives me joy. And I deserve to experience joy after so many centuries of devoted service, do I not?"

"Of course."

"And if he is dead, I will never be able to do the things I now dream about."

His brow furrowed. "What things?"

"Touching him. Curling into his arms." A pause. "Kissing him."

Dangerous desires indeed. Oh, did he know their power. "If you never experience them," he offered, "they are easier to resist." But he hated to think of this wonderful female being without something she wanted.

He could petition the council for Aeron's forgiveness, but that would do no good. A decree was a decree. A law had been broken and someone had to pay. "Very soon, the council will be forced to offer you a choice. Your duty or your downfall."

She gazed down at her hands, once again twisting the fabric of her robe. "I know. I don't know why I hesitate. He would never desire me, anyway. The women here, they are exciting, dangerous. As fierce as he is. And I am—"

"Precious," he said. "You are precious. Never think otherwise."

She offered him a shaky smile.

"I have always loved you, Olivia. I would hate to see you give up everything you are for a man who has threatened to kill you. You do know what you would be losing, yes?"

That smile fell away as she nodded.

"You would fall straight into hell. The demons there will go for your wings. They always go for the wings first. No longer will you be impervious to pain. You will hurt, yet you will have to dig your way free of the underground—or die there. Your strength will be depleted. Your body will not regenerate on its own. You will be more fragile than a human because you were not raised among them."

While he thought he could survive such a thing, he did not think Olivia would. She was too delicate. Too…sheltered. Until this point, every facet of her life had dealt with joy and happiness. She had known nothing else.

The demons of hell would be crueler to her than they would be even to him, the man they feared more than any other. She was all they despised. Wholly good. Destroying such innocence and purity would delight them.

"Why are you telling me this?" Her voice trembled. Tears streaked down her cheeks.

"Because I do not want you to make the wrong decision. Because I want you to know what you're up against."

A moment passed in silence, then she jumped up and threw her arms around his neck. "I love you, you know."

He squeezed her tightly, sensing that this was her way of saying goodbye. Sensing that this would be the last time they were offered such a reprieve. But he would not stop her, whatever path she chose.

She pulled back and smoothed her trembling hands down her glistening white robe. "You have given me much to consider. So now I will leave you to your female. May love always follow you, Lysander." As she spoke, her wings expanded. Up, up she flew, misting through the ceiling—and Bianka's flowers—before disappearing.

He hoped she'd choose her faith, her immortality, over the keeper of Wrath, but feared she would not. His gaze strayed to Bianka, now walking down the aisle toward the exit. She paused at his row, frowned, before shaking her head and leaving. If he'd been forced to pick between her and his reputation and lifestyle, he would have picked her, he realized.

And now it was time to prove it to her.

CHAPTER THIRTEEN

I'VE GOT TO PULL MYSELF from this funk, Bianka thought. This was her youngest sister's wedding day. She should be happy. Delighted. If she were honest, though, she was a tiny bit—aka a *lot*—jealous. Gwen's man, a demon, loved her. Was proud of her.

Lysander considered Bianka unworthy.

She'd thought about proving herself to him, but had quickly discarded the idea. Proving herself worthy—his idea of worthy, that is—would entail nothing more than a lie. And Lysander hated lies. So, according to him, she would never be good enough for him. Which meant he was stupid, and she didn't date stupid men. Plus, he didn't deserve her.

He deserved to rot in his unhappiness. And that's what he'd be without her. Unhappy. Or so she hoped.

"So much for our plan to go naked," Kaia muttered beside her. "Gwen saw me leave my room that way and almost sliced my throat."

"Did not," the bride in question said from behind them.

They turned in unison. Bianka's breath caught as it had every time she'd seen her youngest sister in her gown. It was a princess cut, which was fitting, the straps thin, the beautiful white lace cinching just under her breasts before flowing to her ankles. The material covering her legs was sheer, allowing glimpses of thigh and those gorgeous red heels.

Her strawberry curls were half up, half down, diamonds

glittering through the strands. There was so much love and excitement in her gold-gray eyes it was almost blinding.

"I almost pushed you out a window," Gwen added.

They laughed. Even stoic Taliyah, their oldest sister, who had her arm wrapped through Gwen's. Since it turned out Gwen's father was the Lords' greatest enemy, and Gwen's mom had disowned her years ago, Taliyah was escorting Gwen down the aisle.

"Hence the reason I'm now wearing this." Kaia motioned to her own gown, an exact match to Bianka's. A buttercup yellow creation with more ribbons, bows and sequined rose appliqués than anyone should wear in an entire lifetime. They even wore hats with orange streamers.

Gwen shrugged, unrepentant. "I didn't want you looking prettier than me, so sue me."

"Weddings suck," Bianka said. "You should have just had Sabin tattoo your name on his ass and called it good." That's what she would have done. Not that Lysander ever would have agreed to such a thing. Whether they were together or not.

Which they never would be. Bastard.

"I did. Have him tattoo my name on his ass," Gwen said. "And his arm. And his chest. And his back. But then I casually mentioned how much I'd always wanted a big wedding, and well, he told me I had four weeks to plan it or he'd take over and do it himself. And everyone knows men can't plan shit. So…" She shrugged again, though the excitement and love on her face had intensified. "Are they ready for us yet?"

Bianka and Kaia turned back to the chapel, peeking through the crack in the closed doors.

"Not yet," Bianka said. "Paris is missing."

Paris, who had gotten ordained over the Internet, would be presiding over the nuptials.

"He better hurry," she added grumpily. "Or I'll find a way to make him oil-wrestle again."

"You've been so depressed lately. Missing your angel?" Kaia asked her, pinkie-waving to Amun, who stood in the line of groomsmen beside Sabin at the altar.

Amun shouldn't have been able to see her, but somehow he did. He nodded, a smile twitching at the corners of his lips.

"Of course not. I hate him." A lie. She hadn't told her sisters why she and Lysander had parted, only that they had. Forever. If they knew the truth, they'd want to kill him. And as all but Gwen were paid killers, immensely good at their job, she'd find herself the proud owner of Lysander's head.

Which she didn't want.

She just wanted him. Stupid girl.

"I only would have teased you for a few years, you know," Kaia said. "You should have kept him around. It might have been fun to corrupt him."

He didn't want to be corrupted any more than she wanted to be purified. They were too different. Could never make anything work. Their separation was for the best. So why couldn't she get over it? Why did she feel his gaze on her, every minute of every day? Even now, when she looked like a Southern belle on crack?

"So Sabin doesn't have a last name," she said to Gwen, drawing attention away from herself. "Are you going to call yourself Gwen Sabin?"

"No, nothing like that. I'm going to call myself Gwen Lord."

"What's Anya plan to call herself? Anya Underworld?" Kaia asked with a laugh.

"Knowing our goddess, she'll demand Lucien take *her* last name. Trouble. Or is that her middle name?"

"I here, I here," a voice suddenly screeched. Legion pushed her way in front of Bianka and Kaia. She was wearing a yellow dress, as well. Only hers had more ribbons, bows and sequins. A basket of flowers was clutched in her hands, her too-long nails curling around the handle. Best of all, she wore a tiara. Because she didn't have hair, it had had to be glued to her scaled head. "We begin now."

She didn't wait for permission but shouldered her way through the door. The crowd—which consisted of the Lords of the Underworld, their companions and some gods and goddesses Anya knew—turned and gasped when they saw her. Well, except for Gideon. He'd recently been captured and tortured by Hunters, the Lords' nemeses, and was currently missing his hands. (His feet weren't in the best of shape, either.) Because of his injuries, he was beyond weak, so he lay in his gurney, barely conscious. He'd insisted on coming, though.

From his pew, Aeron smiled indulgently as Legion tossed pink petals in every direction. Just as she reached the front, Paris raced to the podium. He looked harried, pale, and Sabin punched him in the shoulder.

Sabin looked amazing. He wore a black tux, his hair slicked back, and when he turned to face the door, watching for Gwen, his entire face lit. With love. With pride. Bianka's jealousy increased. She wanted that. Wanted her man to find her perfect in every way.

Was that too much to ask?

Apparently so. Stupid Lysander.

"Go, go, go," Gwen ordered, giving them a little push.

Bianka kicked into motion, heading toward Strider, her appointed groomsman. He smiled at her when she reached him. He would be proud to call her his woman, she thought. She tried to make herself return the gesture, but her eyes were too busy filling with tears. She looked around, trying to distract herself.

The chapel really was beautiful. The glittery white flowers she'd hung from the ceiling were thick and lush and offered a canopy, a haven. They were the best part of the decor, if you asked her. Candles flickered with golden light, twining with shadows.

Kaia approached her side, and everyone except for Gideon stood. The music changed, slowing down to the bridal march. Gwen and Taliyah appeared. Sabin's breath caught. Yes, that was the way a man should react to the sight of his woman.

What makes you think you were ever Lysander's woman?

Because she was his one temptation. Because of the reverent way he had touched her. Because she liked how he made her feel. Because they balanced each other. Because he completed her in a way she hadn't known she needed. He was the light to her darkness.

He was willing to show you that light. Over and over again.

Perhaps she should have fought for him. That's what she was, after all. A fighter. Yet she'd given in as if he meant nothing to her when he had somehow become the most important thing in her life.

Bianka didn't mean to, but she tuned out as Paris gave his speech and the happy couple recited their vows, her thoughts remaining focused on Lysander. Should she try and fight for him now? If so, how would she go about it?

Only when the crowd cheered did she snap out of her haze, watching as Sabin and Gwen kissed. Then they were marching down the aisle and out the doors together. The rest of the bridal party made their way out, as well.

"Shall we?" Strider asked, holding out his arm for her.

"She can't." Paris grabbed her arm. "You're needed in that room." With his free hand, he pointed.

"Why?" Was he planning revenge against her for forcing him to oil-wrestle Lysander? He hadn't mentioned it in the days since her return to Buda, but he couldn't be happy with her. He should be thanking her, for gods' sake. He'd gotten to touch all of Lysander's hawtness.

Paris rolled his eyes. "Just go before your boyfriend decides he's tired of waiting and comes out here."

Her boyfriend. Lysander? Couldn't be. Could it? But why would he have come? Heart drumming in her chest, she walked forward. She didn't allow herself to run, though she wanted to soooo badly. She reached the door. Her hand shook as she turned the knob.

Hinges creaked. Then she was staring into—an empty room. Her teeth ground together. Paris's revenge, just as she'd figured. Of course. That rat bastard piece of shit was going to pay. She wasn't just going to make him oil-wrestle. She was going to—

"Hello, Bianka."

Lysander.

Gasping, she whipped around. Her eyes widened. In an instant, the chapel had been transformed. No longer were her sisters and friends inside. Lysander and his kind occupied every spare inch. Angels were everywhere, light surrounding them and putting Gwen's candles to shame.

"What are you doing here?" she demanded, not daring to hope.

"I came to beg your forgiveness." His arms spread. "I came to tell you that I am proud to be your man. I brought my friends and brethren to bear witness to my proclamation."

She swallowed, still not letting hope take over. "But I'm evil and that's not going to change. I'm your temptation. You could, I don't know, lose everything by being with me." The thought hit her, and she wanted to wilt. He could lose everything. No wonder he had wanted to destroy her. No wonder he had wanted to hide her.

"No, you are not evil. And I don't want you to change. You are beautiful and intelligent and brave. But more than that, you are my everything. I am nothing without you. Not good, not right, not complete. And do not worry. I will not lose everything as you said. You have not committed an unpardonable sin."

She gulped. "And if I do?"

"I will fall."

Okay. A small kernel of hope managed to seep inside her. But no way would she let him fall. Ever. He loved being an angel. "What brought this on?"

"I finally pulled my head out of my ass," he said dryly.

He'd said *ass*. Lysander had just said the word *ass*. More hope beat its way inside and she had to press her lips together to keep from smiling. And crying! Tears were springing in her eyes, burning.

Could they actually make their relationship work? Just a little bit ago, she'd been grateful—or pretending to be grateful—that they were apart, since so many obstacles existed.

"I only hope you can love so foolish a man. I am willing to live wherever you desire. I am willing to do anything you need to win you back." He dropped to his knees. "I love you, Bianka Skyhawk. I would be proud to be yours."

He was proud of her. He wanted her. He loved her. It was everything she'd secretly dreamed about this past week. Yes, they could make this work. They would be together, and that was the most important thing. But she told him none of that.

"Now?" she screeched instead. "You decided to introduce me to your friends now? When I look like this?" Scowling, she peeked over his shoulder at them and saw their stunned expressions. "I usually look better than this, you know. You should have seen me the other day. When I was naked."

Lysander stood. "That's all you have to say to me?"

She focused back on him. His eyes were as wide as hers had been, his arms crossed over his middle. "No. There's more," she grumbled. "But I will never live this yellow gown thing down, you know."

"Bianka."

"Yes, I love you, too. But if you ever decide I'm unworthy again, I'll show you just how demonic I can be."

"Deal. But you don't have to worry, love," he said, a slow

smile lifting those delectable lips. "It is I who am unworthy. I only pray you never learn of this."

"Oh, I know it already," she said, and his grin spread. "Now c'mere, you." She cupped the back of his neck and jerked him down for a kiss.

His arms banded around her, holding her close. She'd never thought to be paired with an angel, but she couldn't regret it now. Not when Lysander was the angel in question.

"Are you sure you're ready for me?" she asked him when they came up for air.

He nipped at her chin. "I've been ready for you my entire life. I just didn't know it until now."

"Good." With a whoop, she jumped up and wound her legs around his waist. A wave of gasps circled the room. They were still here? "Ditch your friends, I'll blow off my sister's reception and we'll go oil-wrestle."

"Funny," he said, wings enveloping her as he flew her up, up and into his cloud. "That's exactly what I was thinking."

* * * * *

Lords of the Underworld

A BONUS GUIDE

I, CRONUS, KING OF THE TITANS, powerful warrior god, defender of the people, hereby command you to read and enjoy this guide. I am not mentioned nearly enough, but that is neither here nor there. What you *will* find in the pages that follow: an interview with Gena Showalter herself, conducted by the one and only *New York Times* bestselling author Kresley Cole; notes from those vile fools, the Hunters; once-missing chapters from Gena's first attempt at writing about these immortal warriors (she thought she tossed them, but I, all-powerful god that I am, dug them up); interviews with the Lords of the Underworld, as organized by that irreverent whelp William the Ever Randy; a candid discussion about the Lords of the Underworld among their women; answers to questions readers have been dying to know; a preview of the upcoming novel *The Darkest Passion;* and an intimate look at my very own sacred scrolls.

As I said, you will read and you will enjoy. That is your mission. Nay, your honor. Do not disappoint me. You will not like the results. Just ask Aeron, keeper of the demon of Wrath. Bad things tend to happen.

Yours in the heavens,

Cronus

KING OF THE TITANS

TWENTY(ISH) QUESTIONS WITH KRESLEY COLE

I met the amazing Kresley Cole at a writers' conference many years ago. I'd just read her very first book, The Captain of All Pleasures*—and by "read" I mean "devoured"—and approached her with drool on my mouth to tell her so. Tall, blond and gorgeous—and witty and talented and brilliant—this girl charmed me completely. Somehow, some way, she liked me, too. (Sucker!)*

Now she can't get rid of me. She's one of my dearest friends, a sister of my heart and a bright star in the romantic fiction world. Recently, we sat down together and chatted about the Lords of the Underworld (among other things). We hope you enjoy the results!

Kresley Cole (KC): When I was younger, I would do anything to get out of writing—did you always like it, knowing you'd want to be an author when you grew up?

Gena Showalter (GS): Yes and no. (I know, right? Of course I'd kick things off with a non-answer. Oh, stop shaking your head, Cole. This is typical Gena, and you know it!) I wrote in junior high and high school, but only for myself. And the friends who paid me. Publication wasn't even a blip on my radar.

So, in college, I dabbled with nursing, phlebotomy and microbiology, but never ended up finishing. Like, any of them. After a heart-to-heart with myself—and by "heart-to-heart" I mean slapping myself repeatedly and telling myself to finally get in the game—I realized that writing was what I loved, and the only thing I could see myself doing for the rest of my life.

I decided to go for it, to finally try for publication, no matter how long it took me. Which, as it turned out, was about five ~~painful~~ years.

KC: I'm delighted *phlebotomy*—a word which I totally and completely know the definition of—lost out to your career in writing. [furtively searching Google for "phlebotomy" on cell phone] So what made you decide on the paranormal romance genre? For me, I moved from historicals to paranormals because I couldn't get Lore creatures out of my head. Did character possession affect your decision, or was it something else?

GS: Oh, yes. Phlebotomy. PB, as I called it. When my family would give me strange looks, I would then add: Pulling Blood. Out of people. With needles. I'll stop there. You look pale.

Moving on to PR. I picked paranormal romance—after first trying to write a historical, a couple contemporaries and several series romances—because anything I could imagine, I could write about, and the only limitation was my mind. And yes, I hate my mind for not coming up with the Immortals After Dark first. Damn you, Kresley Cole, you brilliant goddess you! But I do love my mind for envisioning the oh, so seductive Lords of the Underworld. I don't know if they possessed me so much as completely seduced me. The way they tell it, I'm easy.

Anyway. Having all of that beefcake inside my head is pretty delicious some days. Although, to be honest, most of the time they are unbelievably stubborn. And opinionated. And bloodthirsty. (Maybe they were once phlebotomists?)

KC: Brilliant goddess? [Fluffing hair] You shouldn't! But it *is* a perfect segue into our next question: Everybody knows I'm your all-time, one-hundred percent favorite author—and the feeling is mutual in a big, adoring way—but were there any particular writers who influenced your craft or your desire to become a writer?

GS: I love that you love me. Though I love you more. (And do not argue about it. You know it's my turn to win.)

Johanna Lindsey was the first romance author I ever read. I stole *Silver Angel* right out of my grandmother's house and I'm still not sorry! And then, when I read *Warrior's Woman,* also by Lindsey…I fell deeply in love with her strong alpha men and realized I wanted to create men like that. Larger than life, willing to die for their woman, and well, so in love that no other female but the heroine would ever be able to turn them on again.

You know, like our husbands.

KC: Give us an inside peek into a day in the fabulous life of Gena Showalter. Do you write every day? If so, for how long? Does your editor know you spend a great deal of your time entertaining me? If not, how can we make sure that stays secret?

GS: You know that's going to appear on the cover of one of my books, right? "Gena Showalter is fabulous!"—#1 *New York Times* bestselling author Kresley Cole.

Anyway. My writing life. I wake up, mainline coffee and get to work. And as you know, by "get to work" I mean e-mail you a thousand times, maybe call you, chat your ear off—entertaining you, as you said, and not pestering you—and then finally opening my work in progress (the WIP, as writers call it. And it does—whip me). Believe me, the secret of my pester…uh, *entertaining* will remain just that, as I want to continue doing so. Forever.

While crafting a rough draft, I work until I finish a chapter. That could take me two hours or twelve. While editing a finished draft, I tend to work from sunrise to sunset. OCD…sadly, I am her bitch. I can think of nothing else until the story is done. Except for you, of course. And my *entertaining.*

KC: Word on the street is you sold your soul to write these scintillating tales. Tell us this isn't so (since it has already been promised—to *me*).

GS: No truth to the rumors, I swear! Our pact is still applicable. So I'll expect you to give me that—oops. Almost let the terms of our agreement slip. My bad.

Anyway. The rumor about me being an alien with five arms *is* actually true. Right now, all at the same time, I'm answering these questions, drinking coffee, fixing my hair, painting my toenails and drawing pictures to send you. You know, to entertain you. Yes, I am never going to let you forget that you said I "entertain" you.

KC: The Lords of the Underworld are all exceedingly sexy and heart-throbbingly male. Was it your plan to give readers testosterone intoxication by creating, oh, I dunno, TWELVE of them? How did you decide on a dozen main Lords characters (as opposed to, say, five or seven or eighteen)? And how did you make it so that all the warriors have distinct personalities? It must be tough to keep the Lords (not to mention their significant others and the assorted menagerie of friends/relatives/demon companions they collect along the way) straight in your mind as you write....

GS: First, thank you! I'll be smiling for the rest of the day. Three new cover quotes, right there. "Sexy." "Heart-throbbingly male." And "Intoxication."

As for the Lords, I never planned to write about twelve demon-possessed warriors. Believe me, I didn't need all that naughtiness in my head. On top of what was already there, that is. At first, I thought three, maybe four. Tops. But as I wrote *The Darkest Night,* those twelve warriors stood up and said hello in my brain—if only you could have heard how husky and seductive those voices were. I just couldn't say no. Thank God!

And then their friends started to arrive. Irreverent baggage (you know I'm talking about you, William!). I couldn't say no to them, either.

Shockingly enough, it's not hard to keep the growing cast straight. To me, it's like standing in the middle of a room filled with my family. I know them. They look different, act different and even smell different. And sometimes I want to shake them. Some harder than others. (Yes, William. I'm talking about you again.)

KC: So, just between us and a few mil of our closest friends, do you have a favorite Lord? (I've narrowed my fave down—it's a tie between Torin and eleven others.) If you had to choose one of them to come to life and point at you and say *"MY WOMAN!"* who would it be?

GS: I shouldn't admit this, but my favorite warrior is not actually a Lord of the Underworld. I am head over heels for William. Yes, that irreverent baggage! I adore his sense of humor—oh, that wicked tongue! And his cockiness. And his uninhibited nature. And even his temper. To me, there's just something so thrilling about taming a womanizer and becoming the one female in the world he can't live without. And of course, the only woman who turns him on anymore.

My favorite Lord, though, is Strider. The moment he took pictures with his camera phone of a naked Lucien chained to a bed, then e-mailed those pictures to all his friends, I knew he was the one for me. Someday, some heroine is going to have to pry him out of my kung fu grip.

KC: Do your readers seem to have one clear favorite, judging from reader mail you get? Do you have a least favorite Lord, or one who's been tougher for you to write than others?

GS: The reader favorite is, without a doubt, Paris. I get more e-mail about him than any other Lord. And I want to tell his story, I do, but of all the Lords, he truly has proven to be the most stubborn. Finally, though, I know where I want to go with him. It's just going to take some time to get him there. (Please don't hurt me.)

The second most requested Lord is Torin. And I have a very special lady in mind for him....

KC: Hurt you? Why would we ever? It's not as if you had Paris make a heartbreaking sacrifice that got readers a-salivating for his story, yet now you're holding him just out of our reach. Oh, *wait...*[*pummeling Gena*] Next topic! So, I think it's got to be one of the best feelings in the world when a plot twist pops up and takes me by surprise as I'm writing it—something I didn't see coming, but that ultimately was perfect for my story. Tell me about any surprises you've had in the LOTU series.

GS: I have been shocked many times in this series! With *The Darkest Night,* I didn't know that the Greek gods had been overtaken by the Titans until Aeron made his announcement. And I had no idea Danika was the All-Seeing Eye when I made her a painter.

In *The Darkest Whisper,* I didn't know Galen was Gwen's father until she saw that painting of him. You'd think that would drive me mad, not knowing where a story is going while I'm writing it, but I like finding out the truth at the same time the reader does.

In fact, sometimes I'll be writing a scene and wonder why I'm being led in a certain direction. I've learned not to question it, though. The answers always fall into place later.

And as for upcoming plot twists, there are *many* in *The Darkest Passion* and *The Darkest Lie.* To be honest, I have *never* been so shocked by the direction of my stories. What Aeron does, what he gives up…wow, just wow. And what Gideon learns…

KC: You have to tell me!

GS: Well, lean over here and I'll tell you off the record.

[*Whispering. Nodding. Gasps.*]

KC: Wow. Okay. So let's move on before I spill. Personal dish question here. When I'm writing love scenes, sometimes I look over my shoulder and laugh nervously because I can't believe I'm "going there" in certain situations. [cough cough] Icicle [cough cough]. Do you ever do that? Have you ever had to cut or tone down a love scene? If so, will those scenes ever see the light of day?

GS: First, I need to fan myself. That icicle scene in question… genius! And oh, my God was it hot. (Gena just made a funny. Icicle = hot.)

The only love scene that's ever made me blush while writing is between Aeron and his Olivia in the upcoming *The Darkest Passion.* She's a fallen angel, has never known passion before now, and oh, does he show her. Very…enthusiastically. Gymnastics might be involved. Maybe even wings acrobatics. At this point, the details are hazy. I start to sweat every time I think about it, and have to change the subject in my mind.

But I'd like to take this moment to say, "I'm sorry, Mom. Won't happen again." Maybe.

I have had to tone down a love scene, but that scene was in my Atlantis novel *The Nymph King,* and I have since lost the version that was cut. Otherwise, I just might post it! And apologize to my mom again.

KC: Let's talk about the heroines in the LOTU series for a minute. You always find the perfect woman for each hero—your heroes have been paired with everyone from human females with paranormal powers to ancient goddesses to timid Harpies. How do you figure out what type of heroine each Lord should end up with?

GS: With Gwen in *The Darkest Whisper,* it was easy. I dreamed of her, and knew she belonged with a Lord of the Underworld. But she did not like the ones I introduced her to—the ones I needed to be writing about. Like, say, *Paris.* Then Sabin walked through the door. I had no intention of writing about him. Not for a while, at least. But…*Mine,* Gwen instantly said, and it was either write his story or let her ravage my brain. After much thought, I wrote his story. Much thought = two seconds.

As for the others, wild Anya was so different from by-the-book Lucien that I knew they were the perfect balance for each other in *The Darkest Kiss.* Maddox was so consumed by his violent urges, I knew he needed someone gentle in *The Darkest Night.*

Reyes, so far, has been the most difficult to pair. Even in my mind, while writing *The Darkest Pleasure,* he was so against tainting Danika with his darkness that he resisted the match. At one point, I thought I would have to pick someone else for him, but oh, did he throw a fit then. After that, he relented, willing to try anything to keep her.

In terms of the other Lords, I just don't know who they'll end up with. I never know until the sparks start flying.

Oh, wait. I lied. I know who Aeron and Gideon end up with, of course.

Aeron meets his match in Olivia, an angel who tempts like the devil. (You thought I was going to say makes love like the devil, didn't you? Well, gold star for you, because that's what I was really saying!)

And in *The Darkest Lie*, Gideon meets Scarlet, the keeper of the demon of Nightmares, and a woman who claims to be his wife. Just thinking about Scarlet, I'm grinning. I love that girl. She knows he's telling lies, but purposefully takes everything he says at face value. Talk about tormenting him! But then, he needed someone to shake up his world.

KC: On the subject of heroines… Of all the ones in my own series, I probably identify most with Mariketa the Awaited, though people who know me say I'm spacey like Nucking Futs Nïx (and I don't know how I feel about that). Is there one particular heroine so far in the LOTU series that you identify with more than the rest? What about a heroine who was tougher for you to write?

GS: I know what you mean about not knowing how to take things. I identify most with Anya—and readers either love her or hate her. But I identify with her, not because I enjoy chaos or world travel in the blink of an eye—I like calm and as a borderline recluse, I like being home—but because of that smart mouth. Sometimes I can't believe the things I say. (Why are you nodding, Kresley?) I have no filter, no line I refuse to cross. (Stop nodding, Kresley!)

The heroine who might more closely resemble my own personality, though, is probably Scarlet from *The Darkest Lie*.

She's sarcastic (check), faux vengeful (check) and surprisingly vulnerable (check). It'll be interesting—and frightening?—to hear what readers think of her.

The most difficult heroine to write about was, of course, Danika. She underwent such a vast change—from terrified hostage to bait to woman in love to relic of the gods—that I sometimes floundered with what to do with her.

KC: But happily for us, you worked it out with her. Good Gena! Speaking of Danika, I love your character names. Ashlyn, Danika, Anya… How do you come up with them? Is there a name—or a character—from someone else's book or series [*exaggerated stage wink*] that you wish you'd come up with yourself first?

GS: The characters either tell me their names before I start writing the book or I scour baby books until I hear a "That's me!" inside my head. (A fact that horrifies my mother. She tells me I should never admit 1. to having people in my head, and 2. that those people actually talk to me.) All of the ladies mentioned named themselves.

As for a name I wish I'd come up with myself—Mariketa, your heroine from *Wicked Deeds on a Winter's Night*. I freaking love that name. But then, I also wish I was dating Bowen MacRieve, Mariketa's man. Well, and also dating Lachlan from *A Hunger Like No Other.* And Rydstrom from *Kiss of a Demon King*. Yes, I am a romance novel hero slut. I can't be blamed, though. You create such amazing men! I just need to take up residence in your brain. Or your books.

KC: You're one to talk about creating amazing men. But yes, on the subject of your residing in my brain—it would be so much easier if we just morphed into one. And would

really save on our phone bills. Sigh. Anyhoo, so Her Nïxness just got back from an appearance in *The Darkest Whisper* and will tell us nothing about it, just grins mischievously. How did you pick which Lord would catch her wandering from one series to another?

GS: She picked. I believe she said something like, "You can let Torin see me and live, or let someone else and suffer. Your pick, Showalter." That's not an exact quote, you understand, as I swore never to reveal the truth because the "world could implode." But now, Torin wants a taste of those ears. I'm going to have to send in a distraction.

And now the plot thickens…

KC: Let's talk about Cronus's artifacts for a second. The Lords are on a quest to find Pandora's box before the Hunters beat them to it. To do so, they first need to get their hands on four separate artifacts—the Cage of Compulsion, the All-Seeing Eye, the Cloak of Invisibility and the Paring Rod. So far they're two down, two to go. Any hints as to which artifact might be discovered next?

GS: I will tell you that the Lords are actually going to get their hands on all four artifacts—but not for long. Something happens and they lose… Great, now I've said too much. Kresley, you can get me to spill more secrets than anyone I know. It's your smile! It says, *Tell me everything,* and I can't resist!

KC: Do you want to tell us how you came up with these four particular artifacts?

GS: Well, I was perusing mythology books and every time some kind of godly weapon or relic was mentioned, I wrote it down. Then I did the process of elimination. (The Philosopher's Stone got cut, as did the Thunderbolt, different types of armor, shields, swords, the Trident, bows and treasures.) What could be used to hide *and* find something? Why? How?

The four mentioned here stood out the most, only I still have no freaking clue what the Paring Rod does. Cronus is so damn secretive!

KC: Do you know at this point in your writing where Pandora's box might be hiding? Just a thought, but has anyone looked under the "Paring Rod"? (No need to thank me [*fogging and buffing nails*]. I live to be helpful in little ways like this.)

GS: Excellent tip, my sweet! [*curses under breath*] I have no idea where that stupid box is. Oops. My frustration is showing. I really wish I was a planner. I wish I had plotted the entire series so I would know what direction to go in so the Lords could finally find it. They do not like not knowing where that stu—uh, box is, and they let me know about this dislike every day!

KC: So if the gods cursed you to house one of the demons from Pandora's box inside you, which would you pick and why? Which would you absolutely never want to get stuck with?

GS: I would definitely want to be possessed by the demon of Narcissism. You haven't met her yet, but oh…good times! To never doubt yourself? To always know how wonderful you are? Yes, yes, a thousand times yes!

The only downside is that, when you're *that* confident, you tend to get into all kinds of…sticky situations. But with the right warrior at your side—or under you, whatever—"sticky" really means "fun."

As for who I would most want to avoid...let's see...so many choices...but probably Pain. I am a baby and I know it. Stubbed toe? Yeah, I sob like the world just ended.

KC: Do you have a set number of LOTU books envisioned? I **might be happy with an even hundred. (What do you mean that's *a lot?* Work it the *%$& out, Showalter!) [*composing self*] And do you know who the very last book will revolve around?**

GS: I wish! But alas, I'm clueless as to how many Lords of the Underworld books there will be—though I am strongly considering one hundred right now. Really.

Besides that, all I know for sure is that I plan to write a book for every Lord. And William, my sweet William. His heroine might be named Gina. Or Jeanna. Only time will tell. Oh, and I would like to write about Kaia, the Harpy. And maybe Galen. And that's it. Except for, like, ninety others. I mean, the angels are now in play and there are other demon-possessed immortals out there.

The last story will probably be...you know, I actually have no idea. No, that's not true. The correct answer is, the last story will be about the most stubborn warrior. That changes with every story I write. Right now, however, they all rate pretty high on the Mule Meter.

KC: One thing I catch myself doing a lot is thinking back over the first inkling of an idea I had for certain books. With *A Hunger Like No Other,* one of the first scenes I imagined was this massive Highlander werewolf running down this ethereal female and rasping, "Never run from one such as

me. You will no' get away—*and we like it.*" Do you do this, too? What are some of your favorite first inklings?

GS: Those inklings are powerful, aren't they? So, so powerful. I mean, as you were speaking, I had one of the best inklings of my life. *I* was the one that massive Highlander was chasing....

Ten minutes later [coughs]

What were we discussing? Inklings? That's right. And massive Highlanders...

Fifteen minutes later [throws ice water]

Inklings. Right. Yes. I've had them and do I ever love them! I can write an entire book because of one inkling (and those are usually the books I love the most). I have three favorites. In *The Darkest Night,* I saw Maddox being stabbed to death by his best friend, then awakening, then being stabbed to death again.

In *The Darkest Whisper,* I saw Gwen trapped in a glass cage, saw the door to that cage open, then saw her disappear and return holding a man's trachea—and nothing else. (Yes, I have the sweetest dreams.)

In *The Darkest Prison,* I saw a man on his knees, his chest bloody because his skin had just been carved off, and he was screaming at the heavens in fury. I knew a tattoo had just been removed and he wanted that tattoo back. It was only when I sat down to write the story that I realized the tattoo was actually the heroine's name—and he hadn't always liked it.

I just realized that my inklings are violent. What does that mean about me, do you think? Wait, don't answer that.

KC: Veering off topic as we wrap things up, I have to ask you the burning question on every reader's mind: What is your favorite Gena Showalter novel? (Mine rotates on a continual basis—whichever new release is in my hot little hands, about to be devoured!)

GS: Ah, yes. The burning question. This is going to seem mushy and gushy, but I love them all equally.

Okay, okay. Fine. Mama has a favorite, but if Mama were to mention that favorite, Mama would get into trouble with the other babies, so Mama is zipping her lips.

The Darkest Lie. Who said that?

KC: One last thing—you have a LOTU book to write, don't you? If you only had twenty dollars in your purse, what would you buy? Actually, let's make this more challenging: what would you buy—*if not for me?*

GS: A book (yours), a bottle of wine (cheapest white in stock) and chocolate chip cookie dough. And now, every massive Highland warrior out there knows how to seduce me. Come to Mama…

Bestselling author Kresley Cole is a master's grad in English and a former world-ranked athlete, who now concentrates on her dream of writing romance. She has followed her highly acclaimed historicals with the continuing Immortals After Dark *series, a sizzling paranormal romance collection. In 2007, Cole won the prestigious Romance Writers of America RITA Award for best paranormal for her novel* A Hunger Like No Other, *and in January 2009, she became a #1* New York Times *and* Publishers Weekly *bestselling author with her sixth* IAD *installment,* Kiss of a Demon King. *Her latest release is* Pleasure of a Dark Prince *(February 2010), about ruthless werewolf Garreth MacRieve and Lucia the Huntress, the exquisite archer who's become his obsession.*

Kresley invites you to visit her Web site at:
www.kresleycole.com.

FILES FROM THE PRIVATE RECORDS OF DEAN STEFANO,
THE HUNTERS' SECOND-IN-COMMAND

THE GREATER GOOD. That's all I've ever fought for. A life without evil. Without sickness and violence. Without corruption and greed. That life is within my grasp. I know this, and that is what drives me so tirelessly. And yes, you might think me ruthless, the way I kill and seem to use others, but if you knew what could be—peace and hope and love—you would be fighting with me. You would be doing the same "terrible" things.

Who knows? One day you might. One day you might be like me, waking up every morning of every day, thinking, this could be it. This could be the day we find the box. The day we rid the world of Pandora's demons. The day that begins our eternal celebration because we live in a world of absolute bliss.

Am I distressed that we haven't reached that day yet? Yes. We are close, though…I know that, too. Meanwhile, I continue to be vigilant, to study the demons and the men that house them, meticulously documenting my observations in the hopes that someday they can be put to good use.

And just remember. If you aren't working with us, you are working *against* us. Remember also that our enemies tend to die, slowly and painfully….

–Dean Stefano

Maddox

(BUDAPEST CONTINGENT)

Demon: Violence

Height: 6' 4"

Hair: Black

Eyes: Violet (*Note:* eyes glow red when angry)

Butterfly tattoo: Upper left shoulder, wrapping around to his back

Other distinguishing marks: Demon's skeletal face becomes visible through subject's skin when subject is angered.

Preferred weapon: Fists

Demon culpability: The stabbing death of Pandora, and thereby the disappearance of her box, can be traced directly to Violence. In modern society Violence is deemed responsible for street-gang warfare, rape, murder and terrorism.

Notable background: Curse resulting from Pandora's slaying caused the subject to be killed each night and resurrected each day for centuries. Curse has now been broken—methods unclear. Subject still erupts into fits of violence and should be presumed volatile and highly dangerous.

Achilles heel: Recent emotional attachment to human female Ashlyn Darrow, former para-audiologist for the World Institute of Parapsychology who now resides at Budapest fortress. I cannot help but believe that if her mentor, the late Dr. Frederick McIntosh, hadn't hidden from her the true purpose of her work at the Institute, Darrow would not have defected to the Lords' camp. *Note:* Darrow is believed pregnant with subject's child. Due date to be determined.

Objectives: Capture Ashlyn Darrow if possible, use her as bait for subject to rescue, capture subject and imprison him until such time as Pandora's box is found. *Note:* Beware Darrow's ability to stand in one place and hear every conversation that ever took place there. Utter silence will be needed for any recon or capture missions. The element of surprise is crucial.

Lucien

(LEADER, BUDAPEST CONTINGENT)

Demon: Death

Height: 6' 6"

Hair: Black, shoulder-length

Eyes: Mismatched—one brown (normal eye) and one blue (believed to allow subject to see into the spiritual world)

Butterfly tattoo: Upper left shoulder, front of chest

Other distinguishing marks: Face and body are covered in scars. Subject emits an odor of roses presumed to be linked to his demon.

Preferred weapon: Knives. Beware poisoned tips.

Demon culpability: Death is ultimately responsible for deciding which souls ascend to heaven and which are ushered to Hell. It's believed that the subject uses his bias against the Hunters not only to kill their bodies, but to unfairly ensure that their souls never make it to heaven.

Notable background: Subject is believed to have disfigured his own face and body centuries ago in a fit of rage, indicating an unstable temperament and a harmful nature. Subject can travel outside his body and has been known to transport himself from one location to the next faster than the eye can see, making him a unique threat.

Achilles heel: Two of note. The first, when subject's… soul, if that's what it is, leaves his body, that body is left vulnerable. That might be the perfect time to strike. Second, subject seems to have grown attached to Anya, minor Greek goddess of Anarchy. *Also noteworthy:* Anya is believed to have been bound by a curse herself, possibly hampering her powers. Recon team to investigate further in the hopes of exploiting the knowledge for the greater good.

Objectives: Take a divide-and-conquer approach by separating subject from the minor goddess of Anarchy so subject will suffer. If we can kill the goddess, forcing Death to separate soul from body, he will be most vulnerable. *Note:* The minor goddess has a penchant for petty theft, incendiary behavior and general insubordination. Following a recent confrontation in Chicago, she has been deemed a nemesis of the angel Galen and thus her permanent capture is of particular interest to the Hunters.

Reyes

(BUDAPEST CONTINGENT)

Demon: Pain

Height: 6'5"

Hair: Dark brown

Eyes: Brown

Butterfly tattoo: Chest and neck

Other distinguishing marks: Deeply tanned skin; frequently sports scabs caused by self-mutilation

Preferred weapon: Daggers; sword; guns

Demon culpability: Physical pain and suffering throughout the ages are attributed to this demon's acts of random cruelty.

Notable background: Subject has been witnessed going to excruciating lengths to cause himself pain. Jumping off rooftops and cutting his flesh are among his pastimes.

Achilles heel: Subject formed an attachment to human female Danika Ford following her kidnapping at the hands of fellow Lord Aeron. I personally did my utmost to recruit Danika to our cause, even convincing her to stage her own (second) kidnapping so the demons would rescue her and unwittingly bring a spy into their midst. The woman showed tremendous potential but was ultimately seduced by the dark side and aligned her loyalties with the Lords. I count her defection as a personal failure.

Objectives: Separate subject from Danika. Imprison him until Pandora's box can be found. Demonstrate to Danika the consequences of choosing the wrong allegiance in battle.

Paris

(BUDAPEST CONTINGENT)

Demon: Promiscuity

Height: 6' 8"

Hair: Varying shades of brown and black

Eyes: Blue

Butterfly tattoo: Lower back

Other distinguishing marks: Subject is widely regarded as the most physically appealing of all the Lords.

Preferred weapon: Sword

Demon culpability: Out-of-wedlock pregnancy, sexually transmitted diseases and infidelity all can be laid at Promiscuity's doorstep.

Notable background: Subject weakens without frequent physical release and cannot have sexual relations with the same woman twice. Subject has been known to seek out male partners as a last resort if no women are available, though he does not appear to enjoy such forays.

Achilles heel: While imprisoned in Hunters' research facility in Athens, subject formed a fascinating bond with the late female Hunter Sienna Blackstone (R.I.P.) and managed to overcome his demon's aversion to repeated sexual contact with the same woman. Since his untimely escape to Budapest, he has been reported to be relying heavily on ambrosia to regulate his moods and get him through the day.

Objectives: Exploit subject's dependence on ambrosia if possible. Perhaps even arrange for him to receive a tainted batch. Dangle the promise of information about Sienna in order to lure him back to Athens facility for further testing.

Aeron

(BUDAPEST CONTINGENT)

Demon: Wrath

Height: 6’ 6”

Hair: Military-cropped, brown

Eyes: Violet

Butterfly tattoo: Middle of back

Other distinguishing marks: A pair of black gossamer wings hidden by slits in his back when not in use. Face and body are covered with tattoos of war scenes, weaponry and the demon’s victims. Two eyebrow rings.

Preferred weapon: Subject does not discriminate and embraces any weapon at his disposal.

Demon culpability: Wrath ostensibly preys only on victims it considers deserving of punishment. However, this pretense of meting out “justice” is clearly the demon’s twisted attempt to rationalize its killing sprees and evil deeds so it can continue to cause harm without consequences.

Notable background: Subject was taken over by bloodlust due to a curse of unknown origins and nearly killed human female Danika Ford in addition to her maternal grandmother, mother and older sister. Though the bloodlust seems to have passed, subject continues to be considered a menace to society.

Achilles heel: Subject views himself as godlike and humans as fragile and beneath him; however, his current determination to repay his fellow demon Paris for deeds unknown might prove a weak spot to be exploited. Subject is also devoted to the female demon minion Legion and has sworn to protect her from harm. Additionally, subject appears to be having apparent hallucinations that an invisible presence is spying on him.

Objective: Use subject's devotion to fellow Lords and the minion Legion against him. Recon team is also determining ways to turn his hallucinations to the Hunters' advantage.

Torin

(BUDAPEST CONTINGENT)

Demon: Disease

Height: 6' 5"

Hair: White, shoulder-length

Eyes: Green

Butterfly tattoo: Stomach

Other distinguishing marks: Always wears long black gloves

Preferred weapon: As subject is confined to the Budapest fortress he has dubbed "the House of the Damned," he does not generally use weapons but is believed to have gun and sword training.

Demon culpability: Disease is responsible for at least two known plagues that resulted in thousands of casualties. This demon is also at the root of cancer deaths and all additional pestilence, most recently the dreaded Swine Flu pandemic.

Notable background: Subject is unable to touch another living being skin-to-skin without infecting it with disease; subject wears protective clothing at all times and maintains his distance from others to prevent such an occurrence. Subject chooses to hide in the Lords' fortress rather than accept the public blame he deserves for the illnesses he continues to cause, despite his "attempts" to keep the world "safe."

Achilles heel: Subject's battle skills have likely diminished due to his confinement. He could be the weak link of the Lords and vulnerable to capture. A suspected relationship with female Lord Cameo has distracted the subject, and could also be used to Hunters' advantage.

Objectives: Exploit the subject's unique vulnerabilities and use this weakest link to take down the rest of the Lords. If we could somehow arrange for subject to touch the other Lords, they would not be killed, but they would never again be able to touch their loved ones without killing them. Such a realization might just cause them to turn themselves in.

Sabin

(LEADER OF THE GREECE CONTINGENT)

Demon: Doubt

Height: 6' 7"

Hair: Brown

Eyes: Gold-brown

Butterfly tattoo: Right ribcage and waist

Other distinguishing marks: Wears a necklace believed to be a gift to him from his deceased friend, Baden, demon of Distrust, the Hunters' first victim.

Preferred weapon: Subject used to rely on knives, guns, throwing stars et al, but now, like the coward he is, he prefers to hide behind his Harpy bride for protection.

Demon culpability: The vilest of all demons whispers insecurities into the ears of anyone within reach and causes crippling, at times life-threatening self-doubt. This demon and the despicable creature who houses it are directly responsible for the suicide of my beloved wife, Darla, eleven years ago.

Notable background: I find it impossible to write objectively about my most deeply hated foe. This monster who calls himself a man seduced my faithful wife away from me with false promises and dirty lies and coaxed her to betray my secrets. When he'd gotten what he needed from her, he let his demon go to work, and the next thing I knew, my wife had slashed her wrists.

Achilles Heel: His single-minded devotion to Gwendolyn the Timid, his Harpy wife. Due to recent complications at our Chicago training facility, we are uncertain as to the extent to which we might be able to use her against him. But sometimes it is better to ask for forgiveness than permission.

Objectives: Secretly, without Galen's knowledge, separate subject from his wife. Seduce her, as subject likes to seduce other men's wives, and arrange for subject to find her dead, bleeding body.

Gideon

(GREECE CONTINGENT)

Demon: Lies

Height: 6' 3"

Hair: Dyed Blue

Eyes: Blue, kohl-rimmed

Butterfly tattoo: Right thigh

Other distinguishing marks: Multiple piercings and general Goth appearance

Preferred weapon: All of them. Subject seems to have no specific preference, using whatever is nearby.

Demon culpability: Lies has infiltrated politics worldwide, resulting in false promises from world leaders and the disintegration of modern society.

Notable background: Subject is unable to tell the truth without experiencing terrible pain. My forefathers were able to capture and contain subject for a prolonged period of time and, in the course of limb-regeneration experiments, removed subject's feet. Unfortunately, subject ultimately escaped with the aid of his demon cohorts and both his feet have since grown back. The feet we removed, however, we are still in possession of. We exacted revenge in Chicago recently with the removal of both subject's hands, but again were unable to contain him for long. We now have the removed hands, as well.

Achilles heel: Unknown. It is impossible to learn anything of use from this disgusting liar.

Objective: Capture this demon once and for all and rid the world of his offensive presence. Also, continue with experiments of the removed limbs, using them to hopefully create our own immortal warrior.

(GREECE CONTINGENT)

Demon: Misery

Height: 5’7”

Hair: Long, black

Eyes: Silver

Butterfly tattoo: Lower back, wings spreading around to both hips

Other distinguishing marks: Her voice is enough to make you want to kill yourself. Earplugs are needed when around her.

Preferred weapon: Semi-automatic, long-range rifles

Demon culpability: Misery is responsible for mental health issues such as depression and anxiety. The fact that both are reported at higher rates today than ever before suggests that the demon’s reach is increasing.

Notable background: Subject causes profound emotional anguish in everyone around her. Additionally, subject was, until recently, believed to be the lone female Lord of the Underworld. New events suggest that additional female Lords might in fact exist.

Achilles heel: Subject is believed to have a relationship with Torin, keeper of Disease. Subject will be closely observed for any physical or emotional vulnerability that might pave the way for an opportunity to capture her. But because of the supposed relationship with Disease, protective gear will be needed when apprehending her.

Objectives: Recon team is exploring ways to force subject to use her voice to our advantage.

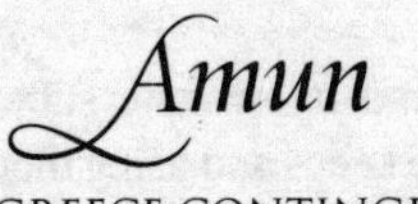

Amun

(GREECE CONTINGENT)

Demon: Secrets

Height: 6' 6"

Hair: Brown

Eyes: Brown

Butterfly tattoo: Right calf

Other distinguishing marks: Dark skin

Preferred weapon: Things of an exotic nature.

Demon culpability: The demon of Secrets fosters a lack of communication that contributes to individual issues such as the breakdown of marriages and global problems such as breaches of national security and the inability to achieve world peace.

Notable background: Subject is unable to speak without the secrets of the world pouring out of his mouth—as I regrettably experienced first-hand at our Chicago facility. Also of note, when he speaks, you hear the voice of the person whose secret he is revealing.

Achilles heel: Subject's fear of speaking might be utilized to our advantage.

Objectives: Capture and interrogate subject in the hopes of discerning the secrets he keeps and using them against the Lords.

(GREECE CONTINGENT)

Demon: Defeat

Height: 6' 5"

Hair: Blond

Eyes: Blue

Butterfly tattoo: Left hip

Other distinguishing marks: Subject was created, not born, yet has a birthmark on the right side of his buttocks. Small, brown and jagged at the edges.

Preferred weapon: Subject embraces all weaponry.

Demon culpability: The demon of Defeat is determined to win at all costs and will do whatever it takes to ensure victory. Defeat has brought about the downfall of athletes worldwide due to its encouragement of illegal tactics like steroids to obtain a win.

Notable background: Subject cannot lose an argument or battle without succumbing to intense physical agony and prolonged sleep.

Achilles heel: Subject's inability to lose gracefully.

Objectives: Issue a challenge the demon cannot refuse, one that leads him straight into a trap.

(GREECE CONTINGENT)

Demon: Disaster

Height: 6' 4"

Hair: Mixture of brown, black and gold

Eyes: Hazel

Butterfly tattoo: Right hip

Other distinguishing marks: We are still searching.

Preferred weapon: Rifles and other long-range weaponry

Demon culpability: Disaster can be held accountable for everything from traffic accidents to construction site fatalities to plane crashes. It is harmful, often lethal, to anyone and anything it comes into contact with.

Notable background: Subject is unable to move without causing ceilings to collapse, vehicles to explode and other assorted catastrophes to occur. Miraculously and despicably, subject seems to escape injury from such incidents, but those around him are less fortunate.

Achilles heel: Unknown

Objectives: Recon team is exploring ways to isolate and capture subject and channel the incidents he causes into a strategy that will be advantageous to us.

BEHIND THE SCENES:
Creating the Lords of the Underworld

I'M OFTEN ASKED HOW I created my Lords of the Underworld series, which revolves around a group of immortal warriors who, cursed by the gods to house demons inside them, embark on a quest for an ancient relic that will take them around the world on a journey beyond their wildest dreams. The answer I most often give is: I had never liked the myth of Pandora, where one curious female was blamed for all the world's misery, so I decided to rewrite that myth—and blame men. But, to be honest, that isn't how the series originated; that's just how it ended up after tons of agonizing.

Let me explain. When I sat down to create the very first Lords of the Underworld book, all I knew was that I wanted to write a story about Death. The Grim Reaper. So, I wrote several chapters of a book where the Grim Reaper swept through Las Vegas to take the soul of a woman destined to die the next day. Only, he woke up married to her instead. But something about that story didn't feel right, and I trashed the pages.

Knowing I needed to start over, I began to question the main character. *Why* was this man Death? What was his history? Had he always escorted souls to the hereafter? To my delight—and frustration—each new question gave birth to another. Those questions, and their answers, were all I could think about.

Then, one day, Death finally opened up and told me about his friends: Pain, Misery, Doubt, Violence, Disease, Secrets,

Wrath, Promiscuity, Distrust, Lies, Disaster and Defeat. Of course, more questions followed. How were they friends? Why were they known as these terrible things?

And then I remembered Pandora's box and the demons trapped inside. Of course, I thought, more excited than I'd ever been. *They* were the demons.

Only, rather than immortal warriors being possessed by these demons, as you know the Lords today, I envisioned the men themselves as the demons and rewrote the first few chapters of Death's new story to reflect that. But again, something didn't seem right. Maybe because Death was no longer the character that claimed my attention. Violence was; he demanded I pay attention to him. I *had* to know more about him, this man who would erupt into fits of madness at the slightest provocation. And so, once more I ditched the chapters I'd been working on and tried again, focusing on Violence, aka Maddox, this time.

Finally. I was on the right path, and I knew it—and yet, after writing the first three chapters of Maddox's story, I realized something *still* was not right. In fact, here's the blurb I had written to describe the book:

> He is the demon of Violence and he's been trapped inside Pandora's box, alone, simply waiting to be unleashed. Then a master thief steals the box and captures his heart, as well. Together they must hunt down the spirits that escaped thousands of years ago, and lock them back up before chaos destroys them both.

And yes, I still have those three chapters. For the curious among you, they are included in this guide. I titled that book *Awakening Pandora.* But you see, I didn't like that Violence was still inside the box—been there and done that with *The*

Pleasure Slave, which I published in 2005—and I didn't like that he planned to lock the other demons back up but would not lock himself up, as well. Where was the fairness in that? What made him so different from the others?

So I sat down and had a heart-to-heart with myself. How could I make the storyline better, yet still utilize the myth of Pandora? And that's when the answer came to me. All of the demons had already been released, and they'd been living among us for thousands of years.

Finally! I wrote the entire book, lost in Maddox's new past and the volatile world around him. And here's another behind-the-scenes tidbit for you: in that manuscript, Paris was originally named Challen; Aeron was Vrede; Reyes was Raine and Galen was Hector. Their names were ultimately changed to make them more accessible and easier to pronounce, and because I wanted names from as many different cultures as possible since my Greek and Titan gods were representing the entire world.

Oh, and in case you're curious, here was my blurb for book two in the series (which ultimately became *The Darkest Kiss*). As you'll see, I was still determined to work in my dying heroine/married in Vegas story:

> Death, the Grim Reaper. Freed from Pandora's Box thousands of years ago, Lucien has spent his time collecting souls and escorting them to their final resting place. Until he encounters his next victim in a Las Vegas nightclub…and, in a drunken haze, marries her instead.

You're probably wondering about my original plans for book three (*The Darkest Pleasure*), as well. Here's that blurb:

> The spirit of pain is unexpectedly given to a modern woman, who suddenly begins wielding powers beyond

belief. The Lords of the Underworld find her with every intention of killing her. Except one of the warriors wants her for his own…

Now, I did not start working on either of those books. I turned in Maddox's story, *The Darkest Night,* and waited to hear from my editor. And oh, I'm glad I did! She helped me see the final remaining problem. With the Lords having been trapped inside the box themselves, they were *too* tortured. They'd never known anything but Hell, isolation and pain, which left a gap between character and reader, and I had not built a bridge between the two.

Back to the drawing board I went, but this time, I brought my editor—brilliant, genius woman—with me. We tossed around ideas and came up with the stories you know today.

Some Lords have traveled easier roads than others, but I promise you, all will eventually get their happily-ever-after. So far Maddox (Violence), Lucien (Death), Reyes (Pain) and Sabin (Doubt) have found their mates. Aeron (Wrath) and Gideon (Lies) are next. Who's after that? you might be wondering. And how do I decide?

Well, to answer the first question: Amun (Secrets) will likely be up next. You'll see why in *The Darkest Lie.* After him, probably Strider (Defeat). To answer the second question: I don't. The men decide for me.

I am not a plotter. At all. Even the thought of planning a story from start to finish makes me want to drop to the floor in the fetal position, sucking my thumb and crying for my mommy. I simply sit down with the grain of an idea (and as you've now read, I've had a lot of grains for this particular series) and allow the characters to take me wherever they want me to go. Which means their stories unfold as they give me the details—and believe me, they are impervious to my begging. 'Cause yeah,

I'd love to write about certain characters before others—*cough* Paris *cough*—but every time I try, I end up staring at a blank screen. Stubborn bastards!

I might torture them in the books, but in the end, they torture me far, far more.

I hope you enjoyed this glimpse into my process. Not to mention the result.

Wishing you all the best!

Gena Showalter

AWAKENING PANDORA

PROLOGUE

AT ONE TIME, HE'D BEEN a man. A warrior. A king. His enemies had trembled in fear, and his lovers had trembled in ecstasy. Both had begged for the sweet release only he could give: death or pleasure. A slash of his blade or a caress of his hand. Life was sweet, so sweet.

But one night, everything changed.

A woman came to him, the most beautiful he'd ever beheld. Seductive, seemingly guileless. Legend would one day call her Pandora. He would one day call her Witch.

The first time she visited him, she wore a white virgin's robe, and the hem danced around her ankles as if the very air around her could not help but touch her. *Know* her. She had hair as dark as a raven's wing, a face so delicate it almost hurt to gaze upon, and eyes so deep a violet that looking into them was like peering into a never ending abyss.

No one understood how she'd entered his fortress, only that she'd demanded an audience with him. He'd granted her one, certain she was one of a thousand others who wished to know the taste of a king. He'd meant to scold her for such daring and send her on her way. Now, seeing her…

"You may speak," he told her, waving his royal hand through the air.

"I come to offer you the world, King Maddox. This one, and any other you might desire." Her voice was lilting, pure enchantment. "Magic will be yours to wield. Time and space will bow to your every whim. Power beyond your wildest imaginings will flow from your hands."

Seated on his throne of gold, Maddox laughed in disbelief. The strongest of his men surrounded him in a half circle and they, too, laughed at her words. Such things were impossible in this dark world of war and sacrifice. Magic and power belonged to those beyond their reach, the gods and goddesses who rarely ventured here. Still, the claim certainly gained his full attention.

Females lied to him constantly as they fought for a place in his bed and at his side. In this, the beauteous creature was no different.

"What do you ask in return for this *gift,* sweet?" he asked dryly. "Marriage? To become queen? The right to bear my child?"

She raised her chin, proud, beguiling. "I ask only that you and your army hide my greatest treasure."

He nearly snorted. Her greatest treasure, in his mind, was her body, and he was more than happy to hide it in his bed. "I accept," he said, grinning. "My men, however, will have to decide for themselves."

One by one his brothers-in-arms stepped forward, each mimicking his acceptance. They, too, were smiling widely.

The woman licked her lips in anticipation. "May I kiss you, great king, to complete our bargain?"

He arched a brow. "I would be most disappointed if you didn't."

Slowly she climbed the marble stairs and onto the dais, her gown still flowing around her like a phantom, alive, separate from her somehow. When she stood before him, a fragrant breeze wafted to his nostrils, a breeze of midnight tempests and...power? The magic she'd sworn to bestow upon him? No. Surely not.

"Your lips," she said.

"Take them." He didn't shift from his reclined position, forcing her to bend, to come to him. She did. Closer. Closer still. And then her lips gently pressed against his. She opened for him, but didn't sweep her tongue into his mouth as he expected. No, she uttered a single word. His new prison. His downfall. His sole reason for existence, he would learn.

"Violence," she said. A gust of wind burst from her mouth and into his, down his throat and into his stomach, his bones. He was suddenly unable to move, locked in place as the brutal wind invaded every corner of his body, *attaching* itself. Becoming part of him. His muscles shook and burned. His stomach quivered. Pain, so much pain.

He wanted to curse, to fight. To kill. What was happening to him? The wind was solidifying, becoming a…no. No! It was becoming a living entity, another consciousness inside him. He could hear the savageness of its thoughts, could feel the darkness of its desires. He gritted his teeth so forcefully, blood filled his mouth. *Grab your sword. Attack!* But he could not. He was still trapped, helpless to the wind-creature as it ravaged him.

The woman moved to the man at his right, and there was nothing Maddox could do, nothing he could say to stop her. Her lips descended upon Baden, a scarred, battle-hardened man with more integrity, more honor, than anyone else Maddox had encountered.

"Distrust," she whispered, and Baden, too, was frozen in place, shaking and under siege.

Over and over, she approached the warriors, kissing them, uttering a different word each time. "Pain."

"Wrath."

"Death."

"Disease."

"Promiscuity."

After a while, her voice faded from his ears and he knew nothing except darkness.

When she left, he didn't know. He only knew that when he awakened, he was stronger than he'd ever been, faster, *better.* The creature, the second consciousness, lay dormant now, so he tried not to concern himself with it. But magic, he learned, was indeed his to command. Time and space did bow to his every whim, and power beyond his wildest imaginings did flow from his hands, just as the woman had claimed.

He reveled in his new abilities, embraced them, enjoyed everything about them—until the beast inside him awoke, no longer content to endure his rule. The beast inside *all* of the men awoke.

That's when the woman began to call upon them.

The beasts were her servants, so in turn, *they* became her servants. When she was angered, it was Vrede she commanded to wreak destruction. He killed without mercy, forced by the beast inside him to unleash a torrent of wrath upon whomever she desired. There was no way to stop it, no way to fight against it.

Challen she called for fucking. Torin she called for plague. Lucien she called for death.

Over the years, he and his warriors lost touch with their humanity. They became wild, nearly uncontrollable, and more vicious than their creator had ever anticipated. Maddox, more so than most. He was the epitome of anger, fury and rage, so lethal a single glance at him could scare the bravest of souls to death.

When Pandora realized she would soon lose all control of them, she locked the essence of them inside a box. They stayed in this box for many centuries, able to observe the world around them but unable to act. Yet, as time often did, memories of their treacherous deeds dulled. Pandora remembered only the good things they'd done for her. They'd punished her enemies, after all. They'd destroyed those unworthy of her. They'd saddened those who did not deserve happiness.

And so, one night she opened the box, meaning to release only one or two of her pets. All but one burst forward before she was able to slam the lid back into place. Yet the beasts were no longer hers to command, and they hated her for what she'd done to them.

Pandora discarded the box and fled for her life, hiding so that none could find her.

The beasts scattered across the world, wreaking havoc. The one still trapped inside the box, well, he waited…and he waited.…

CHAPTER ONE

"YOU GET CAUGHT, AND I'M hauling ass to Mexico."

"Your concern for me is touching. Really." Fighting a grin, Farrah Roberts anchored a small flesh-colored headphone on her left ear and eyed River Jackson, the only person in the world that she trusted. He was also the nineteen-year-old kid responsible for making sure she wasn't caught. "Just watch the feed and warn me if I pick up a shadow."

"Rub it in a little more, why don't you?" he said with a pout. "You're the big, bad thief and I'm the sidekick. I get the grunt work."

"I'm going to leave the target's apartment from the roof. You really want to dangle twenty-nine stories from a thin piece of wire?"

"Hell, yeah," he said, but they both knew he lied. River was afraid of heights. The little shit would pee his pants.

Right now they sat inside a large white van that looked like any other service van parked on Main Street. What was inside *their* vehicle, however, was much different than any of the others. Monitors that revealed much of the activity in and around the apartment complex she was about to enter, as well as computers and blueprints.

Farrah slid a silver ring down her left index finger. If tonight was a success, she would not have to use what was hidden inside it. "You've already hacked into the power system?"

River snorted. “What, I’m an amateur now? Of course I’m in.”

Her lips twitched at his affront. He could hack into anything, anytime, no matter how secure it was, and he wasn’t shy about trumpeting his abilities. Farrah loved his confidence, so different from the lack of self-esteem he’d once exhibited.

She’d found him wandering the streets six years ago, had taken him in though she’d been a child herself, and paid for his education. He’d been a shy little thing back then, unsure, awkward and desperate for attention.

“So…how do I look?” she asked, pinning a small black microphone to the collar of her top.

He eyed her up and down, from the slicked ponytail holding her dark hair captive, to the trench coat hiding the black body suit she’d practically sewed to each of her curves, to the shiny boots on her feet.

“You look like you charge two hundred dollars an hour for bondage and pain. No way you’ll blend with the snobs who live in Crescent Moon.”

“I don’t have to blend. I just have to make it into the elevator without being stopped.”

“Even if you’re stopped, I’m controlling their video recordings here. They won’t get your face on tape. Not permanently, at least.”

“But they will get a description to give the police,” she said dryly.

“Right now, with your makeup and contacts, your face looks like a thousand others.” River hefted the black velvet bag that contained her tools and anchored it on her shoulder. “Get out of here. I’m bored.”

Farrah saw the apprehension in his emerald eyes and bent over to kiss his cheek. He worried about her every time she worked—despite the fact that she’d last been caught ten years ago, at the age of fifteen. “I’ll be fine.”

"Yeah, you will. 'Cause I'm watching your back."

Grinning, she exited the van's passenger door and entered the cold Dallas night. River reached out and pinched her butt just before she shut the door. Her smile widened. She didn't bother turning around to flip him off; the van's windows were tinted so she wouldn't get to see his reaction.

"Testing," she whispered into her mouthpiece. It was taped to her cheek and so thin she often forgot it was there. "Testing."

"Copy is good," River said.

"Asswipe," she muttered, and he laughed.

"You liked it—you know you did."

"If you're not careful, I'll demote you to laundry boy."

"Puh-lease. You need me."

The moon was high, bright, and the street was busy as she maneuvered across. They'd parked a half-mile from the building, and she made the trek through shadows and back alleys without incident. No one paid her any attention. When Crescent's towering chrome and glass came into view, she whispered, "Entering in thirty."

"Tom and John are at the screens, drinking coffee and reading a magazine."

Male names: that meant both of the guards inside the building were armed. Just in case she and River had an unwanted listener, anyone with a weapon was deemed a boy; everyone else got stuck with names like Bubbles and Bambi.

As predicted, Farrah entered the lobby thirty seconds later. Except for the guards, the lobby was deserted. Good. That's why she'd chosen Saturday at midnight. The old were in bed, and the young were out partying. Her boots clicked on the pink-veined marble, bouncing her bag at her side.

Showtime.

"Can I help you, miss?" one of the guards asked. He clanked

his coffee onto the gray countertop and pushed to his feet. He was a burly man in his late fifties. Friendly face, tired eyes.

Farrah didn't slow her steps, but tossed him an I'm-so-innocent smile over her shoulder. "Acting like you don't recognize me? Not funny," she said. "You know I live here."

Maybe he was embarrassed not to "recognize" her. Maybe he was just too tired to care. But he didn't try to stop her as she entered the elevator. And then the doors closed, shutting her inside. Alone. A relieved sigh parted her lips. She would have preferred to have rented one of the apartments and move around freely, without (much) artiface, but all of the apartments were already rented and there was a year-long waiting list. No thanks. She already had a buyer for this particular item, so waiting wasn't an option.

"Which floor is emptied?" she asked River.

Tap, tap, tap. His fingers flew over the keyboard. "Eight is your best bet."

"Pressing eight." She jabbed the button, and the elevator jostled into motion. When it stopped on the correct floor, she strode into the hallway and pretended to dig in her purse for a key. "Hold the elevator for me," she whispered.

"Done," River said. "Alright, the guards are watching you and they see you at the door. I'm switching the feed…now." He paused. "Excellent. All they see now is an empty hallway, so they'll assume you entered the room. I'm controlling the elevator feed, as well. You're good to go."

Farrah hurried back to the elevator and swiped the key card she'd stolen. Anyone who wished to enter the penthouse needed a card to bypass the twenty-eighth floor and reach the twenty-ninth.

"I'm looking at the foyer," River said. "Matt and Mike are waiting for you across from the elevator doors at ten and two."

"Copy that." Farrah dug a black mask from her bag and

pulled it over her face. That done, she stuffed her gloved hands into her coat pockets, wrapping her fingers around the tranq guns anchored inside of each. She was a thief, not a killer, and never carried lethal weapons.

As adrenaline rushed through her, so heady and strong she could have drunk it, she withdrew the guns and held them at her sides. Her heart pounded excitedly in her chest.

It had always been this way. A rush. Addictive.

She'd begun stealing at the age of twelve; her mother had been sick, and they'd needed money. She stole small things at first: food, clothing, wallets. But as her skills increased, so did her targets. Now, her mom was gone and she had a hefty bank account.

There was no limit to what she could take—or who she could take from. Stopping had never appealed to her.

"Awfully quiet in there," River said, cutting into her thoughts. "You imagining me naked or something?"

She snorted. "Funny."

"No. Sexy."

"Arrogant."

"Hold that thought," he said. "Arrival in five. Four. Three. Two." The elevator dinged; the doors opened.

Immediately Farrah raised her arms, aiming her guns at the ten and two positions. She squeezed the triggers before the guards, who were already standing, had a chance to realize she was masked. Red darts pegged them both in the neck. One guy managed to withdraw his weapon, but the tranquilizer was strong, mainly used for wild animals, and he tumbled onto the plush, dark brown carpet without firing a single shot. His friend soon joined him.

"We good?" River asked.

"We're good." Sheathing the guns, she quickly moved to the front door. Unlocked. But she didn't enter. Not yet. "I'm ready for the power surge."

"Overriding power system…now." Lights instantly flickered off, leaving only a dark, dark void. Absolute silence slithered through the air, causing her ears to ring. A necessary evil. It was easier to disable the security system by cutting the power than to use light and sound to cover her actions while she danced around motion detectors and heat sensors. "You have approximately five minutes before they're able to trip the wire and recharge."

"Entering now." She swept inside, time ticking away inside her mind. Here it was lighter than the foyer had been, thin rays of moonlight seeping in from the unadorned windows. For days she'd poured over the blueprint of the apartment, so she knew exactly where to go. The owner, according to her contacts, was vacationing in the French Riviera with his mistress. The wife was here, though—hopefully sleeping.

Silently Farrah moved, rounding corners and taping tiny cameras onto the walls, each one giving River a direct view of her surroundings. "Hallway one, live," he said. A pause, then the clatter of his keyboard. "Living room, live. Uh, you've got a man asleep on the couch."

Farrah backtracked, used a dart on the third guard, or whoever he was, then leapt back into motion.

"Kitchen, live," River said. Pause, clatter. "Hallway two, live."

The study was up next. Reaching the double doors, Farrah's exhilaration intensified. This was it. *The* room. She gave the knob an experimental twist. Big surprise, it was locked. Not with a simple pin-tumbler or a wafer-tumbler, either, but a tubular lock, with pins all the way around the circumference of the cylinder plug.

Usually she preferred museums to private collectors. More of a challenge. This job, however, was proving to be quite fun. "How am I on time?" she whispered, dropping her bag and crouching down. She withdrew the proper tools.

"Four minutes, two seconds."

She inserted the pick gun, a vibrating piece of metal that pushed the lock's pins up to the shear line, all the while working the tension wrench into the bottom hole. *Click.* "I'm in."

Too easy.

"Six seconds," River said. "Not your record, but not bad."

Farrah quietly entered the study, her boots sinking into the thick crimson rug. Even through her mask, she smelled woodsy cigar smoke, leather and freshly polished oak. The spacious room boasted wall-to-wall bookshelves. There was a desk in the center, a cushioned chair and several display cases perched on small marble stands.

"Do you see it?" River asked, his excitement palpable.

Her gaze scanned…scanned…seeing many artifacts and several pieces of jewelry until finally lighting on a small wooden box. Dark, surmounted by a deliciously carved face—a man's face, Farrah realized, when she stood just in front of it—with a glittery golden cord wrapped around the middle.

The gold embossed tag underneath read, *Pandora's box.* Satisfaction hummed inside of her.

"Contact," she said, awed.

Never taking her eyes from the item, she extracted the glass-cutter and a strip of velvet from her bag. The box was certainly beautiful, the most beautiful and detailed she'd ever seen. And the masculine face was a sight to behold, savage, raw, elemental, pulling all of her feminine instincts to the surface. Still, she didn't know why the buyer was willing to pay her a cool mil for it. Especially since Pandora was a legend, a myth, and there was probably nothing inside.

With precise movements, Farrah sliced a circle in the glass, keeping it suctioned to the cutter so that it didn't fall to the ground and shatter. She set the piece on top of the case.

Open the box.

She'd been in the process of reaching out when the words whispered across her mind. Deep, masculine. Seductive… Like the face.

Open it.

Surprised, she straightened and frowned. "Did you just tell me to open it?" she asked River.

"Nope. No time for that. You need to get your ass in gear. Less than three minutes remaining."

Open it. See what's inside.

What was wrong with her? Farrah shook her head, clasped the box, and carefully wrapped it in the velvet. She secured the package inside her bag, part of her hoping to hear the voice again.

"Shit," River suddenly bit out. "The wife is awake and walking into the kitchen."

"She probably got spooked when the power went out and is fixing a midnight snack. We're okay," she said, but she was already moving to the far window. She slipped out of her trench.

"Just get the hell out of there, would ya?"

"Time?"

"Not long," River said. "Less than a minute."

Before he'd finished the last word, the lights flicked on. The heater kicked on, as well, emitting a gentle hum. Farrah swished aside the drapes and raised the window. Cold air blustered all around her as she gathered her coat and bag, then stepped onto the ledge.

"The wife is trying to wake the guard," River said with an edge of panic. Then, "She found the dart in his neck. Damn it, she's running toward the study."

"Good thing I'm leaving." Heart pumping with delicious speed, Farrah slid the ultra-thin wiregun from her bag, raised her arm and squeezed a shot. The sharp tip embedded in the beam above her head. She tugged once, twice, making sure the line was secure. Then she jumped, feet first, and flew toward the ground.

The wire slowed just before she hit—she'd measured the distance before ever entering the building—then stopped altogether, softly lowering her to a stand. She released the handle, removed her mask and casually walked away from the building as if she hadn't a care.

She was smiling.

INSIDE THE BOX, MADDOX seethed with his need to escape. Close, so close. He'd spoken to the woman, and she'd heard him. No one else had ever heard him. But she had hidden him away, cutting him off from her erotic voice. A voice that caused every cell in his body to awaken, to roar, demanding release. How long since he'd spent himself inside a female? How long since he'd known anything except darkness? How long since the beast inside him had experienced the sweet taste of violence?

Eternity.

Did the woman mean to forget him? Oh, he would allow no such thing. He *would* convince her to free him—and she would be able to do so, as no other human had been able, he knew it—and his body's long-denied needs would, at last, be met. And yes, the beast would, at last, be unleashed....

CHAPTER TWO

A TOTAL SUCCESS. AGAIN. Farrah was coming off her adrenaline high, but she couldn't stop smiling. No casualties, no foot or car chase. Just a job well done.

The buyer had insisted she meet with him the same night she "acquired" the box. Perhaps he thought she'd sell it to someone else. Perhaps he simply couldn't wait to hold it in his hands. Either way, Farrah texted him, letting him know the box was in her possession and she would meet him at their agreed upon location in one hour.

"I'll be waiting," was his nearly instantaneous response. He was already in Dallas, had probably flown out before her, three weeks ago.

She didn't know his name or even what he looked like, and she preferred it that way. They always met in the shadows. In the last six months, she'd done several jobs for him, all of them boxes very similar to the one in her bag. What he wanted with them, she didn't know. He paid without balking and never tried to renegotiate. *That* was what mattered to Farrah.

"Wanna see it?" she asked River.

He didn't have to ask what "it" was. "Hell, yeah, I want to see it." He kept his attention on the road as he maneuvered their sedan along the highway. They'd switched out the van in favor of a rental that would blend with every other car on the road. Tall streetlights whizzed past them, illuminating, then drowning in shadows. Trees and buildings flashed in and out of view. "That baby's gonna buy me a kick-ass Lamborghini."

Farrah settled the bag on her stomach. She kicked her legs onto the dash and sunk deeper into her seat. "Why a Lamborghini?" She would have expected him to list all the computer equipment he couldn't live another moment without.

"Owning a ride like that is like stumbling upon an island of naked, horny women whose sole goal in life is to pleasure you."

"No, it's not," she scoffed. "I would never date a guy just because he drives a nice car."

"That's because you don't date, period."

No, she didn't. Men were not a priority for her. They couldn't be. They'd learn her secret and betray her. As she well knew.

In the quiet of the night, as she lay in bed, she might long for one, for strong arms and heat and passion. For sex that was hot and hard, pounding. But she would never allow herself to indulge. There was no one she could trust—except River, but he didn't count. They were best friends, practically brother and sister.

"You're a good-looking kid—"

"Man," he interjected with a pointed glare. His fingers tightened on the steering wheel. "We've had this discussion before. I'm a man. Not a kid, not a boy. You get me?"

"Fine. You're a good-looking *man.*" He was tall and lean, perhaps too lean. He had light brown hair, piercing green eyes and deceptively angelic features. "If a girl—woman—doesn't want you for who you are, you shouldn't want her."

He rolled his eyes. "You act like I'm looking for something serious. I'm a perv looking for action, Farr, that's all. Now show me the box already. Your conversation skills suck."

Fighting a grin, Farrah dug inside the bag and lifted the black velvet mound. Slowly, gently, she unwound the material layer by soft layer. The intricately carved top came into view, the man's face somehow more savage than she remembered. Her stomach fluttered deliciously. If only such a powerful man truly existed....

River darted a quick glance at it and whistled. "That's the coolest one so far. Have you opened it yet? Was it empty like the others?"

"No. And I don't know." The buyer had dictated she not open a single box. Of course, she disobeyed every time, her curiosity too great. Now, however...with the voice... She was a little afraid, which was stupid.

"Ah, come on. Open, open, open," River chanted.

Her hand shook as she reached for the glittery gold ribbon. As if on cue, the voice returned.

Open it, he beseeched. His husky, wine-rich timbre filled her head, invaded her blood, tingling along the surface of her skin. *Open it and see what's inside.*

She jerked her hand away. Incredulous, she blinked over at River. "Do you hear that?"

"Hear what?" He frowned.

"That...voice."

"Don't tell me you actually believe that shit about Pandora and her evil spirits."

"Of course not. I just, I don't know. This very deep, very masculine voice keeps telling me to—oh, never mind!" She waved her hand through the air. "There's no way to explain without sounding crazy."

River's face scrunched and he gave her a brief, you-are-so-weird look. "You been puffing the magic dragon again?"

"Be serious!"

He barked out a laugh. "I am. Come on, tell Brother River what the naughty voice is telling you to do."

One peek. Just take one peek.

Farrah gulped. "You truly don't hear that?"

"No."

I'll give you so much pleasure, you'll feel me inside of you for days. All you have to do is. Open. The. Box.

Farrah's cheeks heated with a blush. Now she knew it was her imagination. Hadn't she just lamented about her desire for a man, for passion and hard, pounding sex? She uttered an embarrassed chuckle. "Never mind. Just forget I said anything."

"Yeah, right. Is the voice telling you to take off all your clothes and dance in the moonlight?" He wiggled his dark brows. "Is the voice telling you to wait for the mother ship to take you home?"

She flipped him off, and he gave another laugh.

Of its own accord, her gaze returned to the box. She removed a glove and traced a fingertip over the man's—warrior's—square jawline, over the slope of his nose, the fullness of his lips. Warmth tingled up her arm. Drugging warmth, electric warmth.

An animalistic purr filled her ears. *Do not stop. Touch more.*

She gasped and snatched her arm away, even tugged her glove back onto her hand. Even knowing she was imagining things, she couldn't stop her tingling reaction.

Woman, I said touch more, not less!

"What's wrong?" River demanded. His arms jerked as he faced her, and the car swerved. Someone honked at them. He hurriedly straightened in the proper lane.

"Nothing, nothing," she assured him. But a wave of need continued to slam into her. Need like she'd never known before, as if she were touching a flesh and blood man and he was touching her in return. That purr… "I'm not going to open it," she said, more for the voice than for River. "That will mess up the ribbon, and the buyer will know we peeked. He might refuse to pay us."

I can smell your arousal, woman. Now I want to taste it.

"Let's just get this thing to its proud new owner," she said on a shaky breath.

"We're almost there." River had lost his teasing air and now hummed with concern. Not that she could blame him. She'd never acted this way before. So…unstable. She was the calm one. She was the one who took everything in stride. *She* was the one who remained unaffected. Yet here she was, lusting after a voice inside her head.

Time to put the box away.

Farrah began to wrap the velvet around the wood, but the voice stopped her. *No. Please, no.* It was tortured this time, a desperate plea. Her mouth went dry, and she stilled. Maybe all of her adrenaline rushes had finally caught up to her and fried her brain. Maybe she needed to take a vacation.

River eased the car into the parking lot of a motel close to the designated nightclub. Even from here, she could hear the bump and grind of the music, a wild, frantic beat that aroused, beckoned. People milled in and out, laughing, talking, flirting.

"I hate these clandestine meetings," River muttered, parking. The meeting place might stay the same, but they parked somewhere new each time.

"We've met with this guy eight other times. Nothing's ever happened." Farrah gently set the box on the dash and wound a thick silver belt around her waist, trying to make her body suit look more sexy and less burglarish.

River twisted and leaned into the backseat, grabbing the Polaroid camera she'd thrown back there. He snapped a picture of the box. The bright flash of light was almost blinding, and for several seconds she saw orange-gold spots.

"Here," he said, handing her the photo. "Proof."

She slid the picture under her belt. "Thanks."

"You prepared for anything?"

"Always." She held up her left hand and wiggled her fingers.

"I have the powdered sedative in my ring and a knife in my boot. Plus, I'll have the dart gun under my trench." Even as she spoke, she was anchoring the gun at her side and tugging her coat around her shoulders.

"Damn it," he suddenly burst out. "I hate sending you in there alone."

"I'm still wearing my headgear, so you'll be able to hear everything that's said. Besides, it's best this way, and you know it. We get the money without giving him a chance to steal the merchandise."

"Yeah, but I don't have to like it," he grumbled. He pulled a Glock from his boot and checked the clip. Every time she saw him with a deadly weapon, she experienced a jolt. She had brought him into this dangerous life, but if anything ever happened to him…

She shuddered. "I'll text you when he's wired the money. You come back with the box, and we'll go home and celebrate."

"When this is done, I'm going to find me a woman. No, *two* women. You won't see me for a week."

Farrah chuckled as she secured her bag on her shoulder. She'd emptied out her tools during the drive and now carried a small, hand-held laptop. With a last, lingering glance at the male face on the box, she emerged from the car. Cold air enveloped her, thick with cigarette smoke and the pungent fumes of alcohol. Farrah walked over to the club, the music growing louder with each step. Her trench billowed at her ankles.

Her adrenaline was spiking again, rushing through her veins like an awakened river. There was as much danger in meeting her buyers as there was in breaking into a building. But this, too, she loved. There was something so…invigorating about knowing that any moment could be her last.

Her mom, God rest her precious soul, used to call her a danger junkie. There'd been admonishment and fear in Jennifer

Roberts's tone, but she'd never asked Farrah to stop. Not even when Farrah was caught the first time. Or the second time. Or the third. But cancer had been eating the sweet woman alive, stealing her energy, destroying it, and she'd been unable to provide for her only daughter—for *herself.* Farrah had quite happily taken up the slack and never looked back.

Farrah entered the nightclub, scanning for any hint of betrayal. There were dancers, couples writhing together with a fluid eroticism that caused her blood to heat deliciously. Damn that sexy voice! She never would have noticed the dancers otherwise. There were drinkers at the bar, and waitresses hurrying from one table to another, taking orders. All under the constant swirl of multicolored strobes, casting a sparkling shower of pinks, blues and greens.

No one aimed a weapon at her. No one tried to grab her.

Farrah paid the cover charge, briefly removed her glove so that her hand could be stamped, and sauntered the rest of the way inside. Per the buyer's instructions, she headed toward the back. The room was filled to capacity, overflowing with eager, lust-hungry men and women. She maneuvered around them. Manufactured smoke billowed in the air, creating a dreamlike haze. Surreal.

Not surprisingly, her contact was waiting for her. He was alone, his table pushed into a shadowy corner.

She knew it was him. Muted beams of light caressed his hand, illuminating a large sapphire ring on one of the fingers clutched around a glass of Scotch. Her heart hammered all the more intently in her chest. She eased into the seat across from him. Without a word, she slipped the photo from under her belt and slid it beside the glass.

A moment passed without reaction. Another.

She wanted to ask him why he was so fascinated with the story of Pandora, but didn't. Early on, she'd learned that questions always made the client nervous. And nervous clients were not good. Most often they became trigger-happy.

The man gripped the photo between shaky fingers and held it closer to his face. Thick, silver hair glinted as a violet strobe passed overhead.

"You may have the item the moment I collect my fee," she said, speaking loudly to be heard over the music.

He cocked two fingers, signaling the need for her laptop. She withdrew it from her bag and handed it to him. It was already booted and ready to go. All he needed to do was type in his account number and press Enter.

The entire transaction took less than sixty seconds.

He handed her the laptop and she double-checked her account. Sure enough, the million was there.

"Uh, Farrah," River said in her ear.

His voice surprised her, and she jumped. Her gaze darted left and right, searching for him. Until she remembered that she still wore the earpiece. "What?"

"I'm being followed," he said nervously. "Had to leave the parking space when I saw I had company. Two cars. Taking turns. I can't shake them."

She cupped her ear with her hand. "Cops?"

"I don't think so."

Trying not to panic, she pushed to her feet. The buyer did the same. He was tall, wider than she'd realized. Muscled. For the first time, she glimpsed his features. He was younger than she'd assumed, too. Probably no more than thirty-five. His eyes were big and brown and devoid of any hint of emotion. His nose was straight, his lips too thin but sexy nonetheless. His hair wasn't silver, as she'd thought she'd seen, but white. Like snow.

He radiated power. Lethal charm.

Not allowing herself to show a single ounce of fear, she flattened her palms on the table and leaned forward. "Do you have a tail on my guy?" she demanded.

"No," was the surprisingly gentle reply. "There has never been a need for that."

He was right. They'd worked together before, and he'd never deviated from plan. So who was following River? "Think you can get home?" she asked her friend. Home, for now, was a motel on the north side of town.

"I'll try."

Her gaze bore into the man's. "I'm afraid I'll have to reschedule with you. Something's come up." She tried to run to the door, but he stretched out his arm and grabbed her, stopping her flat.

"You're not leaving until I have the box." His tone was no longer gentle, but strong, demanding. "I paid you. I want it."

Automatically, her fingers wrapped around the dart gun at her waist. She didn't aim. Yet. But her blood pounded through her veins at full speed. A gloss of sweat beaded over her skin. "I'm afraid that's impossible at the moment. The box stays with me until my boy is safe. And right now, he's being followed."

The man hesitated for a long while. Finally, he said, "Go to him. Help him. But I expect to hear from you before morning. If I do not…" His voice trailed off. Then he added calmly, "I do not want to, Farrah, but I will hunt you down and kill you. Your friend River will be next. Neither death will be quick or easy. Feel me?"

He knew their names. She'd never told him; none of her other clients knew. She'd gone to great lengths to keep them hidden. Lightheaded, Farrah nodded.

The man released her. She spun on her heel and ran. Just ran, shoving people out of the way in her haste. *I'm in way over my head this time,* she thought, as she flung open the front door and sprinted into the night. This was *not* exciting.

Breath burning in her lungs, she hastily searched the cars. When she found an older, unlocked vehicle, she tossed her bag in the passenger seat and jumped inside. She quickly jerked off the dash cover and rerouted the wires. The engine roared to life.

"River," she said, "you still good?"

Her ear was suddenly filled with the sound of screeching tires, then a muttered curse. "I can't shake my shadows, Farr, and they've stopped taking turns. They're both on my ass now."

Who the hell was following him? She bit the inside of her cheek until she tasted blood. Danger directed at herself, she enjoyed. Danger directed at River…different story. She stomped her foot on the gas and sped from the parking lot. "Where are you headed? Maybe I can cut them off."

He rattled off his location and described the cars.

"Slow down, okay, and let them stay close to you. Just not close enough to take a shot if that's their goal." She made the drive in seven minutes, each one ticking slower than the last. She finally spotted River; he was several cars ahead of her. She also spotted his shadows. Black, nondescript sedans, just like River drove. Their windows were tinted, so she couldn't make out the drivers. "I'm here," she said. "I see them."

"What do you want me to do?" There was an edge to the words, a quiet desperation.

I got him into this. I have to get him out. No matter what. "When I tell you, make a sharp one-eighty and hop into the opposite lane. Don't look back, just gas it." Farrah increased her speed, sidling up to one of the cars. "Now," she said, and rammed it. One sedan slammed into the other, and her own car was knocked off course, swerving left and right.

As she fought for control, she heard the squeal of tires, saw River doing as she'd instructed, and felt a wave of relief. The sedans tried to turn, tried to follow him, but she rammed them until they collided with other vehicles, the sound of crunching metal blasting across the highway.

Farrah didn't take her foot off the gas, even whiplashed as she was, but continued north. She was panting, her fingers throbbing from gripping the wheel so tightly, and her skin felt too tight on her bones.

"Farrah? Farrah, are you okay?"

"All's well," she managed to say without any hint of emotion. "Shadows are gone, and I'm on my way home."

At first, he didn't respond. Then he expelled a shaky breath. "What was that about?"

"I don't know. Maybe the box, maybe not. Let's worry about it tomorrow. Right now, I'm wiped."

"Just...ditch the car as soon as you can, and I'll do the same."

"Will do. See you in thirty, Riv."

"Yeah, see you in thirty."

He was upset, she could tell. Nothing like this had ever happened before, and they'd done many, many jobs together. Maybe it was time to get out of the business, go somewhere sunny and safe and relax for the first time in her life. River could "bag the babes" he was always talking about. He could work a normal job, maybe start his own computer business.

Farrah sighed. Yeah, it was time. Past time, probably. She'd miss the rushes, the danger, the excitement, but River was more important. Tomorrow, she'd deliver the box to its new owner—his death threat still rang in her ears—then she'd begin planning a new life for herself and River.

CHAPTER THREE

WHEN FARRAH ENTERED the motel room, she was happy to see that River was already there. He lounged on the bed, flipping channels on the TV. He looked so young, lying there, the stained red comforter fluffed around him, big white pillows under his feet.

The door snicked shut behind her. Their eyes met, his a worried green, hers a relieved blue. Without the contacts, her gaze would have been a relieved brown.

"I'm sorry," she said, locking the door behind her. "So very sorry."

Frowning, he dropped the remote and sat up. "Why? You did nothing wrong."

"I introduced you to this lifestyle. I—"

"Saved me," he interjected. "Time and time again."

She opened her mouth to respond, but he cut her off with a quick shake of his head. "Nope. Not another word on the subject. You're going to relax, catch some Zs, and I'm going to decompress. There's a bar about a block over. They've got pool and loose women, and as you know, that's my favorite combination."

Her lips pursed as she crossed her arms over her chest. "You aren't old enough to get in to a bar."

He hopped from the bed and slipped his feet into his boots, shooting her a wicked grin and suddenly appearing much older than his nineteen years. "My I.D. says otherwise."

True. She'd forged the I.D. herself. But he did not need to be drinking beer, which fogged his brain and made him giggly; he'd proposition everything breathing and—wait. Up close, she could see the lines of tension around his eyes, the tight pull of his lips. She lost her steam. He really did need to decompress.

"Just be careful, okay. Phone if there's any trouble."

"Yes, Mommy."

She anchored her hands on her hips. "Whoever chased you is still out there, smarty."

He nodded, his expression growing fierce. "That's why you're not going to open the door for anyone, no matter who they claim to be."

"Yes, Daddy," she mimicked.

Chuckling, he tossed a pillow at her. She easily ducked, the foam bouncing off the door. River was in front of her in the next flash, kissing her cheek.

"If I'm not back by morning, it's because I've finally found the easy woman of my dreams."

"At least pick one who's had all her shots."

He didn't respond, but whistled under his breath as he left. "Incorrigible," Farrah muttered, bolting the door again. No wonder she loved him so much.

With a sigh, she trekked past the bed and—stopped abruptly. Her gaze had snagged on the mound of black velvet perched atop one of the pillows. *Pandora's box.* Just seeing it made her tingle, made her blood heat and her stomach flutter. But she forced herself to look away, to pad into the bathroom.

She needed to text the buyer. Should do so now. But…*not yet,* she thought. There was still time.

After removing her contacts, she stripped and showered, the steamy water washing away the dark tint she'd applied to her skin. All the while, she thought of the box. What would the voice—her subconscious—say if she touched it again?

Would only silence greet her?

Maybe she was crazy, but she wanted to know. Had to know. She wanted to hear that deep, sensual timbre again. Yes, she *had* to hear it.

Farrah shut off the water and wrapped herself in a stiff white towel. The long length of her hair dripped down her back. Chewing her bottom lip, she exited the bathroom on a cloud of steam and approached the bed. For a long while, she simply stared at the dark bundle. How innocent it looked…how beguiling…

Practically in a trance, she stepped forward. She was reaching down…down…but her toe stubbed on—she tore her gaze away and glanced to the floor—her overnight bag. She and River had stored their belongings here early this morning, having moved from their previous location in preparation for the job.

In and out she breathed. *Dress first, and get your silly compulsion under control. This* need *is ridiculous.* Still eyeing the box, she dressed in a pink tank and matching sleep pants. Her desire to hear the voice was a little frightening. Adrenaline was rushing through her as if she was about to break into a heavily armed fortress.

While a gunfight played on the TV behind her, she reached out once more and clasped the velvet. Slowly she unwound the soft material, inch by agonizing inch. The dark wood finally came into view, and her mouth flooded with moisture.

Open it, woman. I have lost patience with you.

Hearing that, her nerve endings electrified. He hadn't abandoned her. He was still here. But he was no longer seductive, he was now commanding. Wait, she thought, frowning. She was thinking of the voice as a real man now, not a figment of her long-ignored hormones.

Open it! Do not make me tell you again.

"The owner will—"

Not know. I promise you.

How tempting…irresistible. "Fine," she found herself saying. God, she was having a conversation with a nonexistent person. Crazy did not begin to describe her. "I'll open it, but the guy threatened to kill me and the only person in the world that I love. If he realizes what I've done, he'll be pissed and might just try to kill us anyway."

He will not touch you. I'll make sure of it.

A shiver trekked along her spine. The voice was fierce, feral, deadly. And right. She would text the owner, let him know the box was safe and that she would *mail* it to him before disappearing. Even if he decided to come after her and River, he would never find them. They would be long gone, hidden.

With that thought, opening the box was no longer a question. It was a certainty.

Farrah eased onto the edge of the bed and gently placed the box on her lap. The wood was heavy, warm, just as she remembered. The beautiful male face seemed to stare up at her, into her. She untied the golden ribbon and placed her shaky hands over the center seam.

Open, open, open.

She slowly raised the lid. Before she'd raised it two inches, however, it was ripped from her fingers, springing open of its own accord. Something—a butterfly?—gusted from the hollowed center, its flowing cobalt wings flapping furiously.

Farrah watched, open mouthed. Yes, it was a butterfly. But…how? How long had it been inside? How had it survived? As the thoughts poured through her mind, the insect's wings began to grow, expand.

Right in front of her eyes, the insect lengthened…lengthened…taking a solid shape. Bright blue wings became bronzed muscle and sinew, scars and tattoos. Piercings and skin. *Skin!*

Shock rolled through her. Shock and awe and disbelief. She rubbed her eyes, knowing the incredible sight would be gone by the time she refocused. Nope, still there. Shit. Shit! She scrambled backward, all the way to the other side of the bed. She hit the edge and tumbled to the floor, knocking the air from her lungs.

"Woman," the seductive voice said, no longer in her mind but here, with her. Alone with her.

Dear God. She jumped to her feet, knees banging together. There was now a man in her room. A freaking man. Oxygen burned in her throat as she studied him. He was amazingly tall, shirtless and ripped with corded row after corded row of strength. He had hair as black and silky as the velvet on the bed. His eyes were the same color as the butterfly's wings had been, a pulsing blue. Otherworldly. Surreal. They were fringed by spiky black lashes, a deliciously perfect frame.

His face…it was the face on the box. Savage, raw, elemental. Stripes of blue paint slashed his sharp cheekbones. His nose was slightly bent and his lips were too full, but he was exquisite nonetheless.

The rest of him, well…she gulped. Both of his nipples were pierced, completely at odds with the butterfly tattooed on his chest, its wings stretching over his pectorals, his collarbone, and onto his shoulders. He wore crudely made black leather pants and well-worn boots that reached the middle of his calves. A silver cuff circled his left bicep.

He splayed his arms wide and roared. Roared with rage and frustration, relief and need. Her knees almost buckled. Never had she been faced with a more primal, erotic picture: terrifying, yet unbelievably arousing.

"You're…you're…" She didn't know what to say, could hardly breathe. This wasn't happening, couldn't possibly be happening. Who was he? *What* was he? She would have liked to tell herself he was a dream, a hallucination, but couldn't. *Real,* every cell in her body shouted.

"Violence," he purred in that deep, wine-rich voice. There was rage in his eyes, such rage. "I am Violence, and I am hungry."

As he spoke, his blue eyes locked on her face, intense, consuming, and she knew, *knew,* he wasn't talking about food. He radiated heat. Scorching heat. Blistering heat. A hum of zinging energy traveled the length of her body. Her nipples hardened painfully, and a delicious heat pooled between her legs.

She gulped. Who he was and what he was no longer seemed to matter. Slowly she inched backward, trying to reach the door without alerting him to the fact that she meant to bolt.

"Where do you think you are going?" he demanded.

Okay, he'd noticed—and he now looked ready to kill her. Farrah didn't waste another second. She whipped around and sprinted to the door. Locked. Damn it! With her unsteady grip, working the simple lock proved more difficult than the tubular she'd battled only a few hours ago. Finally, though, she made it outside. Cold air bit and nibbled at her exposed, damp skin.

Panting, trying not to panic, she raced through the moonlit parking lot, her bare feet slapping at the frigid cement. Rocks sliced at the sensitive skin, and she grimaced. But she didn't slow. The best way to escape him, she thought, cornering the side of the building, was to lose him in the shadows, in the twists and turns of the back allies. When she was totally safe, she would call River and tell him to meet her in another location.

There were no footsteps behind her, so she dared a quick peek. No sign of him. Good. Maybe he'd decided she wasn't worth the trouble. As she returned her attention in front of her, she slammed into a hard wall—a wall that enveloped her in aroused heat. She was thrown backward and landed on her ass with a hard thump.

"Woman, you cannot escape me. I have your scent in my nose."

How had he gotten ahead of her? How, how, how? With a gasp, she jolted to her feet and bolted in the opposite direction, the same way she'd come. Before she managed three steps, he was blocking her path.

Eyes widening, she ground to a halt. How was he doing that? "Who *are* you?" she managed to squeak out.

"King Maddox. Violence, as I told you." He paused, peering at her with determination. "The man who is going to know the taste of you."

King? Violence? Shaking her head, Farrah backed away from him. "You're crazy. I'm crazy. *This* is crazy. Just…leave me alone." With that, she spun on her heel and ran as fast as her feet would carry her. Again.

MADDOX WATCHED HER GO. He didn't materialize in front of her this time, for he knew that at any time, with a simple snap of his fingers, he could find her. Oh, yes. Wherever she went, he could—and would—find her. He hadn't lied. Her erotic scent, a fragrance of wild passion and sweet female, would instantaneously lead him to her location. The beast's magic gifted him with the ability.

He was hard for her, his blood a molten river inside his veins. For a moment, one breathless moment, she had looked at him and there had been desire in her eyes. Stark, needy desire that had intensified his own.

He could find another woman to slake his body's centuries of denied desires—he smelled several nearby—and maybe he would. Soon. Right now, he wanted that one, with her silky fall of midnight hair, with her dark eyes and lush, red lips. With her delicate curves and siren's voice. Her breasts and their hard little nipples had been made for his mouth. The long length of her graceful legs had been made to wrap around his waist.

At the moment, no one else would do.

Farrah, she was called. An elegant name for a woman of many contradictions. In the time span of a few hours, he'd heard her angry, fierce, tender, teasing, incredulous and afraid. He'd liked the fierceness best. Had wanted it directed at him. In bed.

She'd stolen his box with a skill that surprised him. Tempted and aroused him. He wanted those expert hands on his body, stroking him to full awakening. Yes, he mused again, he would have that woman. Under him, over him, a part of him. But he would have her a little later. Outside now, he simply reveled in the fact that he was free. At last, he was free from the constrictions of that hated box.

He was Pandora's prisoner no more.

He breathed deeply of the night air, its crisp coolness a caress to his skin. And still rage filled him, consumed him. Such rage. How long had he wished for a moment such as this? How long had he prayed to gods who had refused to listen? Eternity, it seemed.

A roar gusted past his lips. Fists tightened, he pounded on the closest wall. The entire structure shook. He kicked metal bins and bent the bars of a staircase. He was glad Farrah was not here to witness his tantrum. But he wanted to destroy everything around him. Everything except, perhaps, the woman. Her, he wanted to fuck. Hard and long. Until the rage was spent.

When he calmed, his eyes closed and he tried to savor the night. He did not know where his men were or what Pandora had done to them when they'd escaped. Were they still alive? He must know, for *he* was responsible for them. No matter where he had to look or for how long, he would find them.

"Free," he shouted to the heavens. Pinpricks of light winked down at him. "Free."

Locked away these many years, with no one but the beast

inside of him for company, he had finally learned to control his need for blood and retribution. He was still dangerous, still more of a weapon than a man, but he could operate in this modern world. He could, at last, forge a life for himself and his men. A life they had been denied because of one foolish mistake. *His* mistake.

He strode back to the room he'd abandoned. As the walls closed around him, he mourned the loss of the outdoors. He hurriedly gathered the box, the material Farrah had covered it with, and her bag. He grinned. She would want that back, he was sure.

"I'm coming for you," he said, knowing she could not hear him. But perhaps she would feel the warning in her bones.

He did not know where Pandora was, but he would find her, too. She would know the taste of his beast at long last. He would kill her as he'd dreamed all these years, without thought, without hesitation, heaping yet another sin upon his already heavy shoulders—a sin for which he must atone when the guilt invariably hit him. But he did not care.

Go. Find the little thief and sate your desires. Afterward, he would begin to hunt down Pandora and his men. One by one.

AT HOME WITH THE *Lords of the Underworld*

YEAH. SO. WILLIAM THE Extraordinarily Amazingly Handsome and Brilliant here. You know, Anya's BFF and an honorary—if not the *best*—Lord of the Underworld. I thought it'd be ~~entertaining~~ enlightening to sit down with the Lords and ask some hard-hitting questions. You know, like what kind of underwear they prefer. So I did what any celebrated journalist would do and ~~kidnapped~~ invited them to ~~the dungeon~~ my office one by one and got the goods. I figured the gods had written an entire book about yours truly—a book Anya continues to hold hostage like the greedy thief she is—so it'd be nice if the Lords had a book of their own. Maybe Anya can steal theirs and give me back mine. Fingers crossed!

Anyway, they didn't always cooperate, the bastards, but I sure had fun. Warning: let's just say things get a little sappy at times. Gag! And yeah, I know you'd rather hear about me—I don't wear *any* undies—but sit back, relax and enjoy. That'll be easy to do since I'm right there with the Lords. And yes, I know you're imagining me naked. Naughty girls. (Call me!)

Maddox
KEEPER OF VIOLENCE

William: What's your nickname?

Maddox: I do not have one.

William: I'm happy to give you one. Captain Ass. What do you think?

Maddox: I can leave.

William: New nickname: Big Baby. Anyway, let's continue. What's your zodiac sign?

Maddox: What is that?

William: Moving on. Choice of weapon?

Maddox: Fists. A fight is more satisfying that way.

William: What are you looking for in a woman?

Maddox: Someone the color of honey from head to toe. Someone who hears past conversations wherever she stands. Someone named Ashlyn Darrow.

William: Favorite food?

Maddox: Ashlyn. And honey. Combine them—heaven.

William: Suddenly I'm starving!

Maddox: Go near her and I'll slice your godsdamn throat!

William: Yep. Big Baby. Moving on again. Favorite moment in the series so far?

Maddox: When Ashlyn came back to life after dying.

William: Least favorite?

Maddox: When Ashlyn died. Showalter almost lost her head for that one. *Literally* lost her head.

William: Describe yourself.

Maddox: No. That's ridiculous. What does my appearance matter?

William: Uh, it means, like, *everything*. But of course *you* wouldn't think so.

Maddox: What does that mean?

William: Nothing. So…any hobbies?

Maddox: Carving wood and building furniture for my future child's nursery, reading romance novels, snuggling—among other things—with Ashlyn Darrow, the love of my life.

William: Household chores?

Maddox: Home repairs.

William: Least favorite household responsibility?

Maddox: Rebuilding whatever Violence made me break.

William: Who is the smartest Lord?

Maddox: We are all equally smart.

William: What do you think of the fact that your home has been invaded by women?

Maddox: I couldn't be more pleased, as long as none of them does something to hurt Ashlyn. And I take full credit for starting the trend.

William: If you knew you only had twenty-four hours before the Hunters found Pandora's box and killed you, what would you do in the time you had left to live?

Maddox: Find ways to ensure Ashlyn's—and my child's—eternal safety.

William: What kind of underwear do you prefer?

Maddox: I am not answering that.

Final thoughts from William: Big Baby is stubborn, disgustingly protective of his woman—would it kill him to share?—and weirdly modest.

William: Nickname?

Lucien: The Grim Reaper, the Dark One, Malach ha-Maet, Yama, Azreal, Shadow Walker, Mairya, King of the Dead. And Flowers—but only Anya can call me that.

William: Fine. I'll call you Roses.

Lucien: You won't.

William: I will. Zodiac sign, Roses?

Lucien: First, how does my woman stand you? Second, I don't think I have a sign. I was created rather than born, and I am unsure of the day, much less the month.

William: I'll just mark your sign as "Roses." Choice of weapon, Roses?

Lucien: You are a bastard. But I like knives. I like to get up close and personal with my kills. Care for a demonstration?

William: Later. What are you looking for in a woman, Roses?

Lucien: Why don't I call you Moron? Anya does. Anyway, I

was not looking, but I certainly found my perfect match in Anya, supreme goddess of Anarchy. Do not call her a "minor" goddess if you know what's good for you.

William: Favorite food, Roses, mate to the minor goddess of Anarchy?

Lucien: You are asking for a beating, you know that? But the answer is, I like anything Anya steals—er, cooks for me.

William: Favorite moment in the series so far, Roses?

Lucien: You are irritating. I shouldn't admit this, but I loved the time Anya and I were in bed—after we'd been fighting—and she proved just how much she, uh, liked me.

William: Tell me more.

Lucien: No. That would be ungentlemanly.

William: All the fun things are.

Lucien: Next question. Now.

William: Least favorite moment in the series, *Flowers*?

Lucien: I hope someone stabs you. Again. As for my least favorite moment, that was when Anya couldn't remember who I was. Talk about tearing my heart in two.

William: Hobbies, Flowers. Besides annoying me.

Lucien: You annoy *me!* But anyway, taking care of Anya is a full-time job. Someone has to put out the fires.

William: Household chores, Flowers?

Lucien: Paperwork.

William: Least favorite household responsibility, Flowers?

Lucien: Escorting Maddox to Hell each night before his curse was broken.

William: Describe yourself, Flowers. Or, if you'd rather, I could do it for you.

Lucien: I can handle this one. I'm ugly, distanced, hard.

William: I would have added annoying.

Anya: [entering the room] What did I tell you about calling yourself ugly, Flowers? Punishment time, big boy, and Mama's not showing any mercy. Although you get bonus points for "hard."

William: What do you think of the fact that your home has been invaded by women, Flowers?

Anya: Allow me to answer the rest of these questions for my man—he's currently…tied up. What does he think about the invasion of estrogen? He loves it. And if you call him Flowers again, I'll rip another page from your precious book.

William: You annoy me, too. Who do you think is the toughest Lord?

Anya: Flowers.

William: Why do you get to call him Flowers but I can't?

Anya: Because I'm special.

William: This isn't even your interview. Get lost.

Anya: There goes another page.

William: Bitch. If you knew you only had twenty-four hours before the Hunters found Pandora's box and killed you, what would you do in the time you had left to live?

Anya: Trick question. No one would be dumb enough to kill him because they would know they'd soon feel the sting of my wrath.

Final thoughts from William: Someone should spank Anya. Hard!

KEEPER OF PAIN

William: Nickname?

Reyes: Painie

William: Zodiac sign?

Reyes: Danika is a Virgo, if that helps.

William: Choice of weapon?

Reyes: Blades. Though I have been known to use a Sig Sauer to get the job done.

William: What are you looking for in a woman?

Reyes: I've found my angel, Danika. She's all I need.

William: Really? That's, like, weird to me. Men should need *many* girls. No one girl should be so important.

Reyes: How sad for you.

William: I'm not sad. You're sad!

Reyes: Why are you so defensive about this?

William: Let's move on. Favorite outfit?

Reyes: First, you said *girls* rather than *women.* Why is that, I wonder? Because you care about one girl in particular? Anyway, clothes are clothes. I don't have any favorites.

William: Go to hell. I care about no one and I'm proud to admit that! Favorite moment in the series so far?

Reyes: The first time Danika looked at me with trust and acceptance in her eyes. I'm still reeling.

William: And just so you know, *girl* was a slip of the tongue. Now. Least favorite moment in the series?

Reyes: Every time I had to kill Maddox.

William: Really? That would have been my favorite. Anyway, hobbies?

Reyes: Do you really have to ask? Yes? Fine. Cutting myself. I've started to draw shapes. Like hearts.

William: You actually admitted that aloud. [snicker] Household chores?

Reyes: Replenishing weaponry.

William: Least favorite household responsibility?

Reyes: When Aeron makes me clean the furniture I've bled on. Cleaning is supposed to be his territory. Right?

William: I bet you'd look pretty in a maid costume. On that note, describe yourself.

Reyes: Happy for the first time in what seems an eternity.

William: Not that you deserve it. Really, I didn't say *girl* for any particular reason. So what do you think of the fact that your home has been invaded by women?

Reyes: As long as I have Danika, I don't care who lives with us.

William: Who do you think is the smartest Lord?

Reyes: Me. Look who I picked to spend eternity with.

William: I think you're the dumbest! Seriously, *girl* was meant to encompass everyone old enough to be bedded by me. Now, if you knew you only had twenty-four hours before the Hunters found Pandora's box and killed you, what would you do in the time you had left to live?

Reyes: Not even death can keep me away from my angel. I would find a way to change such a fate. Again.

William: What kind of underwear are you wearing?

Note from William: Bastard flipped me off and left.

Final thoughts from William: Reyes's thoughts about me and my slip of the tongue were ridiculous and unfounded!

Paris

KEEPER OF PROMISCUITY

William: Nickname?

Paris: Oh, God. Gorgeous.

William: Hey, I've been called both names, too. Zodiac sign?

Paris: I've checked those out. I'm probably a Gemini.

William: Choice of weapon?

Paris: A long, hard sword. Yeah, I went there.

William: So far, you're my favorite Lord. What are you looking for in a woman?

Paris: Here's a better question—*who* am I looking for? And that's Sienna. I don't know if I love her or hate her, but I want her like crazy.

William: Favorite food?

Paris: Female.

William: Me, too! Were we separated at birth? And do you have a favorite outfit?

Paris: Skin.

William: Seriously, what are you doing after this interview? We should head into town and bond some more.

Paris: I'll probably pass out. So, no town for me.

William: Party pooper. Favorite moment in the series so far?

Paris: Having sex with the same woman twice.

William: Who do you think is the cutest Lord?

Paris: Dumb question. Me.

William: Current hobbies?

Paris: Ambrosia, ambrosia and more ambrosia. Got any on you?

William: Yes. And now we've got a date. Reyes said some really dumb stuff to me, and if I share my stash, you can help me kick his ass.

Paris: Count me in.

William: Former hobbies?

Paris: Reading romance novels, watching skin flicks, whipping my boys at Xbox and PlayStation 3. By the way, Willie, you suck at Guitar Hero.

William: Actually, I excel. You just have no rhythm. What are your household chores?

Paris: Grocery shopping and meal preparation.
William: We're out of Cheetos.

Paris: I have a bag in my room. We can trade.

William: Deal. So let's hurry and finish up here. Least favorite household responsibility?

Paris: Cooking. Thank the gods Ashlyn and Danika live here now and actually know how to make things more complex than PB and J.

William: Describe yourself.

Paris: The only way I know to answer that is by using the words women have whispered to me throughout the centuries. Delicious, beautiful, handsome, delicious, extraordinary, brilliant, delicious, strong, brave and delicious.

William: Definitely separated at birth. What do you think of the fact that your home has been invaded by women?

Paris: We need even more women. Not enough of them are putting out.

William: I hope you haven't tried anything on Gilly

because she's too young for you, and I would have to take my blade and—

Paris: Like I would sleep with a teenager! Much less Danika's best friend. Even I'm not that desperate.

William: I was wrong. We weren't separated at birth, because your dad is the devil!

Paris: What crawled up your ass? I just stated a fact.

William: Moving on. If you knew you only had twenty-four hours before the Hunters found Pandora's box and killed you, what would you do in the time you had left to live?

Paris: Get high.

William: What kind of underwear do you prefer?

Paris: I like thongs.

William: You like wearing thongs? I pictured you as a, I don't know, boxers kind of guy. You know, so your boys can hang free.

Paris: No, shithead. I like when women wear thongs. The ones that come up over their jeans. You know what I mean?

William: You've redeemed yourself. I now think you are a man of good taste. Just for that, you get a bonus question. Who would you like to oil-wrestle next?

Paris: Fuck you.

Final thoughts from William: Paris is arrogant, moody, doesn't like girls too young for him and is an ambrosia addict. I may have just found my new BFF.

KEEPER OF WRATH

William: Nickname?

Aeron: Once, in the earlier days, they called me Wings. Well, my friends did. Humans called me Harbinger of Death.

William: Zodiac sign?

Aeron: Sign? I'm not holding a sign. My hands are empty.

William: Are you embarrassed by your cluelessness? Because I'm embarrassed for you.

Aeron: What are you talking about?

William: Never mind. Choice of weapon?

Aeron: Whatever's strapped to my body.

William: What are you looking for in a woman?

Aeron: I'm not. They are too fragile to bother with.

William: Clue. Less. What's your favorite food?

Aeron: Who cares as long as it nourishes?

William: Favorite outfit?

Aeron: Any shirt that tears easily when my wings spontaneously emerge.

William: Favorite moment in the series so far?

Aeron: I do not have one. Too much torture, too much pain. When will it end?

William: And morbid. Least favorite?

Aeron: I'm surprised I have to spell this out. The blood-curse heaped upon me.

William: Hobbies?

Aeron: Punishing wrongdoers.

William: Household chores?

Aeron: Maid duty.

William: Least favorite household responsibility?

Aeron: Ditto.

William: You know, it's okay to elaborate sometimes. Describe yourself.

Aeron: On edge. All the damn time. There. Was that enough of an elaboration for you?

William: Let's just finish this. You're boring me. What do you think of the fact that your home has been invaded by women?

Aeron: I like that my brothers are happy. But do I wish they'd found another way to be happy? Yes.

William: Who do you think is the strongest Lord?

Aeron: Paris. He gave up everything for me. The strength such a gesture required…I am still humbled.

William: If you knew you only had twenty-four hours before the Hunters found Pandora's box and killed you, what would you do in the time you had left to live?

Aeron: I would never allow the Hunters to put me in such a position. Death is for humans.

William: What kind of underwear do you prefer?

Aeron: Did you really just ask me about *underwear?* This is silly. Hunters could be outside our door right this minute and you call me in here like you're dying and you need my help and I….

Note from William: The rant continues for, like, an hour. I *end up having to walk away.*

Final thoughts: I'm just glad it's over.

Torin

KEEPER OF DISEASE

William: Nickname?

Torin: TorTor, and I Need You To— Fill in the blank. Does it matter if I gave them to myself? No? Well, then, there's also Hotness, and The Awesome.

William: Zodiac sign?

Torin: Cancer. Get it? Disease…cancer?

William: Funny. But next time don't ruin the joke by explaining it to me like I'm a two-year-old child.

Torin: Well, I've been watching you, and I've noticed you watching a certain child yourself. Just thought I'd accommodate your preferences.

William: I have not been watching Gilly! And she's seventeen, for gods' sake. Hardly a toddler.

Torin: She's been seventeen for, what, two minutes? Besides, how old are you?

William: Fuck you. Choice of weapon?

Torin: Yeah, I wish. Gods, I love to fight. But I haven't gotten to beat anyone into pulp in thousands of years.

William: What are you looking for in a woman?

Torin: I'm not. Looking, that is. What good would it do me? Not like I can do anything if I see something I want.

William: Things got grouchy fast. Favorite food?

Torin: Anything I haven't had to prepare myself.

William: Favorite outfit?

Torin: Why? It's not like anyone sees me anyway.

William: Grouchy again. Why is that? From what I hear, Cameo gets to see more than just your tightie whities.

Torin: We're just friends. But another word about her, and you'll get to meet my demon.

William: Wow, you're really touchy about this subject. Get it? You can't touch me? Anyway, favorite moment in the series so far?

Torin: I can't say.

William: Translation: you *won't* say. But tell me, does it involve Cameo?

Torin: Yes, now change the subject.

William: Things were just getting interesting, but whatever. Least favorite moment?

Torin: Every time one of my boys comes back injured. I hate knowing I wasn't there to protect them.

William: Hobbies?

Torin: In my spare time, which equals never, I like to bake cakes. Fine, I only bake them in my head, but I've been collecting recipes from the Internet and trying to convince Ashlyn to bake me something with blueberries. Real freaking blueberries. Can you imagine? They'd just explode against your taste buds, man.

William: Household chores?

Torin: Managing stocks and bonds, technology guru, security specialist.

William: Least favorite household responsibility?

Torin: Work keeps me busy, so I'm pretty much grateful for all my responsibilities.

William: Describe yourself.

Torin: Well, I don't like to brag but I am pretty spectacular.

William: Wow, you've got an ego. Everyone knows I'm the most spectacular one here. What do you think of the fact that your home has been invaded by women?

Torin: Freaking torture, man. My poor, neglected body needs a break from the estrogen.

William: Who do you think is the cutest Lord?

Torin: Uh, let me think about that one. Hello, Cameo. And you better keep your mouth shut about her!

William: Put your gloves back on. My mouth is shut. But feel free to describe her breasts and—sit back down. All right, fine. I'll move on. If you knew you only had twenty-four hours before the Hunters found Pandora's box and killed you, what would you do in the time you had left to live?

Torin: Find a woman who's dying and alone and romance the hell out of her and finally lose my stupid virginity.

William: You're a virgin? Wow. Just wow. I probably would have killed myself by now.

Torin: Let me help you with that….

William: Yep, you are too touchy for sure. So what kind of underwear do you prefer?

Torin: Briefs. And no, you can't see them.

Final thoughts from William: Find out for yourself what Cameo looks like naked.

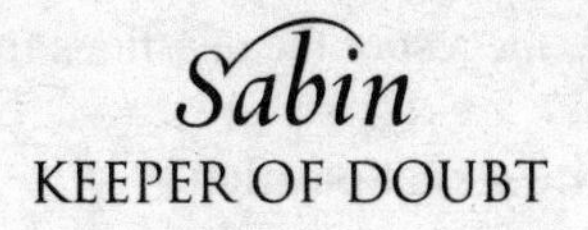

KEEPER OF DOUBT

William: Nickname?

Sabin: Doubtie-poo

William: Zodiac sign?

Sabin: Aries.

William: Why?

Sabin: Because I'm independent and courageous.

William: And short-tempered and impatient.

Sabin: You say tomato, I say shut the hell up.

William: I rest my case. So, what are you looking for in a woman?

Sabin: Straight up *hot.* With a vicious dark side. Red hair, of course. And breasts that fill my hands. Oh, and those breasts have to have hard, pink nipples that are always ready for my mouth. And the woman herself must have legs that—

Gwen: [who decided to sit in on the entire interview, refusing to leave, even after I begged] I apologize for Sabin. Also, I've decided to answer the rest of the questions for him.

William: Favorite sexual position?

Gwen: Pass!

William: Women. No fun. Favorite food?

Gwen: Cheese tots. He's even got me addicted to them.

William: Favorite outfit? Please say "naked" and then offer to model for me.

Gwen: Pervert! The crazier the T-shirt, the more he likes it. But then, he's weird like that.

William: Choice of weapon?

Gwen: Me. But if the weapon kills, he likes it.

William: Favorite moment in the series so far?

Gwen: No question. When he met me.

William: Least favorite?

Sabin: Taking my own interview back over for a sec, and I'm just gonna say it. When Galen got away. Sorry, baby!

William: Hobbies?

Gwen: First, no need to apologize. Second, he loves making me happy.

William: Household chores?

Gwen: Are you kidding? He can't even clean his own room.

William: Least favorite household responsibility?

Gwen: How can he have a least favorite when he doesn't do anything?

Sabin: Hey, now. Who took you shopping? Who helped you plan a wedding? Who calmed you down when you went off the deep end a few thousand times?

Gwen: "Went off the deep end" better be code for "got sweeter by the day."

William: I actually think "off the deep end" means you were a total bridezilla. But we digress. Describe yourself.

Gwen: Sensitive, charming, and utterly caring. When he's not making me angry.

Sabin: None of that is true! I'm a badass, and she knows it. Did you hear the part about how I make her angry? Woman, what are you trying to do to me?

William: What do you think of the fact that your home has been invaded by women?

Gwen: He loves it, of course! He can't imagine his life without me.

William: Who do you think is the toughest/strongest/smartest/cutest Lord?

Gwen: Me. I may not technically be a Lord, but I'm still his favorite *everything.*

William: If you knew you only had twenty-four hours before the Hunters found Pandora's box and killed you, what would you do in the time you had left to live?

Sabin and Gwen (*simultaneously*): Kill our enemies. Every single one of them.

William: What kind of underwear do you prefer?

Gwen: My sisters stole all of his underwear.

Sabin: Along with my weapons. And my cash. And my—

Gwen: But he preferred briefs.

Final thoughts from William: I am never getting married.

William: Nickname?

Gideon: It's not Lies.

William: Big surprise. Zodiac sign?

Gideon: Capricorn.

William: I'll take that to mean you're a Cancer like Torin. Choice of weapon?

Gideon: I hate every weapon I can get my hands on.

William: That's not what I hear. Especially since your hands are still growing back.

Gideon: [*middle finger*]

William: Ah, so a few of your fingers have completely regenerated. Thanks for the visual. So, what are you looking for in a woman?

Gideon: Yeah, 'cause I'm all about permanent. I like 'em ugly, stupid and clingy.

William: Well, aren't you the open-minded one?

Gideon: [*middle finger*]

William: You wish. Favorite food?

Gideon: Fish. Put a plate of sushi in front of me and watch me inhale.

William: Favorite outfit?

Gideon: A dress with ruffles and bows.

William: I'd love for you to show me.

Gideon: [*middle finger*]

William: Favorite moment in the series so far?

Gideon: Let's see. Let me think. I loved the time I got my hands cut off. That was a real party in a box.

William: Is that why you're so fond of showing me your middle finger?

Gideon: [*both middle fingers*]

William: Look at you! Both fingers grew back. Least favorite moment?

Gideon: The moment of my rescue. I wanted to stay strapped to that bed forever, being tortured by Hunters.

William: So you enjoy pain, like Reyes? Interesting. Hobbies?

Gideon: You are a darling man, you know that? As for your question, if I were to say sex, that would be a lie.

William: I'll write down "knitting." Household chores?

Gideon: I can't wait until I'm assigned one.

William: Great. I'll let Lucien know when we're done here.

Gideon: Actually, I'll be busy kissing you silly when we're done.

William: I knew it! I knew you were lusting for me.

Gideon: I love you, man.

William: I know. Now. Least favorite household responsibility?

Gideon: I really hate disposing of my enemies.

William: Describe yourself.

Gideon: Ugly, stupid and clingy. Oh, and weak. Yeah, I'm a real pussy.

William: Sorry, but I have to call off our romance. I don't date ugh-ohs. What do you think of the fact that your home has been invaded by women?

Gideon: I can't stand looking at all that babe candy every day.

William: Who do you think is the smartest Lord?

Gideon: None of us. We're all dumb as shit.

William: Well, we do agree on that.

Gideon: [*middle finger*]

William: If you knew you only had twenty-four hours before the Hunters found Pandora's box and killed you, what would you do in the time you had left to live?

Gideon: Cry, and then go peacefully, without any protest.

William: What kind of underwear do you prefer?

Gideon: I really like it when Leftie and Rightie are bound real tight.

Final thoughts from William: Best interview yet. Gideon let me know on numerous occasions that he's my number one fan.

KEEPER OF MISERY

William: Nickname?

Cameo: Tears. Though no one has called me that in a long time. Maybe because I tend to stab first and ask questions later.

William: I like violence in a woman. What do you think of heading to my room after this?

Cameo: You aren't my type.

William: You don't like beautiful, intelligent, warrior gods?

Cameo: I prefer someone less aware of his appeal.

William: So you admit that I'm appealing. Excellent. Now. Zodiac sign?

Cameo: Why bother?

William: Choice of weapon?

Cameo: Semiautomatics and long-range rifles. I prefer distance with my kills. I don't like when the enemy's misery blends with my own.

William: I like women who prefer long-range rifles. What do you think about heading to my room after this?

Cameo: Never.

William: Just think about it. Now, what are you looking for in a woman? Uh, sorry. I mean, what are you looking for in a man? Unless you are looking for a woman, and in that case, you'll need to describe everything you want to do to her.

Cameo: I'm looking for happiness that I can't destroy.

William: Not exactly the answer I was hoping for. Favorite food?

Cameo: Everything is tasteless. I hate every bite, but know eating is necessary.

William: I like women who think food is tasteless. What do you think about heading to my room after this?

Cameo: No.

William: That's better than "never." We're making progress. Now. Favorite outfit?

Cameo: I wore a dress once. It was silly, frivolous and no good for fighting. But wow, I felt sexy.

William: And I'm sure you looked it. Favorite moment in the series so far?

Cameo: It was nice reuniting with Lucien's team. I guess. I

hadn't seen them in thousands of years, but I'd thought about them. A lot. And I wondered how they were, what they were doing. So seeing them—

William: Wait. Maybe you should keep your answers short and sweet. It's just…your voice…ugh. Least favorite moment?

Cameo: When Club Destiny was blown up—while we were inside it.

William: Short and sweet, woman! Hobbies?

Cameo: I haven't really found anything I enjoy doing. Maybe one day. Well, that's not true. I do enjoy spending time with Torin. I think I remember laughing the other day. Maybe. I'm told I forget when I laugh.

William: Gods, the pain. Do you have a knife handy?

Cameo: No. Why?

William: I would really like to stab myself in the ears.

Cameo: You mean you don't want to head to your room after this?

William: No. Now, household chores?

Cameo: I sometimes help Ashlyn with the cooking.

William: "None" would have sufficed. Least favorite household responsibility?

Cameo: I sometimes help the boys clean their rooms. Pigs.

William: Again, a single word would have done the job. Describe yourself in as few words as possible.

Cameo: The phrase most often tossed at me is "Debbie Downer."

William: What do you think of the fact that your home has been invaded by women?

Cameo: The more the merrier. I guess.

William: Who do you think is the cutest Lord? Please just tell me the name and nothing more.

Cameo: At one time, I had a crush on Strider. Seeing Torin again changed that, however. So my answer is Torin. I just wish he could touch me.

William: We're done here. You can go.

Cameo: But I was told there would be more questions. I'm not leaving until I hear them.

William: I'll give you the final two questions if you promise to kill me afterward.

Cameo: Deal.

William: If you knew you only had twenty-four hours before the Hunters found Pandora's box and killed you, what would you do in the time you had left to live?

Cameo: I doubt my routine would change. Death is much the same as life. You simply are or you aren't.

William: What kind of underwear do you prefer? Now, I know I asked you to be brief before, but as this is the last question, please feel free to elaborate, giving us size, color and just how slowly you pull them on.

Cameo: Supportive.

William: I can honestly say I've never been this disappointed.

Final thoughts: With a roll of duct tape, she'd be the perfect woman.

Amun

KEEPER OF SECRETS

Note from William: Amun remained silent when I asked him these questions. I handed him the questionnaire and a pen, and he walked away. So I went ahead and filled it out for him. I knew, deep down, that he would want me to do so.

Nickname: Spoilsport

Zodiac sign: Half moon (because that's what William showed me as I walked away).

Choice of weapon: Magic wand and fairy dust.

What are you looking for in a woman? I'm not. I'm too attracted to William. He's gorgeous.

Favorite food: Raspberry truffles…spread over William.

Favorite outfit: William. I want to wear his skin.

Favorite moment in the series so far: When William entered my life. I thank the gods every day.

Least favorite: As long as I know William is nearby, I don't care what happens.

Hobbies: Watching William. I even like to watch him while he sleeps. Yes, I'm creepy.

Household chores: If William will let me, I'd love to clean up after him.

Least favorite household responsibility: Anything that doesn't involve William.

Describe yourself: The one thing that defines me is my love for William.

What do you think of the fact that your home has been invaded by women? Have you not heard me? Nothing matters but William.

Who do you think is the smartest Lord? William.

If you knew you only had twenty-four hours before the Hunters found Pandora's box and killed you, what would you do in the time you had left to live? Whatever William wanted me to do.

What kind of underwear do you prefer? Whatever William prefers.

Final thoughts from William: Amun might just be the most intelligent Lord in residence.

Strider
KEEPER OF DEFEAT

William: Nickname?

Strider: Stridey, courtesy of Anya. I suggested Lucien muzzle her, which is why my upper lip is the size of a baseball. Lucien's is the size of a football, though, so it was all good.

William: Sweet! Now, zodiac sign?

Strider: Dude, I'm Sagittarius. For sure. Ruled by the Lucky Star since I'm beauty, brains *and* talent.

William: Funny, that's my sign, too. Choice of weapon?

Strider: Dumb question. Next.

William: Why?

Strider: Any weapon is good. Jeez, when was the last time you actually fought someone?

William: I stabbed your good friend Lucien in the stomach once. Does that count?

Strider: Sure, but if you do it again, I'll gut you.

William: Not if I challenge you to only ever make me smile.

Strider: You're a shithead, you know that?

William: Yes. Now, what are you looking for in a woman?

Strider: Where to begin? I tend to get a bit…possessive with my shit, so I have to be careful with the girls I choose to *honor* with my manliness. Plus, I'm sick to death of girls realizing I hate to lose and then challenging me to keep them happy. So, okay, I think it's safe to say I prefer the clueless variety.

William: First, I'm very glad you realize that saying *girl* doesn't mean teenager. Second, excellent choice. Favorite food?

Strider: Red Hots. Those candies are like heaven in your mouth, man.

William: Favorite outfit?

Strider: Are you kidding? I look awesome in everything.

William: We're both lucky in that regard, I guess. Favorite moment in the series so far?

Strider: Shit. I don't know. Rejoining the other boys, maybe? Next! You're getting mushy on me.

William: Let's see if we can change the vibe. Least favorite?

Strider: You're, like, wanting to make me think and shit, and my brain already hurts. Maybe when I saw what had been done to Gideon, when Sabin handed him over to me while we were at that school for Hunter kids. Damn it. I don't like thinking about that. Thanks a lot. Next!

William: There's no winning with you, is there? Get it. You…winning?

Strider: You're lame, dude.

William: Now you're lying like Gideon. Hobbies?

Strider: Winning. I don't play cards and other games for obvious reasons, but man, I do love to win. It's a rush.

William: Household chores?

Strider: Aeron tried to get me to help him clean up one day. I dodged that bullet, though, and pretended I'd just lost a challenge. I dropped to the ground and didn't get up for an hour. Nice little nap, I must say.

William: Least favorite household responsibility?

Strider: Would be cleaning, if anyone could corner me into doing anything. Can you imagine losing a challenge to a stain?

William: Like the one on your shirt?

Strider: What are you—damn it! Stupid mustard.

William: Describe yourself.

Strider: We already covered awesome. I'm made of the stuff. Intelligent, witty, modest.

William: What do you think of the fact that your home has been invaded by women?

Strider: My entertainment meter hasn't been this high in a long time. My boys are whipped, and it's funny as shit.

William: Who do you think is the cutest Lord?

Strider: Did you ask everyone this question? What'd Paris say? Himself? Shithead. Everyone knows it's me.

William: If you knew you only had twenty-four hours before the Hunters found Pandora's box and killed you, what would you do in the time you had left to live?

Strider: Fuck myself silly, then take a whole bunch of Hunters with me.

William: What kind of underwear do you prefer?

Strider: Boxers. I like me some freedom.

Final thoughts from William: Follow through with that threat to challenge the man to make me happy. Might prove to be amusing.

KEEPER OF DISASTER

William: Nickname?

Kane: Plaster, Unlucky.

William: Zodiac sign?

Kane: Libra maybe.

William: Choice of weapon?

Kane: I most often use long-range rifles. Cameo and I have a stash of them. The further away I am from my target, the less likely I am to meet with a deadly disaster of my own.

William: What are you looking for in a woman?

Kane: I stopped looking a long time ago. I'm no good for anyone, least of all someone I could grow to love.

William: And you let a little thing like that stop you? Five words: You don't want it enough. Now, favorite food?

Kane: Anything without plaster or burns or debris.

William: Favorite outfit?

Kane: Anything without plaster or burns or debris.

William: Your new nickname should be Picky. Favorite moment in the series so far?

Kane: Each time one of my friends has fallen in love and made it work. That means there's hope for the rest of us. Maybe.

William: Least favorite?

Kane: Every time I'm left behind from battle because I'm too dangerous to have around.

William: Why don't you just go anyway? I would.

Kane: I care about my friends.

William: Yeah, but you should love yourself more. That's my philosophy. Any hobbies?

Kane: Don't tell anyone, but I like to draw. I swear to the gods, if you tell anyone, I will rip out a page of your book. Yeah, Anya told me where she keeps it.

William: Like that scares me. You're not the first to threaten me today. Or even in the last hour.

Kane: Anya! Anya, get in here!

[*short recess while a fight breaks out*]

Note from William: We return to our regularly scheduled programming, now that a wall has crumbled to dust and our chairs are in tatters. Oh, yeah. And I won. Or would have, if that chunk of rock hadn't bashed right into my temple.

William: What are your household chores?

Kane: First, the fight was a tie. Second, I've been helping Aeron with the cleaning.

William: What'd he bribe you with?

Kane: Bribe? He didn't bribe. He asked and I agreed.

William: Sucker! Least favorite household responsibility?

Kane: I don't mind any of it, really. The chores make for a clean, well-run home and a clean, well-run home is a happy home. Except when people trying to interview you say they're going to spill your secrets to everyone.

William: It shouldn't surprise you that I don't do off-the-record.

Kane: Anyone ever tell you that you're the male version of Anya?

William: No, but thank you! Describe yourself.

Kane: Catastrophe walking.

William: What do you think of the fact that your home has been invaded by women?

Kane: Honestly? I wish they'd leave. Not to be cruel, you understand, but I'm just afraid I'll hurt them. I should be able to relax at home, you know?

William: Agreed. A man's home is his love nest. And if you can't relax in your love nest, life isn't worth living. Who do you think is the strongest Lord?

Kane: Sabin. He always has been, always will be. That's why I follow him. Boy is ruthless, and you gotta love that in a leader.

William: If you knew you only had twenty-four hours before the Hunters found Pandora's box and killed you, what would you do in the time you had left to live?

Kane: Strider told me you asked him this, as well. He also told me his answer, taking as many Hunters as he could with him. I like that.

William: Copying answers is not allowed.

Kane: What are you going to do? Give me an F?

William: Moving on. What kind of underwear do you prefer?

Kane: It's actually best if I wear a cup.

Final thoughts from William: I had no idea Kane would prove to be the most frustrating of the Lords.

Final *final* thoughts from William: The Lords of the Underworld are loyal, brave and fierce—boring!—as well as ill-mannered, shady and borderline nymphomaniacs. I know, I'm as shocked as you are. But suddenly I'm feeling like a proud papa, as if I somehow corrupted them just right. There might even be a tear in my eye.

But if this interview taught me anything, it's that I actually like the men here. Not that I'll *ever* admit that out loud. What I will admit: they are a shitload of fun to tease. And yeah, I think I'll stick around for a while longer. Hell, maybe I'll even start helping with their little war. Bashing a few heads in could be interesting….

ROUND TABLE:
The Women of the Underworld Speak

GILLY CLAPPED HER HANDS, drawing everyone's attention. Her friends, Ashlyn, Anya, Danika, Gwen, Bianka and Legion, were sitting around her at the dinner table. No food was present. Every morsel would have been flying in seconds, she knew, so she'd purposely trashed the hors d'oeuvres before anyone arrived.

Anyway, she'd called the girls together because, well, William had asked her to do so. And what William wanted, William got. He was *hot* and smart and funny and— Sorry. Digressing.

Anyway, he'd just interviewed the men, and had asked her to do the same to the women. He'd also told her to ignore any rumors about him and some girl. Whatever that meant. So, here she was, and here they were. Much as she lov—uh, liked William as a friend—a very sexy friend—her interview was going to be *way* better than his. After all, everyone knew it was the women of the Underworld who made the series what it was….

Gilly: First, everyone should know I'm videotaping this for posterity, but don't let that deter you from getting personal. A few of you sat through William's interviews with the men, and you know they spilled their guts. Now I'd like you to spill yours. Not literally, of course. Crap! I'm making a mess of this already. I'm so lame! Anyway, to kick off this round table, I have to admit something. When Danika first brought me to stay in the Budapest fortress, I thought she was insane for getting involved with a group of men who were so clearly dangerous, barely able to control themselves and the demons inside them. I was maybe kinda sorta even a little afraid of them. Okay, I still am. But every day I see exactly how tender and affectionate they are with you, and, well, I guess I'm learning to be a little more open-minded in my definition of happiness.

So along those lines, my first question is, what's the best part about dating or marrying a Lord of the Underworld? And remember, no topic is too personal here. Feel free to give us all the juicy details. [*wiggles eyebrows*]

Ashlyn: Well, for me, it's feeling loved for the first time in my life. And the incredible sense of peace. And finding a place I belong. And creating a baby with my soul mate. And—

Anya: If you're not going to mention the sex, then it's someone else's turn. Gilly said juicy details, darling. Juicy. I, for one, think we should play by her rules.

Bianka: Anya, follow the rules? Funny! What next? Angels mating with demons? Hey, wait a sec…

Ashlyn: [*blushes*] Obviously the sex is amazing. Maddox was—okay, I feel really weird talking about this in front of you, Gilly. You're only sixteen.

Gilly: Just turned seventeen, thank you, and believe me, I already know a lot more than I should on the subject.

Ashlyn: All right, well, Maddox was my first, my only, and wow. Just wow. He knows what I want before even I know.

Anya: Me, too! Well, not with Maddox, but with Lucien. He

was my first, and sweet heaven, he rocked my world. The things that man does with his tongue are—

Danika: TMI, goddess. TMI. Reyes wasn't my first, but I'm glad he's my last. No one else could ever compare. The intensity of his touch…[*shivers*]

Legion: Well, I lovesss Aeron 'cause he knowsss how pretty I am. Essspecially when I wearsss tiarasss.

Anya: Tiaras that do not belong to you, by the way.

Bianka: [*laughs*] Like you can chastise someone for thievery, Miss Sticky Fingers.

Anya: You either, Pecan Pie.

Gwen: Girls, stop arguing. It's my turn to talk about Sabin. [*props elbows on table*] I always pictured myself marrying a nice, normal, nonthreatening human man—

Anya: Boring!

Gwen: Exactly right. That's why I'm glad I ended up with my strong, fierce, brave warrior. Who won't let me out of bed until I'm deliciously satisfied.

Anya: I hope you do the same for him. After everything you put him through while planning your wedding, well, you owe him. Big time. I will be a much calmer and more level-headed bride when I walk down the aisle with Lucien.

Bianka: Having strippers at your wedding does not equate with level-headedness. Anyhoodles, I want to talk about Lysander. He's not a Lord, he's a do-gooder angel, but he does turn into a devil while we're in bed. You should all be jealous.

Danika: [*grinning*] I think it's safe to say we're all very satisfied women.

Gilly: Not all of us. But okay, moving on. Why don't you tell us what you find sexiest about the Lords—either your mate in particular or the group as a whole?

Anya: Ooh, me first on this one. Although, I can't just name one thing. Lucien smells like roses, has that deliciously scarred face, and then there are those shiver-inducing mismatched eyes.

Danika: With Reyes, well, you wouldn't know it to look at him, but he is so…sweetly vulnerable. It amazes me sometimes.

Ashlyn: Maddox, too! I know this is a weird thing to say about the man who houses Violence inside him, but I really think the sexiest thing about him is his kindness.

Gwen: Poor things.

Ashlyn: What do you mean?

Danika: Yeah. Do tell.

Gwen: Well, Sabin is anything but kind, and I love it. He goes total warrior on my body, like it's a battleground to be conquered, and I—

Bianka: Eww. Please, no more sex details from you. There are just some things you do not want to imagine your baby sister doing. Or having done to her. But I'm sure you'd love to hear about your older sister and her angel. So I don't mind telling you that what I find sexiest about Lysander is the surprised delight that claims his expression every time I do something naughty to his body. Like last night, when I introduced him to—

Gwen: You were wrong. You can't dish if I can't dish.

Bianka: Hey, I don't make the rules, I just follow 'em. Like Anya. And I'm getting good at that, now that I'm with Lysander. He does like to reward me when I do something nice. Like last night, when I introduced him to—

Legion: Ssshut it, Harpy. I getsss to talk about my Aeron now. He isss sssexy becaussse he hasss them pretty portraitsss on hisss body and sssometimesss I just want to tassste them and—

Anya: Triple eww. If baby sisters can't talk about sex, neither can demon minions. Stick to tiaras next time, ok?

Bianka: Will no one let me tell my story about last night?

Everyone: No.

Gilly: I'm willing to admit I was wrong. Some details I do

not want. So maybe this is a good time to change the subject. We've talked about some of the good things about life with the Lords. But I bet there are some downsides, too. It can't be all sunshine and naked roses living with men like these. Anyone want to give an example of something that's especially difficult to deal with?

Ashlyn: Well, obviously the Hunters can make life difficult sometimes.

Anya: There's the understatement of the century.

Gwen: Yeah, it's tough to deal with the idea that Sabin is constantly on the battlefield and that the enemy is getting increasingly harder to defeat.

Anya: You know what I hate most, though? That Lucien still has to visit Hell on a daily basis because of his soul-escorting duties. He deserves only heaven.

Danika: I know what you mean. Sometimes watching Reyes hurt himself hurts *me*.

Gwen: Yeah, those demons…I've tamed Doubt, but Sabin hates that the beast can hurt his loved ones so deeply. And what Sabin hates, I hate.

Bianka: Yeah, but at least now he has a secret weapon—you! Not to mention the rest of the Skyhawks. Harpies plus Lords equals bye-bye, Hunters.

Ashlyn: I have never loved a math equation more.

Bianka: I know, right? But I'd say a bigger problem here at Chez Demon is just making sure the Hunters don't find Pandora's box before we can.

Legion: Well, I don't like all the visssitsss from rotten angelsss and dumb godsss.

Anya: Hey, watch it. *I'm* a goddess, remember?

Bianka: Yeah, but only a minor one, so you don't count! And angels aren't that bad, minion. They're actually kind of sexy.

Legion: Take that back!

Bianka: Hell, no! I love my man, and no one calls him rotten but me.

Gilly: Before you come to blows, let's move on to the next question. They say that women in love want to see everyone around them happy and in love, as well. But there are still, what, eight unmated Lords in the fortress? Nine if you count William [*blushes*]. Any predictions for who might be the next to find happiness? Anyone you especially want to set up or see happily settled down?

Anya: Was that a blush, Gilly darling? Well, maybe in a few years, when you're older, something can happen with Willie—but gods know that with his prophecy, he's not destined to have good luck with his chosen woman, so be careful.

Gilly: What do you mean? Tell me everything!

Anya: I just did. That's all I know.

Ashlyn: Hey, guys. I think something's wrong with Danika.

Everyone but Danika: What?

Danika: [*gaze fixed*] Aeron. Aeron is next, I think. I see clouds. Flames. Dark hair. White wings. And… blood. So much blood.

Legion: [*bangs table with fist*] You better sssee that dumb angel dying and me in Aeron'sss armsss becaussse he dessstined to marry me.

Danika: [*blinking*] I—I—I don't know. Those wings…they were paired with a flowing white gown and dark curly hair. And Aeron was holding her, and she had a humanlike body.

Legion: I get a white gown, no problem. And a wig. I do that right now. And I can paint myssself peach. [*storms away*]

Anya: Poor Legion.

Bianka: Let's pretend *that* didn't happen—and that trouble isn't heading for our doorstep if Aeron does end up wanting an angel. Legion will fight to the death for him, I think.

Ashlyn: I'd love to see Cameo settled down—she's so lovely and so sad. I was really hoping something would come of all the sparks flying between her and Torin, but it doesn't look like that's going to pan out. Maybe I can make some friends in town and, I don't know, set her up, as Gilly suggested. But is there anyone who's good enough, or strong enough, to deal with Cameo's voice? Anyone our boys would accept?

Danika: Probably not. She's like their kid sister. And you know how brothers protect their sisters.

Bianka: And what about poor Paris? He's so hawt and so miserable—it'd be great to see him happy and settled with one woman. Personally I vote for one of the other Skyhawks—Taliyah or Kaia. Then we can keep it in the family.

Anya: Nah. Kaia's a ho—said with love—and Taliyah, even after all her centuries alive, still isn't in touch with her feminine side. After everything Paris has been through, he needs a soft, sweet, very feminine woman.

Ashlyn: Maybe one of the Skyhawks could date Amun. I want to see him settled down, too. And Kane. And Torin—God, poor Torin. All of them deserve to be as happy and content as I've been blessed to feel.

Gwen: Well, I admit I have a soft spot for Strider. He was one of the first Lords who was actually nice to me—and he's cute, too. Like Ashlyn, I wish I knew someone to set him up with. My year of captivity kind of severed all my human relationships.

Anya: All your choices are well and good, but I can tell you that Gideon's turn is coming, and soon. [*rubs hands together*] That boy isn't going to know what hit him.

Ashlyn: Details, please!

Anya: That's all I know.

Bianka: Yeah. Right. When did you become so secretive?

Anya: When I realized it's fun to know stuff and taunt everyone with the details.

Gilly: On that note, it's time for our next question. Ashlyn, you're pregnant with Maddox's baby. Yay! How do you feel about bringing a new generation of Lords into the world? For that matter, how do all of you feel at the prospect of children?

Ashlyn: [*beaming and softening*] I'm beyond excited, and can't wait to hold my child in my arms. [*grows sober, clears throat*] But am I nervous? Hell, yeah. First, Maddox and I still don't know exactly what kind of baby this will be—a demon? A human with "extra" abilities, like me? A normal human? Some combination thereof? But we do know we'll love it, no matter what. And I swear that this child will have a happier upbringing than I did.

Danika: You know all of us will love this baby as our own. You're going to have more babysitters than you know what to do with. Even the men are getting mushy at the prospect of a child in the house. I think I caught Reyes knitting baby booties the other day—he swore he was just using the knitting needles to cut himself, but I have my doubts.

Ashlyn: [*beams from ear to ear*] That's so sweet.

Gwen: Sabin and I are going to wait awhile. I mean, he's afraid his demon would turn on our kids, and the thought tears him up. What he doesn't realize is, I'd rip through that demon if I even suspected a dark whisper had reached our child's ear. And anyway, with the Hunters out there, willing to capture and kill our offspring—

Bianka: I told you, that's not going to be an issue now that the Lords have the Skyhawks on their team. But Ashlyn, I should warn you that Lysander's had some kind of prediction about your pregnancy. He won't give me the scoop, but he did say you're going to get more than you bargained for.

Ashlyn: Seduce the info out of him! I have to know.

Bianka: On it! Believe me.

Anya: Meanwhile, I don't know about kids. They don't do anything you tell them to do! It's frustrating. Like that one kid we rescued from the Hunter compound? The one who can walk through walls and hurt you when he ghosts through you? Well, I left him with my mom and dad, and I visit him from time to time, and I told him to polish my shoes. Do you know what he said to me? "Polish them yourself." The nerve of the boy!

[*everyone stares at her*]

Anya: What?

Gilly: I think Anya's delusion is a great place to conclude our discussion. I want to thank you guys for meeting with me and sharing way too much. Even though I asked you to do so. But you can't blame me. I'm a teenager, and someone should have told me that was a dumb idea.

So go on. Go get your men and do what I know you're all dying to do. You nymphos! I'll just sit here and think of Will—no one in particular.

FREQUENTLY ASKED QUESTIONS

HEARING FROM READERS is one of my favorite things about being a writer. You guys are supportive, kind, unerringly sweet and my biggest cheerleaders. I can never thank you enough! But I can answer your questions [grin]. *So, I thought I'd share my answers to the top ten most frequently e-mailed questions.*

How do I get the butterfly from the Lords of the Underworld covers so I can have a tattoo made?

Unfortunately neither my publisher nor I can supply you with the actual butterfly artwork. Our best advice is to take the book with you and show the artist. Hopefully, he or she can draw a butterfly to match. Good luck! (By the way, I'm thinking about getting one myself! I'll post pictures on my blog if I do.)

Will all the Lords get a story? Even Paris, who you have tortured and tortured—when are you going to stop torturing him?

Absolutely, all of the Lords will get a story! I want each Lord—and my sweet, sweet William—to get a happily-ever-after. As you said, they've been tortured enough. Well, for the most part. (I'm grinning while I type that because a lot more torture is on the way!)

But I don't know exactly when Paris's story will be told. As I mentioned before, I have finally figured out the direction I want him to go. Not so good news: I have to plant the seeds of his story in other books first. Great news: He deserves the best, and I want to make sure I deliver!

Is Sienna alive?

As you might have read in *The Darkest Prison,* Sienna's soul has been saved and she is in the heavens with Cronus. In the upcoming *The Darkest Passion* and *The Darkest Lie,* you will be given glimpses of what has been happening to her since getting up there. And what Cronus plans to do with her....

Do you design the book covers yourself?

The publisher designs and creates the covers, and I actually have very little say. But I have been beyond happy with the covers for the Lords of the Underworld series. And by "beyond happy," I mean they are covered in my drool. I'm only sad I haven't gotten to meet the models. (Hint hint, Harlequin.)

You should make the Lords of the Underworld into a movie. Why haven't you?

Getting a book made into a movie is a very long process that the writer actually has no control over. I wish, though! I would love to see my big, strong warriors on the big screen. And while writing their books, I try to think of which actors would play them. Weird fact: I can do this for every book I've written *but* the Lords of the Underworld books. I'm utterly stuck. Who do you see playing them?

The women of the series are easier for me to pick. Here's my dream list:

Ashlyn—Jessica Alba
Anya—Charlize Theron
Danika—Sienna Miller

Gwen—Isla Fisher
Bianka—Rachel Bilson
Olivia—Scarlett Johansson
Scarlet—Kate Beckinsale

There's a rumor floating around that you and Harlequin author Jill Monroe actually acted out a scene of *The Darkest Night* for your Internet show, Author Talk. Is that true? And if so, why haven't you posted it?

As embarrassed as I am to admit this, yes, it's true. She played Ashlyn and I played Maddox. We filmed it for Author Talk, and then decided our viewing public was not ready for such…outstanding acting. However, we have been talking about one day posting a clip.

Why did you originally only publish *The Darkest Fire, The Amazon's Curse* and *The Darkest Prison* as e-books? I hate e-books.

The publication of *The Darkest Night* was pushed back by something like eight months and *The Darkest Kiss* close to six to give me time to write *The Darkest Pleasure.* We hated making readers wait and wanted to offer something earlier. The best and only way to go about that was with an e-book.

Why didn't you give Torin and Cameo a happily-ever-after together?

I played with the idea. I did. The sparks are certainly there. He makes her laugh, and he doesn't mind her voice. But in the end, I realized they weren't right for each other long-term. They just didn't…consume each other. He doesn't wipe away her misery and she doesn't make him forget what he is, what he can and can't do. As much as they've gone through, they both deserve a love beyond anything they've ever known. And that's what I plan to give them.

Is Torin going to end up with Nucking Futs Nïx?

I never say never. Except for those times I say never. But this isn't one of those times. Although it might be. Maybe.

Actually, the amazing Nïx will end up with a man in Kresley Cole's Immortals After Dark world, and Torin will end up with a woman in the Lords of the Underworld world. If Torin were to touch Nïx, and Nïx were to get sick, then the Valkyries would have to fight the Lords, and the Lords would, well, possibly die. Therefore, Torin has yet to meet—or see—his lady love. But don't worry, she's on her way!

You've never told us straight-up about the curse concerning William. We only know it involves a woman. So, what's the curse?

To be honest, I don't know yet. The answer will come to me one day, but until then, I'm clueless. And believe me, I want to know about his curse more than I want to know where Pandora's box is. Trust me, that's a lot.

Sneak Peek

AT LONG LAST, IN June and July 2010 respectively, Aeron and Gideon will find the women of their dreams. Or nightmares, in Gideon's case. I had such a wonderful time with these warriors. In *The Darkest Passion* (June), Aeron—stubborn Aeron, who thinks humans are weak—is not prepared for Olivia, an angel who has lost her immortality and is therefore weaker than a human. In *The Darkest Lie* (July), Gideon—sarcastic Gideon, who loves his freedom and thinks himself invulnerable to other people's lies—has no idea what to make of the woman claiming to be his wife.

There are plot twists I didn't see coming, passion that nearly burned the pages and action that left me at the edge of my seat. I hope you'll join me for their journeys! To whet your appetites, here's a preview of chapter two of *The Darkest Passion*.

CHAPTER TWO

"AERON! AERON!"

At the fortress, Aeron's booted feet hit the balcony that led into his bedroom. Jolted by the unfamiliar female voice, he released Paris.

"Aeron!"

At that third ear-piercing feminine cry of terror and desperation, both he and Paris spun to face the hill below them. Thick trees knifed toward the sky, obscuring visibility, but there, amid the dappled greens and browns, he could just make out a figure draped in white.

A figure rushing toward their home.

"Shadow Girl?" Paris asked. "How the hell did she make it past our gate so quickly? And on foot, no less?"

Aeron had explained what happened with the woman from the alley along the way. "That's not her." This voice was higher, richer and far less confident. "The gate…I don't know."

Weeks ago, after he and Paris had recovered from battle wounds inflicted by Hunters, they had erected an iron gate around the fortress. That gate stretched fifteen feet tall, was wrapped with barbed wire and had tips sharp enough to cut glass. It also vibrated with enough electricity to send a human into cardiac arrest. Anyone who attempted to climb it wouldn't live long enough to reach the other side.

"Think she's Bait?" Paris tilted his head, his study of her

intensifying. "She could have been dropped from a heli, I guess."

Hunters had been known to use beautiful human females to lure the Lords out into the open, distract them and capture them for torture. This one certainly seemed to meet the criteria, possessing long, wavy hair the color of chocolate, skin as pale as a cloud and a curved, ethereal body. Aeron couldn't make out her facial features just yet, but he would bet they were exquisite.

His wings folded into their slits as he answered, "Maybe." Just his luck to have to deal with Hunters when half of his friends weren't around to help.

Several of his fellow warriors were in Rome, searching the Temple of the Unspoken Ones. They hoped to find *anything* that would lead them to missing godly artifacts. Four artifacts that, when used together, would then lead to the location of Pandora's box.

Hunters hoped to use that box to lock the demons back inside, destroying the Lords, since man could no longer live without demon. The Lords simply hoped to demolish it.

"There are trip wires out there." The more Paris spoke, the more Aeron noticed a tremor in his tone. Because of Shadow Girl, as Paris had called her, there hadn't been time for him to bed anyone in town, so his strength must be draining. "If she's not careful... Even if she *is* Bait, she doesn't deserve to die like that."

"Aeron!"

Paris fisted the balcony railing and leaned down for a better look. "Why's she calling for you?"

And why was she using his name with such familiarity? "If she's Bait, Hunters are probably out there right now, lying in wait for me. I'll try to help her and they'll attack."

Paris straightened, face suddenly bathed in moonlight. Bruises had formed under his eyes. "I'll get the others, and we'll take care of her. Of them." He was off before Aeron could reply, striding out of the bedroom, boots thumping against the stone floor.

Aeron kept his focus on the girl. As she continued to race upward, closer and closer to him, he realized the white cloth draping her was actually a robe. And the back of it, which he hadn't been able to see before, was bright red.

She wasn't wearing shoes, and when her bare toe slammed into a rock, she fell, that mass of chocolate hair cascading around her face. There were flowers woven through the curls, some of the petals missing. There were also twigs, but he didn't think she'd placed those there intentionally. Her hands were shaking as she reached up and pushed the strands away.

Finally, her features came into view, and every muscle in his body jumped, tensed. She was exquisite, just as he'd supposed. Even splotchy and swollen from tears as she was. She had huge sky-blue eyes, a perfectly sloped nose, perfectly sculpted cheeks and jaw, both just a little rounded, and perfect lips that formed a lush heart.

He'd never met her before, he would have remembered, but there was something almost…familiar about her.

She lumbered to a stand, grimacing and groaning, then started forward. Once again, she fell. A pained sob escaped her, but still she persisted, rising, edging toward the fortress. Bait or not, such determination was admirable.

Somehow she managed to dodge all the traps, weaving around them as if she knew where they were, but when she hit another rock and tumbled to the ground for a third time, she stayed down, shuddering, crying.

His eyes widened as he studied her back. The red…was that…blood? Fresh, still wet? The metallic tang of it drifted on the breeze and into Aeron's nostrils, confirming his suspicions. Oh, yes. It was.

Hers? Or someone else's?

"Aeron." No longer a scream, but a pathetic wail. "Help me."

His wings expanded before he could think things through. Yes, Hunters would purposely injure Bait before sending her into the lions' den, hoping to gain sympathy from the target. Yes, he'd probably end up with arrows and bullets in his back—again—but he wasn't going to leave her out there, injured and vulnerable. Wasn't going to allow his friends to risk their lives to save—or destroy—his little visitor.

Why me? he wondered as he shot from the balcony. Up, up he soared before falling toward her. He zigzagged to make himself less of a target, but no arrows whizzed by and no gunshots sounded. Still, rather than land beside her, he increased his speed, reached out his arms and scooped her up without ever slowing his pace.

Perhaps she was afraid of heights and that was the reason for her sudden stiffening. Perhaps she'd expected him to be killed before ever reaching her and, when he'd actually managed to latch on to her, had stiffened from terror. Either way, he didn't care. He'd done what he'd set out to do. He had her.

"Be still, or by the gods, I *will* drop you." He had her by the stomach, her face aimed toward the ground. That way, she could see just how far she would fall.

"Aeron?" She craned her neck to see him. The moment their gazes connected, she relaxed. Even smiled slowly. "Aeron," she repeated on a sigh of pleasure. "I was afraid you wouldn't come."

That pleasure, undiluted and untouched by malice, surprised—and confused—him. Women never looked at him like that. "Your fear was misplaced. You should have feared I *would* come."

Her smile faded.

Better. The only thing that disturbed him now was the radio silence from his demon. As with Shadow Girl, images and urges should have bombarded him by now. *Worry about it later.*

Continuing to zigzag, he flew into his bedroom, not stopping on the balcony as usual. He needed cover as quickly as possible. Just in case. Except, just as he was retracting his wings, they slammed into both sides of the doorway and fire rushed from the tips to the arches.

Aeron ignored the pain as he skidded to his feet. When he righted himself, he strode to the bed and gently laid his charge atop the mattress, facedown. He ran a fingertip along the ridge of her spine and her heart-shaped lips parted in an agonized gasp. He'd hoped she had been doused with someone else's blood, but no. Her injuries were real.

The knowledge wouldn't soften him. She'd probably inflicted the damage herself, or allowed the Hunters to do it—just for the sympathy it would evoke. *No sympathy from me. Only irritation.* As he stomped to his closet, he drew his wings into his back, but broken as they now were, they wouldn't fit under their flaps. That only increased his irritation with her.

He didn't have rope and didn't want to leave the room to find some, so he grabbed two of the neckties Ashlyn—Maddox's woman—had given him in case he ever wanted to "dress up." He stalked back to the bed.

She had turned her head toward him, pressing her cheek into the mattress, her gaze tracking his every move, as if she couldn't help but peer at him—and not in revulsion as most females did. She watched him with something akin to desire.

An act, surely.

And yet, that desire…there was something familiar about it. Something unsettling. *That's* what he'd noticed earlier, he thought. When she'd called his name, that same desire had been evident, and deep down, he'd known he'd encountered it before. When? Where?

From her?

He continued to stare down at her, and Wrath—was still silent, he realized. This was, supposedly, the first time he'd ever been in her presence, yet his demon still wasn't flashing her sins through his mind. That was…odd. Had happened only once before. With Legion. Why, he'd never figured out. Gods knew his baby girl had sinned.

So why was it happening again? With possible Bait, no less?

This woman, had she never sinned? Had she never said an unkind word to another? Never purposely tripped someone or stolen something as simple as a piece of candy? Those pure sky eyes said no. Or, like Legion, had she sinned but for whatever reason flew under Wrath's radar?

"Who are you?" His fingers wrapped around one of her fragile wrists—mmm, warm, smooth skin—and anchored it to a bedpost with the tie. He repeated the action with her other wrist.

Not once did she protest. It was as if she'd expected—and already accepted—that she would receive such treatment. "My name is Olivia."

Olivia. A pretty name. Fitting. Delicate. Actually, the only thing that *wasn't* delicate about her was her voice. Layer after layer of…what was that? The only word he could think to describe it was *honesty,* and so much drifted from her, he was knocked backward.

That voice had never told a lie, he would bet. It couldn't have.

"What are you doing here, Olivia?"

"I'm here…I'm here for you."

Again, that truth…it was a force that flowed into his ears, through his body, and sent him staggering. There wasn't room for doubts. Not a single one. He was simply *compelled* to believe her.

Sabin, keeper of Doubt, would have loved her. Nothing pleased the warrior's demon more than tearing down another's confidence.

"Are you Bait?"

"No."

Again, he believed her; he had no choice. "Are you here to kill me?" He straightened and crossed his arms over his chest, glaring down at her, waiting.

He knew how fierce he looked, but again, she didn't react as females usually did: trembling, cowering, crying. She fluttered her long, black lashes at him, seemingly hurt that he'd maligned her character.

"No, of course not." She paused. "Well, not anymore."

Not anymore? "So. At one time, you meant to slay me?"

"I was once sent to do so, yes."

Such honesty… "By whom?"

"At first, I was sent by the One True Deity to merely watch you. I didn't mean to scare your little friend away. I was only trying to do my job." Fresh tears filled her eyes, turning those beautiful blue irises into pools of remorse.

No softening. "Who is the One True Deity?"

Pure love lit her expression, momentarily chasing away the sheen of pain. "Deity of you, Deity of me. Far more powerful than your gods, though mostly content to remain in the shadows, and so rarely acknowledged. Father to humans. Father to…angels. Like me."

Angels. Like me. As the words echoed in his head, Aeron's eyes widened. No wonder his demon couldn't sense any wickedness in her. No wonder her gaze felt familiar to him. She was an angel. *The* angel, actually. The one sent to kill him, by her own admission. Though she didn't plan to end him "anymore." Why?

And did it matter? This delicate creature had been, at one point, his appointed executioner.

Suddenly he wanted to laugh. As if she could have overpowered *him.*

You couldn't see her. Would you truly have been able to stop her, had she gone for your head?

The thought hit him and he lost his amusement. *She* was the one who had been watching him these many weeks. *She* was the one who had followed him, unseen, driving a pained Legion away.

Which raised the question of why Wrath wasn't reacting as Legion always did. With fear and even physical agony. Perhaps the angel controlled which demons sensed her, he considered. That would be a handy ability to possess, keeping her intended victims ignorant of her presence—and intentions.

He waited for brutal rage to fill him. Rage he'd promised to unleash on this creature time and time again should she ever reveal herself. When the rage failed to appear, he waited for resolve. He must protect his friends at any cost.

But that, too, remained hopelessly out of reach. What he did get instead? Confusion.

"You are…"

"The angel who has been watching you, yes," she said, confirming his suspicions. "Or rather, I *was* an angel." Her eyelids sealed shut, tears catching in her lashes. Her chin trembled. "Now I am nothing."

He believed her—how could he not? That voice… Seriously, he wanted to doubt her about something, *anything,* but couldn't manage it. Aeron extended a shaky hand. *What are you, a child? Man up.*

Scowling at his display of weakness, he steadied his hand and flipped away her hair, careful not to touch her injured skin. He pinched the scooped neck of her robe and gently tugged. The soft material ripped easily, revealing the expanse of her back.

Once again his eyes widened. Between her shoulder blades, where wings should have protruded, were two long grooves of broken skin, tendons torn to the spine, ripped muscle and even a peek at bone. They were savage wounds, violent and unmerciful, blood still seeping from them. He'd had his own wings forcibly removed once, and it had been the most painful injury of his very long life.

"What happened?" The hoarseness of his voice threw him.

"I've fallen," she rasped, shame dripping from her tone. She buried her face in the pillow. "I'm an angel no more."

"Why?" Never having encountered an angel before—well, besides Lysander, but that bastard didn't count because he refused to speak to the Lords about anything of importance—Aeron didn't know much about them. He only knew what Legion had told him, and of course, there was a very good chance her recounting had been colored by her hatred of them. Nothing she'd described fit with the female on his bed.

Angels, Legion had said, were emotionless, soulless creatures with only one purpose: the destruction of their darker counterpart, the demons. She'd also claimed that, every so often, an angel would succumb to the lures of the flesh, intrigued by the very beings he—or she—was supposed to loathe. That angel would then be kicked straight into Hell, where the demons she had once defeated were finally allowed a little vengeance.

Was that what had happened to this one? Aeron wondered. A trip to Hell where demons had tormented her? Possible.

Should he untie her? Her eyes…so guileless, so innocent. Now they said *help me.* And *save me.*

But most of all, they said *hold me and never let go.*

He'd been tricked by such innocence before, he thought, stopping himself before he could act. Baden had been tricked, as well, and had died for it.

A smart man would learn a little more about this woman first, he decided.

"Who took your wings?" The question emerged as a gruff bark, and he nodded in satisfaction.

She gulped, shuddered. "Once I was cast—"

"Aeron, you stupid shit," a male voice said, hushing her. "Tell me you didn't—" Paris stalked into his bedroom, but ground to a halt when he spotted Olivia. His eyes narrowed and he ran his tongue over his teeth. "So. It's true. You really flew out there and grabbed her."

Olivia stiffened, keeping her face hidden from view. Her shoulders began shaking as if she were sobbing. Was she finally scared? Now?

Why? Women adored Paris.

Concentrate. Aeron didn't have to ask how Paris knew what he'd done. Torin, keeper of the demon of Disease, monitored the fortress and the hill it sat upon twenty-eight hours a day, nine days a week—or so it seemed. "I thought you were gathering the others?"

"Torin texted me, and I went to him first."

"And what did he tell you about her?"

"Hallway," his friend said, motioning to the door with a tilt of his chin.

Aeron shook his head. "We can discuss her here. She's not Bait."

Another swipe of his tongue over his straight, white teeth. "And I thought *I* was stupid when it came to females. How do you know what she is? Did she tell you and you couldn't help but believe her?" His tone was sneering.

"She's an angel, despot. The one who's been watching me."

That wiped the scorn from Paris's expression. "An actual angel? From heaven?"

"Yes."

"Like Lysander?"

"Yes."

Very slowly, Paris looked her over. Female connoisseur that he was—or used to be—he probably knew everything about her body by the time he was done. The size of her breasts, the flare of her hips, the exact length of her legs. That did *not* annoy Aeron. She meant nothing to him. Nothing but trouble.

"Whatever she is," Paris said, far less angry than he'd been, "it doesn't mean she's not working with our enemy. Need I remind you that Galen, the world's biggest blowhard, says *he's* an angel."

"Yeah, but he's lying."

"And she can't be?"

Aeron scrubbed a hand down his suddenly tired face. "Olivia. Are you working with Galen to harm us?"

"No," she mumbled, and Paris stumbled backward, just as Aeron had done, clutching his chest.

"My gods," his friend gasped. "That voice…"

"I know."

"She's not Bait, and she's not helping Galen." A statement of fact from Paris now.

"I know," Aeron repeated.

Paris shook his head as if to clear his thoughts. "Still. Lucien will want to search the hills for Hunters. Just in case."

One of the many reasons Aeron had always followed Lucien. The warrior was smart and cautious. "When he finishes, call a meeting with whoever's here and tell them about the other woman. The one from the alley."

Paris nodded and suddenly there was a sparkle in his blue eyes. "Quite an evening you've had so far, huh? I wonder who else you'll meet tonight."

"Gods help me if there's another," he muttered.

"You shouldn't have challenged Cronus, my friend."

Aeron's stomach clenched as his gaze swung back to the angel. Had the god king actually answered his dare? Was Olivia to be the one who led him on a merry chase? His heart *was* pounding, he realized, and his blood *was* heating.

He ground his teeth. Didn't matter whether she was or not.

She could try to tempt him, but even she, with her fall of chocolate hair, baby blues and heart-shaped lips, would fail to do so.

"I don't regret my words." Truth or lie, he didn't know. He hadn't thought Cronus had any power over the angels. So how then would the god king have sent her here? Or was he not responsible? Perhaps Aeron was mistaken and Cronus had nothing to do with this.

Again, it didn't matter. Not only would the angel fail to tempt him, he would ensure she left before she had time to cause a single moment of concern.

"Just so you know," Paris said, "Torin saw this one on the hill with his hidden cameras. Said she dug her way out of the ground."

Out of the ground. Did that mean she *had* been tossed into Hell, and had then been forced to claw her way free? He couldn't picture the fragile-looking female capable of such a thing—and surviving, that is. But then he recalled the determination she'd displayed while running toward the fortress. Maybe.

"Is that true?" He looked her over with new eyes. Sure enough, there was dirt under her fingernails and smeared on her arms. Besides the blood, however, her robe was perfectly clean.

In fact, as he watched, the tear he'd made wove itself back together, much like his body did when wounded. A piece of cloth with healing properties. Would wonders never cease?

"Olivia. You will answer."

She nodded without glancing up. He heard a sniff, sniff. Yes, she was sobbing.

An ache bloomed in his chest, but he ignored it. *Doesn't matter what she is or what she's endured. You will not soften. She frightens and hurts Legion and has to go.*

"A real, live angel," Paris said, clearly awed. "I'll take her to my room, if you'd like, and—"

"She's too injured for bed sport," Aeron snapped.

Paris eyed him strangely for a moment, then grinned and shook his head. "I wasn't sizing her up or anything, so let go of your jealousy."

That didn't even deserve a response. He'd never experienced jealousy, and wasn't about to start now. "So why were you offering to take her to your room?"

"So I can bandage her wounds. Who's the despot now?"

"I'll take care of her." Maybe. Could angels tolerate human medicine? Or would it hurt them? He knew well the dangers of giving one race something meant for another. Ashlyn had almost died when she'd drunk wine meant only for immortals.

He would have called for Lysander, but the elite warrior angel was currently living in the heavens with Bianka and if there was a way to reach him, Aeron hadn't been told what it was. Besides, Lysander didn't like him and wasn't the type to willingly offer information about his race.

"You want to be the responsible one, fine. But admit it." Paris tossed him another grin. "You're staking a claim on her."

"No. I'm not." He didn't have even the smallest desire to do so. It was just that she was injured and couldn't take care of herself, and was therefore in no position to be anyone's bedmate. And that's all Paris would want her for. Sex. No matter what the warrior claimed.

Besides, she'd called for *Aeron.* Screamed *Aeron's* name.

Undeterred, Paris continued, "An angel isn't technically human, you know? An angel is something more."

Aeron popped his jaw. Of all the things for the man to remember from their earlier conversation. "I said I'm not staking a claim."

Paris laughed. "Whatever you say, *compadre.* Enjoy your female."

Aeron's hands curled into fists, his friend's laughter not so welcome now. "Go and tell Lucien everything we've discussed, but under no circumstances are you to inform the women that there's a wounded angel here. They'll raid my room wanting to meet her, and now is not the time for that."

"Why? Do you plan to make out with her?"

His teeth ground together with so much force he feared they would soon be nothing but a fond memory. "I plan to question her."

"Ah. So that's what the kids are calling it these days. Well, have fun." With that, a still-grinning Paris strolled from the room.

Alone once more with his charge, Aeron gazed down at her. Her silent sobbing had ended, at least, and she faced him again.

"What are you doing here, Olivia?" Saying her name shouldn't have affected him—he'd said it before, after all—but it did. His blood heated another degree. It must be those eyes of hers…piercing him.…

A shuddering breath escaped her. "I knew the consequences, knew I was giving up my wings, my abilities, my immortality, but I did it anyway. It's just…my job changed. Joy was no longer mine to give. Only death. And I hated what they wanted me to do. I couldn't do it, Aeron. I just couldn't."

His name on her lips, uttered with such familiarity, affected him, too. He sucked in a breath. What was wrong with him? *Toughen up. Be the cold, hard warrior you claim to be.*

"I watched you," she continued, "as well as those around you, and I…ached. I wanted you, and I wanted what they had—freedom and love and fun. I wanted to play. I wanted to kiss and to touch. I wanted joy of my own." Her gaze met his, bleak, broken. "In the end, I had a choice. Fall…or kill you. I decided to fall. So here I am. Yours."

The Sacred Scrolls

AS I TOLD YOU EARLIER, I, Cronus, King of Kings, was not mentioned nearly enough in this guide. By now, I'm sure you concur.

But as this compilation began with me, it's only fitting that it end with me, as well. That is why I'm unveiling my ancient scrolls at long last. These scrolls list the contemptible demons unleashed from Pandora's box—well, the demons still at large....

Pay no attention to those who have been crossed out. That is a command! They mean nothing and are of no consequence.

Now then, I've tasked the Lords with finding these...abominations. Better the warriors under my control than those despicable Hunters, after all.

What my men do not know, however, is that a few of these demons are already searching for *them*....

Cronus

KING OF THE TITANS

THE MISSING DEMONS FROM PANDORA'S BOX

Distrust—to regard with suspicion; have no trust in

~~*Greed*—excessive or rapacious desire, especially for wealth or possessions~~

Hate—to dislike intensely or passionately; feel extreme aversion for or extreme hostility toward; detest

Indifference—lack of interest or concern

Intolerance—lack of toleration; unwillingness or refusal to tolerate or respect contrary opinions, beliefs or persons of different races or backgrounds, etc.

Irresponsibility—said or done with, or characterized by, a lack of a sense of responsibility

Jealousy—resentment against a rival, a person enjoying success or advantage, or against another's success or advantage itself

Narcissism—inordinate fascination with oneself; excessive self-love; vanity

Nightmares—a terrifying dream in which the dreamer experiences feelings of helplessness, extreme anxiety or sorrow

Obsession—the domination of one's thoughts or feelings by a persistent idea, image or desire

Selfishness—devoted to or caring only for oneself; concerned primarily with one's own interests, benefits and welfare, regardless of others

~~*Strife*—vigorous or bitter conflict, discord or antagonism~~

LORDS OF THE UNDERWORLD

Glossary of Characters and Terms

Aeron—Keeper of Wrath

All-Seeing Eye—Godly artifact with the power to see into heaven and Hell

Amun—Keeper of Secrets

Anya—(Minor) Goddess of Anarchy

Ashlyn Darrow—Human female with supernatural ability

Baden—Keeper of Distrust (deceased)

Bait—Human females, Hunters' accomplices

Bianka Skyhawk—Harpy, sister of Gwen

Cage of Compulsion—Godly artifact with the power to enslave anyone trapped inside

Cameo—Keeper of Misery

Cloak of Invisibility—Godly artifact with the power to shield its wearer from prying eyes

Cronus—King of the Titans

Danika Ford—Human female, target of the Titans

Darla Stefano—wife of Dean Stefano, Sabin's lover (deceased)

Dean Stefano—Hunter, Right-hand man of Galen

dimOuniak—Pandora's box

Dr. Frederick McIntosh—Vice President of the World Institute of Parapsychology

Galen—Keeper of Hope

Gideon—Keeper of Lies

Gilly—Human female, friend of Danika

Greeks—Former rulers of Olympus, now imprisoned in Tartarus

Gwen Skyhawk—Harpy, wife of Sabin

Hera—Queen of the Greeks

Hunters—Mortal enemies of the Lords of the Underworld

Hydra—Multiheaded serpent with poisonous fangs

Kaia Skyhawk—Harpy, sister of Gwen

Kane—Keeper of Disaster

Legion—Demon minion, friend of Aeron

Lords of the Underworld—Exiled warriors of the Greek gods who now house demons inside them

Lucien—Keeper of Death, Leader of the Budapest warriors

Lysander—Elite warrior angel and consort of Bianka Skyhawk

Maddox—Keeper of Violence

Olivia—Fallen warrior angel

Pandora—Immortal warrior, once guardian of *dimOuniak* (deceased)

Paring Rod—Godly artifact, power unknown

Paris—Keeper of Promiscuity

Reyes—Keeper of Pain

Sabin—Keeper of Doubt, Leader of the Greece contingent of warriors

Scarlet—Keeper of Nightmares

Sienna Blackstone—Female Hunter

Strider—Keeper of Defeat

Taliyah Skyhawk—Harpy, sister of Gwen

Tartarus—Greek god of Confinement, also the immortal prison on Mount Olympus

Titans—Current rulers of Olympus

Torin—Keeper of Disease

William—Immortal, friend of Anya

Zeus—King of the Greeks

BL_199_TDP

AERON, KEEPER OF THE DEMON OF WRATH, FINALLY MEETS HIS MATCH...

An angel – demon-assassin – has been sent to kill immortal warrior Aeron. But Olivia claims she fell from the heavens, giving up immortality because she couldn't bear to harm him.

Now, with an enemy on his trail and his faithful demon companion determined to remove Olivia from his life, Aeron is trapped between duty and consuming desire.

www.mirabooks.co.uk

BL_169_TDN

HIS POWERS – INHUMAN.
HIS PASSION – BEYOND IMMORTAL...

Ashlyn Darrow has come to Budapest seeking help from men rumoured to have supernatural abilities and is swept into the arms of Maddox.

Neither can resist the instant hunger that calms their torments and ignites an irresistible passion. But every heated touch and burning kiss will edge them closer to destruction – and a soul-shattering test of love.

www.mirabooks.co.uk

BL_170_TDK

SHE HAS TEMPTED MANY MEN...BUT NEVER FOUND HER EQUAL. UNTIL NOW.

Anya, goddess of anarchy, has never known pleasure. Until Lucien, the incarnation of death, draws her like no other.

But when the Lord of the Underworld is ordered to claim Anya, they must defeat the unconquerable forces that control them, before their thirst for one another demands a sacrifice of love beyond imagining.

www.mirabooks.co.uk

BL_171_TDP

HE CAN BEAR ANY PAIN BUT THE THOUGHT OF LOSING HER...

Although forbidden to know pleasure, Reyes craves mortal Danika Ford and will do anything to claim her – even defy the gods.

Danika is on the run from the Lords of the Underworld who want her and her family destroyed. But she can't forget the searing touch of the warrior Reyes. Yet a future together could mean death to all they both hold dear...

www.mirabooks.co.uk

BL_172_TDW

THE NEXT INSTALMENT OF THE LORDS OF THE UNDERWORLD SERIES

Gwen, an immortal, always thought she'd fall for a kind human who wouldn't rouse her darker side. But when Sabin frees her from prison, battling their enemies for the claim to Pandora's box turns out to be nothing compared to the battle Sabin and Gwen will wage against love.

www.mirabooks.co.uk

BL_204_BT_TT

AVOID SUNLIGHT.
DRINK BLOOD.
HATE YOURSELF. FOREVER.
WELCOME TO IMMORTALITY.

I became Dr Carrie Ames eight months ago.
Now I'm a vampire and have a blood tie to
the monster who sired me.

Drinking blood, living as an immortal and being
a pawn between two warring vampire groups
isn't how I saw my future. But the only way to
conquer my fear is to face it. Fangs bared.

www.mirabooks.co.uk